A DANGEROUS DIAGNOSIS

A DANGEROUS DIAGNOSIS

A THRILLER

SHANTANU RAI

NEW YORK

Published in the United States by Crooked Lane Books, an imprint of
The Quick Brown Fox & Company LLC.

Crooked Lane Books and its logo are trademarks of The Quick Brown Fox & Company LLC.

Library of Congress Catalog-in-Publication data available upon request.

ISBN (hardcover): 979-8-89242-499-8
ISBN (paperback): 979-8-89242-500-1
ISBN (ebook): 979-8-89242-501-8

Cover design by Hayley Warnham

Printed in the United States.

www.crookedlanebooks.com

Crooked Lane Books
34 West 27th St., 10th Floor
New York, NY 10001

First Edition: February 2026

The authorized representative in the EU for product safety and compliance is eucomply OÜPärnu mnt 139b-14, 11317 Tallinn, Estonia,
hello@eucompliancepartner.com, +33757690241

10 9 8 7 6 5 4 3 2 1

To patients everywhere,
and the doctors and nurses who
fight for them.

PROLOGUE

Dr. Tom Carpenter is standing by the window of his clinic, contemplating Occam's Razor—the centuries-old principle that the simplest explanation is often the right one—when he begins to feel lightheaded.

In his medical career, he's often said that the cardinal sin is diagnosing a patient with multiple conditions when one would suffice.

But the sins he's confronting today are far graver.

He looks out over the neighborhood that once housed the working-class community his free clinic was built to serve. Now his patients are scattered across the city, displaced by the biotech companies and high-end coffee shops that followed the rapid expansion of Mount Beacon Hospital—the institution his clinic is affiliated with.

The sun setting behind Boston casts his reflection in the glass. His bald head and oversized white coat make him look more ghost than man.

When did he get so old? When did he get so damn tired?

He shakes his head, trying to will the exhaustion away.

Around the room are reminders of his younger, more energetic self. A medical diploma from Mount Beacon Medical School. His residency certificate in internal medicine from Mount Beacon Hospital. Photos of himself as a young medic in Vietnam. Of Maria before breast cancer ever entered her mind. And of Emma, his daughter—bright, shining—her arms wrapped around him. Looking at the image, he has to steady himself.

Doc, can you see one more patient?

Doc, can you make one more house call?

Tom loved being the savior. He knew how to play the role—and he played it well. But being a father? He never had a clue. So he put his patients first, even when he didn't need to. Even when he shouldn't have.

His gaze drifts a mile away to Mount Beacon Hospital's newest building: a state-of-the-art ICU. When it opened six months ago, half the beds were empty. Now they're full. To the hospital's board of trustees, it's a testament to MBH's value.

To Tom Carpenter, it's a symptom of a broken system—one that measures success by how many sick people it treats, not by how much sickness it prevents.

He turns to his whiteboard, where he usually puzzles out complex medical cases. But instead of symptoms and diagnoses, it's cluttered with names—dozens of patients who've been harmed—and a tangled web of clues connecting them. He's uncovered so much these past few weeks, but there's no single culprit or explanation. *Occam's Razor be damned.*

A knock at the door. Before he can answer, his new secretary steps in.

"Dr. Carpenter, you won't believe—" She stops short. "Are you all right?"

The edges of his vision blur. He grips the desk to steady himself. His mind races, piecing together the symptoms: nausea, vertigo, weakness—

"You look pale—"

"I'm busy," he snaps—then instantly regrets it.

Her face reddens. "Oh, I didn't realize you were working on something . . . important."

Her eyes trace the whiteboard behind him—a chaotic sprawl of text and half-erased diagrams. No doubt she's heard the rumors. *Has dementia finally caught up with the great Tom Carpenter? Or paranoia?*

She's only been with him a couple of months. Kind. Steady. Loyal. He likes her more than he lets on. But his staff never last long. Few of the people in his life have—through his exile from MBH, through the tantrums, the rages.

He opens his mouth to apologize, but bile chokes his words. He gestures for her to stay, but she's already halfway out the door.

He swallows hard, steadies his voice. "What won't I believe?"

She turns, her face brightening. "Mrs. Joseph called. The new baby came. She named him after you. Said it's thanks to you Gerard got clean. Thomas Brunel Joseph."

A flicker of warmth cuts through the haze. He pictures Gerard—eight years old, fresh from Haiti. The boy had hardly flinched during his shots, then beamed when Tom unveiled a red lollipop.

Tom closes his eyes. This—*this*—is what's at stake.

He curses himself. If he hadn't overstepped with Maria, if he hadn't pushed away the people he trusted most—maybe he could've prevented this.

Now, he can only hope Community Cares survives, that the anonymous donors behind his free clinic keep funding its mission, no matter what happens to MBH.

He needs time to think. He'll send a copy of his files to Paul Klein, his longtime patient—now a reporter at *The Boston Globe*.

In a matter of days—weeks at most—hundreds, maybe thousands of patients could be at risk.

Paul is a start. But only a doctor can put the pieces together.

As his secretary leaves, another wave of dizziness sends Tom staggering for his desk chair. Ever the internist, he runs his own differential diagnosis—ranking the conditions that match his rapidly advancing symptoms.

Dehydration. Hemorrhage. Stroke.

The room keeps spinning. A darker thought takes hold: What if this isn't a coincidence?

He rewinds the past few days: the visit from that clinic. The fight with hospital administrators.

Is this how they've chosen to silence me?

He has too many enemies. Some envious of his career, others who simply want vocal doctors gone.

As his legs give out and he hits the floor, one last diagnosis comes to mind.

One that explains everything.

He fumbles in his pocket for his pen and prescription pad. This is his last chance to save his patients. He prays it's also the cure for the doctors he's hurt—and for his daughter, Emma.

On the blank page, in a scrawl only his office staff can read, he writes out his final instruction.

CHAPTER 1

"NOW, JUST RELAX."

"Relax?" The accent seems heavier than usual. "How the hell am I supposed to relax when you have my life in your hands?"

The patient has a point. Dr. Sanjay Patel hovers above the three-hundred-pound billionaire Muscovite, about to insert a needle into the man's penile shaft.

A sixty-three-year-old with severe coronary artery disease and gout, Yuri Petrov has—in an effort to please his fourth wife, a Hungarian model—taken a triple dose of Viagra.

"It was an emergency, Doctor!" Petrov had laughed when he called Sanjay an hour earlier.

It is now, thinks Sanjay. Every hour that Petrov's penis is stuck in an erection, he risks losing it. They're at the six-hour mark, and the chance of irreversible damage is 20 percent. At twenty-four hours, it'll be 90 percent.

Sanjay had been only thirty minutes away by air. A short ride in a private car, then a final approach by Vespa to the cliffside villa, and he was at Petrov's Ravello compound. He found Mrs. Petrov sitting on the balcony outside the sprawling master suite, high above the Mediterranean, scrolling on her phone. Two bodyguards insisted on a pat-down. The routine was familiar, but given his patient's situation, Sanjay chafed at the delay.

The setting called for improvisation. The exam table is a massage bed. Reclined thirty degrees, it allows for a decent reverse Trendelenburg position. To complement the local anesthetic, Sanjay rolls up a Hermès tie and places it between Petrov's teeth—to keep him from biting off his tongue, though the silence is a welcome side effect.

Everything else Sanjay needs is in his high-tech medical bag, midnight black. Thanks to Cassie, his roving assistant, both the bag and its contents would be the envy of the Mayo brothers.

Holding Petrov's engorged penis with his gloved left hand, Sanjay uses his teeth to pop the top off the lidocaine syringe in his right hand. "A stick and a burn," he says.

Petrov bleats a Russian expletive into his four-hundred–euro tie.

"Okay. That was the numbing medicine."

Sanjay directs a second needle through the skin, careful to avoid any major blood vessels. "Hold still."

For the first time in years, Petrov follows his physician's instructions.

"All done." Sanjay stands back to observe Petrov's face. "Now just stay down for another ten minutes so I can monitor you."

"Monitor me? Doctor, I am a Petrov. We need no monitoring."

Petrov is already swinging his legs around when Sanjay pushes him back down. One guard barrels toward Sanjay; the other reaches for his holster.

"Okay, Doc. Okay," says Petrov, waving off his goons. "Is all right."

He lies back down. Out comes his phone. *From where?* Sanjay wonders. The man's stark naked.

Pulse is reasonable, pain and stress considered: 92 BPM. But Sanjay has a feeling. He digs into his medical bag for the blood pressure cuff.

"Boris, vodka. Chilled," Petrov's voice sounds different. Weaker. "And what's with the fucking A/C?"

Beads of sweat appear on the big man's forehead.

Uh-oh.

Sanjay drops the cuff and lunges forward as the patient's eyes roll into the back of his head. He catches Petrov before he falls off the table, grabs his wrist, and puts two fingers on the radial artery, simultaneously lowering the table to get gravity on his side.

The guards are in a full-blown panic, one gripping a bottle of Beluga Gold while the other stands frozen, his mouth agape.

"Ambulance!" yells Sanjay. "Helicopter, if they've got one. Tell the operator he's in cardiac distress."

The guards look at each other.

"Now!"

Petrov still has a pulse, but it's thready. Sanjay places his stethoscope on the man's chest. In seconds, it delivers a three-dimensional ultrasound to Sanjay's phone. Ejection fraction is 20 percent, down two-thirds from normal. Not enough forward blood flow.

The medicine Sanjay gave Petrov must have gotten into his general circulation, a rare and unavoidable complication.

"Dammit." Sanjay looks to the remaining guard. "My bag!"

Petrov's heart should be racing to compensate, but it's not. Years of calcium and cholesterol buildup have weakened its rhythm. He'd ignored Sanjay's recommendation to take a stress test.

But that's the problem with being a concierge doctor to the uber rich. The patients aren't the listening kind.

Sanjay jams a sixteen-gauge IV into Petrov's left arm and pushes half a milligram of atropine. Then he grabs a bag of saline and hops up on the table, squeezing fluid out as fast as possible.

A few minutes later, Petrov comes to. Sanjay eyes his blood pressure cuff. BP 90/58. The man needs more fluid, but nothing the ambulance crew can't handle.

"What happened?" Petrov asks, rubbing his head.

"Your heart isn't as strong as it used to be. You need to slow down. And by the next time I see you, I want an exercise stress test done."

"Exercise? Doc, we Petrovs don't . . ." Petrov turns to his guards for approval. But their aghast expressions stop him cold. His eyes scan the medical equipment, open syringes, and medication bottles strewn across the floor.

"Okay, Doctor," he says, putting his hands up. "I'll take your advice." He turns to one of his guards and snaps, "Bruno, since the doctor is here, give him his retainer."

Bruno vanishes, returning seconds later with a Gucci tote, dark green. He unzips it and shows the contents to Sanjay—stacks of US hundred-dollar bills, packed to the brim.

"Half cash," says Petrov. "The rest we'll wire to—"

"The 703 account."

"Yes, yes. We know. Bruno will call your secretary to arrange the transfer."

Before Sanjay can take his leave, Petrov's wife comes into the room, her high heels clattering as she steps around the paraphernalia on the floor.

"Yurochka," she whines, "can we go? If we don't hurry, we won't even make the second half of the show."

"Of course, my sweet. Of course." Petrov starts to rise from the table, but Sanjay's scowl drops him back down. "Actually, kedvesem, you go. Take Gorevich. I need to stay here. Doctor's orders."

Her face flushes. "He works for us. My husband doesn't take orders from him!"

"He does now!" snaps Petrov. "And you take orders from me."

Tears form in her blue eyes. Petrov softens. "I'm . . . advising you to treat our doctor here with respect. He just saved your husband's life."

She turns to Sanjay. A cold expression on her face. "Thank you for saving my husband. But since you do work for us, I have a job for you. A friend of mine. A quick visit. You can do that, right?"

Sanjay ignores the malice in her voice. That, too, is part of the job.

"I'm afraid I have to pass. I have a full patient load."

Her eyes cut to her husband.

Petrov sighs. "Please, Doctor. It's just by the water. Lots of beautiful women, I promise."

* * *

Twenty minutes later, Sanjay steps down from Petrov's armored Mercedes onto the marina.

Rising from the sapphire waters ahead are the dramatic coastal cliffs that make the Amalfi Coast so breathtaking—and so treacherous to drive. Sanjay can just make out a yellow Lamborghini convertible winding around a curve, a bright red Ferrari not far behind.

"Dr. Sanjay," calls a voice from behind him. "Please, if you'll follow me."

He turns to see a muscular young man in an Armani suit coming down the gangway. Stretching in front of him is a yacht a hundred feet long, stem to stern. A Heesen, by the look of it.

Sanjay follows the man to the portside deck. A steward waits with a tray bearing a cut-crystal tumbler and a tall, jet-black ceramic bottle with platinum and silver accents. Clase Azul Ultra. Nearly impossible to find. Cassie must have called ahead.

He swirls the caramel flavors on his tongue. Distilled from 100 percent blue agave at one of the highest altitudes in Mexico, this tequila is nothing like the ones college kids imbibe that give the drink a bad name. It's pure taste, no hangover. The benefits of a liquor made from a green plant. He takes a couple sips and returns the glass. An unnecessary precaution, but better to wait until after his last patient of the day.

Ushered into the main salon, Sanjay feels transported to a club on South Beach. Scantily clad dancers gyrate in bird cages while beautiful women deliver bottles of Dom to businessmen and their runway-model girlfriends.

"Please, Doctor," the attendant shouts above the pounding bass. "Wait here. Ms. Jansen is finishing her swim."

Cassie had briefed him by phone on the ride down. Sophie Jansen is the twenty-four-year-old daughter and only child of a Dutch shipping magnate. College at NYU, part-time model, scattered tabloid stories. Apparently, she has an errant wrinkle and is due for Botox.

His phone rings. It's Cassie. "You have an urgent call."

He sighs. In concierge medicine, everything is urgent. "Which patient?"

"Not a patient—a Dr. Emma Carpenter-Flores. She says you know her?"

Emma—twelve years, and not a word. Now it's urgent? "Uh, yeah. Med school."

A memory of their first time listening to a patient's heartbeat together flashes through Sanjay's mind. The way Emma's eyes widened in wonder. Then those same eyes, sparkling, when their lips touched for the first time.

The line cuts over.

"Emma?"

"Hi." Just one syllable, but he'd know her voice anywhere. Full of warmth and surprisingly deep, only more tired now.

"Wow. It's . . . It's great to hear from you." Sanjay doesn't need to check his pulse to know it's racing.

"Where are you?" She sounds strained. "It's loud. Sorry. I didn't realize you were . . . out."

Sanjay needs to get away from this crowd and the pulsating beats from the DJ booth. Not the best impression, given the rumors Emma's likely heard about him. He puts a finger to his ear and steps outside, onto the main deck.

"Nowhere. It doesn't matter. I'm glad you got in touch."

"I didn't, exactly. My father did."

Sanjay masks his surprise. After the way they'd left things, he never expected to hear from Tom again. "Good old Tom Carpenter! How is he these days?"

"Dead."

CHAPTER

2

PAGE DR. SANJAY.

Those are the words Tom Carpenter wrote as he breathed his last? On a prescription pad?

Sanjay heads back to the ship's bar. The only seat available is tucked behind a couple who are drunkenly groping each other. He grunts at them, and they stumble away.

Head spinning, he orders himself a drink, his fingers trembling as he takes the glass. It's hard to imagine that Tom, the man who taught him everything he knows about medicine, is dead, of a stroke no less. He takes a sip, the burn of the alcohol not enough to numb the ache inside.

Strokes don't just pop up out of nowhere. They're the result of years of uncontrolled blood pressure or high cholesterol, neither of which Tom could have had. He was an avid cyclist and obsessed over what he ate, more to set an example for his patients than anything else.

But Sanjay recalls the adage Tom drilled into him: *Not every patient reads the textbook.* Plenty of patients present with illnesses that defy medical knowledge. Why not Tom Carpenter, too?

Tom's secretary found the "Page Sanjay" note next to Tom's body. She called Emma. There were plenty of others who could have delivered the message from there. But Emma chose to do it herself. That means something, doesn't it? The last time Sanjay tried to contact Emma, after she'd dropped out of med school and moved to Sweden for her PhD, she wanted nothing to do with him.

But that wasn't the biggest mystery. The real question is why Tom asked for Sanjay. As if they were separated by a few floors or zip codes—not by an ocean and a decade.

He hears himself laugh before he can stop it. Not that anyone can hear him over the ship's techno beats.

Tom. Calling on *him*. Sanjay, the protégé he disowned. The parachute-in doctor to plutocrats and the spoiled rich, the man whose practice is antithetical to everything Tom stood for—at least on paper.

That Tom paged him, after everything that went wrong, must mean it was something important.

But what?

Whatever it was, Emma made it clear she didn't know and didn't care. In clipped sentences, she mentioned a funeral near MBH, followed by a memorial service at the clinic. The vibe of the call was corpse cold.

Then came the frostbite: "But of course, you'll be too busy prescribing Xanax to billionaires."

"Screw it," Sanjay says now, under his breath.

He's not going back. MBH—like the modern healthcare system it represents—is rotten to the core. With Tom gone, it'll only get worse. Whatever he paged Sanjay about, assuming it wasn't the hypoxia-induced delusions of a dying brain, couldn't possibly be worth getting sucked back in.

MBH screwed him. Twice. The third time won't be any more charming.

Besides, he has patients waiting. Fall is his busy season. Dubai tomorrow, then Oslo for a round of annual physicals. *Patients first, right, Tom?*

Sanjay raises his glass to the ceiling, downs his Clase Azul, and stares out at the dance floor. An olive-skinned beauty in a deep V-neck dress saunters past. She answers his stare with a smile.

Just the distraction he needs.

But a moment later, a muscular blond man, heavily inked, steps between them, blocking Sanjay's view. "Shopping, bruv?" His raised chin makes the challenge clear.

Sanjay makes a rapid assessment. Six four, maybe two-fifty. Respiratory rate elevated. A walking medical atlas—brachioradialis, brachialis, biceps, triceps, deltoids—every muscle clearly etched through the skin. The perfect teaching dummy for anatomy students.

"Oi! You deaf?"

"No. And no. Not deaf. Not shopping." He knows the type. Better not to engage.

A step forward. "Yeah? Too good for 'er, then?" Fists clenched. External jugular veins popping out.

Sanjay fixes his gaze on a point over the guy's shoulder. "I'm afraid I can't tell you. I have myopia."

"Myo-whuh?"

"Eye condition."

"Oh, sorry, bruv." The man claps a flank-steak-sized hand on Sanjay's shoulder, then turns to the bartender. "This man drinks what he likes. On me."

Once he's out of earshot, the bartender leans in. "Myopia. That's just nearsightedness, yeah?"

Sanjay nods.

"So, basically, you told him you wear glasses."

Sanjay grins. He'd learned the hard way growing up—nerdy, immigrant, undersized: brains were the better defense. "Contacts, actually."

* * *

On the aft deck, a rainbow of swimsuits adorns an ensemble of sunbathing women. The attendant introduces Sanjay to Sophie Jansen, his new patient. She's a textbook heiress. Scandinavian features, tanned body, thousand-dollar calfskin sandals.

"Dr. Patel, this is Ms. Jansen. Ms. Jansen, this is—"

"Dr. Sanjay," the doctor interrupts. Noticing her confusion, he adds, "Where I'm from half the doctors around are Patels, so it's easier."

"You're the doctor?" Sophie ogles his six-foot-two frame and broad chest. He has his personal trainer to thank for that. "You're too cute to be a doctor," she says, soliciting giggles from her girlfriends.

"Ms. Jansen—"

"Oh, come on!" she teases. "We're practically the same age. Call me Sophie."

"Okay, Ms. Sophie," says Sanjay. "Is there somewhere private we can do this?"

She presses her right hand to his chest and laughs. "Let's just do the shot right here. That's how my regular doctor does it."

Sanjay's right eyebrow goes up. "I'm not a regular doctor."

In a small lounge off the sundeck, he has Sophie sit across from him. He begins by asking about her previous Botox treatments and allergies to medications.

"Wow, this is fun!" She giggles. "It's like I'm a real patient."

In spite of himself, he rolls his eyes. It's clear no one has asked her these questions before. *Why do so many doctors cut corners?*

The Botox injections to her forehead and crow's feet go well, but as he's wrapping up, Sanjay notices something.

"How long have you had this?" He pulls out his phone and reverses the camera so she can see the dark mole on her neck.

His look of genuine concern seems to amuse Sophie. "I don't know. Since forever."

"Has it changed recently? Gotten larger or darker or anything?"

She frowns, wrinkling her nose. "Come to think of it, it's gotten a bit bigger."

"Okay. It needs to be checked out. Most moles are innocuous, but yours has features that warrant a closer look."

Her breath catches. "Features?"

"In med school, they taught us ABCD. Asymmetry: Draw a line down the middle of your mole; it should be the same on both sides. Yours isn't. Border irregularity: Your mole doesn't have a consistent edge; parts of it seem to be spilling over. Color: It isn't just one but several colors and tones. Diameter: Like you said, it's gotten bigger."

"So . . . What are you saying?"

"Only that it needs to be biopsied. I can do it now, if you like."

She nods, and he goes to work, glad he only had one drink and that the procedure is straightforward. Reaching into his medical bag, he injects lidocaine to numb the area, excises the mole into a sterile container, and closes the wound with Steri-Strips.

"We'll have the results back in a week or so," he says. "I'll have my assistant Cassie send the sample to a pathologist I trust at the Royal Marsden in London."

Sophie's face is blank. Sanjay waits. He thinks he knows what's coming.

"Could this . . ." She blinks her large eyes. "Could it be cancer?"

"That's what we'll be testing for. If it is, we're looking at melanoma."

"My mom had melanoma. I was ten when she died. She was really sick at the end. I . . ."

Sophie buries her face in her hands, suddenly sobbing uncontrollably. Sanjay resists the urge to take her in his arms and console her. For a longtime patient, maybe, but not someone he doesn't know well, and certainly not a young woman, with no nurse or chaperone present.

He remembers the first time he had to tell someone they had cancer. A woman in her forties, Mrs. Coretta. When he entered the exam room, she was extra chatty, asking about his weekend and his family, as if she sensed what was coming and was trying to delay the inevitable.

He'd been dreading the conversation since he got the call about her mammogram from the radiology office. A 3.5 centimeter spiculated mass with multiple enlarged lymph nodes—not good. All he had thought about was whether she'd get angry; whether he'd lose control and get emotional.

But rolling his chair up to hers, seeing the deep lines etched in her forehead and the gold locket necklace with photographs of her two young children, all he thought about was her. This was a moment she'd replay in her mind for years to come. The most important message she needed to hear—and feel—was that he was there for her, no matter what came next.

Now he gazes down at Sophie, never letting his eyes leave hers.

"If it is melanoma, we caught it early, right?" she asks.

"It's premature to say it's cancer. But yes, we'd have caught it early."

She looks up at him, her face brighter. "My regular doctor, he never said anything."

"Like I said before." Sanjay smiles back. "I'm not a regular doctor."

"I can see that," says Sophie, laughing through her tears.

Back on the sundeck, she trills, "How many drinks behind am I, ladies?" giving her friends no hint of what just transpired.

"You two were gone a long time for a couple of Botox injections," one of the women says, provoking knowing looks from the crowd. "And is that a hickey on your neck?" she adds, pointing to where Sanjay took the biopsy.

Sanjay has to dismiss that notion—and fast. "I don't get involved with patients."

"Good thing I'm not your patient," calls a voice.

He turns. It's the woman from the bar with the deep-cut dress, minus the rugby player.

"Good point," Sanjay says, smiling.

* * *

"Who's Emma?"

"Hmm?" Sanjay is half-awake. Daylight leaks in under the pulled-down window shades.

"Emma. You were saying her name in your sleep."

He rolls over. Right. The woman from the yacht. He does a quick rewind. *Drinks, dancing, the drive back to the Gulfstream, the competitive sex.* Nataliya. That's her name.

He uses every doctor's favorite excuse. "Just a patient."

She doesn't seem convinced, but it doesn't matter. More troubling is why his mind is stuck on Emma.

"Anyways, coffee?"

He looks at her blankly.

"Have. You. Got. Coffee?" she repeats.

Sanjay throws the covers off. "Of course." He slips out of the aft cabin and pads toward the cockpit. She follows him. But the capsule espresso machine doesn't meet with her approval.

"I mean coffee. That's. . . . product."

He starts a cup for himself anyway. Years of burned nursing station coffee has made him immune.

Last night, Nataliya was stunned to learn that his plane didn't have a flight attendant. Besides the pilot, the plane only has two regular passengers—him and Cassie. And they both know how to make a sandwich and pour tequila.

Now Nataliya asks, "Do you live here? On the plane?"

He turns to find her standing over one of the leather bins, pawing through his stuff. His jaw tightens in irritation.

"And where are your things?" She props a hand on her hip. "No family photos? No mementos?"

The questions annoy him, but she's not wrong. He has two apartments—in Zurich and Manhattan—but they are just as barren. Sanjay prefers not to be reminded of his past. More often than not, he sleeps on the plane. He flies nearly every day, often multiple times. Not the cheapest way to live, but worth every euro. His clients tend to be in locations at least two connections away, and they have little patience for delays—or anything else.

Now he hands Nataliya a toiletry kit. She frowns at it, but heads to the back of the plane. When she's gone, he puts his nose in a book, or more precisely, a magazine. *The New England Journal of Medicine*. He loves trying to crack the diagnostic mystery at the back of each issue. It keeps his diagnostic skills sharp, given how mind-numbing his practice often is.

This week's case: *A forty-year-old man with abdominal pain, low platelets, and fragmented blood cells. Thrombotic thrombocytopenic purpura*. Fun, but easy.

Nataliya comes back, toweling her hair dry. "I know where we can get real coffee."

He reaches for his phone. "Let me get a car. You know the address?"

She struts past him. "I'll tell the pilot."

Ninety minutes later, they land at Caravaggio Airport, Bergamo. The helicopter Nataliya apps up delivers them to a spot on the south shore of Lake Como, near Bellagio.

"I can't believe you don't know Nene's," she says. "It's the best."

Sanjay gazes across the lake, at the low-ranging Alps. In front of them is an outdoor café, wrought-iron tables scattered around a dozen water fountains, each with a bucket of rosé being chilled against the warm breeze. He looks up to see a copper green lion's head over the entrance gate.

He does know this place. He didn't remember the name.

Or he chose not to.

His sister Neela was the one who pushed him to come. When she flew into Chicago to visit him his last year of residency, she burst into tears at baggage claim. It wasn't just the fifteen pounds he'd lost. He was hollowed out emotionally, too.

Neela had never been to Lake Como—their family wouldn't spend that kind of money on frivolities. But Neil, Sanjay's closest friend from med school, had been twice, and the way he described it sounded perfect. So Neela used her savings to buy Sanjay a non-refundable ticket. He stayed a short walk from this café. He couldn't afford much, but the brisk morning swims in the lake and espressos were enough.

For two weeks, nightmares about patients he hadn't been able to save tormented him. The most distressing was Louise, an uninsured woman in her fifties who came to the ER with chest pains. What he remembered most were her feet. Her toenails were three inches long and twisted, many ingrown, a sign of severe functional decline. The community hospital Sanjay was rotating through was one of the few that had podiatrists on call. While Louise's hospitalization had nothing to do with her feet, he consulted them anyway; the next day on rounds, she proudly showed off her neat toes and bright pink nail polish, her excitement fogging up her oxygen mask.

But that was all he was able to do for her. Within days, her heart failure spiraled. She needed valve surgery his hospital couldn't perform, so he requested a transfer to the city's major teaching hospital. After multiple phone calls, he received a late-night fax denying the request.

"Due to the advanced progression of the underlying disease," it stated, "surgery would be futile and risk unnecessary harm."

Sanjay was livid. There was clear-cut evidence to support surgery. He debated driving over to the teaching hospital and demanding to speak to the chief of cardiac surgery himself. But before he mustered the courage, Louise's heart stopped. Sanjay jumped into CPR, but after thirty minutes, his attending forced him to call it.

He doubted a surgeon had ever been consulted on her case—probably an administrator denied the transfer. Not because there was little they could do to save her, but because without insurance there was little money in saving her.

On her death certificate, he signed cardiac arrest as the primary cause of death, followed by heart failure as the secondary cause and valve disorder as tertiary. But years later, after witnessing again and again how the healthcare system mistreated patients and marginalized doctors, he knew he should have written: *cardiac arrest due to corruption and greed.*

"Hell-lo! Are you listening to me?"

He looks up from his coffee and apologizes to Nataliya. She seems unaware of his inner turmoil.

Yet, in bringing him here, she's done something almost psychic. From where he's sitting, he can nearly make out the spot across the lake where he knelt and cast a flower onto the waters for Louise. Bright pink, like her toenails.

Tom had paged Sanjay, which meant he was asking for his help as a doctor.

Nataliya's talking about her parents. Rich and overbearing, they've never accepted her. To rebel, she became a model. "I've learned that fighting and losing is better than not living," she says, tossing her hair over her shoulder.

He looks up curiously, then turns away, glancing back at the lake. His coffee is cold.

The decision was made even before he got the call from Emma. The moment Tom scribbled those three words. Maybe even earlier. He just had to catch up to it.

"I called a car," Nataliya says. "I'm heading to Milan. You want to come and—"

"I'm sorry. I can't. I have to go to Boston."

CHAPTER

3

PROFESSOR EMMA CARPENTER-FLORES slams the phone down in disbelief.

First, they tell her the autopsy's been declined on her behalf. Then they say that her father's body won't be embalmed before cremation. Now the entire guest list is—what's the word the funeral director used? "Locked"?

It's her father's funeral and she's his only living kin, but apparently no one got the memo. Her only choice in the matter? Whether to give a brief eulogy, and even then, she's been granted no more than five minutes.

Well, no eulogy, thank you very much. She won't give them the pleasure.

She slumps down at her desk and buries her face in her hands. MBH owned her dad when he was alive. Apparently, they own him in death, too.

Her eyes return to her desk, and she sighs. Around her are a pile of overdue scientific papers to peer-review from *Cell* and *Science*; sticky notes reminding her of letters of recommendation she's promised to write (three yellow notes, two red, the color signifying the lateness); and her next R21 grant to the National Cancer Institute, stuck on page two.

She groans. When exactly did she go from discovering cures to pushing paper?

A gentle knock.

"May I come in?"

Peeking through the doorway is Janelle White, Emma's most promising postdoc. Emma wants to politely turn her away, but through the glass wall that separates her office from her laboratory, she can see the faces of her postdocs, doctoral students, undergrads, and research assistants. Nearly two dozen women, all staring at her. Faces full of worry. Did she slam the phone down that hard?

"Sure, Janelle. Come in."

"We, uh, are just concerned about you. How about I pick you up a London Fog?"

Emma smiles despite herself. Since founding Flores Lab five years ago, she's prided herself on building more than just a research team—she's built a family. Her office walls are lined with photos: group hikes up Pitcher Mountain, happy hours at Pisco y Nazca, the closest thing she's found in Boston to her grandmother's Peruvian cooking. That same sense of togetherness drives the work itself. The lab decodes the mechanisms of cancer with a single goal: to prevent what happened to her mom, Maria Flores, from happening to anyone else.

To stay true to the lab's ethos, she needs to say something to them.

"Hi, everyone." She gets up, presses her tunic down over her jeans, and stands against the doorway to her lab. "As you know, this has been a . . . difficult time for me. But I'm going to keep working. There are things I need to get done. Then I promise—" She puts her hand on her heart. "I'll take some time off and leave you all alone." Smiles. "Until then, I hope you can pardon my dust . . . and the occasional F-bombs."

Emma's crew breaks into laughter. "We love you, Emma!" yells a research technician.

"I love you all, too." She means it. "I don't say this enough, but—"

"Professor Carpenter-Flores?"

Emma turns toward the deep voice to her right.

"Sorry to interrupt. I have a package for you. It needs your"—the FedEx deliveryman's face reddens when he sees the room full of women, all looking at him—"signature."

One glance at the thick manila envelope, "Confidential" emblazoned on it, and Emma feels herself tighten up. *It's here? Already?*

"All right, back to work, everyone. Tiffany, please let me know as soon as you rerun those gels, and Aliya, we need the new spectrometer calibrated and ready to go by Friday."

Emma turns back to her desk, manila envelope in hand. The FDA wasn't kidding when they said the new drug application was being fast-tracked. She sighs. This means she has less than two weeks before the closed-door meeting near Washington, DC.

"Thanks," comes a whisper. "They needed that."

Emma looks up, startled. She forgot about Janelle.

"What's that?" her postdoc asks, gesturing toward the envelope.

"Remember how I was asked to advise an FDA review panel on a new drug?" Janelle nods. "It's related to that. I'll tell you more when I can."

Emma wishes she could just tell her now. She could use the extra pair of hands, and Janelle, who's graduating soon, would benefit from the exposure. But the drug being evaluated was developed at MBH, and while the review process is confidential, Emma can't risk jeopardizing Janelle's future here if the drug fails to get approved. MBH, like most medical institutions, can be vindictive.

"FDA. So cool. You are a badass woman of science, Professor Carpenter." Janelle's voice is light, teasing.

Emma laughs. "You and me both, girl. Now if you don't mind . . ."

Janelle smiles at her and nods. "Message received. I'll close the door behind me."

She goes, and Emma picks up the envelope. It's heavier than she expected. In it are the in vitro results of absoluxir, the most promising new drug to come out in two decades.

Despite everything going on, Emma feels a rush of excitement. Absoluxir is the brainchild of Dr. Henry Ecker and Dr. Matthew DeSalvo. Dr. Ecker is a personal hero of Emma's—and nearly every other researcher at MBH. Matt is Ecker's number two and Emma's med school classmate. Although they had a falling out of sorts in med school, she can't deny his brilliance.

Here, in this review process, is her chance to use her PhD to directly help patients.

Not that her dad cared, Emma thinks. To Dr. Tom Carpenter, there was only one kind of doctor worth being.

The heavy envelope slips from her hand to her desk, almost knocking over a flower arrangement. Emma steadies the vase and sighs. How Neil remembered that yellow daffodils were her favorite, she'll never know.

The card reads, "I'm sorry about your dad. I'm here for you. Always."

Poor Neil. He's left her so many voicemails in the past week. She's returned none of them. The two dates they went on were nice, sure. After a decade of friendship, starting from medical school, being with Neil was easy and uncomplicated.

Maybe that's how love's supposed to be? Right now, she doesn't have the emotional energy to find out. Emma locks the envelope in her desk drawer and prays for no further distractions.

Then of course, her phone buzzes. A text. From Sanjay Patel.

—Just landed. Cafecino's at 1?

She sighs. *Great. The prodigal doctor returns.*

Cafecino's is too gaudy for her taste. Which fits—of course Sanjay would be paying nine dollars for a cup of coffee. No, if he wants to meet, he'll need to work around her schedule. She can spare a few minutes between her lecture and lab meeting.

—No. Third Cup at 2:00.

Of all people, why on earth did her dad ask for him?

CHAPTER 4

THE DUNKIN DONUTS at Terminal E in Logan Airport is proof that Sanjay is back in the land he used to call home. Thousand-calorie treats and gallon-sized cups of coffee. *"America dies on Dunkin!" Isn't that the slogan?*

He's grateful to be off the plane. Wailing babies and weak drinks, even in first class. He's used to flying private. But he wasn't going to leave Nataliya in the lurch. His pilot is delivering her from Bergamo to Orly so she can skip Milan and hit her favorite stores in Paris. After that, Jacqueline, the nurse practitioner who will cover for him, needs the plane to get to his patients.

Sanjay has never taken a full week off before, and certainly not without notice. It's unclear how his patients, ever demanding, will react. But it's a risk he has to take. He can video call most of them from the US to take histories and diagnose—something they're used to after the Covid-19 pandemic. The few that need a physical touch, Jacqueline will fly to and see. Cassie will stay a couple more days to collect his monthly retainer from those who insist on paying in hard cash, then join him in Boston to be available at a moment's notice.

His plan is to attend the funeral, stay until Tom's memorial, and in between catch up with Neil Desai, his best friend from med school and the only consistently good thing from his time there. Sanjay's tempted to pop over to New York to see his parents and sister, too, but he can do without the guilt trip.

Outside baggage claim, he sees the car Cassie has arranged for him. She went with his favorite, a Range Rover SV Sport. Black.

"You with me the next few days?" he asks the driver, ducking into the back seat.

"That's what Ms. Cassandra tells me," says the man in a thick Boston accent. He waves a finger toward Sanjay in the rearview mirror. "Let me tell you. That lady. She don't mess around."

You don't know the half of it, Sanjay thinks. "What's your name?"

"John Collins, but John is good. You?"

"Sanjay." Sanjay extends his hand, and John turns to meet it. His shirt sleeve pulls up, revealing a tattooed skeleton of a frog on the inside of his upper right arm. *Former Navy Seal,* thinks Sanjay. Overkill, but for Cassie, old habits die hard. He shakes his head, smiling.

"Mount Beacon Medical School please—MBMS," he says, leaning back in his seat. "You good with hip-hop?"

"Yessir. What should I put on?"

"No worries. I got it." Sanjay connects his phone to the car's Harmon Kardon speakers. Soon Kendrick Lamar reverberates through the leather seats.

As they turn onto I-93, his eyes snag on an enormous billboard. The slogan screams, "Next Health: We're democratizing the future of medicine!" The image is of a doctor looking at a body scan on his iPhone, next to a blown-up photo of the abdomen and a patient in a CT scanner giving a thumbs-up.

Sanjay groans. Full-body scans are a scam. Never mind that the photo on the billboard shows the patient's liver on the wrong side of the body.

They get closer, and he sits back, blinking. The doctor in the photo is Nikhil Bansari, a classmate from med school, now identified as "Dr. Nick Bansari, Chief Medical Officer, Next Health." But Nikhil dropped out of residency to work in consulting—he doesn't even have a medical license.

He's back in America, all right. Home of the medical-industrial complex that puts profits before patients.

* * *

Twenty minutes later, they arrive at Mount Beacon Hospital—or as the residents and doctors here smugly call it, "Man's Best Hospital." Sanjay barely recognizes the place. What was once a series of small outpatient clinics and administrative offices is now a cluster of towering medical buildings and research labs. Everywhere he looks, there's more construction.

Four blocks past the main hospital, John pulls over at the entrance of Mount Beacon Medical School. First and second years with backpacks and smiling faces fill the summery quad, alongside harried-looking third and fourth years, their white coats bulging with reference guides.

It's not much of a disguise, but Sanjay dons a blue baseball cap before he darts from the vehicle and checks Cassie's text for the location of the lecture hall. It's unlikely anyone from his past will recognize him, but he doesn't want the hassle.

At Room 10–250, he peers in through the door's square window. Stepped rows of seats lead down to a podium. Perfect. He slips in and stands at the back. If Cassie is right, which she always is, the advanced organic chemistry class still has twenty minutes left.

Emma is facing the whiteboard. Her wavy hair is shorter but still jet black. In dark jeans and a loose-fitting blue blouse, she has a cool professor vibe about her. Moving electrons from one molecule to another, she draws a series of chemical compounds that Sanjay vaguely recalls from pharmacology.

With a final flourish, she caps her marker and asks, "What have we derived?"

She turns to face her class, and his breath catches. She's even more stunning than he remembered, with her perfectly oval face, dark eyes, and caramel skin.

"A purine," a voice calls out.

"Ah, yes, but which one?" Emma smiles, tapping the marker on her jeans.

A hand goes up.

"Once again, no need for hands in my class, but please go on."

"It looks like a mercaptopurine, and the SH group is at position 6, so 6-mercaptopurine?"

The class of fifty murmurs excitedly.

"Wait, is that 6-MP?" a student yells.

"Yes!" says Emma, beaming.

"Oh my God, I think my grandfather took that!" says another student.

"For what? What was 6-MP initially used for?" Emma prompts.

"Acute leukemia. It was, like, the first effective treatment for leukemia in kids," says the same student.

"Yes, exactly. And why was its discovery so important?"

The murmuring is louder now.

"No wrong answers. At least, not until the test." Emma smiles, then goes on. "Before 6-MP, drug discovery was trial and error. Alexander Fleming and the serendipitous discovery of penicillin ring a bell? But with 6-MP, that all changed. It was designed, with intention, and not just by anyone. By a woman. Gertrude Elion, born in New York City in 1918. Of Jewish descent. Her grandfather died of cancer when she was fifteen. The experience . . . shaped her career."

Sanjay wonders if he's the only one who notices the break in Emma's voice.

"Her family was bankrupted by the crash of 1929, so she couldn't afford grad school. And scholarships? They weren't for women, not back then. World War II provided her big break. Not enough male chemists, so women finally got a shot. Gertrude didn't waste hers. She discovered 6-MP in her early thirties. Azathioprine by forty. Acyclovir, the first drug to fight a virus, in her sixties. Won the Nobel at age seventy. All with impeccable ethics and integrity."

Emma takes a moment to look around the room at each of her students. "I expect great things from you all, too . . . including turning in your next problem set on time." Laughter. "See you next week!"

She puts her marker down and wipes her hands on her jeans—likely a habit left over from the days of chalk—then looks up and spots Sanjay. He waves, enjoying her look of surprise.

She mouths two words: "You're here."

* * *

Sanjay finds Emma's coffee shop across the street while she speaks to stragglers after class.

As he stands in line, he examines the artwork on the walls. Bright red and bold black canvases: a phone saying, *Have you checked your privilege lately?*; a woman whispering in a man's ear, *Silence is not a yes*; and a series of fierce portraits. For him the most striking is of a woman with a black beret, fist raised to the sky, her Covid-style face mask reading, *I will fight until I die*!

A part of Sanjay can relate. The rest wonders, *Why bother? You can't win, anyway.*

He orders a drip coffee and takes a seat.

Growing up in rural Michigan, Sanjay was often the only brown kid in class. He vividly remembers the prettiest girl in grade four, Catherine Moore, coming up to him on the playground and bellowing, "DO YOU SPEAK ENGLISH?" then asking, "What's that smell?" and wrinkling her nose. Worse than looking different was constantly smelling like Indian spices—a side effect of living above his parents' grocery store and stocking the shelves before school.

Later, when his parents had to shut down the Michigan store and move in with his uncle in New Jersey, Sanjay was no longer the only South Asian. But he was the only poor one. His classmates were children of doctors, engineers, and businesspeople, and they looked down on his beat-up shoes and secondhand clothes.

Whenever Sanjay or his older sister Neela complained, their mother would calmly repeat: "Head down. Heart up. Go." It was her response to every challenge, big or small. *Need new shoes?* Keep your focus, work hard at your dreams, and one day you'll have everything you need. *Want more friends?* Follow the path, and they'll come. *Want justice?* Stick to the mantra, and in time your success will make the world treat you fairly.

As a teenager he constantly hustled—juggling the family store, shifts as a junior EMT, and school. But he isn't sure he ever got new shoes. Or friends. Or justice.

He lifts the mug to his lips. Empty.

Where's Emma?

He's surprised to feel his anxiety building. Hasn't he been with plenty of beautiful women in the last twelve years? He isn't the same scrawny, out-of-place immigrant kid. He's dating supermodels, heiresses.

But even as he thinks this, he knows he's fooling himself. Emma is beautiful, yes, but that wasn't where the attraction came from. Like her dad, she always strove to do right. Unlike Dr. Tom Carpenter, she managed to do it with kindness and grace, in a way that made people into better versions of themselves.

Sanjay has no interest in a relationship. He has a growing medical practice to get back to and too much respect for Emma to engage in a one-week fling.

Yet, there's that pit in his stomach.

Is he worried she'll criticize his career choices? Or is this about how things ended between them?

Sanjay shakes that thought out of his head. He's here to pay his respects to Tom and follow through on whatever duty that final "page" requires of him. Emma is special, but she's part of a different life; one that might have been but wasn't. If he hadn't failed that crucial anatomy exam and needed a break from school, who knows where they'd be?

Now here she is, greeting him with a nod through the picture window of the coffee shop.

The hug is over before Sanjay realizes it. Mechanical. More like distant colleagues than old friends. He expresses his condolences for Tom and answers questions about his family. Then he asks, "How's Neil?"

Emma's shoulders tense up. "Why would you ask about him?"

"The third pea in the pod? He texted me yesterday, said you told him we spoke."

"He's good." She exhales, sits back in her chair. "You know, he's president of MBH now?"

Sanjay does know. Reading about US healthcare is depressing, but he enjoys seeing articles about his friend Dr. Neil Desai—MBH's rising star, the youngest president of a top ten hospital, and a frequent honoree in industry "Top 40 Under 40" lists. As president, Neil directs all operations across MBH, including the hospital's three thousand doctors. Though the physician-in-chief is technically the hospital's "top doctor," it's largely a ceremonial title. The president—Neil—is the one in charge.

"He's why you can't recognize this place anymore," Emma says. "Without him, the new ICU tower never would have gotten off the ground. They're calling it 'the last place of hope for the sickest patients in the country.'"

When the small talk runs dry, she turns to Tom's death, telling Sanjay that his secretary heard her father hit the floor and called EMS. Tom arrived at MBH in under ten minutes, still with a pulse. But a stat head CT showed a massive stroke, and he coded minutes later, she says, her eyes filling with tears.

Sanjay reaches for her hands before he can stop himself. Emma looks down, then pulls them back and fishes around in her purse. Out comes a paper prescription.

Page Dr. Sanjay.

It's handwriting Sanjay would recognize anywhere. Tom always said with pride that it was legible enough for a pharmacist to read accurately, but illegible enough for the pharmacist to know that the writer was truly a physician.

He takes the slip of paper and turns it over. The front side is empty under the preprinted text "Community Cares, Dr. Thomas Carpenter, Executive Director and Internist." He flips it a couple more times, staring at the blank spaces, before Emma takes the prescription back and puts it in her purse.

"Why did he ask for you?" she asks.

"I'm wondering the same thing," Sanjay says. He sighs.

She eyes him carefully. "You really have no idea?"

"Not a clue."

"When did you last talk to him?"

"Tom and I hadn't spoken since . . . I emailed him about a case a few years ago, but no answer."

Emma's eyes narrow. "You meant something to him. To us. But you just . . ." Her voice wobbles.

"Just what?"

"Left. You left, Sanjay."

He sighs and sits back in his chair. "Look, Emma, I left because the system's corrupt."

Her face scrunches up. "Yeah, so? You take off when things get hard? Run away to the land of bimbos and billionaires?"

He crosses his arms. He didn't come to Boston to be lectured, and certainly not by a Carpenter.

"Forget it, Sanjay." Emma's eyes are cold. "It's all in the past."

It doesn't seem to be, he thinks, but says nothing.

"Anyway," she says, rubbing her nose. "A medical question. The last few weeks, my father was acting erratic. Is that normal before a stroke?"

Sanjay feels his eyebrows go up. Strokes can be preceded by TIAs, transient ischemic attacks. Mini strokes. But aberrant behavior is an unusual symptom. "Tell me more."

"I got calls from his old colleagues at MBH—said he was back at the hospital, working in the dark, mumbling to himself. I didn't think much of it. But then one of his clinic nurses called—someone who actually knew him, who cared. She said he was flying off the rails, even worse than normal."

"What was he mad about?"

"You remember how my father would get," Emma says, looking away.

Sanjay does. Carpenter's temper was almost as legendary as his diagnostic prowess. Sanjay was on the receiving end only once—and that was the last time he saw Tom.

That temper, people said, was why Tom got banished to the free clinic a year later. Something about him blowing up at an MBMS student, although Sanjay never got the full story.

"I went to his office to check on him," Emma continues. "This was about ten days ago. It was a mess, marked-up papers and sticky notes everywhere. As soon as he saw me, he pushed me out, saying, 'We can't talk here. It's not safe, it's not safe.'"

Her pupils dilate. Whatever she witnessed that day still scares her. "Do you think it's possible that someone . . . ?"

"That someone what?" he asks.

"Nothing. Never mind." She's wringing her hands. "I mean, he had a stroke, right? That's not one of those diagnoses that doctors get wrong."

She was about to ask, Sanjay thinks, if it's possible someone hurt him. But she's right. Clinically speaking, strokes aren't something anyone can inflict on another person.

He nods for her to continue.

"Anyway, I think it was stress, but I want to . . . I need to know what he was stressed *about*. The last time we spoke, about a week ago, he was distracted. Confused, even. He kept mumbling, 'My files, my files.'"

Sanjay leans forward. "What files?"

"That's what I asked. But he brushed me off, like always. You know him. His head was buried in patient charts all day, every day. But he never referred to those as files."

"He lived under stress," Sanjay says. "He put his patients first."

"That he did," Emma says, looking away, her face suddenly sullen. "I just don't get why he asked for you. He had high hopes for you once, you know? He thought you'd run the free clinic. He thought—"

She stops and rakes her hands through her hair.

"Emma, I want you to know—"

The words come fast, like she's been holding them in for years. "He still talked about you after you left. Said you were the best diagnostician he'd ever trained. And he trained a lot of people."

Sanjay rubs his chin. Things are coming together for him. But as often happened back in med school, Emma gets there first. "He'd say that if he ever needed help with a difficult case, you were the first person he'd call."

"So that's it, isn't it?"

Emma looks squarely at Sanjay for the first time. "Of course. He must have been trying to crack a difficult diagnosis. That's what the files are about. That's why he was so stressed."

Sanjay nods. "A medical mystery. But who's the patient?"

CHAPTER 5

IT MAKES SENSE now. Tom summoned him to consult on a patient with a mysterious illness.

His first thought is whether the patient might have been Tom himself. But Tom was too skilled a physician not to know, even as he scrawled Sanjay's name, that his time was measured in hours, if not minutes.

He and Emma agree to meet later at Tom's office, hoping the files he mentioned would be there. With any luck, they'll lead to the mystery patient. Emma has a research meeting, which gives Sanjay a couple hours to kill. He debates heading over to Tom's office now. On the flight to Boston, he fantasized about walking into the free clinic's waiting room, maybe seeing a patient or two. But the look in Emma's eyes when she described her run-in with her father is gnawing at him.

No one could cause a stroke, but what if the ER missed something?

Almost without thinking, Sanjay leaves the coffee shop and heads to MBH. At the employee entrance, he slips in behind a resident wearing AirPods.

As he steps into the twenty-four–room ER, he reflexively eyeballs the patients in the waiting room. Other than a couple of cuts and scrapes that need to get sutured, most of the people out front don't need ER-level care. And he knows from experience that the ones brought directly to the back by ambulance likely needed to be seen by a doctor weeks ago. But that's one of the catch-22s of the American healthcare system. Because hospitals like MBH refuse to see uninsured patients in clinic and cap the number of low-income patients they take, patients have only two choices: go to the ER for nonurgent problems or be brought there too late.

A group of doctors cluster around the tracking board. Sanjay checks his watch: It's 3:05 PM. Change of shift time. The 7 AM to 3 PM crew is leaving, the 3 PM to 11 PM coming in. The outgoing doctors look worn-out, a bit dazed. The incoming ones are giddy, wired on adrenaline and caffeine.

The standout is a striking blond, her hair up in a ponytail, who's barking orders to the residents. "What about room seven? We need to street him."

"I'm waiting for CT. They're backed up," says a hapless resident.

"Not as bad as your patient is. That's the only reason he's got abdominal pain. Get him on MiraLAX and out of my ER."

The other residents laugh.

"You got it, Chief," one calls.

Ah, the chief resident, thinks Sanjay. An honorific for the best physician in the residency program. In his experience, females make better ER docs. They're cooler under pressure and quicker at sniffing out BS.

The residents disperse, and Sanjay stiffens as a voice calls out, "What are you doing in my ER? You a drug rep or something?"

He turns to find the chief resident eyeing him. "Nah," she says, stepping closer. "You're good-looking enough, but I'd say you're too smart."

He puts out his hand. She eyes it skeptically.

"Dr. Patel."

"I'm Dr. Jenna Ciroli. Back to my question. What are you doing here?"

"Tom Carpenter was my mentor. When I worked here."

She sighs. "We always knew when a patient of his was coming in, because he'd call and give us a heads-up. Even so, the first thing you'd hear was, 'I'm a patient of Dr. Carpenter's.'"

He smiles. "That was our guy."

"We should've been able to save him. With all this, I mean." She waves a hand across the telemetry monitors, mobile CT scanners, and respiratory machines cluttering the room.

"You were there?"

"No, I was off that day. But I heard it was like his body just gave up."

Sanjay rubs his chin. "Do you mind if I look at his chart?"

The questioning eyes are back. "It was textbook, I can promise you that. The attendings wouldn't let a resident or intern in the room. Not even to do chest compressions."

Sanjay nods. "I wouldn't normally ask. Or be here. But right before he died, he asked to have me paged."

She purses her lips, likely weighing the risks. Then she strides to a computer on wheels a foot away, types in her password, and pushes the machine toward him. "You have five minutes while I change into something that doesn't have blood on it."

The best way to learn what happened to Tom, of course, is to check his electronic health record. Sanjay knows it would contain everything that happened from the moment he arrived in the ER to the time he was pronounced dead, including blood tests, X-rays, and reports.

Sanjay clicks in and is met by a pop-up: "This patient is deceased. Are you sure you want to open this record?"

A throbbing sensation lurches up from his abdomen. He knows it's just the pulse of his aorta, but it feels like his heart has dropped into his stomach. Tom's death suddenly feels more real, more final.

He takes a breath and clicks past the warning.

The ER note confirms what he's already learned. Tom came in unresponsive, but with a pulse. Blood pressure was low normal, heart rate elevated. The left side of his body was paralyzed. Minutes after his head CT, he coded. After twelve minutes of CPR, they called it.

Sanjay checks every medication and lab result. Everything was done as it should have been. Next, he opens the CT scan, rapidly scrolling through slices of Tom's brain. *It's a stroke, all right. A massive one.*

"Time's up."

Dr. Ciroli is back. In tight jeans. Hair down. When she leans across him to log out of her computer, she smells like rain.

"Nice meeting you . . ." she says, and arches an eyebrow. "Unless you want to buy me coffee?"

He looks at her, and she meets his gaze with a crooked smile. *She may not be talking about coffee*, he thinks.

"I'd love to, but I'm meeting up with a . . . friend."

"Well, if you want a new friend, page me. Ciroli, pager number 4721. Dr. Patel is a pretty common name around here. Your first name is?"

"Sanjay. I usually go by Dr. Sanjay."

Her expression flickers. Maybe it's recognition. It's definitely a flicker.

Without another word, she turns and walks off.

* * *

As the Range Rover pulls up, Sanjay takes in the bright blue banner stretched across the building: "Community Cares Clinic." Just beneath the name, in Spanish—Tom's quiet tribute to his wife Maria: "Abierto para la salud de todas nuestras familias." Open for the health of all our families.

He takes a moment to get his bearings. What was once a modest neighborhood of Haitian and El Salvadorean immigrants is now lined with biotech firms, glassy research centers, and upscale coffee spots. MBH is metastasizing.

From the outside, the free clinic hasn't changed since the last time he and Tom worked together—it's the same diminutive two-story brick building with grimy windows and sun-faded children's paintings covering the front wall.

But inside, Sanjay knows, things are different. Ten years earlier, the building was chiefly occupied by MBH's billing department. Tom never tired of the irony. Medical bills are the number one source of bankruptcy in America. And where do the poor go for medical care? Free clinics. Now the clinic is fully staffed and modernized, and it fills the whole building.

When Sanjay worked here as a medical student and again as an attending, the patients reminded him of his parents. Many were recent immigrants, and they were poor and uninsured. The system made their lives nearly impossible, yet they were gracious to a fault. It wasn't uncommon for them to rise to their feet when Sanjay entered the room, and offer pupusas and handmade scarfs.

They were also sick. Most had put off seeing a doctor until the last possible moment—they couldn't afford to pay for medical care or to miss work, get childcare, or arrange transportation. Then the foot sores or wheezing would get so bad that neighbors would ask, "Have you gone to the free clinic?" Often, that's how word spread about Community Cares.

But Sanjay was no savior. He loved working at the clinic because that's where he felt most free to practice medicine. No insurance had an upside: no insurance companies. Which meant no bogus paperwork, no endless justifications for routine decisions. When he prescribed a medication, rather than wondering if the patient had enough money to fill it, he'd go to the back room and count pills—free samples donated by pharma companies—into white envelopes. No mindless electronic health records; no litany of checkboxes and unnecessary documentation. Instead, he kept tabs on his patients using a gray box of index cards, arranged alphabetically with the most relevant medical history and treatment plans jotted down.

The clinic ran on a shoestring, but it delivered on its mission—offering what was needed to care for patients and nothing else.

As long as it had the funding to do so.

"Dr. Sanjay?" Across the parking lot, a fiftyish woman in blue scrubs locks a Nissan Altima and jogs toward him. "You're back!"

"Nurse Kay! A sight for sore eyes, as ever."

"If your eyes are sore, then I need cataract surgery," she says with a laugh.

Stooped over fifteen degrees, she is still steady on her feet and, he's willing to bet, still strong enough to lift a patient. Nurses are built different. They have to be.

She pulls him into a hug, then pushes him back for a once-over. Satisfied, she gets right to business. "I got a bad diabetic ulcer I could use your help packing." She starts for the door, then stops, her face asking, *What?*

"I'm . . . I'm just here for a minute."

She peers at him and takes a breath. "About Tom?"

"Not exactly, but yeah."

"Best damn doctor I ever worked with. One of the best men, too." Her eyes get misty, but she holds it together. "You'd have been close in line. If you stuck around, I mean. I hear . . ."

Whatever she heard, she thinks better of passing it on. "You know, I was the first nurse on the scene. When Tom collapsed."

His eyebrows go up.

"Yep. When he went down, he knocked over his chair. His secretary heard the thump and called for help. I ran up as fast as I could and started stabilizing him. Not that it mattered. What was it Tom would say about a stroke? Time is—"

"Time is brain."

Tom had a saying for everything. Sanjay first assumed it was just his quirky way of talking. But over the years, he realized Tom's mnemonics were verbal talismans, prescribed to ward off medical errors.

In his mind, Sanjay can see the scene unfolding. "It must have been hard," he says softly.

"Hard?" Kay frowns at him. "He wasn't Dr. Carpenter then. He was a patient in need of help."

Sanjay can't help but smile. He misses working with professionals like her. "And what was your assessment?"

She hesitates. Considers. "I've seen my fair share of strokes. I was *sure* it was his heart."

Sanjay cocks his head.

"His toes were blue. You know Tom; he loved walking around barefoot like he was still on mission in Peru. Never seen a stroke patient with blue toes. Course, I'm just a nurse. Dr. Carpenter's case would be way above my pay grade. Leave that to you MDs."

Sanjay isn't so sure. Any doctor worth his diploma learns the first week of internship to listen to nurses.

"Anyway, I'm due in. Sure you don't want to come?"

Sanjay can already picture himself packing the wound, counseling the patient on how to check his feet to prevent another ulcer. But he's frozen. Is this his body's way of telling him he's too tainted for this place now?

He begs off to head up the side entrance to Tom's office, leaving Nurse Kay to go in alone. Standing in the parking lot, he considers what she just said. Blue toes and strokes don't usually go together, and unless the jet lag is hitting him harder than usual, the ER note made no mention of blue toes. He'll have to go back and review Tom's chart line by line.

When a nurse's sixth sense is fired up, it's almost always right.

CHAPTER

6

TOM'S OFFICE IS unrecognizably quiet without a rush of staff flowing in and out, and without Tom's booming voice doctoring patients by phone in Spanish with his distinctive Bostonian twang.

When Sanjay flips the lights on, his eyes go to the whiteboard, where he and Tom used to crack their toughest cases. They'd list the patient's symptoms and lab results on the left and keep a running list of diagnoses on the right, ordered from most to least likely.

Looking at the empty board, he can almost see himself and Tom jockeying for the black marker, racing to underline key findings or cross out diagnoses—then stepping back, satisfied, when they cracked a case.

In his private practice, Sanjay doesn't have a whiteboard, but he often writes out tough cases on a blank sheet of paper.

He was hoping to see some of Tom's infamous chicken scratch today, but if there was anything on the board when he died, the janitorial staff must have cleaned it off.

When did he first witness Tom's brilliant medical mind at work? Sanjay crosses his arms, staring at the board. The memory comes almost instantly: second year of med school, clinical skills, the first time they practiced histories and physicals on real patients.

The patient was a twenty-six-year-old Marine who'd been stationed in Southeast Asia when she began experiencing nightly fevers. During the day, she felt fine, but every night she woke with bone-shaking chills and sweated through her clothes. Given the jungle setting, doctors on base tested her for a wide range of tropical infectious diseases. When the tests came back normal, they ordered rest, but the fevers continued. So they gave her a course of antibiotics. That didn't work, either.

Over the coming months, the young Marine became a medical mystery, transferring from medical facility to medical facility: Okinawa, Japan, then Germany, then Walter Reed—each time with a new battery of tests and treatments, but no improvement. Finally, she arrived at Mount Beacon Hospital, often the last resort for patients with medical conditions that couldn't be solved elsewhere. But after two days of extensive testing, the doctors there, too, couldn't figure out what was wrong.

As Sanjay and his classmates were finishing their practice session, Dr. Tom Carpenter entered the patient's room. After asking her a series of questions and examining her skin and reflexes, Tom announced, "I know exactly what this is, and you'll be better in no time." He explained to the patient that she didn't have an infection. The fevers and tropical setting were red herrings. She had adult-onset Still's disease, an autoimmune condition that happened to start while she was stationed overseas. The key was a telltale salmon-colored skin rash that had disappeared early in her illness, which no other doctor had thought to ask about.

With two weeks of high-dose ibuprofen, Tom expected a full recovery.

Sanjay was in awe. The woman had seen dozens of doctors and received hundreds of tests and X-rays, all without a diagnosis.

Dr. Carpenter was able to crack the case in minutes, with just his mind and his bare hands.

Tom was equally skillful in the way he treated the patient. When she told him about her family history, he shared a bit of his own and got her talking. When she cried describing how the illness was affecting her life, he held her hand. When he gingerly bent to examine her knees, he joked about his old age and got her laughing. By the end of the encounter, he didn't just know her diagnosis, he'd earned her trust.

In that moment, Sanjay found the doctor he wanted to model himself after.

Afterwards, he asked Tom if he could start shadowing him. Tom agreed, but only on one condition: that Sanjay put patients first. Hand over his heart, Sanjay met his new mentor's gaze and said, "I promise to always put patients first."

Now a sharp knock yanks him back.

Emma slips through the door. "I bet the files my father was fretting about are actual paper files. He always hated computers."

He suspects it's her first time here since her father died. He wants to say something, but her face is tight, unreadable. She hasn't had time to process this—or she doesn't want to.

"I'll check here," she says, nodding toward one side of the room. "You start over there."

They open cabinets and shuffle through reams of old medical journals, looking for any recent patient records. Emma mentions that the office is surprisingly messy for her dad, ever the army man.

"Maybe all part of the stress that caused his stroke?" she asks.

Sanjay doesn't know. He wonders if he should tell Emma what Nurse Kay saw, then decides to wait. He isn't sure what to make of it, and he doesn't want to add to Emma's worries.

After an hour, they admit defeat. Emma sighs and slumps back against a cabinet. "I was sure the files would be here."

"It's okay," Sanjay says. He tries to put his hand on her shoulder to comfort her, but she takes a step back, and he awkwardly misses.

They tidy up in silence. Before they leave, Emma opens her dad's well-worn appointment book and flips back and forth through the final entries.

"Huh," she says.

Intrigued, Sanjay walks over.

"Here, look." Emma hands him the book. "In the past month, my father saw MBH's general counsel three times."

"That is odd." In Sanjay's experience, it's never a good thing to meet with lawyers of any kind. Especially hospital lawyers. "Your dad wasn't working at MBH anymore, right?"

Emma shakes her head, thinking. "After he was pushed out, he continued seeing a handful of patients from his old practice. But otherwise, no. He had very little to do with the main hospital."

Had Tom's temper gotten him in trouble again? Sanjay wonders.

Emma takes the book back, runs her fingers over her dad's handwriting. "Maybe this is why he was stressed? We should ask Dr. Ecker."

"Ecker? Is he still chair of medicine? I thought Tom didn't like him." In Sanjay's experience, Ecker was the best of the lot when it came to hospital administrators, but at MBH, that was a low bar.

Emma rolls her eyes. "My father didn't like anyone who didn't see patients anymore, but that was a Tom Carpenter problem. I trust Ecker, and as the highest-funded researcher at MBH, he's even more powerful than Neil or the physician-in-chief. If my father talked to the general counsel, Ecker's our best bet to find out why."

Before Sanjay can say anything, she grabs her coat. "I gotta go check on my team at the lab. I'll meet you in the hospital lobby in an hour."

* * *

Sanjay ditches the Range Rover and tells John, the driver, he'll be on foot the rest of the day. After eight hours crammed on a plane, he's glad to be moving his muscles.

Nurse Kay saw blue toes, but the ER note made no mention of them. Likely a harmless clerical error or nurse overread, but Sanjay had learned from Tom to never let the sun go down on a medical mystery.

Tom's secret sauce wasn't his intellect. It was that he unfailingly followed up with patients—to see what happened to them and find out whether his diagnoses were right or wrong. He'd say that most doctors didn't *practice* medicine.

"Not like you practice the piano or your backhand in tennis," Sanjay can almost hear him saying. "When you play a wrong note or over-hit the ball, you know it, and you improve. But in medicine, most of the time, doctors don't get feedback. They aren't practicing; they're playing God. It's foolishness."

Tom was obsessed with feedback. Once, a patient of his was deported a day after he diagnosed her with migraines. He badgered immigration authorities until they gave him her contact information in Mexico. Only when he finally got hold of her and confirmed his treatment was working—which meant she didn't have something worse, like cancer—did he let it go.

The memory reminds Sanjay of Petrov. He texts Cassie a quick reminder to have his nurse practitioner check up on the oligarch. If Petrov doesn't get a stress test by next week, Sanjay will fly back and drag him to one personally.

He slips past a security guard glued to his phone. MBH's exterior has gotten a facelift, but Sanjay hopes the guts are the same. He takes a sharp left, heads down the basement stairs, and pushes through a heavy, unmarked set of double doors to his right.

The stench of formaldehyde hits his nostrils, knocking him back. No question—it's still the autopsy room. Plastic bags of organs rest on metal workbenches or dangle from ceiling-mounted scales. A high-pitched buzz hums from the far corner, interrupted by the occasional thump. Sanjay grabs a pair of oversized goggles and heads toward the sound.

Standing over a metal table, driving a chainsaw through a naked body, is a man in goggles and a bloody white coat. He's cracking open the sternum of a dead male in his late sixties. Protuberant belly and edema up to the thighs. Anasarca. Likely diastolic heart failure.

Having reached the pericardial sack, the man throttles off the chainsaw, and the room goes abruptly silent. Sanjay clears his throat, and the man turns, takes down his mask, and pushes his goggles up. His red beard has more gray in it now, but his eyes are still full of kindness. Sanjay always thought he looked more like a farmer than a pathologist.

"Dr. Sanjay! In the living flesh?"

Sanjay lets out a short laugh. "More or less. I'm impressed you remember me, Dr. Feldman."

"Remember you? Heck, you and Carpenter were the only doctors who ever bothered to come down here. God forbid doctors talk to each other anymore. They're all just typing away at their computers these days. Like playing a goddamn video game." Feldman tears off his right glove and wipes his hand on a cleanish section of his coat before extending it.

Sanjay opts for a fist bump. "You know what Tom used to say: 'The internist knows everything and does nothing. The surgeon knows nothing and does everything. The pathologist knows everything—'"

"'—but is always a week too late.'" Feldman laughs, shaking his head. "He was a good man, Tom. Damn shame."

He kicks at imaginary dirt on the lab floor. Sanjay gives him a moment, then asks, "Listen, what did Tom's autopsy show?"

Dr. Feldman eyes Sanjay and takes a deep breath. He speaks slowly, as if he's not sure he should be telling him this. "I don't know. I never got a look."

Sanjay shakes his head, confused. "What do you mean? Who did the autopsy?"

"Nobody."

"What?"

Feldman drags a stool over and slumps down on it. "I don't know what to tell you. The ER docs, us, everyone wanted an autopsy. It's protocol, and besides, Dr. Feedback would have insisted."

Sanjay nods. Tom often lamented the modern trend away from autopsies. *The dead's way of serving the living*, he'd say.

"We were ordered not to do one," Feldman says in that same thoughtful voice.

"Ordered? By whom?"

"Dunno. A call from upstairs, someone high on the food chain. One of the intake clerks took it. The caller was a woman. Said it was out of respect for Tom's privacy. Something about his family wanting it that way."

No. Not possible. Emma was all the family Tom had left, and she knew how her father felt about autopsies. Besides, as a scientist, she'd want answers, too.

"What did you make of his blue toes?"

Feldman blinked. "Sanjay, I never saw the body. But I don't have to tell you—blue toes in a stroke don't make any damn sense."

Sanjay bites his lip and looks up at the ceiling, thinking over his next move.

Feldman says, "You know Tom's other saying, right?"

Sanjay looks at him and cocks his head.

"'The tissue is the issue.'" Feldman scoffs. "Get me some—a test tube of blood, even, and we'll talk."

With that, he pushes his goggles back on his face, stands, and fires up his chainsaw.

CHAPTER

7

THE MAIN LOBBY of MBH has been completely renovated since Sanjay was last here. The marble and flooring are all black, and the space is divided into dozens of sitting areas, each partially enclosed by two ten-foot walls set at right angles. The intent must have been to give families privacy, but it comes across as cold and disconnected. Adding to that effect are the doctors, who wear stark white lab coats over dark ties and pants, a new mandatory dress code, according to the security guard who waved Sanjay in.

To Sanjay it feels more like a bank than a place of healing. But then, he thinks, in many ways, it is. Healthcare costs the American people over $4 trillion a year, a third of which goes to hospitals like MBH. He read once that if the entire US healthcare system were its own country, it would have the fourth-highest GDP in the world—and MBH would be its capital. As a nonprofit that pays no federal taxes, the hospital clears over $1 billion a year in profits. Last year it paid its CEO a tidy salary of $10 million.

In the corner, Sanjay sees a mom and dad cradling a child no older than two in their arms, a large surgical dressing covering her head. Brain cancer, he figures. They look so small in the open-air atrium.

As he draws closer, he sees the worry etched on their faces. From the bits of Spanish he can make out, they're fretting over the hospital bill.

Sanjay's stomach twists with a familiar sense of dread. He's witnessed this scene too many times. How many families like theirs could MBH's billion-dollar profits help? How many could be spared the agony of choosing between care for their loved ones and making ends meet?

Instead, it's the opposite. The hospital's profits come *from* these families. Because in this infuriating healthcare system, it's those with the least, the uninsured, that pay the most.

"I'm sorry I'm late," a voice calls. It's Emma, hurrying in through the lobby door, still wearing a long lab coat. "We had an equipment failure. A real mess." She pushes her bangs from her eyes.

He's looking at her, but thinking about the family. His own, too.

"What?" she asks, eyeing him suspiciously.

He shakes his head. "Nothing. Let's head up."

* * *

They take a glass elevator to the executive offices on the top floor. When Sanjay sees a sign for the Office of the President, he detours, feeling his spirits lift.

"Sanjay! Emma!" Neil exclaims, jumping up from his chair. He drapes his arms around them. "Look at us. Three peas in a pod!"

Sanjay steps back to examine his old friend. It's only been a year, but Neil's hair is thinner in front and his little paunch has grown. Too much cortisol, not enough vitamin D, no doubt the cost of his promotion to hospital president. But his smile is the same, and Sanjay feels more whole in his presence.

Neil takes Emma's hands. "I'm so sorry about your dad. I've been trying to get hold of you. Did you get my flowers?"

"I did, thank you, Neil. I meant to call you back," says Emma.

Sanjay notices her blush.

"Dr. Carpenter was a legend," Neil says simply. "He taught me so much. Brilliant and compassionate. Unquestionable integrity. He truly was the best of us."

"Thank you, Neil," Emma says again, and this time her voice quivers.

"And Sanj, I'm so glad you came. Though she may not admit it—" Neil gently elbows Emma. "This one wants you here for the funeral."

Emma blushing and Neil speaking for her? Sanjay's antennae go up. *Are they a couple?*

"Plus, I just want to hang out with my buddy again." Neil elbows Sanjay, grinning. "Remember Zurich last year, that medical conference? Emma, you wouldn't believe how this guy rolls. Yachts, the best tequila—"

"You've seen each other recently?" asks Emma, her voice going up an octave.

"Yeah, over the years, I've referred patients to Sanj, and of course we text. But last year we finally met up. Speaking of which, are you guys coming to our class reunion?"

"Class reunion?" Sanjay repeats, confused.

"Oh, come on, Dr. Patel. Our ten-year med school reunion? It's this weekend. Don't you get the emails?"

"You should go together," says Emma, suddenly colder. "I'll sit this one out."

Neil frowns. "At least come out for drinks with the gang the night before." He looks at Sanjay. "I won't take no for an answer."

Emma looks annoyed but gives Neil a shrug. Sanjay knows that when his old friend's heart is set on something, it's easier to give in. They make plans to meet the following night.

"So, what are you doing up here?" asks Neil, waving his arm around the executive offices.

Emma tells him about the mysterious files and Tom's meetings with the general counsel, then says, "We're hoping Dr. Ecker can point us in the right direction."

"I hope so, too. But since you don't have a hard stop, want to visit the new ICU? Emma, you only saw it for the ribbon-cutting ceremony, before we had patients."

Emma's face lights up. "You have to see it, Sanjay. It's amazing."

"You remember the old one, Sanj? Total disaster. If a patient on the far side of the unit was coding, you couldn't even see them from the nurse's station. Well, we finally decided to do something about it."

"You mean, *you* decided to do something about it," says Emma, patting him on the shoulder.

* * *

A few minutes later, they're crossing the glass bridge that connects the administrative offices to the ICU. Sanjay trails behind. Halfway down, Neil stops, touches Emma's shoulder, and points her gaze toward something ahead. Sanjay can't make out what he's saying, but the gesture reminds him of their first visit to Community Cares—how Neil excitedly led the way in.

It was the day before classes started. Sanjay and his classmates stood outside the campus bookstore, the mood somber. Tomorrow loomed—the start of hours of dry lectures, followed by even more hours of mind-numbing memorization.

"I can't wait to see patients!" he said, hoping to brighten the mood. "When do we start on the wards?"

"Never!" scoffed one of the students.

The rest laughed. Clearly, Sanjay didn't get it.

"You have to wait," said another. "We don't see patients until our third year."

The first two years, they explained, were strictly for classroom-based learning—anatomy, physiology, pharmacology. Most of them were the children of doctors and already knew the lay of the land.

Then, from behind him, came a voice.

"Actually, if you want to see patients, I know a free clinic where we can go."

He turned to see Emma Carpenter-Flores. He'd noticed her during orientation—it was hard not to—but they hadn't yet met. Her father, Dr. Tom Carpenter, was one of the most talked about doctors at MBH, renowned for his diagnostic skills and his high expectations of medical students.

"Hi, I'm Emma." Her heart-shaped face, doe eyes, and thick dark hair were mesmerizing. "It's Sanjay, right?" she added, smiling.

Behind her stunning facade, he felt an incredible warmth, like she was good through and through.

"Um, yeah," he managed, extending his hand. She shook it gently. "Hi."

"I gotta go get my textbooks, actually. Looks like you already have yours," she said, pointing at Sanjay's bags. "Are you in the dorms?"

Why was she asking? "Yeah, room 2012."

"Okay, great. How about we head to the free clinic tonight? It's open from seven thirty to nine. Meet you outside the dorm around seven?"

He reached the lobby at 6:50 PM, wearing his nicest slacks and button down and a whiff of cologne, an unopened Littmann stethoscope box under his arm. As soon as he stepped outside, an idling BMW out front blasted its horn. The front door opened and out popped Neil Desai, another first year. They'd met at the buffet line and briefly bonded over their Midwestern roots.

"Hey hey, Sanjay, it's Neil!" he said, jogging over and giving him a fist bump. "Let me get your stethoscope set up. You're gonna need it tonight."

As Neil opened the box, Sanjay gave him a confused look.

"Oh yeah, Emma mentioned you guys were gonna check out the free clinic, so I had to come. I'm raring to see patients. I don't care what everyone else says." Neil swung the stethoscope around Sanjay's neck, then inched it forward and smiled, satisfied. "There. Perfect."

It was the first time Sanjay had ever worn a stethoscope, but he could hardly savor the moment. Had he made a faux pas already, not even a week into medical school? What was wrong with going to the free clinic?

"What does everyone else say?" he asked.

Neil rolled his eyes dramatically. "That volunteering at Community Cares is a waste of time. Like we should be doing research in a lab and getting published."

Sanjay would soon learn that taking care of patients isn't the only mission of academic medical centers, or even the primary one. It's one of three—often described as the tripartite mission—research, teaching, and patient care. And research—basic science, drug discovery, and clinical trials—was what the institution truly prized.

"So why did you want to be a doctor?" Neil asked Sanjay that long-ago night.

"Because of my mom. She has an autoimmune condition that was misdiagnosed when I was a kid, and she's never recovered."

Neil's face scrunched up. "I'm sorry to hear that. In a way, that's why I'm going into medicine, too."

Sanjay took a step back. "Really?"

"Yeah, there are so many problems in healthcare. I want to be the best doctor I can be, and help other doctors be their best, too."

Just then Emma arrived, already looking like an attending physician in a crisp white coat, her stethoscope perfectly arranged. "What are we talking about?" she asked, smiling.

"The reason we wanted to become doctors," said Neil.

"What's yours?" asked Sanjay, unable to look away from Emma.

"All my life," Emma said, eyes distant, "my dad has worked hard to be a good doctor. But still his patients die. And every time it happens, my mom and I lose him for weeks." She straightened her back. "I want to be a physician-scientist and make discoveries that save more lives than any one doctor can on their own."

When they arrived at Community Cares, Neil led the way in. It was a mess. An overflowing line of patients at the door was the waiting room; the "exam rooms" were clusters of bar stools scattered across the fifty-by-fifty-foot space.

But to Neil, Sanjay, and Emma, it was heaven.

From that day on, the "three peas in a pod" were inseparable. They studied and ate together—Emma and Neil often footing the bill from their generous allowances. After each exam, they binged their favorite show, *Grey's Anatomy*.

Sanjay loved Emma because she always did the right thing—and did it with kindness. If someone stopped her on campus—often a panicked patient or a worried family member, lost in the hospital maze—she wouldn't just give directions. She'd walk them to the right entrance herself, even if it made her late to class.

Neil, he loved for his helpfulness. Sanjay had never gone to an elite school and initially struggled to keep up. Neil stayed up late helping him, explaining concepts everyone else seemed to know and sharing study tricks he'd learned in private school.

Initially, the trio went to the free clinic every week. They took their first medical history together, listened to their first heartbeat, wrote their first prescription. Then school and life got in the way.

Neil bent to pressure from his parents, who were angry that he wasn't the top student in class. He began skipping clinic—once a month, then every other week—and then took a two-year gap from med school to take a prestigious research fellowship at the National Institutes of Health in Maryland.

After her mother was diagnosed with metastatic breast cancer, Emma became her primary caregiver—her father was too consumed by his practice. She still tried to show up, but more often couldn't. Then her mom died, and she dropped out of med school.

Still, those early days at Community Cares are what Sanjay remembers best—the raw joy of becoming a doctor, of serving those in greatest need. Of feeling, for the first time, like he was exactly where he was meant to be—with the people he was meant to be there with.

* * *

"Here we are!" Neil announces now, as they arrive at the new intensive care unit.

The glass door slides open, and Sanjay hears a hissing sound, signaling that they're entering a positive pressure space, designed to keep outside contaminants from entering.

Each room is housed in glass and arrayed around a central nursing station for maximum visibility. The rooms themselves are large, with ample space for families to stay the night. As they pass, Sanjay notices one innovation after another—a middle-aged woman on a ventilator, walking on a treadmill to reduce muscle wasting; a twenty-something woman, likely with cystic fibrosis, receiving mechanical thumps to her back to clear mucus from her lungs.

They reach the room of an elderly patient. A younger woman—probably her daughter—gestures through the glass, trying to get Neil's attention. Unlike the others, this patient just seems to be sleeping. She's breathing on her own, her vitals are stable, and there's only one IV.

Neil steps inside, pulls up a chair, and rests a hand on the patient's leg as he turns to the daughter. A minute later, she begins to cry. He gently pats her shoulder, says something Sanjay can't hear—and she laughs. A moment later, they hug.

Sanjay turns to Emma, who's observing Neil with tears in her eyes. Maybe she's remembering the long weeks she spent in the ICU with her mom. Or maybe she's missing Tom.

He reaches over to comfort her, and thankfully, this time she doesn't withdraw.

"Neil was always such a good doctor," she says.

Sanjay nods. "Yes, he was. He is."

Neil steps back into the main hallway, and Emma asks, "What were you talking to the family about?"

"The patient is medically ready to be transferred out of the ICU, but the daughter wants her mom to stay another night. She loves the nurses here, and she's scared that if we transfer her mom to the floor, she'll bounce right back. I told her she can stay, and that we'd fight to make sure her insurance company covered the bill."

"I love how you care for your patients," says Emma, her eyes shining.

A twinge of jealousy hits Sanjay hard, catching him off guard.

Then Neil looks at him and says, "Sanjay, I see that look in your eyes! You miss real medicine. If you want a job here, just say the word."

"I practice real medicine," he protests lamely.

Neil slaps him on the back. "Oh, I know you do. But what you're doing out there . . ." He pauses. "Look, this is Man's Best Hospital, and you're one of the best doctors we've ever had. This—" He waves his arms around the gleaming ICU. "This is where you belong."

Sanjay has to admit, as he sees the pathology around him—congestive heart failure, post-transplant rejection, sepsis—he can't help but feel his talents are being wasted.

To come back to MBH, though? The thought's absurd. He turns to Emma, expecting her to agree. But for the first time since he's arrived, she's smiling at him.

They reach the last room on the tour, and Neil gives Sanjay and Emma a thumbs-up. "It's fantastic. We're at capacity!"

Internally, Sanjay cringes. But he reminds himself that "heads in beds" is the mantra of every hospital administrator in the country. Hospitals don't get paid for making people healthier. They get paid for filling beds. And given what he's seen, he has no doubt these patients are better off in Neil's beds than in any other ICU in the region.

"So, what do you think, Sanj?" asks Neil.

"It's impressive, no doubt. Not just the building—the level of care you're delivering. Have your parents seen it yet?"

Neil's parents, both physicians, were good people, but they were hard on their son. Top of the class, top of his field—that was the expectation. Sanjay hoped the ICU made the case for him at long last.

"No, not yet," says Neil. "Hopefully soon."

"Well, we're here. And we're proud of you," says Emma, smiling up at him.

Neil rubs his neck, his brown skin reddening. He waves them off. "Thanks, guys. You've always been on my side."

Sanjay feels the same—at least about Neil. When Sanjay couldn't match at MBH for residency because of his anatomy grade and wound up in Chicago, Neil was the one he'd call on his dark days. Days when attendings, wide-eyed that he went to the top medical school in the country, asked why he'd "settled" for Chicago.

"It isn't the name on the hospital," Neil would say, "it's the doctor in the exam room who matters."

Sanjay feels his eyes sting and shifts gears. "So how'd you pull this off? Can't be a small investment, even for MBH."

"You know how hospital boards are," Neil says, swatting the air with his right hand. "They don't know anything about medicine. I had to explain how the aging population and new procedure codes would make ICUs more profitable. But they still spent two million dollars on high-priced consultants who just repeated my analysis with prettier slides." He fake rolls his eyes. "After that, it was a done deal."

"But it was tough at first, right?" Emma says. "When it opened?"

"Yeah." Neil's eyes darken. "Six months ago, the tower was practically empty. We were hemorrhaging money. At first, the execs were all pointing fingers at each other, but then they turned on me."

"It was just awful, Sanjay." Emma cups Neil's shoulder, her face warm and open.

"It wasn't even my fault," Neil says with a sigh. "Over the past few years, referrals from other hospitals have been drying up."

Sanjay's head jerks back. "What? MBH has always been busy. Too busy, even."

Neil lowers his voice. "MBH wasn't playing well in the sandbox. We were buying up community hospitals. Those we didn't acquire saw us as a threat and boxed us out. We raised our prices too much, so insurance companies started incentivizing patients to go elsewhere. And our relationships . . . Man's Best Hospital became too arrogant, if you can believe that." He half-laughs. "We didn't think we needed to cater to referring doctors anymore, so they stopped catering to us."

"And then?" asks Emma.

Neil's whole body lightens. "Then we turned it around. We got this place humming."

Sanjay scratches his chin and asks, "Where did the patients come from?"

But Neil doesn't hear him. He's looking at his pager. *It must be on vibrate*, thinks Sanjay. He didn't hear it go off.

"Sorry," Neil says, "I gotta take this."

Sanjay wants to repeat the question, but Neil is already walking over to the nursing station, and there's something more pressing to ask.

"Hey, Neil," he calls. "Have you ever heard of an administrator canceling an autopsy?"

Neil pivots, frowning. "What? Which patient are you talking about?"

"Just something I heard. A rumor, maybe." He eyes Emma, who's half-listening.

"Gotta love hospital gossip," Neil says, shrugging. "It'd have to be someone pretty high up; higher than me, maybe. If something like that ever happened?" He raises his eyebrows. "We'd all be screwed."

CHAPTER

8

"DR. ECKER ISN'T JUST 'available' to meet. As you can imagine, he's very busy."

Ecker's secretary seems offended—mad, even—that Sanjay and Emma have dared to show up without an appointment.

"I'm Emma Carpenter-Flores. Dr. Tom Carpenter is . . . was my father." Emma's voice quivers. "It's important that I speak with Dr. Ecker."

The secretary's scowl vanishes. She steps out from behind her desk to shake their hands. "I didn't realize. I'll see what I can do." She motions them to follow her to a door on the far side of the room. "Wait here."

The conference room she leads them to is massive. In the center is a twenty-foot-long table with an inlay of MBH's crest, the three-sided dome, at the center. On the nearside wall are banners for each year MBH has been ranked the number one hospital in the country by *US News and World Report.* There are eleven of them, dating back to the year Dr. Ecker was named chair of internal medicine, MBH's largest department. But either the banner from last year hasn't arrived or MBH isn't number one anymore. Sanjay will ask Cassie to check on that later.

On the far wall is a series of black-and-white photographs of Ecker with movie stars, politicians, and business leaders—likely famous people who came to MBH for healing, then became major donors.

The last photo is of Ecker's medical school graduating class. Nearly every face in the photo is of a white man; only two are white women. No Sanjays, Neils, or Emmas in the crowd back then. In the front row is Ecker, all bow-tied up. Next to him is a young, full-haired Tom Carpenter, flashing his farm-boy grin.

"How is Ecker?" Sanjay asks Emma. "Still all about research?"

Although Ecker is one of MBH's most famous doctors, Sanjay suspects he hasn't seen a patient in decades.

"Now more than ever." Emma's voice rings with admiration. It's how she used to talk about her dad, before her mother got sick. "For years, he was one of the world's experts in blood clotting. Lots of grants and big papers. Then, five years ago, he had a breakthrough. He discovered a new drug that prevents clotting. He named it absoluximab"—the standard naming convention for monoclonal antibodies, Sanjay knows—"but everyone calls it absoluxir." She pronounced it as if it were *absolute-xir.*

"I read the early report in *Nature.* I didn't realize Ecker's lab was behind it."

"There was some controversy over who discovered it first," Emma says. "MBH or Johns Hopkins. But we won out. It's an antibody that blocks a novel protein in the blood-clotting pathway. The hope is that it will prevent clotting without excess bleeding. As you can imagine, there are a lot of applications."

Sanjay nods. The majority of cardiovascular diseases—heart attacks, strokes, peripheral artery disease—result from unwanted clotting. A drug that could stop harmful clotting without inhibiting good clotting would be a groundbreaking achievement—one that could secure Ecker's place in history and possibly win him the Nobel Prize.

"He decided to go after heart attacks first," Emma went on. "It's personal for him. His dad died of a heart attack when he was nine. He and DeSalvo got funding for a major clinical trial to prove—"

"DeSalvo? Matt DeSalvo?"

"Yeah, from med school. He and Ecker co-run the lab together." Emma takes a deep breath, and Sanjay catches something in her eyes, a look of hurt.

Matt DeSalvo was an MD-PhD, part of an elite group of students who got full scholarships to pursue dual degrees in medicine and science. Most MD-PhDs practiced medicine and led research labs, but from the first day of school, Matt made it clear that he never planned on seeing patients. He was a self-proclaimed "lab rat," a moniker Sanjay thought fitting, given Matt's pale skin and beady eyes.

Sanjay always found Matt's lack of interest in patient care irksome. Maybe Emma did, too. He's about to ask when Dr. Ecker's secretary returns.

"Dr. Ecker will see you," she says, and scowls at each of them in turn. "He's in the lab. Follow me and don't touch anything."

The secretary is more than just irritated. Something is off. As they cross the glass walkway from Ecker's office to the research building across the street, Sanjay observes her closely. Her eyes are bulging out of their sockets. She keeps fidgeting with her dress. And when they shook hands, hers felt noticeably warm. Hyperthyroidism? It would also explain the moodiness.

When she opens the doors to the research building, he looks at her neck. Right at the midline, below her Adam's apple, is a well-healed surgical scar. So she's had her thyroid removed, which means she's taking thyroid replacement medication. Is she taking extra doses on purpose? More people now know that thyroid hormone is responsible for metabolism, and it's become a fad to take extra thyroid pills to lose weight.

But no; her red dress is sagging, and her makeup is smeared. Not the picture of someone desperate to look better.

What if she's accidentally taking higher doses of thyroid medication? What if her doctor isn't monitoring her blood levels regularly, and she's on too high a dose?

"Here we are," she says.

Standing in front of the door is a heavily inked, burly man nearly a foot taller than Sanjay. He resembles a bouncer at a dive bar more than a hospital security guard.

"Professor Emma Carpenter-Flores and Dr. Sanjay Patel," says the secretary. "Here to see Dr. Ecker."

The man grunts, sizes Sanjay up, and gestures for their IDs.

As he pulls out his wallet, Sanjay turns to Emma, who looks equal parts uncomfortable and confused. *What kind of research lab needs security?*

The guard grunts again and waves them in, swiping the door open with an electronic key card. Emma walks inside, but Sanjay stays back to speak to the secretary.

"You need to get your thyroid level checked," he says softly.

"I'm sorry?" Her eyes bulge out even more.

"Your dose is too high." He points to her neck scar. "It's why you're having difficulty remembering things."

Her face turns red. "How do you know about that?"

* * *

Ecker's twenty-thousand-square-foot lab is filled with row after row of lab benches. Everywhere machines hum, and scientists and lab techs run gels, pipette solutions, and sketch in spiral notebooks.

In the corner of the room, away from the hubbub, on a spartan lab bench with wooden cabinets and a gray granite top, Dr. Henry Ecker hunches over a microscope. He wears the same white lab coat as the dozens of researchers who work for him, but somehow on him it gives off an air of sporty refinement.

Ecker looks up. His thick, dark brown hair seems wet, and his face is glowing, as if he just stepped off a treadmill.

"Come, take a look!" he says, waving them over.

On the plate, Sanjay sees dozens of bright purple dots floating in a sea of red circles. An old memory from pathology class stirs. He's looking at platelets, the cells in the blood that form clots and stop bleeding.

"Coagulation. This little process holds the key to life." Ecker launches into his latest hypothesis about platelets and the proteins involved with blood clotting, but Emma gently cuts him off.

"Fascinating, Dr. Ecker. Really. But I was hoping to talk to you about my father."

Ecker looks directly at them. His eyes are a very deep blue. "Tom was a great physician." He sighs, folding his hands together. "The institution is heartbroken. I am heartbroken."

Emma smiles sadly. "Thank you so much, Dr. Ecker. I got the voicemail you left me. Very thoughtful."

"It's the least I can do. I only wish I'd gotten absoluxir out sooner. This drug—well, it didn't have a hope of saving my father, but it could have saved yours."

Emma's eyes start to well up.

Though Ecker's being dramatic, Sanjay doesn't think he's wrong. Most strokes are the result of a blood clot forming in the brain. If absoluxir could prevent blood clots in the heart, in theory it could also prevent one in the brain.

Ecker extends his hand to Sanjay. "Dr. Sanjay, I hear you're doing well for yourself these days. Many of your clients are people I've been trying to get to for years. There's so much more we could do for patients if we could fund more brilliant scientists like Emma. We should talk."

Sanjay looks at Emma, but she's lost in thought. He's shocked that Ecker's openly soliciting his patients as donors. Then again, at least Ecker's being aboveboard about it. He reminds himself of that low bar at MBH and stifles an ironic smile.

"So, Emma, how can I help?" asks Ecker.

"Dr. Ecker, the last few weeks, my father was very stressed, more than usual, which may have contributed to his stroke." Emma's voice sounds heavy, sad. "I thought you might know why."

Ecker's eyebrows shoot up. "Me? As you know, your father wasn't my biggest fan."

"I know. I'm sorry."

"No need to apologize." He smiles, shakes his head. "Tom was a man of principle. I admired that."

Emma nods. "His appointment book showed three meetings with the general counsel in the past month. I know you're close to the board. Any idea what those meetings were about?" Her face flushes. "I know it won't change anything. I'd just like to know."

"I don't know anything that would be of any use to you. But Emma, since you're here . . . I know it's not the best time, but I'd like to talk to you about something."

"Of course."

"What do you think about merging our labs?"

Seemingly in spite of herself, Emma gasps.

"I know, I know." Ecker puts his hands up. "It requires serious discussion. But I've long been impressed by your research. I told Tom as much. And I worry about you and your team. NIH funding isn't what it used to be—we both know that. My lab has ample resources. It's a great opportunity for brilliant scientists like you to focus on the science and leave the paper pushing to old dogs like me."

Emma's speechless at first. Then she manages, "That's very flattering, Dr. Ecker. Truly. My lab is actually doing okay. In fact, we're about to get a grant to—"

"A grant to what?" asks a nasal voice.

Sanjay whirls around to see Matthew DeSalvo. He's as pale as ever, his thinning hair streaked with gray.

"Matt, it's been a while." Emma nods to him, seeming to expect a response, some form of acknowledgment or condolences. None come.

"Hello, SAN-jay," Matt says, pressing his cold hand into Sanjay's palm. Despite his brilliance, he remains part of the 1 percent of people who can't seem to get Sanjay's name right.

"Matthew, I was just telling Emma that our labs should join forces," says Ecker.

"Well, that's an idea." Matt smiles, but it doesn't reach his eyes. "Dr. Ecker, we have that donor meeting, followed by the CFO of Next Health, then a meeting with—"

Ecker's cheeks flush. "—our partners," he finishes Matt's sentence. "Yes, of course. Emma, Sanjay, I apologize, but we'll need to continue this later. Perhaps after the funeral tomorrow?"

"I'll show them out," says Matt, already moving toward the door. He strides behind them, almost shoving them along. Sanjay is more than willing to leave.

As they approach the exit, Matt says, "Emma, I appreciate your interest in our work, but now's not the right time for us to be bringing in new people."

"Sure, Matt. It wasn't my idea. I—"

"Security will assist you if you need anything else." He turns and leaves.

Sanjay finds himself face-to-face with the bouncer, who gestures for them to raise their hands.

"You've got to be kidding me," he says.

"What's going on?" Emma asks, puzzled.

The bouncer frisks Emma, then Sanjay, lingering around Sanjay's belt. It takes every bit of restraint Sanjay has not to punch him.

What is this about? And what has become of this damn hospital?

* * *

Later that day, Sanjay goes for a workout, hoping to clear his mind. Tom's funeral is tomorrow, and after that, he plans to turn in early and catch up on sleep.

Cassie's made arrangements at an old-school boxing gym. Sanjay hates the frou-frou hotel fitness centers where guests make conference calls or watch C-SPAN from ellipticals.

The moment he steps inside, the clang of iron and deep grunts tell him that Cassie has struck gold again. He opens FaceTime and dials his trainer, Mike.

"Hey hey, good morning, good morning. Look who the cat dragged in," says a jovial man in a tight-fitting tee and baseball cap.

In five years of training with Mike, Sanjay's never seen him in a bad mood—and already, his own is lifting.

"Hey, what's up, Mike?"

"All good, all good. Where you calling in from today?"

"Boston." Sanjay starts high knees.

"Boston, Beantown. That's old school—I'm talking *Mayflower*!" Mike laughs. "You ready to get it before you hit some clam chowder?"

Sanjay smiles. "Yes, sir."

"Okay, show me what we're working with."

Sanjay pans his phone to show Mike the equipment.

"I like it! All right, today we're going to get into the heavy."

For the next hour, Sanjay does a mix of weights and Filipino martial arts, sprinkled with some life lessons from Bruce Lee and hip-hop.

As he does his final stretches, Mike asks, "So what's on the docket the rest of the week?"

"I don't know, man. Everything's upside down."

"What's up, man? That doesn't sound like you."

Sanjay picks up his phone to look Mike in the eyes. "I'm back at MBH—where I did med school, and then worked briefly after residency. I loved this place, but . . ." He stops and shakes his head. "Let's just say it didn't love me back. Now I'm here and . . ."

He pauses again, trying to put this strange feeling into words. "Something's still off."

"Sounds like you need to get outta there."

Sanjay nods. "You're right. But I can't, not yet. I kinda promised someone I'd do something for him. I'm not sure what that is, exactly. But I have to stay until I do."

"That sounds like a lot. But here's the key. How are you feeling?"

"On edge. But focused. Like I'm supposed to be here, even if it's hard."

"That's okay. Let the universe come to you."

It's good advice. Sanjay just hopes there are no black holes lurking.

CHAPTER 9

EMMA NEVER IMAGINED this day would come. Certainly not so soon.

Yet here she is. In her apartment, getting dressed for her dad's funeral.

My father is dead. My father is dead. The words make sense in her mind, but her body rejects them. This is just another day, another funeral. Of someone she knew, but not her dad.

She spent the early morning immersed in the absoluxir data, poring over pages and pages of protein purification and binding assay results, looking for any inconsistencies or anomalies in the drug development process. She wishes she could get her hands on the drug itself, but her role is limited to reviewing the preclinical data sent to the FDA before it was used on any patients.

The science is fascinating. Riveting, even—and impeccably done. The only question in her mind is her encounter with Ecker. Was his offer to merge their labs genuine? A nagging voice inside her keeps asking if he knows she's advising the FDA review committee and is trying to influence her.

Or is that her impostor syndrome talking?

She stands in front of her bedroom mirror, checking the fit of her black dress. *This is what denial looks like*, she thinks. Years ago, when she was still in med school, she learned about the stages of grief. She recalls a professor of psychiatry—tweed jacket, bowtie, and all—standing at the lectern, saying, "The stages of grief are a misnomer. They don't progress one after another, nor do they proceed in a set order."

She tries to remember them: denial, bargaining, depression, acceptance. *Isn't there one more? Oh yes, anger.*

As if on cue, rage blazes through her. For most of her life, her dad put his patients first, and for what? In the end, the stress of diagnosing a mystery patient literally killed him. And that wasn't the only cost. The piano recitals he missed to make house calls. The empty stares at the dinner table when he was puzzling through a case. Those she could forgive.

But what he did to Mom?

When her mother, Maria, got cancer, Emma assumed her dad would spend more time with them. Mom was a patient now, after all. But the sicker she got, the more her father threw himself into work, leaving Emma to be her mother's sole caregiver.

It was a slap in the face. All those years, it wasn't that patients came first. It was that she and Mom came second.

After her mother died, Emma decided that if she ever had a family, she didn't want a career that made her spouse or children second-class citizens. Nor did she want her dad brooding over her, disappointed she'd put her own needs ahead of a patient's.

So a month after the funeral, she quit. She quit medical school and—if she's being honest with herself—she quit her father. She went as far away as she could for her PhD, all the way to Uppsala, Sweden. Its long winters, she'd half-joke to old friends over text, were an apt metaphor for her emotional state.

She never regretted dropping out of med school. Except for one thing: losing the chance to see what might have become of her and Sanjay.

But not anymore.

Years ago, a friend forwarded her a British tabloid headline: *Handsome Doctor Makes Life-Saving Diagnosis at the Beach*. Sanjay, now a "concierge doctor to the uber-rich," had been sunbathing in Saint-Tropez with a runway model when a young man walked by. Dangling arms, long fingers, and sunken chest—classic signs of Marfan syndrome, a rare genetic condition affecting connective tissue. The man turned out to be Lukas Vanderhaus, son of shipbuilding magnate Adnan Vanderhaus. After Sanjay's beachside diagnosis, a CT scan showed the man had developed the most dreaded complication of Marfan, severe aortic aneurysm. But thanks to Sanjay's keen eye, Lukas wouldn't drop dead in a matter of months.

Emma had always known Sanjay was capable of that kind of diagnostic feat. But she'd never thought he'd turn his back on patients in need.

Not until she saw him at the coffee shop in his tailor-cut suit and designer shoes.

He's a doctor, sure, but to rich pricks and plutocrats? What a waste.

She shakes her head and checks herself in the mirror one last time. She's no runway model, but not half-bad.

* * *

The outdoor ceremony will be closed casket, so the funeral home is her last chance to see her father.

When the pastor asked two days ago who she wanted with her, she surprised herself by saying Sanjay, not Neil. She told herself it was for Sanjay's sake. That he'd appreciate the opportunity to have a moment alone with Tom, that Neil was too busy with work and that they'd only started dating a few weeks ago. Truthfully, though, she didn't know what she wanted or why.

The funeral director leads her to the private viewing room. She isn't ready to face the body alone and is grateful to hear that Sanjay has already arrived.

The room is well lit with an arched ceiling and a simple pew in the back. Directly in front of her is the casket. As she enters, she sees Sanjay, his back to her, kneeling beside it. Perhaps sharing some last words of gratitude with his mentor.

The door swings shut behind her, and Sanjay abruptly stands. She didn't intend to scare him, but what did she expect, coming unannounced into an empty room with a dead body? As he turns, Emma's eye catches a flash of something bright blue in his hands.

A moment later, he's in front of her, hands empty. Her grieving mind must be playing tricks on her.

They embrace, and Emma feels the weight of her grief soften.

This time Sanjay is the first to let go. "I'm so sorry for your loss, Emma," he says. "I'll let you be alone with him."

Emma approaches the casket and looks at her father for the last time. She lets emotion wash over her, and after a few moments whispers goodbye and leaves. She's truly alone now.

* * *

Nearly all her life Emma has been surrounded by the MBH community—her childhood friends, college and medical school mentors, now colleagues and staff. For years she's had a love-hate relationship with the institution, but today she's grateful. Funeral arrangements sprang up almost automatically. Invitations sent; food catered; logistics handled without her having to ask. Sure, she would have done things differently—starting with how her dad's remains were handled—but in her grief, she remembered something her mother used to say: "A caballo regalado, no se le miran los dientes." Don't look a gift horse in the mouth.

As the black Cadillac carries her from the funeral home to the cemetery grounds, she sees hundreds of people, fashionably dressed in black suits and dresses, talking and laughing. *Dr. Tom Carpenter's funeral has become the social event of the season*, she thinks, sighing. A place to see and be seen. Hospital administrators talking shop. Board members fundraising in Tom's name. Junior faculty cozying up to senior faculty.

When she steps out of the car, she has to steady herself against the door. Many of the faces she recognizes. Many more she does not. All at once she's awed by the number of people her dad touched in his life—and saddened by how much of that life he kept from her.

Neil is in the front row, deep in conversation with MBH's former chief financial officer, Jim Hadley. Emma blinks, surprised. Jim once tried to shut down the free clinic, take away its funding, and there was no love lost between him and her dad.

Janelle and the rest of Emma's research team are toward the back, outside the unspoken VIP section. They wave vigorously at her, and she smiles at them.

Briefly, she scans the crowd for Matt DeSalvo. Thankfully, there's no sign of him.

Just as she's about to find a seat, she notices two dozen men and women standing on the lawn behind the seated crowd, silent. She squints, taking in their ill-fitting clothes and uncomfortable stances. *Patients from the free clinic*, she thinks, and her heart swells. She raises a hand to wave. Then, to her surprise, she sees Sanjay standing among them.

Dr. Ecker catches her eye and beckons her to an empty chair in the front row. When she takes her seat, he squeezes her shoulder and says, "You're gonna be okay." It's a phrase she's heard many times today, but now she has to stifle tears. Ecker also lost his dad at a young age. But it's more than that. Ecker was her dad's classmate and decades-long colleague—and now he's the closest thing she has to a father figure.

The funeral program begins with an invocation from MBH's head chaplain. Speeches by the hospital CEO, chief nursing officer, and dean of the med school follow, all glorifying the virtues of physicians, MBH, and her dad. No mention of her mom or the sacrifices she made for that glory.

Emma is glad she's not giving a eulogy. She always speaks the truth, and hers would be too much for this crowd. This funeral is a show. Her part is that of the perfect, grieving daughter, and she'll play it. If she needs to shed tears or scream, she'll save it for another time and place.

* * *

The crowd disperses. Two hospital board members, Janet Scully and Dave Stoddard, approach.

"We're so saddened by your dad's death, especially in light of our recent decision," says Janet, her voice trailing off, as if nothing more needs to be said.

"Recent decision?" asks Emma.

Janet's eyebrows furrow. "You didn't know?"

"Didn't know what?"

Janet locks eyes with Dave, who nods. "Your father was about to become MBH's next physician-in-chief," she says.

"What? That must be a mistake." Emma shakes her head vigorously. "My father didn't do research."

"Times are changing," says Dave. "The board wanted a more mission-oriented leader, someone who could refocus the institution on patient care."

Emma leans in to ensure that no one overhears. "But what about his temper?"

"That was a risk some of us were willing to take," says Janet, glancing again at Dave. "We call ourselves Man's Best Hospital, yet our ranking fell to number two this year. In Neil, we've found an effective operator who can keep the trains running on time. But we wanted an elder statesman to complement him, someone to set the direction."

Emma covers her face with both hands. "I'm sorry, but this is a lot to take in." She forces the words out, head spinning.

Why hadn't he told her? They'd had dinner twice in the past month. She'd let herself believe they were finally reconnecting—that he was becoming her father again.

And all the while, he'd been hiding this. Why did he always shut her out? Why did near-strangers know more about him than she did?

"To be clear," Janet is saying, "your father didn't want the job. He was chosen. Classic Tom—after much debate and delay, he agreed, but on one condition."

"Condition?" asks Emma, half-listening.

"Yes, that's why we hadn't announced it yet." Janet's voice is noticeably quieter. "Tom didn't care about titles. He only wanted the job if he could use it to improve the quality of care at the hospital. He insisted on doing a 'diagnostic workup'—a review of our medical records—to see where things stood before he accepted the role."

"Had we known he had a health condition, we wouldn't have pushed the job on him." Dave shakes his head and sighs. "I'm so sorry for your loss."

"My loss?" Emma says, her voice rising above the din in her head. "What loss?"

Dave takes a step back.

"MBH suffered a loss. The free clinic suffered a loss. Me? I lost my father a long time ago. *To* MBH."

Dave looks at Janet, seeking help. Finding none, he turns and walks away. Seething, Emma waits for whatever Hallmark card sentiment Janet will offer.

"I know better than most people that your dad wasn't a saint," says Janet quietly. "And I know with my own children, I wasn't either."

Emma's eyes burn. Janet looks both ways, then leans in. "Come by the executive offices in the morning. There's something else you should know."

CHAPTER 10

SANJAY HATES FUNERALS. To him, they're proof of modern medicine's shortcomings. Sure, everyone has to die, but did they have to die when they did?

Tom's funeral brings up memories of his first funeral, his grandmother's. Being awakened before dawn by Baba. Shuffling through Newark Airport in his pajamas. Hawkers crowding the New Delhi airport terminal; snow globes of the Taj Mahal, despite the 110-degree heat.

What he recalls most are the smells. The sweat of the porters and rickshaw wallahs navigating them through narrow alleys. The ginger and cardamon chai served at every relative's house. The gobs of ghee, purified butter, that the priest flecked onto Nani's white shroud, mixed with dhoopbatti, incense, either to keep the flies away or to transport his grandmother to nirvana—maybe both.

He didn't know her well. Though she visited them each year in the United States, he couldn't speak Hindi, the only language she knew. His parents' greatest fear was that he'd have an Indian accent when speaking English, so they refused to teach him. And yet, when the priest instructed him to sprinkle holy water over Nani's body for the last time, he felt lost and confused.

Tom's funeral stirs the same feelings in him now.

Thanks to Neil, though, he has a welcome distraction. He's heading to his first shift at MBH's primary care clinic. Half the doctors at MBH attended the funeral, so the clinic needs all the help they can get. And Sanjay can't think of a better way to honor Tom than to practice the craft Tom taught him.

He doesn't have an MBH badge to swipe, so he asks the front desk clerk to notify the head nurse that he's arrived. In the waiting room, he watches as arriving patients pull a ticket, then are called by number. The brainchild of an overpaid consultant, he thinks. It may well optimize efficiency, but it makes the clinic seem like a deli counter—or worse, the DMV.

The patients are mostly white and dressed in professional clothes. For many people, it's too hard to miss a half day of work to find parking and wait to be seen. Telemedicine would be a better option. But then MBH would miss out on charging for labs and X-rays. Sanjay shakes his head. The ideal would be house calls, like he does in his practice. No need to ask if a patient smokes or wonder about their diet. Just take a whiff or open the fridge.

But insurance companies rarely cover house calls, and even when they do, doctors can't make as many visits per day, which means less revenue. In the U.S. healthcare system, what gets paid for is what gets done, even if it's worse for patients.

"Dr. Sanjay, we're ready for you," calls the head nurse.

His first patient is in her late sixties with multiple risk factors for heart disease. She wants to transfer her care to MBH in hopes of getting into the next clinical trial for absoluxir. "That Dr. Ecker," she says. "He's a godsend."

Sanjay modifies her medications to better control her blood pressure, then heads one room over to see his next patient. There's a bounce in his step. Taking care of the rich means a lot of vanity medicine—Botox, anxiety treatment, acne cream. Here, he's already encountered a real person with real medical problems that actually utilize his level of expertise.

But an hour later, he's disgusted and ready to leave.

The exam rooms literally have a light that flashes yellow after his ten minutes with a patient are up—no doubt another consultant recommendation. At fifteen minutes, the light flashes red—something Sanjay finds out when his second patient tears up talking about the recent loss of her husband, and he ignores the yellow light to hold her hand. The electronic health record is intrusive. For the third patient's leg ulcer, he spends more time clicking through screens, documenting a wound wrap, than he does administering one.

As he gets to his last patient of the day, an MBH ICU nurse in her early sixties, he heaves a breath of relief. The nurse explains that she's come to transfer her medical records to another clinic, and Sanjay assumes she's moving out of Boston or retiring.

But no. She got laid off.

"They said they didn't need as many ICU nurses." She shrugs, pressing her lips into a line. "I'm not stupid. They only fired the older ones."

"What does age have to do with it?"

She looks at him like he's an intern asking what dose of Tylenol to prescribe. "Experienced nurses earn more. Management knows they can cut costs by fifteen percent just by replacing older staff with younger ones."

"But the most experienced nurses are the ones who can tell when a patient is about to crash."

"That doesn't show up on a spreadsheet," she sneers.

He tries to print out her records so her new doctor has her complete medical history, but the computer won't let him. He asks the front desk clerk, who explains that to get a copy of her medical records—her own information—she has to pay a fifty-dollar processing fee.

"At what point did MBH become a cash register?" he mutters with a groan.

The clerk shoots him a wry look and shrugs. "It got worse after the new management team took over three months ago."

Around the time Neil became president. Sanjay makes a mental note to tell his friend what hospital administrators are doing under his nose.

* * *

"He was going to be made *what*?" Sanjay can hear the shock in his own voice.

Emma had called just as he was leaving clinic to tell him about her conversation with the board members.

"Physician-in-chief of MBH. I know. I'm as shocked as you are."

"That makes no sense. Those jobs go to researchers."

"The board said they wanted a new kind of leader. Someone to bring MBH's focus back to patients."

The irony of a hospital needing to prioritize patients. Then again, after what he saw today, MBH clearly does.

How many people knew about the decision? he wonders. The job was coveted, and Tom had no shortage of enemies. Sanjay's probably being paranoid, but the news makes him even more eager to dig into the unusual circumstances around Tom's death.

"If you were my father, how would you run a diagnostic on the hospital?" Emma asks.

"I'd start by doing chart biopsies."

"Chart biopsies?" Emma sounds horrified.

Sanjay chuckles, remembering she left med school before learning all the jargon.

"Sorry. Doctor-speak for going through medical records and looking for something off. Like a biopsy of a body—but of the chart instead."

"MBH sees tens of thousands of patients a week. Where would you even start?"

Sanjay pauses, rubbing his five o'clock shadow.

"With the dead ones."

CHAPTER 11

. . . *Enter Password* . . .

"Try your mom's name," Sanjay says.

Emma nods and types.

. . . *Incorrect Password* . . . *Two attempts left before your account will be locked*

"Damn it!" groans Sanjay.

They're back in Tom's office, standing over his computer. Emma's new theory is that the files her dad kept mentioning—and his diagnostic workup of MBH—are one and the same. If she's right, then Tom wasn't paging Sanjay about a single mystery patient, but a whole cluster—something systemic.

To find out, they'll need access to MBH's electronic health record. And for that, they need to get into Tom's account. Normally, MBH requires users to change their password every four weeks. But Tom had an exemption. He hated passwords almost as much as he hated computers, so he convinced the hospital's chief technology officer to give him a permanent one.

"He must have told you his password at some point," Sanjay says, hoping to jog Emma's memory.

"He didn't. All I remember is that he wanted it to have no capital letters. But the CTO insisted it have at least one, so it's all caps."

"Try your name."

. . . *Incorrect Password . . . One attempt left before your account will be locked*

"Uh-oh," says Emma.

"Uh-oh is right." Sanjay sticks his thumb in his mouth and chews on his nail, an old habit from med school he thought he'd left behind. "No more guesses until we're as sure as we can be."

Neil could get us in, he thinks, but doesn't say. He doesn't want to risk Neil being accused of abusing his powers. Doctors at all levels of MBH have enemies. The last thing Sanjay wants is to give Neil's detractors the firepower to take him down.

Emma pulls her hair back and twists it into a bun. Sanjay remembers she does this when she's stressed or deep in thought.

"I should call my grad student from MIT. I'm sure she knows a computer genius who can hack us in," Emma jokes.

"That's actually a good idea," Sanjay says, reaching for his phone. "I'll call Cassie."

"Who?"

"My EA. Short for Cassandra. She's . . . ah . . ."

Emma squints at him.

"Let's just say she has a storied past." He starts dialing. "More importantly, she knows as much about computers as any MIT engineer."

Cassie picks up.

"Hey, I need you to break into an EHR for me . . . Send you what? An IP address? Okay, okay, slow down."

Sanjay mutes the line, switches to speaker, and sets the phone on Tom's desk. From the other end comes the sound of rapid typing—like torrents of rain.

"I guess we wait." He leans back in Tom's chair and takes a breath. For the first time since the coffee shop, there's silence between them. "So?"

Emma frowns at him. "So?"

He picks up a piece of paper from Tom's desk, takes a quick glance, puts it back down. "You and Neil seem close."

Emma crosses her arms. "We are."

"That's nice." Sanjay's voice inflects up.

"Yeah, it's nice to have friends who stick around."

He grits his teeth. He isn't gonna let it go this time. "Friendship goes both ways, Emma. Sometimes we have to give people a second chance."

Emma's lips tighten. He can feel her stewing, but he can't resist. "So, just friends?"

Emma huffs. "Yes."

"Does he know that?"

She stands and marches over to the bookshelf, putting her back to him. "Look, Sanjay, I'm not doing this now."

"Fine. But when are we gonna have the conversation?"

"About Neil? Never."

"Not Neil. Us." He takes a breath and lets it out audibly. "Look, Emma. I'm sorry for how things turned out when we—"

She spins around, knocking a book off the shelf. "Turned out? Turned out?" Her eyes pierce him. "You left, Sanjay. Nobody forced you to go, and you didn't give a damn about the consequences of leaving."

"I did care. You've never given me a chance to tell you—"

"All for a stupid test."

"It wasn't the test! It was—"

"I don't want to talk about it, Sanjay. I—"

"Hey!" a voice yells. They look over at Tom's desk, remembering Cassie, then look at each other and grit their teeth.

Sanjay takes a deep breath and taps the unmute button. "Hey, you're on with both of us."

"You won't believe this," says Cassie. "The password is EMMASANJAY, one word. All caps."

Sanjay and Emma just stare at one another. Speechless.

"Hello! Can you hear me?"

Sanjay blinks twice. "Uh, yeah, we hear you."

"He must have set the password—" whispers Emma.

"Years ago," Sanjay whispers back. "When I was still here."

Did Tom know that Emma and Sanjay were dating—and does this mean he approved?

Sanjay hangs up and turns to Emma. Before he can speak, she grabs the keyboard and enters the password. A moment later, a loading bar appears. Emma claps her hands.

"Now what?" she asks.

Logging in—hard as it was—is the easy part. Now they'll have to retrace Tom's steps.

Sanjay's plan is a brute force approach: search for patients recently hospitalized at MBH and comb through the records of any patient who died to see if mistakes were made. It'll take days to figure out—if he's lucky.

He clicks around to find the search bar.

"Wait. Stop." Emma points at the right side of the screen. "Who are these patients?"

In the corner is a small window labeled *My Lists*. Expanding it to full screen, Sanjay sees multiple pages of names. Tom must have added these, like bookmarking a site on a web browser. Sanjay clicks again. In addition to the open tab, there are two more lists.

"Why three?" Emma muses, shaking her head.

"It's a good question. I don't know if you've ever used one, but electronic health records are notoriously difficult," Sanjay says. "They're designed for billing, not patient care. You can create lists of patients, but you can't label them, so there's no way to know why your dad created these, or when. For all we know, they might just be old patients of his."

"Let me take a look," says Emma, nudging him out of the way. "I know a lot of my father's longtime patients from doing house calls with him."

Each list has a couple of dozen names, and it doesn't take long for Emma to scroll through them.

"No one looks familiar," she says. "Does this mean they were part of his diagnostic work up of MBH?"

"There's only one way to find out."

* * *

Sanjay is getting cross-eyed.

He glances at the clock. It's 3:48 AM. He gently slaps his face and takes a swig of coffee, then grimaces. *Yuck.* Freezing cold.

From residency, he's used to staying up all night—admitting patients, responding to pages, running codes. His current practice is similar. Jetting from one country to the next and mastering multiple time zones often means long days. But staring at a computer screen? He has no idea how radiologists, who spend hours in dark rooms reading X-rays and CT scans, manage it.

He puts on his headphones and cranks up "Juicy" by Biggie Smalls.

He's been at it for eight hours now. Emma insisted on helping, but after an hour, the exhaustion from the funeral hit hard, and she took a rideshare home. She urged him to call it a night, too, but he couldn't. He's made up his mind to get through the first list, which, in his tired state, he's unimaginatively dubbed "List A." If he has time, he'll dip into List B, too.

Sanjay has a routine now. One by one, he opens each patient record, then goes in reverse chronological order through each clinic visit and hospital discharge summary. Some of the patients have only a handful of records; others have hundreds. He isn't sure what he's looking for, exactly, but whenever he spots something out of the ordinary, he jots it down in a spiral notebook from Tom's desk.

The repetitive task frees his mind to drift over the past forty-eight hours. Two days ago, he was savoring an espresso with a stunning woman in Lake Como. Now he's back at the institution that betrayed him, stuck in a dark room, trying to unravel a mystery that may not exist.

Somehow, he feels more like himself than he has in years.

MBH, though? It's worse than he remembers. He can only imagine the sweeping changes Tom would have made had he gotten the chance to serve as physician-in-chief.

But change, even good change, would disrupt the status quo—and the people behind it.

Something in a patient's record catches his eye. He's only halfway through List A, but a clear pattern has emerged.

He jumps up to get a fresh cup of coffee. He's going to need it.

CHAPTER 12

EMMA GENTLY KNOCKS on the door to her dad's office. Hearing no reply, she eases it open, careful not to spill the coffee in her hands.

There's Sanjay, right where she left him eleven hours earlier. At her dad's desk, fast asleep. Head slumped over a pile of books he's using as a makeshift pillow.

It takes her back to med school, when she'd find him in his dorm room—collapsed over textbooks and stacks of highlighted index cards. She usually waited a beat to wake him. He was such a ball of energy, endlessly optimistic, seemingly invincible. That he needed sleep was a reminder that he was just a man. That maybe one day he would need her, too.

But it wasn't until their first date that she saw him as someone she could spend the rest of her life with. After an electrifying, unexpected kiss in her apartment, he finally asked her out. The plan was to catch a movie in Harvard Square, then grab dessert.

Unfortunately, two hours before the date, Emma came down with a blistering migraine.

Sanjay sensed something was off the moment he saw her. He sat her down on a bench in front of John Harvard's statue and gently brushed a strand of hair from her face.

"Are you okay? Emma, if this date isn't what you want..."

Emma was embarrassed to tell him—but she could already see the concern in his eyes.

"I have a headache, and I forgot my Advil. I'm sorry. I think I crammed too hard this week."

He stood and held out his hand. "Then first stop: pain relief."

They wandered through Harvard Square together, Sanjay scanning storefronts until they found an Indian grocery store. Emma was reluctant—they'd be late for the movie—but he was already grinning as they stepped inside.

"Ah, the smell of home," he said, eyes lighting up at the scent of turmeric and incense.

Within a minute, he found a packet of paracetamol—"The name they use for Tylenol in India," he explained—and grabbed a drink box of mango juice for her.

In the checkout line, they noticed the storekeeper's wife struggling with a heavy trash bag. Sanjay immediately stepped in to help. When he returned, the shopkeeper refused to take their money. Instead, he nodded to his wife, who pressed a dot of red tikka on each of their foreheads and blessed them.

They missed the start of the movie, but Emma didn't care. She was in love.

Then, a month later, it was over. Sanjay failed his anatomy test—and ghosted her. No goodbye, no message. Just gone. Emma was devastated, but more than that, she was bewildered. Had she misread his feelings? Had she done something wrong?

In the end, the only explanation was the test and his desire to put med school first. Her dad had chosen his work over her, time and again. Now her first love had done the same.

Her mom passed away a few weeks later, and Emma left Sanjay a final voicemail. "If you care about me at all, you'll call back. If you don't, I never want to see you again."

He never called.

Neil was different. They'd been friends for years, but something shifted the night of the ICU tower's ribbon cutting. They stayed up talking in his condo until 3 a.m., rediscovering their shared passion for making healthcare better—hers through science and new medicines, his through leadership and clinical excellence.

For Neil, making his new ICU the best in the country was just the beginning. He wanted to build a first-of-its-kind clinic for sickle cell patients, most of them Black and low-income. He also planned to remove barriers for foreign medical graduates to work at MBH—a personal mission shaped by his parents' journey as immigrant physicians.

Her whole life, Emma heard her dad lament the demise of medicine. But it was mostly complaining. Here was Neil with an actual plan to fix it.

So when he asked her out a few months later, she said yes.

Now she looks at the rise and fall of Sanjay's chest and shakes her head. Juxtaposing the memories confirm that something was missing in her two dates with Neil. That spark. Sanjay isn't the right guy for her, not anymore, but neither is Neil. She'll have to let him down gently, and soon.

"Sanjay," she says.

He bolts upright, takes a deep breath through his nose, and blinks his eyes widely, as if rebooting himself. "Yeah?"

She hands him a coffee and asks, "What did you find out?"

"I got through the first two lists. List B is a bunch of patients referred to MBH for specialty care. Nothing out of the ordinary. But List A? I have a working theory."

"Which is?"

"Better to see for yourself. You up for a house call?"

* * *

Their destination is a small two-story house, the front yard littered with plastic toys and beer cans.

Emma parks her car, and Sanjay grabs his medical bag from the trunk and half-jogs up to the porch. "Let's go see some patients!" he shouts, grinning.

Watching him, she's transported back to Saturday mornings growing up, when she and her dad would go on house calls in neighborhoods just like this. When she was nine or ten, she'd wait for him in the car, reading Baby-Sitters Club books, but later, she'd go into the house to assist.

She used to remember those days fondly. But after Mom got sick, the memory spoiled. To her dad, she realized, the house calls weren't a chance to spend time with her. They were the beginning of her apprenticeship. She was less his daughter and more his intern. Taking care of her dying mom alone? That was medical residency.

Sanjay knocks on the door. From inside, a woman's voice calls out, "In a minute!"

A middle-aged woman in a stained apron opens the door. "Yes?" she says, peering at them through the broken screen.

"Good morning, ma'am. We're two doctors, just coming in from MBH," says Sanjay.

Emma wasn't thrilled when Sanjay shared his plan with her on the ride over. Her one condition was that they not lie. Now she appreciates the effort he's making. Technically, they are two doctors. She has a PhD. And technically, they're coming from MBH, even though they don't work there.

"Mrs. Pulaski, I assume?"

"That's me," the woman says.

"We're here to follow up on the quality of medical care your husband received at MBH."

"Nicholas!" the woman yells, walking back to the kitchen. "Two docs are here from the big hospital!"

Emma hears heavy footsteps charging down the stairs. A moment later, Nick Pulaski appears, his AC/DC T-shirt barely covering his bulging abdomen.

"Come in! Come in!" He has a big grin and a wide gap between his two front teeth. "We weren't expecting company, but you're welcome here."

As Emma turns to close the door behind her, a dark green car catches her eye. It looks like something from a 1970s cop show—low slung, all chrome edges.

She can't see the driver clearly, but he's holding a phone up through the sunroof—as if searching for a signal.

Or was he taking photos of her? And of Sanjay?

Sanjay calls out to her and she rushes inside, slamming the door shut behind her.

* * *

At the kitchen table, Sanjay explains the reason for their visit. Several months ago, Nick received an endoscopy ("the camera down your mouth to look at your belly from the inside"). They want to hear about his experience at MBH before and after the procedure.

Nick's clearly itching to jump in but manages to let Sanjay finish. "Everything was amazing!" he blurts. "You guys saved my life!"

Emma turns to Sanjay. She's still feeling on edge about the car outside, but the calm look on Sanjay's face makes her feel safe.

"It started at work. I'm a butcher, you know? Bill's Meat House off Patrick Street." Nick searches Emma's eyes for recognition. There isn't any. "I started getting these bad stomach pains. Real bad. Right here." He points at his stomach. "It was worse after meals, especially dinner, and on the weekends.

"The first doctor I saw at the hospital . . . Oh, man, he was the worst! He asks me this, he asks me that. Then you know what he says? That I have to lose weight! Can you believe it?"

Sanjay, Emma, and Mrs. Pulaski nod along, trying not to draw attention to the fact that in Nick's excitement, his T-shirt has popped over his belly, exposing his midriff.

"But then I get a call from a second doctor at MBH. He says, 'I believe you. I know you're in pain, and I really want to help you.' He took me seriously! The next day he schedules me for an appointment. He doesn't ask too many questions, like the first guy. He just tells me they're going to do an enda-scopee."

"Ad-noscopy," corrects Mrs. Pulaski.

"Yeah, whatever, the camera in your mouth. The docs know what I'm talking about."

Emma nods.

"And they found—" his wife says.

"Something fishy, something in my effa-fagus." Nick pauses for effect. "And guess what? Whatever that goombah was, they lasered it. Twice!"

"The doc said if he'd waited any longer—" his wife starts.

"My stomach would have EXPLODED!"

Emma jumps back in her chair. Nick looks at her face and quiets down. "Or something like that, anyway."

He rubs his elbow and looks at his wife, who is eyeing him sternly.

"Wow," says Emma, breaking the awkward silence. "And how are you now?"

"After the laser—" Nick says.

"—and those acid pills the doctor put you on," adds his wife.

"I'm much better. As good as new!"

"That's great to hear, isn't it, Dr. Sanjay?" says Emma.

"Yes. Great," says Sanjay in a deadpan voice.

They make small talk, then get ready to leave. As they put on their jackets, Sanjay asks Nick if the person who recommended the procedure was Dr. Johnson, the doctor who signed the endoscopy report in Nick's chart.

"No, no. He was the one who did the procedure. He was great, too, but it was a different doc who saved my life."

"You remember his name?" asks Sanjay.

"No, I don't. If I did, I'd send him a care package of our best cuts."

Emma takes out her phone, swipes through, and pulls up an old photo on Facebook of her and Neil, their arms wrapped around each other's shoulders. "Is this the guy?"

"Yeah, that's him!"

Sanjay looks over and frowns. Mrs. Pulaski takes a peek, too, then says, "He your boyfriend or something?"

* * *

Emma is back in the car with Sanjay, headed to their second house call. No sign of the dark green car. *Probably nothing*, she thinks, exhaling with relief.

She shifts focus to the positive. "Neil did such a great job. That family loves him."

A small smile crosses her lips. Modern medicine really is a marvel. It's what motivates her research. Despite her dad's cynicism, she's always believed most doctors want to do the right thing. If anything, it's the system that's broken.

And Neil isn't just any doctor. He's a good man—and a good friend.

She's so lost in thought, she doesn't notice Sanjay's expression—until he speaks.

"He didn't do a great job, Emma. Far from it." Sanjay's voice is tight and controlled, anger lurking beneath. "All Nick had was GERD. He didn't need that procedure."

GERD, Emma knows, is short for gastro-esophageal reflux disease, or what most people call acid reflux.

"He's medically obese," Sanjay continues. "The weight of his abdominal fat is increasing intra-abdominal pressure, pushing stomach contents back into his esophagus. Large meals overstretch the stomach, and alcohol—especially in excess—relaxes the lower esophageal sphincter, which normally keeps acid where it belongs. That's why he's worse on the weekends."

Emma is speechless. She's heard about Sanjay's diagnostic acumen but seeing it firsthand is something else.

"The first doctor had it right. Mr. Pulaski needs to lose weight, cut back on drinking, and avoid late-night eating."

At the next traffic light, Emma glances over. "But what about the laser? And whatever they found during the endoscopy?"

"Untreated GERD can cause changes to the esophageal lining—what's called Barrett's esophagus. It's a marker of chronic reflux, not a disease that needs fixing. A clinical trial in *BMJ* about ten years ago showed that laser therapy for Barrett's doesn't just fail to help—it actually increases the risk of complications."

Emma takes all this in. Medicine is full of treatments that seem promising—until rigorous studies prove otherwise. Plenty of hyped drugs crash and burn. Some are even approved by the FDA or other international regulatory bodies, only to be pulled from the market after causing widespread harm. Thalidomide. Fen-phen. Oxycontin.

A reminder that she needs to be careful with her review of absoluxir. No shortcuts.

"That's disturbing," she says carefully. "Especially because Mr. Pulaski is so happy with his care."

"Most patients assume more care is better care." Sanjay is massaging his temples, looking tired. "And doctors? We're all too happy to oblige, because we don't get paid for quality. We get paid by the yard. So what do patients get? More yards."

His voice is distant now, darker. "Mr. Pulaski should never have gotten that procedure. And Tom knew it."

* * *

Their reception is very different at their second house call.

"Your hospital is treating me like a common criminal. Why should I let you in?"

Emma is on guard, half expecting the front door to slam on her nose. All Sanjay did was say the word "MBH" to the patient.

"We know about your GI procedure at MBH, Mr. Franks," Sanjay says, not backing down. "And we believe it may not have been medically necessary."

Mr. Carl Franks grunts, then steps back, leaving the door open. They follow behind cautiously. The apartment is dark and colorless, except for a photo collage of a happy toddler on the TV mantle.

"I went in for a simple thing—hemorrhoids—something I've had a million times before," he says once they sit down on his faded couch. "I was just bleeding a little more than usual and wanted to make sure it was okay. Next thing I know, the doctor's saying the 'c' word. You know? 'Cancer.' I got scared. I mean, I'm no doctor. So he gets me to sign one of those forms and schedules me for a colonoscopy. The procedure went fine, but then I got hit with a huge bill. I'm a carpenter. I make an honest living. I can't afford to pay the hospital fifteen thousand dollars!"

Carl is choking up. He swipes angrily at his cheeks, says, "Eighteen months later, I'm still paying it off. I couldn't even get my grandson a gift for Christmas. And all for nothing. My hemorrhoids are still acting up."

Emma feels a deep ache in her chest. "I'm so sorry," is all she can manage.

Seeing the pain on his face brings up memories of patients she met during her mom's cancer treatment—those who couldn't afford their co-pays and were waiting for financial relief from the hospital or who lost their jobs because they didn't have enough time off to make all their appointments. While her mom napped through chemo, they'd tell Emma how they felt like a burden on their families—or worse, that they'd failed them.

The inequities in the healthcare system sometimes made her research feel futile. Even if she discovered a new treatment for cancer, she worried she'd hurt patients more than she helped them.

"Now your hospital's sending me letters saying my payment's past due!" Carl is shouting. "They even got collections involved. Collections! If they'd told me the price beforehand, I would have shopped around or not gone through with it. Now, in addition to hemorrhoids, I'm having chest pains. But I'm not going to the doctor. No, sir. I won't go to the hospital again, even if I'm bleeding from my eyeballs!"

His new symptoms alarm Emma, but she can't blame him. Her dad always said, "Medicine is a public trust." If patients don't trust doctors, they won't get the care they need.

"I mean, collections! How can hospitals even do that?" Carl asks Sanjay, who sighs.

"Collections unfortunately are now as routine a part of medical care as mammograms," he says. "At least in this country."

Carl shakes his head. "My daughter found this report online about how much MBH donates to charity care. I applied, but they won't even return my calls."

Emma and Sanjay exchange a knowing glance. Then Sanjay says, "Charity care is a sick joke. It's supposed to mean hospitals offer free or discounted treatment to people who qualify *before* they get care. But that's not how it works."

"These days, too often 'charity care' is what they call it when patients can't pay their bills," he adds.

"Bills plus interest," Carl mutters, the corners of his mouth pulling down.

"They don't stop until they've taken you to court and garnished your wages. Every paycheck—hospitals take the first cut."

Carl's face turns white. "If that happens, I'm done for. I won't be able to buy food."

A wave of nausea hits Emma.

"If that's not enough, the hospital writes it off as bad debt. That's what MBH's annual report calls 'charity care.'" Sanjay aggressively makes air quotes.

The color in Carl's face returns. "As a carpenter, sometimes customers can't pay, and my tax guy has to write off the materials."

"Exactly. But imagine getting to call that job charity—and then using it to claim you're a nonprofit and avoid paying taxes."

"Sign me up," says Carl, with a wry smile.

"Me too," says Sanjay, smiling back. "Listen, Carl, if you ever want anyone to look at your hemorrhoids or address your chest pains, you can go to Community Cares. It's a free clinic."

"A free clinic? Do you think I'm an ox and a moron?" says Carl, chuckling. "I'll believe it when I see it!"

Emma can't imagine maintaining a sense of humor through this. But in her career, one consistent truth she's found is that the patients give *her* hope, not the other way around.

"Here's the card for the clinic," says Sanjay, fishing it out of his wallet. "Just in case."

He keeps one with him? Emma thinks, surprised.

Carl takes the card and reads it. "It looks good, but I don't know . . ."

Sanjay pulls his chair closer. "I'll do you one better. Why don't you meet me there the day after tomorrow? Say, eleven AM?"

Carl shakes his head with a smile. "Not gonna let me off easy, are you?"

"No, sir."

"Okay, Doc," says Carl before putting the card in his breast pocket. "It's a deal."

Emma feels herself tear up. Given everything Carl's been through, she feels her heart getting lighter.

"But before we leave, Mr. Franks, just one more question," says Sanjay.

"Sure, Columbo." Carl laughs again.

"Who was the doctor who said you needed the colonoscopy?"

"I don't remember his name, but he kind of looked like you . . ." His face reddens, and he scratches the back of his neck. "If you know what I mean."

"Gotcha, no offense taken," says Sanjay, putting his hands up. "I'm a South Asian male. Medicine's kind of our sport. We're no good at the real ones."

He breaks out laughing and Carl joins him, adding a few knee slaps.

Emma pulls up the photo of Neil on her phone again. Carl peers over his glasses at the screen. "That's him, all right. He's not your boyfriend, is he?"

* * *

Ten minutes later, they're back in the car, heading to Emma's apartment with Sanjay driving. For the first half of the drive, he's been uncharacteristically quiet. Now Emma breaks the silence.

"So that's what List A is about? Patients who got medical care they didn't need?"

"Yes. Last night it was just a hunch. But after seeing the patients myself, I'm sure of it." He hangs a left. "And List A? They're all GI cases."

"Gastroenterology? That's a procedure-heavy specialty. Endoscopies, colonoscopies . . ."

"Exactly." Sanjay pulls over and looks directly at her. "It's also Neil's specialty and the department he was chair of before he became president."

Emma gasps. "You don't think Neil is behind every patient on List A, do you?"

Sanjay says nothing, but his gaze is fixed on her. Emma takes a deep breath in and out, trying to calm herself.

"I mean, just because Neil was involved with the two patients we saw today doesn't prove anything. All the patients on List A are in his field? Fine. It's a big department."

"Sure, but it doesn't look good."

Emma hates how he sounds. So cold. So clinical. The way her dad sometimes got. She feels her anger rising. "You're jealous of

Neil. Why, because you think he and I are dating? Is that what this is about?"

"No. I'm not jealous of Neil. He's been my friend for years, just like you were." Sanjay's choice of tense isn't lost on Emma. "But he did always put being first ahead of putting *patients* first."

Emma huffs. She almost spits back, *At least Neil's helping real patients*. But she bites her tongue.

Instead, she says, "So you suspect a whole group of patients got unnecessary care at MBH. What are you going to do about it?"

Sanjay blinks, surprised. "Me? Nothing. I have my own practice to worry about. In a week, I'll be back in Europe." He merges into traffic and looks straight ahead.

"It makes sense now." Emma's voice is flat.

"What does?"

"What my father said about you once, after you quit MBH. That you don't have the stomach for real medicine."

Sanjay's hands turn white on the steering wheel.

"You turn up your nose at what's wrong with this place, but you aren't willing to do the hard work to make it better."

At the next red light, Sanjay lets go of the wheel and folds his arms against his chest. "Yeah, well, when you try to make things better, people get hurt."

Emma's eyebrows furrow. "What's that supposed to mean?"

He turns away. "You wouldn't understand."

Minutes later, he pulls up to his hotel in silence. They had planned to grab lunch in the lobby restaurant. But Sanjay hops out of the car and closes the door without a word, and she lets him go.

CHAPTER 13

SANJAY HAS THE afternoon to kill before he and Emma are due to meet Neil and their former classmates for drinks at Bombo's, their old hangout, though he wishes now he could get out of it.

The List A patients are weighing on his mind. That they point to a quality problem at MBH tells him the three lists he and Emma stumbled upon are part of Tom's diagnostic work up of the hospital. It may even be why Tom paged him, Sanjay thinks. Not to help diagnose one patient, but to figure out what went wrong with *dozens* of them.

But to what end?

He checks in with his nurse practitioner, Jacqueline. Mr. Rosulli's gout has flared up again. He's taking his allopurinol but is still eating cured meats and drinking a gallon of wine a day. *Like opening the drain of an overflowing sink, only to keep the faucet on*, Sanjay thinks.

Ms. Zhang is insisting she needs antibiotics for sinusitis before traveling from Paris to Saltzburg for a Mozart festival. She has a runny nose and a cough at night, but no fevers, no improving then worsening course of symptoms, and no focal tooth pain. Jacqueline made the right call in not prescribing anything, he assures the garment factory boss.

The rest of the practice is quiet, aside from a handful of patients grumbling about his "two-week, last-minute vacation." As if their lives aren't a perpetual vacation. He video calls the ones who complained, forcing a smile.

Afterward, he heads back to the boxing gym, this time without his trainer. He sets up a high-intensity interval circuit: jump rope, high knees, plank, burpees, mountain climbers. *Rinse, repeat.*

He isn't mad at Neil—he's sad for him, and disappointed.

Over the years, Sanjay has watched many doctors lose sight of why they went into medicine. Burnout is everywhere, but not because doctors can't hack it. Making it through medical school and three to seven years of residency takes enormous resilience.

No, the real problem is *moral injury*—not being able to care for patients the way you know you should.

Ten-minute visits. Hours of mindless data entry. No mental health resources. Endless fights with insurance companies. Exorbitant drug prices. It's hardly surprising so many doctors are miserable.

For some, the solution is quitting medicine. For too many, it's quitting life. The last time Sanjay checked, the United States was losing one physician to suicide every day.

Moral injury, he thinks, *is a dangerous diagnosis.* Even the survivors don't get away clean. Many become jaded to the point where they compromise care and, in effect, perpetuate the failings of the system.

He acted unfazed in front of Emma—but the truth is, he *was* surprised to find Neil in that camp. Neil's competitive, sure—but also always amazing with patients. Brilliant *and* kind.

But Neil's carried burdens Sanjay never had to. Neil's parents gave up thriving practices in India so their son could grow up in

America—but at a cost. Despite doctor shortages, U.S. medical boards require doctors from other countries to repeat their medical training. And most hospitals don't even interview foreign-trained candidates, no matter how qualified. So Neil's parents ended up as general practitioners in rural Ohio, a field looked down on back home.

In India, they'd been highly respected specialists. Here, "GP" was a label they wore like a scar. Their only hope, their redemption, was Neil.

And they made sure he knew it.

At the end of first year, when Neil didn't finish at the top of the class, his parents skipped his white coat ceremony. For most parents—Sanjay's included—watching their child don a white coat and take the Hippocratic Oath is one of life's proudest moments. Not Neil's.

That night, Sanjay's parents invited Neil to their celebratory dinner.

Sanjay was embarrassed they insisted on eating Indian. At least they followed his request not to ask about Neil's parents.

Instead, his dad did the next most Indian thing: tell bad jokes.

"How many steps does it take to put an elephant in a fridge?" he asked, his eyes twinkling.

Neil looked over at Sanjay and shrugged. "I don't know. A lot?"

"Three," Sanjay's dad said, holding up his fingers. "Open the door, push the elephant in, close the door."

The boys rolled their eyes—then cracked up.

"Now, challenge question," his dad said. "How many steps to put a giraffe in the fridge?"

"Three!" shouted Neil without hesitating.

"No, no," Sanjay's dad said and laughed. "Four. You open the door, tell the elephant to move over, push the giraffe in, then close the door."

Neil nearly fell out of his chair laughing.

When they said goodbye, Sanjay saw his dad hug Neil then tousle his hair. Afterward, Neil's eyes were red. A lone tear streaked down his cheek.

"Oh no," said Sanjay. "What did my parents say?"

"Nothing," said Neil softly. Then, after a pause: "Tonight . . . felt familiar. The tastes, the smells, the mix of Gujarati and English. But that feeling of being accepted, of people being proud of me—I'd never felt that before."

He looked at Sanjay and smiled sadly. "For the first time, I felt at home."

That night they became more than friends. They became family.

Now, as Sanjay finishes his last gym circuit, he feels his heart lifting.

He knows Neil. He's not a bad person.

There *has* to be an explanation.

And Sanjay has just enough time to find it before they meet for drinks.

* * *

John is standing in front of the Range Rover when Sanjay steps out of the gym. It's the first time he's seen him in the open. John's taller than he expected.

"Couldn't resist some fresh air," John says. He opens the rear passenger door for Sanjay, then walks around to the driver's side.

Sanjay notes a slight limp. John's favoring his left side.

"Bum right knee?" Sanjay asks.

"An old navy injury," John replies, swatting the air. "It's nothing."

"Have you seen a doctor about it?"

"Nah. Don't do doctors." John slips into the driver's seat.

"A quick X-ray would tell us what's going on. I imagine that knee doesn't make driving much fun."

John grunts. "X-rays? Hospitals? You won't catch me dead in one."

Sanjay just nods. He knows the type. "Let me ask you something: When it's about to rain, can you tell?"

John jerks his head toward the rearview mirror, eyes wide. "How the heck did you know that? My wife swears I'm psychic."

"You may well be, but you also have osteoarthritis." Sanjay smiles, remembering the patient, a retired physics professor with severe arthritis, who first explained the phenomenon to him. As barometric pressure drops before a storm, the reduced air pressure causes tissues around the joints to expand, triggering pain in people with arthritis—like having their own built-in weather forecast.

"I have just the thing for you," Sanjay adds, "but I need a couple supplies. Lucky for us, we're heading to a doctor's office."

To get to the bottom of List A, Sanjay needs to talk to someone who was actually there with Neil—a doctor, ideally one who no longer works at MBH and can speak freely.

Between gym sets, he looked up the names of the doctors who signed patient notes in the list. Most are still at MBH. The few who've left now appear on the websites of hospitals on the other side of the country.

But there's one exception: Dr. Fuki Olopade. He's across town at Boston Medical Center and, according to his online faculty page, primarily practices at a community site. Sanjay directs John that way.

Thirty minutes later, the Range Rover stops in front of a church, the parking lot filled with Black and Latino children playing hopscotch. A sign for the clinic directs Sanjay toward the basement stairs.

After explaining to the front desk staff that he's a colleague of Dr. Olopade's, Sanjay makes his way past the waiting room and down a narrow hallway lined with doctors' offices. Toward the back, he arrives at a door with a removable placard: Fuki Olopade, DO.

Sanjay knocks firmly.

"Yes?" asks a deep male voice from within.

"Dr. Olopade, it's Dr. Sanjay."

The door opens, and a man appears. His face is serious but kind, his forehead deeply furrowed.

"Dr. Olopade," Sanjay says, "you're not expecting me, but I need your help. I'm from MBH, and I have some concerns about the GI department. I know you used to work there, and you probably don't want to talk to me, but—"

"I don't mind talking to you. You wouldn't come to this side of town unless it was important." Sanjay nods, appreciating Olopade's deductive reasoning. "But I have this patient I'm in the middle of seeing that I can't figure out." He scratches his head sheepishly. "My wife is annoyed that I keep coming home late, and—"

"What's the case?"

Olopade furls his lips. "Hmm?"

"You said you have a patient you can't figure out. Tell me the story."

Dr. Olopade looks at him quizzically, then shrugs. He ushers Sanjay into his small but tidy office and gestures for him to sit down.

"Okay, she's a 55-year-old housekeeper with coronary artery disease and hypertension who's been having abdominal pain for about a month. It comes in episodes—bad enough to double her over—but then it goes away completely. Often happens after meals, but not always. Exam benign, labs normal. Her scope was clean. Her last doctor thought it was reflux, even hinted she was exaggerating. But I believe her. I just think—"

"Is she a smoker?"

Fuki looks startled. "What? Why?"

"Humor me. Does she have a history of tobacco exposure?"

"I think so. Let me be sure." He spins around to his computer, puts on his reading glasses, and pulls up her record. "Yes, yes, she has a thirty-year history of smoking a pack a day."

"You need to check a CT angio."

"She's had a CT of her abdomen—"

"No, she needs a CT*A*. It's mesenteric ischemia."

"Mesenteric ischemia?" Fuki chews at the end of his pen. "My gosh, that makes complete sense. It's not in her gut. It's in the *arteries* of her gut. You might just be right."

"I am right," Sanjay says, smiling.

Dr. Olopade slips his glasses off and looks at Sanjay. "Who *are* you?"

* * *

Ten minutes later, Dr. Olopade returns from the patient's room much more at ease. "CTA's ordered. They say when you hear hoofbeats, think horses, not zebras. But sometimes, I guess, it's a zebra."

Sanjay smiles. That had been a favorite saying of Tom's.

While Olopade was out of the room, Sanjay leafed through the papers on his desk. He needed to know if he could trust him before asking about Neil. It only took a few patient notes to see that he could. Olopade is generous in his descriptions, writing not "35-year-old Latino diabetic" but "35-year-old carpenter and father of three, Latino descent, with type 2 diabetes." And his medicine is impeccable. He orders enough tests to take patients' concerns seriously, but not so many that he is practicing cookbook medicine or racking up frivolous bills.

"So tell me, Dr. Sanjay, how can I help you?"

"Why did you leave MBH, Dr. Olopade?"

"Please, call me Fuki. And I've been waiting a long time for someone to ask me that." Fuki takes a deep breath. "I chose MBH for fellowship because of a specific doctor. Neil Desai. He was a rising star in interventional gastroenterology. His paper on the impact of balloon endoscopy on gastrin-producing cells was brilliant. It's still one of the most cited papers in our field. And he was renowned for his technical skill."

Sanjay keeps his expression even. He doesn't want to let on that he and Neil are friends and risk Fuki clamming up.

"At first, things were great. Neil loved patient care. He was a brilliant clinician and a tireless researcher. He was ambitious, but so was I. I'm not sure he had a clear purpose for his ambition, but he wanted to be the best. That's for sure."

Fuki's eyes become darker. His voice heavier.

"Then things changed. The head of the GI department died. It was sudden; stage four pancreatic cancer. Neil got wind that the job wasn't going to the best researcher, as it had in the past. The chair of medicine was looking to promote the best administrator. What mattered was revenue, not grants. Basically, the game was RVUs."

RVUs—relative value units. Fittingly, Sanjay thinks, it was Tom Carpenter who first explained the concept of RVUs to him. Sanjay had just been slammed by his new boss, the chief of hospital medicine, for his low numbers. He'd told Tom, who'd frowned.

"Relative value units are a measure of physician productivity," he'd said. "The more patients a doctor sees and the more complex the care he delivers, the higher the RVUs."

"Okay, but how am I supposed to increase my numbers?" Sanjay asked. "My only options are to spend less time with each patient, so I can see more people per day, or to order more tests and procedures than the patients actually need. Neither makes any sense."

"You're right," Tom quipped. "It only makes dollars." More somberly, he'd added: "RVUs are at the root of why medicine has gone so wrong. They reward doctors for doing more *to* a patient than *for* a patient."

Fuki's explanation supports Sanjay's suspicions about Neil.

"Neil was determined to earn as many RVUs as possible, so he'd be named chair?"

"Yes. It started innocently enough. He worked longer hours. He fought with insurers when they denied a procedure a patient needed, which increased the complexity level of our care." Fuki slumps back in his chair, shakes his head. "Then he started lying to insurance companies to get things approved. I didn't agree with his approach, but at that point, he was pushing for things patients needed, and we convinced ourselves that the ends justified the means."

"Then?" Sanjay asks, his stomach turning.

"Then he started doing procedures patients *didn't* need. He'd put things in their charts that just weren't true. All to get the insurance company to pay. When that didn't work, the patients had to pay out of pocket."

Like Carl Franks. No insurance company would cover a diagnostic colonoscopy for simple hemorrhoids—nor should they. It's a procedure that carries real risks.

"I voiced my dissent, but in the end, I deferred to him." Fuki's voice gets quieter. "It didn't help that I was the only Black doctor in the department. Some of the attendings already thought I didn't belong. That I was a diversity hire. The last thing I wanted to do was stand out." He looks at the ground, clears his throat. "I regret it now."

Sanjay watches as Fuki gathers a stack of papers in his hand, squares them against the desk.

"We had a patient, Mr. James Blake. He died during an endoscopy. I'll never forget his name. Or the faces of his two children." Tears gather in Fuki's eyes, and he blinks rapidly. "James had bad esophageal varices. They got nicked during the procedure, and he bled out. Neil wasn't the one holding the scalpel, per se. But he pushed the doctor to do a procedure the patient didn't need, and he created a malignant culture of overdiagnosis and overtreatment. I did blame him for that. So, I quit."

Sanjay leans across the desk and puts his hand on the man's shoulder. He knows too well the toll on doctors who feel they've contributed to a broken system.

They sit in silence, letting Fuki's story sink in. Then Sanjay says softly, "You said you *did* blame Neil. You don't anymore?"

Fuki smiles. It reminds Sanjay of the small Buddha statue his mom keeps in her prayer room. "No. I'm a big believer in the saying, 'Every system is perfectly designed to achieve the results it gets.' MBH rewarded doctors that did more procedures, so Neil did more procedures. If there's someone to blame, which there isn't, they'd be higher up than Neil. The CEO, even the board . . ."

"Sometimes leaving is the only way forward," Sanjay offers.

"Maybe." Fuki strokes his chin. "I'd still like to change healthcare on a larger scale. But here, at least, I can practice medicine the way it's meant to be. That's enough for now."

Fuki doesn't seem convinced, but Sanjay lets it go. He's taken enough of Fuki's time. "Before I leave you to your patients, can I ask a favor?"

Fuki raises an eyebrow.

"Can I borrow some lidocaine?"

* * *

Sanjay trudges back to the car. He can't believe what's become of Neil.

"Your face is scaring me, Doc." John's leaning against the Range Rover, massaging his knee. "Is that for me?" he asks, pointing at the tray of medical supplies Sanjay is holding.

Sanjay puts on a smile. "Yup. We're gonna get you fixed up." He points to the driver's seat, directing John to sit and face the street, then roll up his pant leg. He injects corticosteroids into John's knee and, for good measure, puts on a bandage.

"That it?" asks John. "We're done?"

"It'll take the medicine a day or two to kick in fully, but after that, you should be good for six months."

John flexes his knee in and out. "I feel better already. You're amazing, Doc!"

"That's the lidocaine talking—and a bit of placebo. But yeah, your arthritis isn't bad yet. If you lose some weight, it'll be even better."

"Lose weight, huh? I have let myself go a bit since I got out of the service." John slaps his gut, chuckling, then says, "Tell me what I gotta do, Doc."

This time, Sanjay can't bring himself to smile. If only fixing the mess with Neil—and MBH—were that simple.

CHAPTER 14

"Paging Dr. Sanjay, paging Dr. Sanjay . . ."

It's Neil, calling from across the bar at Bombo's. Beside him are Bill Shires, Sylvia Cannes, and Mohinder Singh—all classmates from med school.

Just past Sylvia is Emma, looking stunning in a bright blue jumpsuit with a deep neckline.

Bombo's is one of those moody, New York-style cocktail bars: low lighting, a glowing amber backbar, bartenders in crisp white shirts and black pants. The crowd is a mix of thirty- and forty-something professionals—meeting someone from a dating app or getting a head start on the weekend.

Before Sanjay's eyes can adjust, Neil is upon him with a bro hug. He stiffens, then relaxes. He greets the others. Then Emma.

He braces himself—but she surprises him, taking his hand and leaning in to deposit a light kiss on the cheek. *Maybe this night won't be as bad as I thought.*

Within minutes, Neil has Bill, Sylvia, and Mohinder doubling over and Emma laughing so hard she's covering her mouth with her hand. He's onto a favorite pastime: naming diagnoses that could double as rock bands.

"Rocky Mountain Spotted Fever," Neil says with a laugh. "Or just Spotted Fever."

"Ground Glass!" shouts Mohinder. "Or . . . I got it! The Opacities."

"How about Ankylosing Spondylitis?" suggests Sylvia.

"Good one!" says Neil, high fiving her.

"The Alleles," adds Emma.

Now Neil is doubling over. When he catches his breath, he says, "Emma, you definitely win for the nerdiest band name ever."

And just like that, for a moment, Sanjay lets go—of the anger and the disappointment at Neil, the three lists. He pulls out a stool, slides into a high top, and orders another round.

"I forget, what specialties are you all in?" Sanjay asks the group.

"Sanj, these guys are on the R-O-A-D to happiness," Neil says.

Seeing Emma's puzzled look, he adds, "Specialties with predictable hours, minimal overnight shifts, and still great pay."

"I'm in radiology," says Mohinder. "That's the R."

"I'm optho. O," says Sylvia.

"Derm," says Bill.

"All we're missing is an A for anesthesiologist," says Neil with a big smile. "Emma, it's not too late!"

"Sanjay, I still can't believe you went into primary care," Sylvia says.

Sanjay almost forgot how often he used to get the question: Why primary care? Although a family doctor is what most people envision when they think of a physician, few medical students, especially at top schools like MBMS, choose it as a career. The pay is much lower than in other specialties, thanks to the absurdly low value the RVU system assigns to primary care compared to procedure-heavy fields.

"Yeah, man, you were top of the class second year. You could've done anything you wanted," says Mohinder. "Or was it because of that anatomy test?"

It lands like a sucker punch, knocking the air out of Sanjay's lungs. He grips the edge of the table, steadying himself.

Bill chuckles, oblivious. "Oh man, I almost forgot about that exam!"

"You did? I still have nightmares about it," says Sylvia. "That creepy room full of cadavers, all those numbered flags?" She mock-shudders.

Sanjay's jaw clenches. "That test . . . ruined everything."

He glances at Emma—she gives him a faint, pained smile—then at Neil, who grimaces sympathetically.

"If I hadn't failed . . ."

He stops himself from saying the last part aloud: If he hadn't failed, maybe he'd still be at MBH. Still seeing patients at the free clinic. Still with Emma. Maybe he wouldn't have tried to . . .

No. *That* is something he can't even think about.

His face burns. He shouldn't have brought it up. They're all staring at him now, the air suffocating. He stares down at his drink.

"But honestly . . ." He clears his throat, forcing the words out. "That's not why I chose primary care. I love taking care of whole families. Watching them grow up, being part of their lives."

Emma, clearly sensing his discomfort, smiles gently. "I think that's sweet, Sanjay. Human connection is what's missing for so many patients." She reaches out and places her hand on his shoulder.

Neil watches her and takes another sip of his cocktail.

They move on, start talking shop. Bill's practice in Atlanta was part of a recent "roll up," he tells them. A private equity group bought it, along with two other dermatology practices. Now it's raising prices on insurance companies and replacing doctors who took early retirement with physician assistants, who are lower paid.

"Selling was the best financial decision I ever made—twice the pay for half the work," Bill says. Then he winces. "But I'm not so sure about the patients. Our quality scores look great on paper, but I don't believe them. We keep missing serious diagnoses, and every week there's some new device or cream we're told to push."

Sylvia and Mohinder stare down at their plates. Sanjay suspects similar things are happening to their practices, too.

"I wish I'd asked more questions about the buyout," says Bill, shaking his head.

This is how medicine gets worse, thinks Sanjay. Businesspeople making all the decisions, while doctors stand by and do nothing—or are silenced.

"I wouldn't assume it's all bad." Neil's voice is matter-of-fact. "Things look different from the boardroom than the exam room. Sometimes you have to keep the big picture in mind."

Sanjay scoffs. "What's bigger than taking care of patients?"

Neil's face reddens. "Oh, come on, Sanj—"

"Speaking of which," Emma cuts in, her eyes pleading with Sanjay. "I forgot to ask earlier. How was clinic at MBH?"

"Oh, what were you guys up to earlier?" asks Neil, stirring his drink aggressively.

Sanjay ignores him. "The patients were great. The nurses, too." He turns to Neil. "But I have some concerns I wanted to share. The clinic seems way too productivity driven, and I don't think it's good for patients. I think—"

"We're a *business*, man," snaps Neil. Emma glares at him, and he sets down his drink with a *thump*. "C'mon!" he says to her. "You think Sanjay is any better? Sanj, how much do you charge your clients?"

"That's beside the point."

"No. It *is* the point. No margin, no mission. We *all* want to make healthcare better, but it takes resources." He turns to Emma. "If we want to build cutting-edge research facilities, we need donations." He looks at Sanjay. "If we want to pay our support staff more, we need to cut costs elsewhere. That's the mission. But without the money, we're stuck."

"Sure, but at what cost?" Sanjay asks.

Neil doesn't seem to hear him. "Doctors like us—" He waves his arms, encompassing the five of them. "We all want a seat at the table, but we have to earn it. Speaking of which, you still haven't answered my question. What are your usual and customary fees, Doctor?"

Sanjay looks at Emma, his face getting hot. She seems to be waiting on his answer, too.

"See?" taunts Neil. "Let he who casts the first stone . . ."

Sanjay can't hold back. "At least I don't do procedures on patients who don't need them."

"Sanjay!" gasps Emma.

Neil looks intently at her, then at his friends, then back at Emma. They're all staring at him.

After a brief moment, his shoulders relax, and he forces a laugh. "Good one, Sanjay. Ease up on the tequila, will you?"

"This has nothing to do with—"

Sanjay's cellphone starts to ring. He pulls it out of his jacket pocket and sees Cassie's name on the screen. "It's from my practice. I need to take this."

* * *

Sanjay puts his phone to his ear as soon as he steps out of the bar. "Hey."

"Sorry to bother. Mr. Kosaac called for an emergency. I tried to get him to see Jacqueline, but he insists on you. Even more so when I told him you're unavailable."

Sanjay grits his teeth. Not only does Mr. Kosaac have an "emergency" every few weeks, by taking care of him Sanjay's pretty sure he is indirectly abetting a criminal organization. The way Kosaac's eyes constantly dart around the room; the urgent, whispered phone calls in the middle of appointments; the multiple last-minute changes in location—all of it is more than Sanjay wants or cares to know about the man.

Back in the Range Rover, he taps the Call Accept button on his laptop. In an instant, he's confronted with a screen-size scrotum.

Lovely, thinks Sanjay. *Glad my eleven years of schooling are being put to good use.*

He quickly spots the lesion. It's perfectly round and red. No ulceration. A textbook case.

"Can you see it? Can you see *it*!" asks Kosaac, as he pulls back on his sack to give Sanjay a better view.

Now Kosaac's face flashes on the screen. No neck; beady, dark eyes.

"I need you to fix it. *Now*," he says, jabbing a finger at the screen.

Sanjay's irritated by the display of aggression but checks himself. "Tell me what happened."

"What happened? You saw my balls. That's what happened. Do you need me to show you again?"

"No, I got that part. But how did it start?"

"Nothing happened. I woke up a few days ago with this. I don't know where it came from. You're the doctor!"

"Any fevers?"

"No."

"Any discharge?"

"No."

"Any new sexual partners?"

"What does it matter?"

Bingo.

"Look, we need to examine you and get some tests. But just looking at it, I think you have syphilis."

Kosaac is eerily quiet. Sanjay tries again. "Syphilis. It's a sexually transmitted infection—"

"I know what syphilis is, damn it! Just get over here and fix it!"

Sanjay raises his voice. "—and if it's syphilis, we'll have to notify the public health authorities and each of your sexual partners."

"What! Authorities? Sexual partners? What the hell are you talking about?" Kosaac's face goes beet red.

"Syphilis is dangerous. If your wife has it, she—"

"My wife! Don't bring my wife into this! What the hell do I pay you for? You work for me!"

"Yes, I do, but I also have an obligation to the public."

"The public! Are you a fucking politician?"

"No, I'm a doctor. And if you'd just shut up and listen to me for a minute—"

"Fuck you, *Doctor*—"

Sanjay hangs up. "Why the fuck do I even bother?" he yells into the car.

He's sick of the phony emergencies, the sketchy patients. He curses himself for ever getting into this business—

Cassie calls, interrupting his train of thought.

"I wish you hadn't done that," she says.

"He complained?" Sanjay huffs out a bitter laugh. "Look, there's no way I'm gonna treat him and not notify his partner. It's unethical."

"I'm not asking you to do anything unethical. I'm asking you to be nice. This is a service—and you're in the service business."

Yeah, well, maybe I don't want to be in the service business anymore, he thinks.

Cassie exhales. "I've been trying to keep them at bay."

"Keep who at bay?"

"You don't need to worry about it. You've got enough on your plate."

His pulse spikes. "Worry about what?"

"Your patients, Sanjay. Mr. Kosaac and some of your other Eastern European patients are in a group chat."

"How do you know—"

"They've been discussing cheaper options."

"Cheaper options! What am I, Costco?"

"There are new players now—high-end spas, even salons, getting into concierge medicine."

"Treating cancer with facials?" Sanjay scoffs.

"All I'm saying is play nice. If Kosaac badmouths you, we could start losing patients."

Sanjay puts the phone down, a pit opening in his stomach. Billionaires and oligarchs are like lemmings—if one veers off, the rest will be quick to follow. No more freedom to practice on his own terms. No more extra cash to help those in need.

* * *

Emma's lingering by the entrance of Bombo's when he gets back inside.

"Got a sec?" she asks.

He wants to be done with this night, but that's not her fault.

"Matt DeSalvo just got here. Apparently he and Neil are close."

"Okay. So?"

"So things may be tense between Matt and me," Emma says slowly. "I wanted you to know the full story."

What? Sanjay has to struggle to keep his face still. All this time, he's been worried about Neil. *Don't tell me you and Matt are a couple*, he almost says.

"Remember the rumors about my father leaving MBH? The student he lost his temper with? That was Matt's partner, Jaewon Kim."

A wave of relief comes over Sanjay. Followed by a sense of dread.

Her dad was attending on the wards that month, Emma tells him, and Jaewon was one of his students.

"In the rush of everything, Jaewon discharged a patient with an antibiotic she had a known allergy to. The next day she was back in the ER, her hands and feet so swollen she couldn't walk. The worst part? She didn't even have an infection—he'd misdiagnosed her." Emma grimaces. "The next day on rounds, my father exploded. He humiliated Jaewon in front of the entire team. By the end of the week, Jaewon had dropped the rotation, and a month later, he left med school for good."

Words fail Sanjay. He remembers his own fight with Tom, the last time he saw him, the way the shame and guilt bubbled up in his throat.

"I don't think Matt's ever forgiven him," Emma says, voice steady. "Or me."

* * *

When they get back to the bar, Matt DeSalvo is sitting in Sanjay's chair, staring down at his phone, texting. He's wearing an ill-fitting Armani suit and a gold Rolex. *Who says science is all work and no pay?* Sanjay thinks wryly.

"Everything okay with your patient, Sanjay?" asks Bill, as he pulls up a bar stool for himself.

"And how much did you charge?" Neil's tone is needling; he's still pissed.

Matt drops his phone on the table and cuts in. "That was the CMO of Next Health. They're gonna push absoluxir hard." He flashes a grin. "I mean, a once-a-month injection that cuts your heart attack risk to nearly zero? It's a no-brainer."

"What's Next Health?" Emma asks.

"A startup delivering high-tech primary care," Sylvia says. "We get a lot of referrals from them. They've got clinics all over the country now."

Sanjay pictures their billboard by the airport, the idiotic CT scan. Ecker mentioned them too. But he's seen the name somewhere else—where?

As Sylvia talks, he pulls up Next Health on his phone. The first article online shows their CEO in a classic tech-bro pose—maroon hoodie, arms crossed, smug grin. The headline reads: *How This CEO Plans to Disrupt a $4 Trillion Industry and Heal America*. Sanjay rolls his eyes.

"They're technically a startup, but already they're a unicorn," Sylvia adds.

His ears perk up. "Unicorn?"

Neil's tone is condescending. "Privately held company worth over a billion dollars. About to go public, I hear."

Sanjay is about to ask another question when Matt leans forward, cutting him off. "SAN-jay," he says, locking eyes. "You should think about prescribing absoluxir. We're doing a buy-and-bill. Charge insurers thirty percent over what you pay—on a drug that'll run two hundred grand a year." He smirks. "Sixty K. Not bad for an honest day's work."

But Sanjay's barely listening. He's remembering one of the clinic notes in List B: *The patient is a thirty-nine-year-old man with atrial fibrillation referred by Next Health.*

The coincidences are piling up—Tom was looking into a patient from Next Health, and now Matt's partnering with them in some kind of money-making scheme.

What Neil did was bad, but not enough for Tom to page him. All the cases in List A were over a year old, and unnecessary procedures—while abhorrent—are sadly routine in American healthcare.

No—Tom was chasing something bigger. And maybe more dangerous. Sanjay needs to get back to Tom's office and finish reviewing List B.

He looks over at Emma, who's awkwardly avoiding eye contact with Matt. He can't just leave her here.

"Emma, want to get something to eat?" he says, standing. "I hear the restaurant next door is decent."

"You're leaving?" Mohinder squints up at Sanjay from his hummus dip. "We just ordered more appetizers."

"Let him go," Neil says. "He'll be back. It's impossible to get a reservation at Il Paloma."

Emma stands, too, and gathers her purse. "He's right, Sanjay. That place *is* impossible. Let's just get takeout."

CHAPTER 15

"Right this way, Dr. Sanjay," says the maître d'.

Emma gawks at Sanjay, but he just folds her arm into his and follows the gentleman in a black tux to the back of the restaurant.

A moment earlier, despite Emma's protests, they made their way into Il Paloma, and Sanjay gave the hostess his name. She was just glad to be out of that bad scene at Bombo's. "Two minutes, and if we don't get a table, we're out of here," he said.

Now the maître d' leads them past the main dining area, where men in black ties and women with Louis Vuitton clutches speak in hushed tones over bottles of wine and crudité. He pushes through a set of double doors; a moment later, the bright fluorescent lights of the restaurant kitchen nearly blind them. Squinting, Emma and Sanjay make their way past harried sous chefs in messy aprons juggling pans over blazing fires to the far corner, where they're seated at a butcher-block countertop.

"Chef will be with you momentarily," he says.

Emma is about to ask Sanjay what is going on when the maître d' returns with a bottle of red wine, a corkscrew, and two glasses.

"Do you like red?" Sanjay asks her.

"Um, yes . . ."

"Here we go." He pops the cork with a flourish and gives her a small pour. "What do you think?"

"I think . . . Oh, you mean, the wine?" She swirls it in her glass. "It's good. Really good."

"Great," Sanjay says, topping up her glass. "Château Lafite is one of my favorites."

Before she can ask how he arranged all this, a line of servers pass through—one bearing a bottle of water and glasses, another with baguette and butter, a third with table settings.

"Sanjay, how did you—"

"Dr. Sanjay! It's you!" Out of a doorway pops a heavyset man with a bushy mustache and powerful arms. Sanjay jumps up and embraces the man like an old friend. "What have people been feeding you! You are all muscle and no fat. So sad." The man laughs heartily.

"And who is this fine entrée?" He nods toward Emma.

"Chef Eze Abara, this is Professor Emma Carpenter-Flores, my . . . my classmate from medical school."

"Well, if I had known my classmates would look like her, I myself would be a doctor right this very instant," says the chef, laughing again.

"And then your parents would finally be proud of you."

"Sanjay!" Emma chastises.

"It is true," says Eze, waving off her concern. "I'm from Nigeria. When my mother was pregnant with me in Abuja, people would stop her at the bus stop, point at her belly, and ask, 'What are you having?' And she'd say, 'I'm having a doctor.'"

Sanjay laughs for the first time since he's arrived.

"You see, Professor Carpenter," says the chef, "one of Dr. Sanjay's and my favorite pastimes is talking about our immigrant childhoods."

Sanjay finally stops laughing, and Eze asks, “Doctor, did I tell you about the time my father caught me cheating on an exam? Oh boy, he whooped me good. But when I told him I only got an eighty-eight, he whooped me even harder. ‘Boy,’ he said, ‘if you’re going to cheat, at least do it properly!’”

More gales of laughter. Gathering himself, Sanjay says, “Did I ever tell you about the time my father tried to take me to the movies?”

Eze shakes his head and smiles. Emma does the same.

“I was in tenth grade, about to get on the school bus home, when his beat-up Toyota Camry pulls to the curb. My dad hardly ever left the store, so my first thought was that someone had died. But he gets out of the car and says—loudly, mind you, so all my classmates can overhear—‘Beta, I got us tickets to see a movie. All the kids in the store are talking about it, so I got us tickets to the early show for a cheaper price.’ And I said, ‘Okay, sure, which movie?’ And he answered, ‘*Pokémon*!’”

Now Emma is laughing, too.

The next hour flashes by. Chef Abara cooks one incredible dish after another, his staff keeps their wine glasses full, and Sanjay and the chef exchange stories from their childhoods.

Despite the large portions, Sanjay is scraping his plate. Olives, beef tartare, bone marrow, cheese, whatever is thrown his way, he eats. And he keeps emptying his wineglass as well.

“My father always told me, ‘Never trust a skinny chef.’ That’s why I maintain my physique, just so,” says Eze, pounding his belly. “But this doctor? In my country, we’d say this man eats like he has a tapeworm in his belly!”

“A drunk tapeworm at that,” adds Sanjay with a laugh.

“In all seriousness, Sanjay, you look really good. How do you do it?” Emma asks.

Sanjay reddens. “When I started my practice, I decided to stop taking my health for granted. I work out daily and eat keto.” It’s true, Emma notes; his bread is untouched. He's only eaten proteins and fats. No carbs.

"Speaking of health, I need to go to the little doctor's room. Which way, Eze?"

The chef watches him leave, then turns to Emma, his voice gentle. "That boy is into you. I've never seen him so at peace."

"That's funny, Chef. I was just thinking I've never seen him as happy as he is tonight, but because of you."

"It's not me, I'll tell you that much."

Emma feels herself blush.

"Right now, you're wondering how we know each other," he says.

"Yes."

The chef tells his story. He grew up in Nigeria, then moved to the Bronx. He had a knack for cooking and soon found himself shucking oysters, then working his way up at any restaurant that would try him out. Eventually, he got an offer to train in Naples with some of the best chefs in the world. Right as he was making a name for himself, he was diagnosed with tongue cancer.

"I never smoked a day in my life. It was curable, but they said they would have to cut out my tongue. They might as well stab me in the heart."

A well-heeled patron told him about Dr. Sanjay. "He said, 'He's the doctor to the rich and famous. He can do things no other doctor can.' I doubted him, but what choice did I have? I was desperate. After examining me, Sanjay told me I was a candidate for a new approach that would save my tongue. Radiation and a special cocktail of chemo. He found a doctor in Chicago willing to do it, and although he didn't tell me at the time, he paid for my treatment. And it worked! I'm six years cancer-free and living the dream. At least, my dream. My parents are still holding out for medical school," Eze adds with a laugh.

Then, more seriously, "That man is not only my friend. He's my brother."

Emma is buzzing. The whole evening feels like a dream. Sanjay is both the man she knew and fell in love with and the man she envisioned him becoming one day.

Was everything she heard about him just rumor? Was their estrangement some big misunderstanding?

Someone clears their throat. She turns to see Sanjay, smiling at her with his deep brown eyes. "What are you two talking about?"

Emma fans herself, the warmth from the nearby kitchen suddenly rising.

"Oh, nothing," replies Eze, winking at her. "Just debating what I'm serving for dessert."

* * *

"Want to come up for a nightcap?" Emma asks, her hands spilling over Sanjay's biceps.

The Range Rover's outside her place. It's late, and Emma is tipsy. Sanjay insisted on dropping her off at home. Now he wonders if this is the right note to end a perfect night on. He needs to get back to List B and see if there's any connection to Next Health. But he isn't ready to say goodbye yet. Sanjay lets John go and tells him that he'll find his own way back.

After fiddling with her lock, Emma opens the door to her apartment. The key gets stuck, and when Sanjay tries to step inside, they collide. He feels her breath on his neck as she lingers. She smells like the Emma he remembers.

Then the key comes out, and Emma unfurls from Sanjay. "I'm going to freshen up and get us a bottle of wine. You stay here," she says, directing him toward the living room.

Her apartment is exactly as he imagined it, a mix of her two sides. The clean lines and simplicity of Northern European design, enlivened by the brightly colored paintings and walls of a Peruvian villa. Oak tables and shelves, a cloth sofa, fluffy pastel pillows. On her bookshelf: *Siddhartha* by Hermann Hesse; *Eat, Pray, Love*; a biography of Marie Curie. Hanging on the wall, her BA in biology from Harvard and her PhD from Uppsala. A collection of photos of her mom. Only one has her dad in it—a trip to Lima, perhaps to visit her mother's family. The rest are intimate portraits of Maria, taken by Emma. The last of these shows Maria lying in bed. Despite the sunken eyes and hairlessness, Emma's features are clearly visible in her mother's.

Missing is any medical school diploma or trace of the two years she and Sanjay were classmates—and more.

He hears Emma in the kitchen, opening drawers. "Red or white?" she calls.

Standing there, he regrets his decision. A part of him wants this so badly. But Emma needs to know that he isn't coming back. He's worked too hard to leave his practice, even if the patients infuriate him at times.

Emma appears in silk pajamas, her hair down, bearing two glasses of red wine.

But something is wrong. Her movements are more measured, and her lips form a frown.

"Sanjay." She takes a deep breath. "Tonight was special, but last time . . . You hurt me. I want whatever this is to be different. And I don't know if I can trust you yet."

He just nods. She has every right to feel that way.

"There's something else you should know." She sits on the couch and gestures for him to join her. She waits to speak until their eyes meet.

"I didn't tell you everything about me and Neil. We went on two dates. Recently. I don't know how he feels, but . . ." She stops, looking for the words. "I love Neil; I do, but only as a friend. And with work, my father, I haven't had a chance to talk to him yet. I need to do that first."

Sanjay tries to hide his surprise. He makes polite conversation, finds an excuse to leave. On the elevator ride down, he wonders why Neil or Emma didn't tell him earlier.

He arrives back at the Four Seasons just before midnight. The cheerful greeting from the bellhop seems forced, and he's more than a little irritated when his room key is demagnetized and he has to trudge back down to the front desk for a new one.

The room is freezing cold. Monochromatic paintings on the wall. No photos or personal effects. Just chocolates on the bed from the turn-down service and no one to share them with.

Life was so different growing up. Potlucks at a new Indian auntie's house every weekend, the kids running around in the basement while the adults played cards upstairs—or, if a bottle of Johnnie Walker was involved, sang old Hindi songs. They didn't have much, but in the ways that mattered, they had it all.

He thinks about calling Neela or his mom, but they'll only sense his loneliness and pity him. Or, worse, try to cheer him up.

Other than a one-day visit here and there, he's been away from his family for ten years—delinquent in his filial obligations to them, at least the nonfinancial ones. He's strayed from his mission of caring for those in need. He's disconnected from Neil—and from Emma.

Is he living a lie? Has he made the right choices?

Is the life he left behind truly in the past?

* * *

The next morning, a ringing phone jolts Sanjay awake. His brain scrambles to remember where he is—his plane? Paris? Monaco? Then he peers out the window, sees MBH in the distance. He can almost make out the ICU tower.

Boston. Tom's office. The three lists.

His eyes find Tom's office phone just as the ringing stops. A telemarketer, probably.

Stretching his back, he replays the last eight hours. After tossing and turning in his hotel bed, he took a cab to Community Cares and powered through lists B and C.

List C was troubling but not unexpected in a hospital chart audit. All the patients were ICU transfers, routinely investigated because they can point to quality problems. Why Tom was digging into these particular cases, Sanjay didn't yet know.

List B was more baffling. He's pieced together that every patient was referred to MBH from Next Health—the clinic Matt mentioned. Beyond that, the cases seem ordinary: patients were sent to a wide range of specialists, not just GI, and many underwent procedures, though none overtly unnecessary.

At least the two lists have nothing to do with Neil, he thinks, sighing.

Tom's office phone rings again. *A patient?* wonders Sanjay. He picks up, just in case.

"Dr. Carpenter, is that you?"

"No, I'm sorry, it's not. Who is this?"

"It's Paul Klein, I'm . . ." The man pauses. "I'm a patient of Dr. Carpenter's."

Sanjay glances at his watch. It's 8:10 AM. Maybe Klein had a phone visit scheduled? Tom often gave patients his direct line.

Sanjay breaks the news straight. "I'm sorry to tell you that Dr. Carpenter's dead."

"Oh my God." The line goes silent. Then the man says, voice shaky, "What happened?"

Sanjay gives him the brief story. Sudden collapse. Stroke. Failed resuscitation.

"I, uh . . . I'm shocked. I just talked to him a week ago." Paul's voice trails.

"What was he helping you with? I'm a doctor, too."

"I'm sorry, but I have to go."

"Wait. If you change your mind, my name is Dr. Sanjay Patel. My number is—"

"Sanjay Patel? As in Dr. Sanjay?"

Sanjay is as surprised as the patient is.

"Tom talked about you. Said you were the best doctor he'd trained. A good man."

Sanjay's throat tightens. Then Paul lowers his voice.

"Listen, I'm not actually a patient of Tom's. At least not anymore."

"I don't understand," Sanjay stammers, his pulse quickening.

"I'm a reporter at the *Boston Globe*. Tom asked me to help him investigate MBH."

Sanjay's mouth goes dry.

"I've been digging into a connection to a startup here in Boston—Next Health—and have been off the grid, chasing leads." Paul's voice speeds up. "And now he's dead? Days after he was threatened?"

"Threatened?" The word slams into Sanjay, his vision narrowing.

"Tom got a call—telling him to back off. But after he visited a Next Health clinic and pressed their doctors, men showed up at his office. That's when he called me."

Sanjay recalls Emma saying Tom looked frightened when she visited his office just before his death. It fits. "Who were they?"

"That's . . . all I know." Paul suddenly sounds afraid, as if the line itself isn't safe.

Sanjay senses he's about to hang up. Then Paul rushes: "I'm no doctor, but most people who have a stroke don't die, right? Especially at a place like MBH?"

The line goes dead.

Sanjay hangs up the receiver, his heart pounding in his ears. He checks his pulse—120 beats a minute—then strides to the clinic bathroom and splashes cold water on his face. It's an old trick from residency to break an abnormally fast heartbeat.

It doesn't work.

In his zeal to figure out the three lists, he bypassed the oddities around Tom's death: the blue toes, the skipped autopsy. Now he adds in what he's just learned from the reporter: Tom's investigation into MBH, the death threat.

What if these aren't coincidences? What if someone went after Tom for what he discovered?

What if Tom Carpenter was murdered?

CHAPTER 16

SANJAY'S TALKING INTO his cellphone, rapidly pacing Tom's office. He's just finished updating Cassie on what he's learned.

"Sanjay," she says. "This is crazy. You need to go to the police."

"The police? We have an old man, seemingly dead from natural causes, and a bunch of theories. They'd laugh me out of the room."

"Fine, then go to the hospital lawyer. Didn't you say Tom spoke to him? Doesn't that mean we can trust him? Or what about Ecker?"

A shiver goes down Sanjay's spine. MBH's lawyers tried to fire him years ago. And Ecker? He stood by and did nothing.

"No. I don't trust anyone in this place."

Cassie exhales. "Then leave. You've said yourself how much you hate it there. Your practice is hanging by a thread. Why risk everything—for this?"

She has a point. Crap like this is the exact reason he left MBH the last time. Now he's letting the place suck him back in. *Fool me once, shame on you. Fool me twice . . .*

Still, he remembers the promise he made Tom Carpenter the day they met: to always put patients first. Walking away could mean patients get hurt.

"I could, but—"

"Sanjay, please. You need to let this go."

But he isn't listening. He's looking around Tom's office, remembering the last time he saw him alive: William Barnett, the hospital disciplinary committee, the fight. In this very room.

"Cassie, I have to do this. Tom called me here. After what happened between us, there's no way he would have done that without a good reason." Sanjay walks across the room to Tom's whiteboard, picks up a black marker and palms it in his hand. "I'll work it up like any other case. Put the pieces together."

Her voice sharpens. "Sanjay, this isn't a puzzle. It's real—and it's dangerous. I know the kind of people who get involved in things like this—"

He ends the call.

His concierge patients often ask, "How'd you get into this line of work? How did you become a doctor to the uber-rich?" Invariably, he gives a witty answer: "To pay off my gambling debts" or "To be the first international man of medicine." It's all part of the act.

But it's never the truth. For years, he's blocked out the memory of the day he left MBH for good.

Now it all comes flooding back.

CHAPTER

17

Ten Years Ago

SANJAY WHIZZES PAST the ER nursing station. "Morning, Marla!"

"Morning, Dr. Sanjay," the charge nurse calls after him. "Don't be ordering any fancy tests in my ER today!"

He and Marla have butted heads a couple times, but after three years of residency in Chicago, he's just happy to be back at MBH—this time as a freshly minted attending physician.

Even better, he's back at the free clinic with Tom and spending every free evening with Neil: late-night Chinese takeout, binge-watching *Scrubs*. Almost like good times—minus Emma. She's in Sweden and still not returning his calls.

He quickly sorts out his first three patients: staples removal for a gangbanger who lost a knife fight; a nursing home admission for kidney infection; strep throat in a brittle diabetic. The last patient is Pakistani and uninsured. Before discharging him, Sanjay gives him his cell number and sets up an appointment at Community Cares.

Then, over the PA, he hears, "Code blue."

Adrenaline floods him. A second later, Marla's there, grabbing him by the arm, rushing him to trauma bay six. "Fifty-two-year-old guy—finance—woke up forty minutes ago with acute-onset dizziness," she says. "No motor or sensory loss. Head CTs ordered, stat."

Stroke's the obvious concern. But Tom reminded him just last week that the biggest mistake a doctor can make is premature closure—narrowing in on a diagnosis too early.

Now he casts a wide net of possible diagnoses: dehydration, orthostatic hypotension, migraine, hemorrhage. In the fifty-odd seconds it takes to walk to the trauma bay, he comes up with thirty possible conditions, ordering them in his mind from most to least likely.

Pulling back the curtain, he says, "Clear the room, please."

The patient, William James Barnett, is lying on the bed, clutching his head.

"Mr. Barnett," Sanjay begins, "tell me what happened this morning. In the most exact detail you can."

"When I woke up, my head was spinning. I can't control it. I sit down, but it doesn't make a difference."

As he talks, Sanjay scrolls through Barnett's electronic health record. Mildly overweight; recent physical turned up high cholesterol; family history of high blood pressure. All typical for an overworked fifty-something professional.

Barnett pauses, and Sanjay nods for him to continue. The average patient gets eleven seconds to lay out the reason for their visit before the doctor interrupts. Those lost seconds are where the gold is found.

"I don't know what happened," Barnett says. "I'm an early riser. Up before the markets, you know? But I have a big board meeting today. They're trying to sell my company out from under me. So I was up most of the night with my CFO, putting a deck together. It wasn't until my alarm went off that I got up. I jumped out of bed to get ready, and I felt it."

"CT!" someone yells from behind the curtain. The transport team barges in. *Not much time left.* Sanjay leans in.

"When you woke up," he asks, "was the alarm clock on your left or right?"

"Huh? What difference does it . . . ?" The transport team starts moving the bed, and Barnett looks up at Sanjay, who's waiting for an answer. "On my right."

Sanjay follows the gurney. "Did you wake up facing the alarm clock? Or away from it?"

Barnett is almost out of sight when he yells, "Away!"

There it is. The gold.

A few minutes later, Sanjay's on his way back to Barnett's room when three gray-haired men in white coats flag him down.

"Dr. Patel. Great job with this case," says the first. He looks familiar.

"I haven't solved it yet," Sanjay says, rocking back on his heels.

"We've been following your work at MBH," the man continues. "That case of extra-pulmonary tuberculosis you diagnosed last month made the rounds in the doctors' lounge. Great stuff. But we got it from here."

"Thanks," Sanjay says reflexively, more confused than flattered. He looks at the man's ID badge. Dr. Henry Ecker, the chair of medicine. Frowning, he glances at the other two badges. Why are the chair of medicine, chair of neurology, and chair of radiology down here?

"It's not a stroke," he adds, having just come from the CT scanner.

"The head CT was negative, but that doesn't necessarily mean it's not a stroke," says the chair of neurology.

"Yes, but based on Mr. Barnett's history, it's more likely his diagnosis is BPPV. Perhaps we can discharge him, and he can follow up in clinic tomorrow? He mentioned something about a meeting he needs to—"

"You know patients," says the radiology chair. "They never make their health a priority."

For a man who sits in a dark room all day, never actually talking to patients, this guy seems to know a lot about them. Sanjay opens his mouth, about to erupt.

Dr. Ecker heads him off. "Dr. Patel, the truth is no diagnostic test or fact obtained on patient history is perfect. Would you agree?"

Sanjay nods.

"And there's a chance, however small, that he has something serious going on."

"There's always a chance. I—"

"What you don't know is our patient here is a VIP. If we discharge him too soon, we risk our reputation, not to mention a lawsuit. Conversely, if we keep him here a day or two to ensure we have the right diagnosis, we create an opportunity to fund the next breakthrough and save millions of lives. A small price to pay, if you ask me."

"VIP?"

Ecker gives him a tight smile. The two other doctors look at each other like their young colleague has just strolled into their country club in nonregulation socks.

"Ah. You don't know. William James Barnett? As in Barnett & Smith, the biggest private equity firm in town. He's one of the richest men between here and Palm Beach."

Now it makes sense. They're hoping to extract a huge donation. If Sanjay discharges Barnett, he might be letting a $10 million—even a $100 million—check walk out the door.

It's not lost on him that if Barnett were Black or brown, even if he were rich, he'd still be in the waiting room.

Taking a deep breath, he uses the only card he has left. "I didn't get a chance to complete my physical exam. Don't want the insurance company to hassle us over the bill." He nudges his way past them and into Barnett's room.

"Your head CT is negative," he says to Barnett. "To me, that says you didn't have a stroke." Pointing toward the spot where the three senior physicians just stood, he adds, "But to be on the safe side, they want to admit you."

"Admit me?" Barnett waves his hands in the air. "No, no, no. I have to leave as soon as possible. Can't you just prescribe something?"

"It's a couple days at most. To run some tests."

Barnett rubs his chin. "You said, 'they.' '*They*' want to admit me. You're my doctor in here. What do *you* want to do?"

Sanjay pauses. He wants to put his patient first. Hospital politics be damned.

In one breath, he makes his decision.

He directs Barnett to sit on the side of the bed, his head turned to the left. Gently, Sanjay lays him down from behind until his head hangs over the edge. "Now open your eyes."

It's textbook. Barnett's eyes keep drifting to the left, then jerking back. His body thinks it's turning right; to keep his gaze fixed on the same point, the eyes move left, only to skip back to their original position a moment later.

"Now we're going to cure you in one fell swoop." Holding Barnett's head, Sanjay instructs him to roll right until his head is facing downward.

"Okay, now, let's sit you up. Slowly."

Barnett gets upright and turns his head from side to side. "It's gone! The dizziness is gone!" He looks at Sanjay, incredulous. "How did you do that?"

"You have what's called benign paroxysmal positional vertigo. BPPV. It's caused by a crystal in your inner ear getting stuck. Like a kidney stone, but from the fluid in your ear. That maneuver we just did—it dislodged it."

Barnett looks impressed. "Now what?"

"Now you're fine. There's a chance, about five percent, that the crystal will cause problems again in the next week. If that happens, you can do that maneuver on yourself." Sanjay points toward the ceiling. "The higher-ups will still want to admit you."

"Forget that. I have a board meeting to get to." Barnett yanks the EKG leads off his chest, winces, and gets up.

Sanjay watches him walk out of the room and smiles.

* * *

The next morning, Sanjay wakes to his alarm clock. Outside the window of his tiny studio apartment, rain pummels the city.

Down in the lobby, he nearly trips over a bucket. The roof is leaking. Again. He sighs. Having taken out loans to pay for what his scholarships didn't cover during eight years of college and med school, he has a narrow choice of places to live close to the hospital.

Staring through the lobby door at the rain, now coming down in sheets, he wishes he could afford a car. Or even a cab.

Just as he steps outside, a black stretch limo pulls up to the curb. The driver's door opens, and a man gets out. In his fifties, Caucasian, wearing a dark suit and a black hat, he opens a large umbrella, then says, "Dr. Sanjay, my employer, Mr. Barnett, respectfully requests a small dose of your time."

The rich BPPV patient? thinks Sanjay. *That would explain the limo.*

"Is he okay? I told him the stone could recur—"

"He's very well—thanks to you. This is another matter entirely."

Sanjay feels the urge to pinch himself out of a dream—or a nightmare. He isn't sure which. "I need to go to work," he says.

"We know. His home is a quick ride from here, and he's very busy, so I assure you: The meeting will be brief. Afterward, I'll deposit you at the hospital. Dry."

Sanjay stares up at the flooding sky. No end to the rain in sight. And he's forgotten his extra pair of scrubs. "Okay, let's go."

He tries a couple seats before settling into the rear bench of the limo, sinking into the buttery leather. He feels like an intruder in someone else's living room. Through the intercom, the driver instructs him to help himself to breakfast.

In front of him, a foldout tray holds a stainless steel carafe nestled into a fitting ring, along with a small basket lined with linen napkin. Sanjay hesitates, then pours himself a black coffee, opens the basket lid and grabs a powdered scone.

He's just discovered the champagne cooler when the limo stops fifteen minutes later. They're on a circular cobblestone driveway in front of a massive house. At the entrance is a large water fountain, a statue of a naked child at its center. *A curious way to greet visitors.* The face of the stone child is tranquil, gazing up at the sky without any hint of yearning. He's exactly where he belongs.

Sanjay can't say the same.

The limo door opens. "After you, Doctor."

A second man in a dark suit leads Sanjay through several grand rooms to a library unlike anything he's seen. The domed ceiling soars up three stories over bookshelves on two levels, accessed by a rolling ladder. As someone who spent much of his childhood scrounging for books from neighbors and at used books fairs, Sanjay's in awe. Money has never mattered much to him, except when there isn't enough for basics. In an instant, he begins to appreciate all that riches can, in fact, buy.

At the far end of the room, rising from a mahogany desk, is the man who summoned him.

It takes Sanjay a moment to recognize him. Yesterday, William Barnett seemed old and weak, like patients often do in their flimsy hospital gowns. Today, he looks ready for a round of polo, complete with the strong aroma of musk, a perfectly fitting gray sports jacket, and a crimson handkerchief in his left breast pocket.

Mr. Barnett's first order of business is to thank Sanjay. "While my condition didn't necessitate saving my life, by getting me out of there, you saved my company."

Kind, but not enough reason to ambush him. Sanjay waits.

"Your background is impressive," Barnett continues. "The son of immigrants. Got into the country's best universities but went local on scholarship. Then the best medical school. Top of your class by your second year—until something happened. Went on to win a national diagnostic competition in residency, landing you a plum job at Man's Best Hospital."

This is more than just his chart. It's a full biopsy.

"I'm not a man who wastes time." Barnett takes out a sheet of paper. "I could use a doctor like you. Here is what I'm prepared to pay." He writes fast, flourishing his pen. "You quit your job, and I put you on retainer. Available on reasonable notice, which I hope is no more than two to three times a year."

He folds the paper and hands it to Sanjay.

A single number stares back at Sanjay: a one with five zeros.

"A hundred thousand a year!" Sanjay's hand trembles. "For two to three visits? That's what I make at MBH, working sixty-hour weeks—"

"Nonexclusive, of course," Barnett continues. "You're free to take on other clients. My name alone should bring in another ten."

The room spins.

In three months, he could clear his debts. He could send money to Neela. His parents could pay off the store.

He'd heard of lawyers and accountants pulling in absurd fees from the ultrarich, but doctors? Then again, what's more valuable than health? How many dying patients had told Sanjay they'd pay any amount of money for more time?

Still—ditch the hospital, the free clinic? Tom?

"It's a generous offer, Mr. Barnett, but I can't. And I really need to get to my ER shift."

Barnett hands him a gold-foil business card. "My offer is good for two weeks. That little episode yesterday made me realize I need a concierge physician as soon as possible. I hope it's you."

* * *

Three days later, Sanjay is back outside the glass entrance to the ER. He's early, and it's raining, as usual. But when he swipes his ID badge, the door doesn't slide back.

"Again," he grumbles. Unless he finds a security guard who'll bypass the bullshit, he'll be late. And wet.

As he's considering this, another doctor arrives. Sanjay scoots in behind him. But when he swipes his ID badge again—this time to unlock the computer and order labs on his first patient—it doesn't work. *Of course. It's all one system.*

He goes to find Marla, the charge nurse.

"The hell are you doing here?" she asks.

"Nice to see you, too." This is more than their usual banter. "My badge isn't working."

She puts her hand on her hip. "Oh, it's working."

"Sorry?" Sanjay is genuinely confused.

"Have you checked your email?"

"Uh . . . no." The hospital forbids doctors from emailing patients, so Sanjay seldom bothers to check his account.

"You've been put on administrative leave."

"What? Why?"

If she'd been wearing glasses, she'd have looked at him over the top of them. "As if they'd tell me."

Sanjay stumbles out of the ER. Taking refuge from the rain under an awning, he pulls out his phone. The email is hard to miss. "PRIVILEGED AND CONFIDENTIAL, NOTICE OF LEAVE, EFFECTIVE IMMEDIATELY."

The message itself has little useful information; it's boilerplate language likely vetted and re-vetted by the hospital's battery of lawyers. Sanjay skips to the attachment. The key phrases are "unnecessary risk to a patient's health" and "refused warnings from senior physician leaders." It doesn't mention Barnett by name, but it's obviously about him.

Toggling back to the email, he reads that he must report to the hospital disciplinary committee.

Which might result in his medical privileges at Mount Beacon Hospital being restored—or terminated. In the latter case, the Massachusetts Board of Registration in Medicine will be notified, and could conduct an independent review.

Which might result in Sanjay's medical license being permanently revoked.

How could they put him on involuntary suspension? His breath catches. Would the committee listen to his side of the story, or is the hearing a formality, his termination a given? Either way, it would be a permanent black mark on his record.

A cold sweat breaks out on his forehead. This might be the end of his medical career. And for sticking his neck out to do the right thing?

His first instinct is to call Neil. But after a two-year gap doing research at the NIH, Neil's still a junior resident. A faculty favorite, sure, but there's nothing he can do beyond offering sympathy.

There is only one person who can reverse this. Though he's become a bit of a pariah since being pushed out of MBH, he's still the go-to physician for MBH executives' own care. Sanjay prays that counts for something.

He runs to the free clinic and sprints up the stairwell. Every other time he's shown up unannounced, Tom's secretary has waved him right in.

Not this time.

Tom must already know.

As he waits, Sanjay wonders what Tom Carpenter said to the hospital administrators when they called. Did he defend his protégé?

After ten excruciating minutes, he hears Tom yell through the closed door, "Come in!" Without preamble or greeting, Tom demands an account of the ER episode with Barnett. "Spare no detail," he says, and listens with crossed arms.

When Sanjay's finished, he says, "When you made your diagnosis, did you base it on your own read of the CT or the radiologist's?"

"I read it myself. I know how to read a C—"

"After Mr. Barnett left, did you call him that day or the next to make sure his symptoms had in fact resolved?"

"I didn't call him, but I saw him the next day." Sanjay fills Tom in on the meeting with Barnett and the job offer. He isn't seriously considering it, but he still wants Tom to know.

"So you didn't proactively follow up with the patient."

Is Tom on MBH's side?

"Sanjay, I've always told you to keep your differential diagnosis as broad as possible for as long as possible. You can never be sure."

Sanjay runs his hands through his hair. "We're really doing this? You're really lecturing me on the basics of diagnosis?"

Tom uncrosses his arms. "I'm getting you ready for the disciplinary meeting."

Sanjay feels a wave of nausea. "I'm not sure if I can go through with it."

"What does that even mean?" Tom's eyes narrow.

"Worst case? I get fired and lose my medical license. I won't be allowed to practice anywhere in Massachusetts. In any state I move to, I'll have to report that my last license was revoked. I may never get to practice again. Best case? I get my job back, but my reputation's ruined. Pretty soon everyone will be talking about me getting put on leave. Colleagues won't send me patients. Nurses will second-guess my decisions."

"So, that's it? Towel thrown in?" Tom's tone is brusque.

Sanjay tries to visualize himself standing in front of the disciplinary committee. Ten to twelve of his peers, asking these same questions. Staring at him, judging him. His stomach churns.

Tom seems to sense his mounting anxiety. "In a career where you put patients first, there'll be thousands of fights like this."

Sanjay's breath is becoming short. "I just want to do my job. Take care of patients. Not fight the system."

Tom scoffs. "Fighting the system *is* the job. If you don't fight, we all lose. Patients lose."

Sanjay can't speak.

"Or maybe you just *want* to be a doctor to billionaires. Wouldn't be that different from the rest of the goddamn profession."

The words are a gut punch. Tom knows better than most Sanjay's commitment to serving the poor.

Without looking at him, Tom sits back down at his desk. He puts on his reading glasses and picks up a chart.

Sanjay's breath is coming fast, heavy with growing anger. "And you?"

Tom looks up, eyebrows raised.

"Did you fight for me when they called? Or do you only fight for yourself? Is this all part of the *Dr. Tom Carpenter Show*?"

Tom's fists slam against the table. "What the hell are you talking about?"

"Ever since I got back, I've wondered: Why is Tom running a free clinic affiliated with MBH? If all you wanted was to help patients in need, you'd practice at a community clinic or a homeless shelter. But the truth is, you're no different. Reputation and prestige are everything to you. Fuck anyone who risks making you look bad—including me. Including Emma."

Tom grabs his copy of *Harrison's* and throws it. The medical tome hurls past Sanjay's head and knocks a diploma off the far wall with a crash.

"Get the fuck out of my office, Sanjay!" he bellows. "And never come back!"

"Glad we're finally on the same page."

As he opens the door to leave, Tom shouts after him, "They were right about you all along! You aren't cut out to be a doctor."

Sanjay pounds down the stairs, all the greed and corruption he's witnessed since starting medical school flashes through his mind.

There's no point in fighting the system. Or even being a part of it.

He digs out his wallet and finds Barnett's card.

CHAPTER 18

The memories confirm Sanjay was right to leave MBH. But he can't walk away this time. He has two mysteries on his hands: Was Tom murdered? And what had he uncovered about MBH?

He jumps up and down in place and throws a few punches—a habit he picked up in med school. It came in handy when he'd been up all night studying or caring for patients and needed to refocus. He smiles, remembering the time Emma walked in on him. Her look seemed to say, "I'm glad to know you're just a silly boy after all."

The punches are tighter now, thanks to Mike, his trainer, but no doubt if she were here, Emma would still laugh at him.

With his body calmer, a new thought crosses Sanjay's mind: Write it all out. He's made the mistake of narrowing his diagnosis too soon once before. He can't afford to do it again.

Tom's whiteboard is tempting, but he needs something more mobile. He grabs a sheet of paper out of the printer and scribbles down what he knows:

	What?	Who?	Why?
List A	Unnecessary procedures	Neil	To be department chair
List B	Referrals from Next Health	?	?
List C	ICU transfers	?	?
Tom	Stroke; Murder?	?	?

Should he bring in Emma or Neil? He leans back in his chair, weighing the risks.

Emma's out—he has no proof Tom was murdered, and the last thing he needs is an indignant Carpenter raising hell and drawing attention from whoever threatened him.

And Neil? Tempting, but with List A pointing in his direction, Sanjay needs to keep his distance.

It's him and Cassie for now. During the day he'll focus on Tom's death, and at night the three lists.

Satisfied, he slips the paper into his medical bag and heads for the hospital, mentally retracing the clues as he goes.

Tom definitely had a stroke—that much is certain from his CT scan. But strokes have different causes. The vast majority come from an artery in the brain that suddenly gets clotted from within—just like a heart attack. Less common is a blood clot in the heart or the arteries of the neck, which flicks off other tiny clots—emboli—that travel to the brain and stop blood flow. That could explain Tom's blue toes: The same clot that sent an emboli to his brain could have sent one to his foot.

But it doesn't explain the missing autopsy. Sanjay thinks of Occam's Razor, the principle that the simplest explanation is often the right one. He needs a theory that pulls all of Tom's findings together.

What if the doctors at MBH misdiagnosed Tom's condition, then covered it up? It's a stretch to think someone would go to that much trouble to hide an error—especially since the misdiagnosis wouldn't have changed the outcome. But what if someone made a mistake not just in diagnosis, but in *treatment*, like giving Tom the wrong medicine in the ER?

As that reporter at *The Boston Globe* said, strokes don't usually kill people.

The reporter also said someone threatened Tom. What if someone slipped Tom the wrong medicine in the ER on purpose, then covered it up?

That's something that would show up in an autopsy and—with any luck—in a blood test, too.

* * *

The pathology lab still reeks of formaldehyde, but this time, it's quiet. Feldman's in the corner, hunched over his desk, charting. Sans bloody apron and chainsaw.

He looks older today, more tired. Like Tom, he's a relic from a time before the corporatization of medicine, before the mountains of paperwork and the tedious demands of billing and coding. A time when doctors were in charge and medicine was more art and science and less of a business.

Sanjay clears his throat, and Feldman lifts his head slowly. When he sees Sanjay, his eyes light up. "Dr. Sanjay. Twice in two days! To what do I owe the honor?"

His hands look clean enough. Sanjay offers him a handshake, then a cup of coffee.

Feldman eyes it suspiciously. "'Timeo Danaos et dona ferentes.' I fear the Greeks even when bearing gifts. Know who said it?"

"Nope."

Feldman shakes his head and smiles. "None of you young docs learn the classics these days. The Trojan priest Laocoön, who warned the city when they were gifted a wooden horse? Virgil's *Aeneid*."

Sanjay shrugs. His parents were too busy recounting tales from the *Mahabharata*. "It's not poison, if that's what you're thinking."

"Ha! Poison I could cure." Feldman laughs, takes a gulp.

Sanjay plops his medical bag onto the cleanest surgical tray in reach, grateful once again that Cassie added a cold storage system to transport vaccines and patient samples across continents. Opening it, he takes out a plastic specimen bag full of ice. In it is a vial of blood.

"Is that what I think it is?" Feldman whispers.

Sanjay nods.

"Jesus Christ!" Feldman glances over his shoulder. "You know when I told you to get me a vial of Tom's blood, I was just horsing around, right? How'd you pull it off?"

It wasn't easy. Knowing that Tom would prefer cremation to burial, Sanjay gambled on the funeral home not embalming the body, which meant there'd be some blood left. He arrived early and convinced the caretakers to let him into the viewing room alone. Kneeling beside Tom, his back to the door, he'd pulled a tourniquet out of his pocket—hospital grade, bright blue.

Blood filled the vial more slowly than it would from a living patient. When he heard Emma open the door, he took the needle out quickly, praying he had enough. He'd hoped to examine Tom's feet and say a few words, but all he had time for was, "Thanks, Doc."

"I didn't think I'd actually use the sample," he says to Feldman now. "I just figured, why not?"

Feldman is smiling. "The apple didn't fall far from the tree. Tom would be proud."

Sanjay has his doubts, but he appreciates the sentiment.

Feldman picks up the vial and eyes its contents. "This about the blue toes?" he asks. When Sanjay nods, he purses his lips and says, "So what do you want me to test it for?"

"Everything."

* * *

Sanjay jogs up the basement staircase from the pathology lab. Now that Tom's bloodwork is cooking, he needs to follow up on the blue toes. With such an unusual symptom, why didn't it show up in Tom's electronic health record?

He swipes into the resident workroom off the lobby entrance and logs into his account. Clicking past the dead patient admonition again, he opens Tom's record and finds his ER note. The physical exam section makes no mention of blue toes. Nor, for that matter, does it contain any real details—something he knows is increasingly common as doctors are compelled to prioritize efficiency. *Turn that crank.*

He's rereading it for the third time when something catches his eye.

It's signed by a physician assistant.

Sanjay sits back, crosses his arms. Technically, physicians, physician assistants, and nurse practitioners are all considered providers; they can make diagnoses and prescribe medications. But physician assistants don't have the same privileges as MDs. When Sanjay last worked here, PAs weren't allowed to sign medical charts. He doubts that's changed. MBH isn't that progressive—or inclusive.

Back in the ER, he tracks down the chief resident, Dr. Ciroli, the striking blond he met his first day back at MBH. She's at the nursing station, signing a stack of paperwork.

"Hello again," she says with a smile. "If you wanted to hang out, you could have just paged me."

"I'm old-fashioned that way," says Sanjay, smiling. "But unfortunately, this isn't a social visit. Who's Ana Nunez?"

Dr. Ciroli looks up from her papers and shrugs. "No clue. She a patient in the ER?"

"No, she's the physician assistant who signed Tom Carpenter's ER chart."

"Not possible. Only MDs can sign notes down here."

A minute later they're standing over a computer, Tom's chart open on the screen.

"See? 'Ana Nunez, PA,'" says Sanjay, pointing at the line.

"Weird." Dr. Ciroli opens a browser and searches. "I'm not seeing her in the paging directory, either." More typing. "But she does have an email address here."

"Great, thanks. I owe you."

"You sure do," she says, flashing him a smile as he walks away.

He heads to the main lobby of MBH. He has to find Ana Nunez.

CHAPTER 19

Emma arrives at MBH's administrative offices to meet Janet Scully, the board chair. Though she wants to avoid Neil, she feels obligated to drop by. Thankfully, his secretary says he's spending the morning at one of MBH's satellite hospitals across town.

But Neil isn't why her insides are turning. *I know better than most people that your dad wasn't a saint.* What had Janet meant by that?

Last night, Emma tossed and turned in bed, unable to put the question out of her mind. Finally, at 3 AM, she found herself scrolling through articles about Janet on her phone. To Emma's surprise, she wasn't a physician or a nurse, nor was she a scientist or a community leader. Instead, Janet's bio fit the mold of an industry titan: Stanford undergrad, Harvard MBA, investment banking at Goldman Sachs. One of the first female CEOs of a regional bank before a national acquired it—earning Janet a $50 million payout.

All interesting, but it didn't offer any clues about what Janet needed to tell her.

Going back further, Emma learned that Janet was a champion rower at Harvard College. Even in the grainy newspaper clippings, she could see Janet was a beauty. Tall. Thick blond hair. And, as Emma knows from the funeral, eyes the color of methylene blue.

Everything Mom was not.

Over the years, rumors abounded about her dad having affairs, but Emma always chalked them up to gossip or jealousy. Though Tom was often distant, he prided himself on being a person of integrity. He would never cross that line, she thought, if only for his own reputation.

Janet doesn't actually have an office at MBH, so their meeting is in the boardroom, an imposing space with wood-paneled inlays and full-length glass windows overlooking the city. Emma immediately feels underdressed, and even more so when Janet stands to greet her in a gray pinstripe suit and no-nonsense white blouse.

Janet offers a firm handshake and motions her to sit down. She dives right in. "Fifteen years ago, Tom Carpenter made an egregious error," she says flatly. "He used his position at MBH to get a patient into a clinical trial for a promising new cancer drug. The problem was, the trial was already closed and the patient was ineligible to participate. What Tom did was a massive breach of ethics, if not outright illegal."

The incident was brought to their attention last month, Janet says, during Tom's vetting for physician-in-chief. An anonymous tip.

"I was in the room when the board confronted him," she tells Emma. "To his credit, he immediately admitted it."

Emma tries to picture her dad in that moment. Would he bow his head in shame? Apologize? Clinical trials are sacred. They're also risky. Most new drugs fail, and some cause serious side effects. The patient Tom helped could have died.

"The board was divided. It got very heated. The worst I've seen." Janet shakes her head, as though pushing away the memory. "We did a preliminary vote. The recommendation was termination for cause. MBH's reputation was our overarching concern. We were sympathetic to Tom's situation and the fact that this happened so long ago, but if news got out, it would further tarnish our ranking."

Emma's suppresses a gasp. Her dad would have lost his position as executive director of Community Cares. And his privileges as a physician. No more patients.

No more Dr. Tom Carpenter.

"We scheduled the final vote for the next day. That night, Dr. Ecker called me. He demanded to speak to the board in the morning, before our deliberations."

Emma lifts her head.

"Ecker made an impassioned plea. Said Tom was an outstanding doctor, that he always did the right thing for patients. Called him a tireless advocate for the underserved."

Emma's eyes well up.

"We appreciated his testimony. But it was ultimately unnecessary. We'd already decided not to fire Tom and instead name him physician-in-chief. We needed him to right the ship, and we thought the risk was manageable."

Emma feels the tears streaming down her face. "Why are you telling me this? To explain why my father was stressed before he died?"

"No, Emma." Janet's voice is different now, caring, more nurturing. "I'm telling you because that patient Tom tried to help? It was your mother."

CHAPTER 20

SANJAY STEPS INTO the elevator and eyes the white coats crowded inside. The thought of a rogue physician assistant somewhere in the hospital, harming patients, sends a chill up his spine.

He had gone to the doctors' lounge, hoping to ask about Ana Nunez, but it's closed for the next hour—housekeeping—so he's headed back to the lobby. After his second all-nighter in three days, he needs caffeine. Stat.

The brightly lit wood-paneled coffee shop is the busiest franchise east of the Mississippi River—a byproduct of the hundreds of doctors who practically make the hospital their home. It reminds Sanjay of the origin of the term "residency"—back in the day, doctors in training lived in the hospital; they were *literally* residents.

The sound of the coffee grinder and wafting aroma of freshly brewed coffee welcome him. He grabs a disposable cup and lines up for the communal pot.

"Dr. Sanjay!"

It's Neil, with a gaggle of residents and medical students in tow.

"Trainees, meet Dr. Sanjay," Neil booms out. "He was one of the top students in my class. Renowned as an attending for his diagnostic prowess before . . ." He stumbles over his next words, settling on, "before he transitioned careers."

The trainees, four women and two men, their short white coats overflowing with pocket-sized reference books and medical instruments, turn toward Sanjay. He can easily pick out the senior resident, the junior resident, the intern, and the medical students—each one conditioned from the first day of med school to look up the next rung of the ladder with awe and jealousy.

He plans to keep this exchange—the only thing standing between him and caffeine, and then looking for the mysterious Ana—brief.

"Dr. Sanjay, care to join us on rounds?" Neil asks. "'To study medicine without books is to sail an uncharted sea. To study medicine without patients is to not go to sea at all.'"

Neil is baiting him with one of Tom's favorite sayings, one he adapted from Sir William Osler, the father of modern medicine.

Sanjay's about to decline when he realizes it's an opportunity. He can't get his head around what's become of Neil. Maybe observing him on rounds will offer some clues. Seeing patients together—like they used to—might even give them a chance to make up.

Besides, after a two-day drought, he's itching to see patients.

* * *

"Mr. Hancock is a forty-eight-year-old African-American man with congestive heart failure, type 2 diabetes, and stage 3 chronic kidney disease, who presented to the ER with shortness of breath and leg swelling."

They're at the bedside of the final patient on morning rounds. What started lighthearted—Neil and Sanjay trading jokes and wowing the students with their medical knowledge—has grown increasingly tense. The two attendings are butting heads more often, and the barbs have gotten progressively sharper—and more personal.

Earlier, Neil dazzled the group by nailing the diagnosis of Plummer-Vinson syndrome after just three symptoms—fatigue, pain on swallowing, and mouth sores. Then came the jab: "Spend less time reading *GQ* and more time on *Harrison's*."

It was a GI case—Neil's specialty—but it still stung. Years of concierge medicine had dulled Sanjay's edge, and they both knew it.

Mr. Hancock is propped against three pillows—a telltale sign of fluid backing up from his heart to his lungs.

"Classic volume overload," says Dr. Tiffany Pinkston, the intern who admitted him. She's been on shift for over twenty-four hours without a break. She's pale, fading. "We're diuresing with IV Lasix. Dispo Friday."

"Excellent," Neil says. "Martha, what are the three most common causes of acute heart failure exacerbation?"

Mr. Hancock's eyebrows rise at "heart failure."

Martha, one of the medical students, straightens. "Um, dietary indiscretion, heart attack, then arrythmia?"

"Very good," says Neil. "His EKG's clean. Labs show decreased kidney function but normal cardiac enzymes. That leaves diet. Dr. James?"

James—the senior resident, mid-thirties, shaggy hair—says, "You need to reduce your salt intake. The American Heart Association recommends two thousand milligrams a day, although the way I read the literature, I'd advise no more than fifteen hundred. Also limit your fluid intake to a liter daily." Then, blandly: "I know it's not easy, but you can do it."

Can he? Sanjay wonders. He doubts any of them has been taught how to explain milligrams and fluid ounces to someone who likely has no kitchen scale or measuring cup.

"And has the patient been following the diet?" asks Neil.

"Yes, the patient reports being compliant," Martha says, flatly—like the man wasn't inches from her.

Sanjay fights the urge to grimace. It's not her fault. Or the others'. This was how Neil—and MBH—were training them to practice medicine: detached, objective, impersonal. More technicians than healers.

"Hmm," says Neil. "Dr. James, your thoughts?"

"I suspect he hasn't been fully compliant. I'd recommend—"

"I disagree," Neil cuts in, eyes narrowing. "If reversible causes are ruled out, we must consider irreversible ones."

"A biopsy?" Martha asks.

"Precisely," says Neil.

She beams—brownie points earned.

Sanjay clenches his jaw. The cause of Mr. Hancock's condition is obvious. A heart biopsy is not only unnecessary—it's reckless.

This was the same pattern Neil followed with patients in List A, Sanjay thinks. *But he's president now. What else is he trying to achieve?*

Sanjay looks at the faces of the residents, sensing their unease. Martha is still early in her training, but Tiffany and James have enough expertise to know that a biopsy isn't necessary. They've also seen enough to understand that sometimes hospitals have motives beyond medicine.

Each of them had likely entered medicine idealistic, only to find themselves trapped in a system that doesn't always put patients first—and rarely empowers doctors to speak up.

"Given his risk factors, notify the ICU he'll be coming post-biopsy," Neil says. Then, turning to Sanjay: "Unless you have additional observations?"

Sanjay nods. He's not missing his chance to help the patient—and these students.

He finds a chair and pulls it up next to Mr. Hancock. He sits, looks the patient in the eye. The man is clearly scared.

"Mr. Hancock, I'm Sanjay Patel," he says, extending a hand.

"Nice to meet you, sir."

"Oh, I'm no 'sir'. Last I checked, I haven't been knighted by the Queen."

Mr. Hancock chuckles.

"At least not yet." Sanjay winks, and Mr. Hancock laughs harder. "Call me Sanjay."

"All right, Sanjay."

"What your medical team is talking about is how we can prevent this from happening again. We can fix you up today, but I'm guessing you'd rather not end up back here. Even though I know you love our company. And the fine hospital cuisine."

They both laugh. The med students smile silently.

"We're not exactly sure why this happened. Most likely, you haven't been able to follow the heart doctor's instructions, like cutting down on salt. But if you have, then something else may be going on." Sanjay softens his tone. "Anything you want to share?"

Mr. Hancock hesitates. "Sir?"

"It's Sanjay, remember?" He smiles then nods towards the man's wrist. "Maybe something to do with that?"

Everyone follows his gaze to a dark blue silicone bracelet.

Mr. Hancock looks down. "Well, yeah. It's just . . . It's just that I'm homeless right now." Martha inhales sharply. "I haven't been taking my meds because there's no fridge. I'd like to watch my salt, like you said, but I don't make my own food. The cook there, she don't care about me."

"Thank you for telling us," Sanjay says gently. "We all need help sometimes." He turns to the group. "That bracelet's from Sisters of Hope. It's a shelter nearby."

Mr. Hancock's voice cracks. "I lost my job because of my heart. My medicines, they help me, but they make me run to the bathroom a lot. My manager on the line, he said I was taking too many breaks. He's an old friend, but the next round of cuts, he said he had no choice. I'm not lazy. I work hard. Real hard. It's just—my heart, it gets in the way."

In the hallway afterward, all eyes turn to Neil.

He says nothing.

So Sanjay steps in. They consult social work to apply for medical respite, which will get him a place of his own for three to six months. They adjust his medications so he won't go to the bathroom as much during the day. Finally, they outline a letter to his former employer, which Martha will later draft, reminding them that in the state of Massachusetts, a person cannot be fired for medical reasons.

"We're totally fixing this patient," says Pinkston, finally smiling.

"So this means no biopsy, right?" asks Martha.

Before Sanjay can give a resounding yes, Neil's pager goes off. "911—ICU tower, bed five. Let's move!"

* * *

Moments later, Sanjay and Neil burst out of the ICU stairwell, breathless and on high alert.

"I'm so sorry to page you, Dr. Desai! We didn't know what to do!" says a resident, frantically gesturing them over to bed eleven.

Through the glass wall, Sanjay sees a middle-aged man being held down by two male nurses and an orderly. The patient is thrashing violently, grabbing at the respiratory tube that's keeping him alive. In the far corner, a woman his age and two young girls are clasping each other, their faces aghast.

"Forty milligrams of propofol, stat. We need to get Mr. Vasquez sedated," barks Neil, sending the nurses scrambling. Turning to the residents, he adds, "You two, hold him down. We can't lose that ET tube."

While the team jumps into action, Sanjay enters the room, gives the family a slight nod, and swiftly examines the patient's neurologic function and ventilator settings.

As he finishes, the nurse returns with the sedative and looks to Neil for confirmation before administering it.

"Do it," Neil orders.

"Wait," says Sanjay. He turns to Neil. "I wouldn't do that if I were you. This patient is ready to breathe on his own."

The nurse stares openmouthed at Sanjay, then at Neil.

"Take the tube out," Sanjay tells Neil.

Neil laughs, incredulous. "Sanjay, you don't know the first thing about this patient. My team and I have been taking care of Mr. Vasquez for days, and he's not ready to be extubated. Stick to Botox, will you?"

Sanjay ignores the slight and states his case. The patient's wife is now standing against the door, listening in. A couple of residents nod in agreement.

But Neil remains adamant. "We extubate him now, chances are he'll end up here again in no time. But, of course, you'll be back on your private jet by then, so not your problem, right?"

Neil's being a jerk, but he's not being unreasonable. It's a call very few attendings would make in this situation. And Neil is a GI doctor, not a pulmonary and critical care specialist.

"If I'm wrong," Sanjay says, looking at the wife, "he goes back on the ventilator, and nothing changes. But if I'm right, he gets out of the ICU. He's one step closer to getting his life back."

Now all the residents are nodding. The wife, too. Neil's face turns beet-red.

A woman in blue scrubs and a long white coat steps forward, her dark hair pulled into neat braids. She moves with the alert composure of someone used to running toward crises. The ICU fellow, Sanjay guesses.

"Dr. Desai," she says. "Do you feel strongly about re-sedating him?"

Neil looks at the faces of the residents. The tide has turned. "I do, but this is a teaching hospital. He's your patient."

The perfect out, Sanjay thinks, as Neil turns and leaves the room.

When he's out of earshot, the ICU fellow turns to her team. "Cancel that propofol order and prepare to extubate Mr. Vasquez on my count."

The patient isn't his, but Sanjay wants to be kept in the know. And the ICU fellow is no-nonsense, which he loves. "I'm Sanjay," he says, extending a hand.

"Williams," she says. "Dr. Harper Williams."

He pulls one of the waveform strips off the ventilator, scribbles out his phone number, and hands it to her. "Dr. Williams, call me when he's talking."

As he walks out of the room, he checks his phone. A missed text from Emma. But before he can read it, he hears a voice from behind him say, "That was incredible."

Sanjay turns. "Thanks, I—"

In front of him is a woman so stunning he swallows his words.

"I'm still new here," she says, offering him her hand. "I'd love to be mentored by you."

His eyes fly to her silk turquoise blouse, her white coat. Stitched in bold lettering on the breast pocket are her name and credentials: "Ana Nunez, PA."

CHAPTER

21

EMMA PACES THE MBH lobby, phone in hand, waiting for Sanjay to reply. The news about her father has her reeling—shock, anger, grief colliding at once. It feels like losing both parents all over again—at the same time.

Beneath it all, a flicker of catharsis: proof her father may have loved her and her mother after all.

Before she can process any of it, she needs to see Ecker. The scientist in her desperately wants to corroborate Janet Scully's account. Ecker was there for all of it.

But the human part of her dreads facing it alone. When it comes to her father, she trusts only Neil and Sanjay. But with the board involved, she won't risk dragging Neil into it.

Where is Sanjay?

She takes a gulp of air, trying to quiet her mind, but it doesn't work. So she heads to the coffee counter for a London Fog, her comfort drink of choice.

She orders a large and turns to find a table.

And there he is. In the far corner, a smile lighting up his face. She waves, but he doesn't notice.

Because he's not alone. Across from him is a dark-haired woman with blond highlights. She is folded over the table; every few moments, she lightly brushes her fingers against Sanjay's shoulder or arm, pausing only to type something into a phone and hand it to him.

So this is why he hasn't been answering.

Trying to keep her voice cool, Emma approaches their table. "Hey, Sanjay."

He looks up, surprise flashing across his face. The woman turns around. She, too, is Latina. Early twenties, perfect skin. It's like looking in the mirror ten years ago.

"Emma," Sanjay says, gesturing between them. "This is Ana. Ana, Emma."

Ana extends a hand, but Emma just crosses her arms. "I've been trying to reach you, Sanjay."

"I should get back to the ICU." Ana stands, smoothing out her perfectly pressed white coat. "Bye, Sanjay. You have my number. Nice to meet you, Emma."

As soon as she's gone, Sanjay turns to Emma. "Ana is—"

"I don't care," she snaps, the words bursting out before she can stop them.

"Emma, it's related to your dad. At least, I think it is. I was just about to find out more."

Emma's breath catches, a mix of frustration and anxiety surging through her. "Look, let's talk about it later. I need your help with something."

* * *

When they open the door, Dr. Ecker's secretary is sitting at her desk in what looks like a brand-new dress. Her hair looks different, too.

She looks up from her computer, and Emma braces herself.

"Dr. Sanjay!" she says, jumping up out of her chair. "So nice to see you again!"

It is? Emma blinks, taken aback. This is a big change from the cranky secretary of a couple days ago.

The secretary comes around her desk and gives Sanjay a hug. "Thank you for your . . . advice. You were right." She winks at him. "Listen, Dr. Ecker's in his office. If you bear with me, I'll try to reschedule his next appointment and get you in."

While she checks on Ecker, Sanjay fills Emma in on his suspicions about the secretary's thyroid condition. Emma's impressed.

"Done," says the secretary when she returns. "It'll be about ten minutes."

"Thanks. I see he's very busy these days," says Sanjay.

"You can say that again. It's been stressful around here since . . ." She lowers her voice to a whisper. "The investigation."

"What investigation?" asks Emma, her brow furrowing.

The secretary waves them to the far side of the room, away from Ecker's door. "About a month ago," she says, speaking softly, "they realized some vials of absoluxir were missing. Now they think someone from the lab took them."

Emma gasps. "Why would someone steal an experimental drug?"

Beside her, Sanjay looks as shocked as she feels. He collects himself, then says, "If the drug works as well as you say, I suspect some of my patients would pay top dollar for it on the black market."

"I wish I'd thought of that," the secretary says with a laugh. "I'd give a dose to my dad—he's had two heart attacks already—and sell the rest for a Birkin."

Emma gets what they're saying, but it seems crazy to her. The drug isn't FDA approved yet. Who knows if it's safe?

"So the theft, that's the reason for the security guard?" asks Sanjay.

"Yes. MBH insisted. Dr. Ecker wasn't fazed, but Dr. DeSalvo?" The secretary's eyes widen dramatically. "He was *livid.* He demanded there be no guards at night. That's when he likes to do his quiet work. They both drew the line at security cameras. Something about their research data being too valuable." She looks both ways, then lowers her voice. "You didn't hear this from me. As you know, Dr. Ecker is very protective of MBH's reputation—and his own."

* * *

Ecker's behind his desk, wearing a dark suit and tie, Montblanc pen in hand. Although he has his usual air of refinement, Emma can sense he's on edge.

"I'm sorry, Emma, but I only have a few minutes," he says, gesturing for her and Sanjay to sit down. "I have a meeting with a pharmaceutical company across town. Matt was going to take it, but he's . . . preoccupied today."

"Is he okay?" asks Emma.

"Yes. Let's just say it's hard to find people to trust." He looks to the side, his face worn down. "Money has everyone too excited. They've forgotten why we're in this work in the first place."

Sanjay shares a dubious look with Emma.

"This won't take long," she says, changing subjects. "I talked to Janet Scully."

"I know. She called me."

Emma is surprised, but only for a moment. She suspects little at MBH gets past Henry Ecker.

"That's the real reason my father saw MBH's lawyers, right?"

Ecker sighs. He comes around his desk and sits on the edge, facing Emma. "Yes. I'm sorry I didn't tell you earlier. I wanted to protect you from all that. Your father was . . . a remarkable doctor, Emma, but he was also a human being."

"Tell me everything."

Ecker explains. Tom was overwhelmed by Maria's deteriorating condition, he says. Her cancer hadn't responded to treatment, and she was dying. Tom couldn't imagine his life without her—or Emma's. So he was eager to enroll her in the clinical trial. Even though there were only 50–50 odds she'd receive the still unproven drug, he saw it as her only chance.

But when the trial opened for volunteer patients, it was immediately oversubscribed. Clinical trials are notoriously difficult to recruit patients for, but it had been years since a new treatment had come out for breast cancer, and people were desperate. The institution was forced to develop new criteria to determine who got in—patients who were less likely to respond to the drug and more likely to suffer serious side effects were excluded.

Emma's mom narrowly missed the cutoff.

Desperate, Tom went to the principal investigator, Dr. Abigail Steinmetz, a former classmate of his and Ecker's, and convinced her to admit his wife. He went so far as to ensure that Maria was put in the treatment arm, not the placebo, so she'd actually get the drug.

But it was all for naught. The cancer kept spreading. Maria went into hospice, and Tom buried himself in his work.

"I told him to slow down," Ecker says, shaking his head. "That Maria didn't have much time left, and you both needed him more than ever."

This part of the story Emma knows all too well. She feels a wave of emotion coming and steadies herself, trying not to be taken under.

But she isn't prepared for the bombshell Ecker drops next.

"As penance, your dad left his beloved practice at MBH and took the long-vacant job as executive director of Community Cares."

"Wait. He wasn't forced to leave?" Emma feels herself sinking. "I thought it was because he verbally abused a student—"

"What happened with Matt's partner wasn't great, but it blew over. Mostly. The student did drop out of MBMS, which was unfortunate, and Matt has no love lost for Tom. But your dad leaving? No. That was Tom's decision, his way of atoning."

Emma's shocked. She looks over at Sanjay. For most of the conversation, he's been sitting, motionless, but now he stands and strides out.

"Sanjay—"

"Let him be," says Ecker, the command in his voice surprising Emma. Then it softens. "Your dad loved you and Maria." He leans down and places a comforting hand on her shoulder.

The tears come, hard.

After handing her a tissue, Ecker makes his way back to his side of the desk. Emma takes it as a sign that the meeting is over.

As she gathers her things, he says, "Tom wasn't always there for your mother, but he was always faithful to her."

Emma stops in her tracks. "Why are you telling me that?"

"Your dad's not here anymore, Emma, and I feel I have an obligation to tell you to be careful. I've known that boy a long time." Ecker points toward the door, through which Sanjay vanished. "He can't be trusted."

CHAPTER 22

SANJAY IS IN the waiting room of the hospital, his face in his hands.

Is everyone in this godforsaken place corrupt?

When Emma told him what she'd learned from Janet Scully, he didn't want to believe her. How many times did Tom remind Sanjay that medicine was a public trust? That doctors must adhere to the highest moral and ethical code?

Now there's no denying it. Tom betrayed his own values. Tom, who was Sanjay's North Star. That Sanjay failed him—or, more precisely, didn't meet his standards—has haunted him every day of his life since.

Was all that pain for nothing?

He gets that Tom acted out of love. But by giving his wife an unproven drug and bypassing the guardrails of a clinical trial, Tom risked her life. Worse, by cutting the line, he may have deprived another patient of a life-saving treatment.

All his career, Tom lectured other doctors about putting the needs of patients first. But when it came down to it, Tom put himself first.

Not only that, he was forgiven. When the hospital found out, he wasn't put on involuntary leave or fired. *He was promoted!* To the highest role in the hospital, no less. Sanjay did something far less grave, yet the outcome was entirely different. Had Tom been a person of color, would the all-white board still have forgiven him?

Worse than MBH, *Tom* didn't forgive Sanjay.

Well, fuck Tom Carpenter. And fuck MBH. This institution is sick, and he's been a fool to think Tom or anyone else was immune.

Cassie was right. He needs to get out—and soon. Whatever happened with the three lists and Tom is in the past. And he doesn't owe Tom anything. Not anymore.

He pushes through the hospital doors and takes a big breath of fresh air. Ahead, in the roundabout in front of the entrance, a young man helps his elderly mother out of the car, her walker in tow. Sanjay watches them, smiles, then picks up his phone.

After only half a ring, his mother answers. "Beta, so nice to hear from you. Are you eating?"

Before he can answer, she launches into the latest gossip. A water leak in the store; a new neighbor who, like Sanjay, is into "rapping music"; a friend's daughter newly engaged. Usually, this type of chatter bores him and he passes the time by thumbing through journal articles on his phone, but today he's thankful for the distraction.

"Where are you now?" she asks.

"Boston."

"Oh *vow*, are you seeing Emma?"

"Yes, but not like that." He's glad she doesn't mention Tom. Just the thought of him brings the taste of bile to Sanjay's mouth.

"Hmm, too bad. I need a grandchild to hold before my hands hurt too much."

Classic Indian mom guilt, he thinks, shaking his head. He takes the opportunity to press her on finding a new doctor—he doesn't like this one. She refuses. "A doctor is a doctor is a doctor."

The irony is his mom has more reason than most not to trust doctors. When Sanjay was eleven, he began noticing that in the mornings, she'd rub her hands together, even when it was warm outside, and that she was constantly massaging her fingers against the kitchen counter.

His parents were uninsured, but eventually his dad realized they needed to see a doctor. Baba wore a suit and Mama a sari; the four of them, including Sanjay and his older sister, Neela, sat in the waiting room for two hours before being called in. When they were finally brought into the exam room a little after 6 PM, Sanjay could see the excitement in his parents' eyes. The doctor was wearing a business suit. To them, that meant they had chosen a good doctor. An important doctor.

Almost immediately, Sanjay sensed something was off. The doctor wouldn't sit, muttering about being late for an important dinner. Neela barely got through the first three bullet points of their mom's symptoms before he pronounced it run-of-the-mill joint pain from old age and scribbled out a prescription.

A year later, his mom woke up with her fingers bent to the side. Sanjay begged one of Neela's friends to drive him to the library, where he found *Harrison's Principles of Internal Medicine.* Although he didn't recognize many of the words, he was able to piece together from the medical illustrations how dangerously wrong the doctor had been. After his parents saved up enough for a second opinion, a new doctor confirmed Sanjay's diagnosis: rheumatoid arthritis, an autoimmune disease. But by then, his mom's hands were permanently disfigured and she had developed inflammation in her lungs, a serious complication.

Her story is why he modeled himself after Tom, from the first day they met. Tom was the perfect doctor. He never missed a diagnosis. He always put patients first.

Or so Sanjay thought.

Sanjay starts sobbing—for his mom and for the loss of his mentor—but quietly, so his mom can't hear. She's never been one for self-pity, and as an immigrant, she's never expected her life to be perfect. Just better for her children.

She seems to sense his distress. "Beta, what have I always told you: Head down, heart up, go. Remember?

He feels the corners of his mouth curl up. "Yes, Mama."

"Good. Now you have to do something for me."

"Okay . . ."

"There's this wedding. Your cousin Reeju—

"No, Mama. I—"

"Tonight. If I knew you were going to be in Boston, I would have told you sooner. But you never call."

"I can't. I'm actually thinking about leaving soon. I—"

"I'd go, except my hands make it difficult to travel."

He hears the shop door chime in the background. A customer has arrived.

"I have to hang up now, but you must go, nah? And be sure to look out for your sister."

Neela's in town, too? At least she'll know what to do about Emma, thinks Sanjay.

"And, beta? Please wear something nice."

* * *

The wedding isn't till later in the evening, so Cassie suggests he take the opportunity to visit his most important patient, the man who started Sanjay's concierge practice. "If anyone can tell you more about Next Health," Cassie says, "it's William Barnett."

The billionaire is kind enough to schedule Sanjay immediately. Of course, he insists on sending his own driver to pick Sanjay up.

As the limo pulls into the circular driveway outside Barnett's house, Sanjay once again finds himself staring at the naked boy statue. How curiously blissful he seems. Sanjay always assumed the fact that he had no clothes on was a nod to the ancient Greeks. But perhaps the boy's nakedness—him being himself, unabashedly—is the secret to his happiness?

The car door opens, and he's greeted by Barnett's butler. "Here we are, Dr. Sanjay. I've set you up in the library. I know it's a favorite of yours."

As Sanjay follows the butler into the house, he reflects on how far his practice has come since his first visit. He sometimes jokes that, like a contagion, Barnett was patient zero, the index case. From him, Sanjay's services spread from one close contact to another, as people got sick and passed his contact information along. After Barnett, Sanjay was hired by his attorney, Charles Beacon, whose wife had developed dementia; then by Beacon's fellow Museum of Fine Arts board member Michael Dubey, who'd decided to lose weight. Christine Canery, Dubey's mistress and the executive creative director of one of the major Paris fashion houses, was next.

From there, the practice spread across Europe. At first, Sanjay was surprised by the interest. Most EU countries have universal healthcare. Then he realized "universal" meant everyone was treated the same, and people were frustrated with the healthcare system everywhere. For those who viewed money as no object, retaining a top doctor who was available to them whenever and wherever they wanted was an easy decision.

His practice is enviable now, but it took years of hard work to build. His concerns about patients leaving the practice bubble up, and he takes a deep breath to push them back down.

Barnett rises from his desk, extending his hand. "Dr. Sanjay. Always good to see you."

His grip strength is striking. He has taken Sanjay's recommendation to go on a ketogenic diet, and his body fat composition is now under 10 percent. *Sugar truly is the other white powder, the legal one.*

"Here," he says, handing Sanjay a copper-colored tumbler and motioning him to a seat by the fireplace. "I know you prefer straight tequila, but trust me, you'll enjoy this."

Sanjay sniffs the drink skeptically. The mint and lime juice are a thoughtful touch, but why mess with perfection?

"Before we begin, I need to get your ear on something."

Sanjay straightens, scanning Barnett from head to toe.

Barnett waves him off. "Not me. You taught me that an apple—and a protein shake—a day keeps the doctor away, and that works for me. But your other patients?" He pauses, his face tightening. "They're demanding to know where you are."

Sanjay's heart skips a beat. *This has gotten to Barnett, too?*

"My advice: Lawyer up. Your contract says you'll be available 'on reasonable notice.' Hard to say if this sabbatical to Boston qualifies."

Sanjay nods, numb.

"If you're in breach, you might have to refund your retainer. Worst case scenario: for the full year."

Sanjay bolts upright. The money's gone—there's essentially nothing to return.

"But forget the money. You can earn that back. Reputation's different. If word gets out that you're neglecting your clients, the rest will walk. I care about you, Sanjay, but selfishly? I doubt you'll stick around if I'm your only client. You need to fix this."

Sanjay's mind races. His parents own the store now; his nieces have a college fund; he can live frugally. But the 703 account? That one can't run dry.

If his patients all leave, he'll have to go back to the MBHs of the world. Red tape. Insurance companies. Check-the-box medicine. No more freedom. No more putting patients first.

Even more reason to get out of here as soon as this wedding is over. Hiring a lawyer? He isn't ready for that, not yet.

"I'll let you know," he says.

Barnett checks his watch. Sanjay takes his cue and explains his interest in Next Health, the startup company that is setting up doctors' offices around the country.

"Certainly, I know of them. They keep coming to us for money." The founder is a tech guy who knows nothing about healthcare, Barnett explains. The real boss is the chief financial officer, Jim Hadley, who left his position as MBH's CFO three years ago because "he was tired of being a millionaire in a room full of billionaires."

Sanjay rolls his eyes. He remembers the name. Jim tried to close Community Cares multiple times. He and Tom fought constantly, and a few times it got ugly.

Remembering the Next Health billboard featuring his med school classmate, Sanjay asks, "What about Nikhil Bansari? He's their chief medical officer."

Barnett shrugs. "Never heard of him. I don't have to tell you, Dr. Sanjay, most docs at these kinds of companies are flies on the wall. They keep 'em around for photo ops."

Next Health was in trouble when they hired Jim, Barnett continues. They'd spent so much on billboards and Facebook ads that they were basically losing money with every visit. Jim was charged with charting a new financial path. If he could make a nonprofit hospital like MBH profitable, imagine what he could do with a for-profit startup like theirs.

Jim had the right idea—shift from getting paid for visits to delivering value—but neither he nor the CEO had a clue how to pull it off. Matters came to a head when Next Health couldn't raise its fourth round of funding. They had no choice but to take money from shady investors overseas. "Thugs in Armani suits," Barnett says, shaking his head.

In the process, Jim got control of the board, and the CEO officially became a puppet. Now the company is on a fast track to a lucrative IPO. They filed their S-1 just this month, Barnett explains, and are set to go public in a matter of weeks.

It's unclear to Barnett how they turned the business around. But he's curious.

"I hope this was helpful, Sanjay," he concludes. "Given the circumstances, I'll have my secretary email their confidential investment documents to your assistant. The financial data is rudimentary, but it's a start."

The meeting is over. Sanjay stands, sighing. "I still don't get why Tom was tracking their patients, or the connection to MBH."

"I don't know, but watch your back."

Sanjay is about to laugh, but the look on Barnett's face stops him dead.

"Seriously, Sanjay. These kinds of investors don't want anyone messing with them or their money."

Sanjay can almost feel the cortisol pumping out of his adrenal glands, making the hairs on his arms stand on end. "What are you saying?"

"Just this. I've spent years managing risk. All it takes is one bad egg for the whole carton to rot."

With that Sanjay takes his leave, wondering if Ana Nunez, the physician assistant, could be the egg he's looking for.

CHAPTER 23

She's seated at the bar when Sanjay arrives. Bright red dress, plunging neckline, all leg. Looking at her, he catches himself picturing a younger Emma. It reminds him of all the years they've missed.

Ana doesn't strike him as the kind of person who would intentionally harm a patient, but he needs to find out why she signed Tom's ER note. Feldman is running Tom's labs; Cassie's digging into Next Health's financials; List C seems to be a dead end. This is the last thread left to pull.

"How'd you know?" she asks after a generous hug.

He's thrown off guard. "Know what?"

"That this is my spot."

"Lucky guess." Behind him, cologne-drenched men clamor for drinks; women at a high-top table line up shots. A week ago, this would have been Sanjay's scene, but now it just seems loud and dark.

Ana raises an eyebrow seductively. "Or . . . ?"

He looks at her blankly.

"Or you were checking out my Insta." She flashes him a smile.

Instagram. He's never figured that one out. He'd rather live in the moment than relive the past.

No, Cassie picked the place. But if he has any hope of making this meeting productive, he'll have to play along.

"You got me." He puts his hands up, smiling sheepishly. "What's my penalty?"

"All in due time, Doctor," she says, laughing. "Now, you gonna explain the outfit? It's cute."

Sanjay looks down. He'd almost forgotten. He's wearing a kurta for the wedding. Bright red with gold hand-stitching.

When he was a kid and his parents forced him to wear Indian clothes to temple or a dinner party, he'd get stares—or, worse, people yelling, "Go back to your country!" These days, the more common reaction is, "I love the colors!" and "Where can I get one?" Maybe some things *have* gotten better.

After Ana snaps a selfie of them, Sanjay figures it's time to get to the reason for the meeting.

"So how did you decide to become a doctor?" he asks.

She giggles. "Um, news flash, I'm not a doctor. I'm just a PA."

"Just a PA? Ana, I had this professor in med school. He used to call all of us doctors, and we loved him for it. One day on rounds, a senior physician corrected him. 'They aren't doctors yet. They're just medical students.' And you know what my professor said?"

Ana leans forward.

"He turned to us and asked, 'If I were to fall to the ground right now and stop breathing, which of you would try to save me?' We all raised our hands. Then he turned to the old physician and said, 'See, doctors.'"

Ana laughs. "I like that, but let's be real. Most doctors don't think that way."

Sanjay nods in agreement.

She sips her wine and leans in closer. "We didn't grow up with much, and my abuela had bad diabetes. I saw her suffer, and I thought if I became a doctor, even if we didn't have any money, I could always take care of her myself."

Sanjay can't help but smile. He thought the same about his mom.

"I didn't realize how expensive it was. Four years of college, then four years of medical school, all before your first paycheck? And as a resident, you earn less than a high school teacher. With these huge loans to pay off! My family needed me to support them sooner than that, so I turned down med school and became a PA."

He nods. It's a common story.

"And now?" he asks. "How do you feel about medicine?"

"Oh, I love it." She touches his wrists. "I mean, I love the patients. The other parts . . ." She rolls her eyes. "Let's just say it's a j-o-b."

"What don't you like?"

"Can you keep a secret?" She tosses her hair, looks both ways. "The part where I'm Dr. Desai's chief of staff."

Sanjay startles back in his chair. Ana blinks, surprised by his response. If he's not careful, he's gonna lose her. He steadies his voice, clenches his fists to rein in his emotion. "How did you end up there?"

Ana sits back, swiveling her wineglass. She seems to be considering—wondering whether she can still trust him.

A moment later, her smile returns. "I wanted a clinical job, to see patients, but MBH is slow to credential PAs. I needed something in the interim, and Neil liked having a chief of staff who understood the clinical side."

That explains why Ana isn't in the paging directory but still has an MBH email.

"Neil's brilliant, but he's always making me do things that have nothing to do with my training." She clears her throat. "Like, a few months ago, he decided to fire a bunch of older nurses—and had me do it."

Sanjay recalls the nurse he saw in clinic, the one MBH let go. He tries to picture her sitting across from Ana, being told that the hospital where she'd spent decades caring for patients was cutting her loose. Neil was behind that, too?

"That's terrible," he says, feeling queasy.

"It was awful," Ana says, putting down her glass of Merlot. She forces a smile. "But it's not all bad. A year ago, I got to work on a clinical trial."

Sanjay's hands start to tingle.

"Have you heard of absoluxir? Everyone was calling it a miracle drug, so when Dr. Desai asked if I wanted to be the one to administer it to patients, I jumped at the chance. That's how I started working with Matt . . . I mean, Dr. DeSalvo."

Again, Sanjay's blood pressure shoots up, but he manages to stay still. He takes a sip of his tequila, swallows. *Ana works for Matt, too?*

"How was working with Matt?" he asks coolly.

Her eyes return to her wine. "I loved the patients. To qualify for the trial, you had to be at increased risk for a heart attack. Many had already had one, so they were really grateful to be there. Dr. DeSalvo? He was okay, I guess. Quiet. He wasn't around much—always off meeting with some pharmaceutical company. I guess they're all gonna make a lot of money once absoluxir gets approved."

"The drug companies will," Sanjay says, raising an eyebrow. "The scientists won't."

She shrugs. "I don't know. Matt seemed pretty excited. He joked a lot about the kind of yacht he'd buy."

Sanjay grimaces. He's heard of universities giving faculty a share of the profits from research they commercialize—a clear conflict of interest—but he didn't think MBH had stooped that low. The institution used to pride itself on scientific integrity. It wouldn't risk its reputation by creating an environment where hospital scientists might manipulate data for financial gain.

"But why are you asking me so much about him?" Ana's smile is playful, but he can detect a hint of concern.

He pretends not to hear her and looks around the bar. All Matt's talk about making money from absoluxir, his grudge against Tom, and now a connection to Ana? Sanjay might be getting somewhere. He has yet to ask why she signed Tom's ER note, but her guard's already up, and he needs to get his head around what he's learned. One misstep, and he may lose his chance.

"Listen," he says, glancing at his watch. "I have to go."

"What? So soon?"

"Yeah, you know Indian weddings. Real sticklers for punctuality."

She doesn't get the sarcasm. Indians have their own time zone, IST, "Indian Standard Time," their excuse for being perpetually late.

"I'll call you soon. I promise." He leaves a $100 bill on the bar and gives her a peck on the cheek.

CHAPTER 24

"WHERE TO NOW, Doc?" John asks when Sanjay steps out of the bar.

Sanjay gives him the address, and John looks down at his phone, scratching his head. "I was expecting a hotel or something. Looks like the middle of nowhere."

"Don't worry," Sanjay says. "This is what Indians do. We dance our way to marriage. In the street."

"With how good my knee is feeling, I might just join you." John laughs.

As they drive, Sanjay feels himself lightening up. He still has misgivings about his investigation into Tom's death and the three lists, but who knows? Maybe the wedding will do him good. How did Mama know?

He's excited to see Neela, too. If anyone will know what he should do next, it's her. She practically raised him. When he was eight and she was ten, Mama and Baba figured she was big enough to take care of her little brother while they kept the store. She was too young, according to the law, but nearly every immigrant family did it. Besides, Neela and Sanjay loved being alone together after school—riding pillows down the stairs of their apartment building and fixing themselves their favorite snack, Campbell's tomato soup with half a bag of shredded cheese thrown in.

He smiles at the memory.

"Hey, Doc, we might have a problem." John's eyes are darting back and forth between the rearview mirror and the highway. "I thought I was imagining things earlier, but I'm pretty sure we have a tail." His voice is taut, his face tight with tension. "Dark green Pontiac Skylark, two cars back, one lane over."

"What?" Sanjay's laugh sounds nervous to his own ears.

"That same car was behind us yesterday when I took you to that clinic where you injected my knee. And again at the bar. Twice might be a coincidence, but three times?"

Sanjay wheels around, scanning the traffic. There, a dark green Pontiac, just as John said. The car seems ordinary enough, but his insides are turning.

"If they wanted to hurt us, they'd have done it by now. They're probably just keeping tabs on us." The calm in John's voice is a stark contrast to how Sanjay feels. "What do you want me to do, Doc?"

Barnett's warning echoes in Sanjay's head: *All it takes is one bad egg for the whole carton to rot.*

He can't risk anything happening to Neela.

"I don't want to put you on the spot, John, but you think you can lose them?"

John's knuckles tighten on the steering wheel. "These guys are good, Doc, but not that good," he says, eyeing the rearview mirror.

In the next breath, the car shoots forward, veering sharply into the leftmost lane of the four-lane highway. Sanjay checks his seat belt, then the odometer. It syncs with his racing pulse—122 and climbing.

"Okay, Doc. Hang on!"

Before Sanjay can react, they veer right, and he's thrown left. Hard. He sees a blur of lights, hears a cacophony of screeching tires and blaring horns.

A moment later, his head bumps against the roof as the car jumps a lane marker and thuds off the highway onto a side road. They slow, and John turns around and eyes him up and down. "You okay, Doc?"

Sanjay's heart is pounding, but he forces a shaky breath. "I'm fine. Just—let's never do that again."

* * *

They pull up to the address his mother sent, the car idling in the middle of the street. Sanjay looks over his shoulder for what feels like the hundredth time. They're alone. John is certain they've lost their tail, but tension is gnawing at Sanjay's gut.

Who the hell is following him? And why? Next Health is the obvious suspect, but with List C still a mystery, he can't be sure.

Suddenly Tom's investigation feels all too present, looming over him. It shifts everything—his plans to leave Boston feel more urgent. But so does whatever Tom paged him about.

If only Tom had left more clues. He needs to find Neela, then get back to Tom's office. Fast.

—*Where are u?* He texts his sister.

—*Tailgating. Come around the truck.*

Sanjay steps out of the car and scans his surroundings. Sure enough, there's an eighteen-wheeler on the far side of the street. He can just make out feet on the other side of it.

When he gets there, he's enveloped by a throng of twenty- and thirty-somethings, all colorfully dressed in traditional Indian clothes, drinking pink lemonade out of plastic bottles. A big Sikh guy in a pink turban greets Sanjay with a slap on the back and hands him one.

After what he just went through, Sanjay takes a big swig, then nearly coughs it back up. On the back, a printed-out label lists its contents: gin, tonic, love. Tasty, but not at all what he expected.

"Hey!"

Sanjay looks up, startled. It's Neela, dazzling in a dark green lehenga. You'd never guess she was a tenured professor and full-time mother of two.

She gives him a big hug, and he feels his blood pressure come down. "When Mom told me you were here, I didn't believe it. My little brother wouldn't visit the East Coast and not come see us."

"Neela, I—"

"I'm messing with you, punk." She punches his arm. "Ouch, what do you have in there? Metal?'

Sanjay laughs despite himself.

"I *am* a bit pissed, you know. Meena is four now. Almost the age where she'll remember you."

"I'll come. As soon as I'm done with—" But Sanjay isn't sure where to begin.

"Done with what, Sanj? What *are* you doing in Boston? I thought you were never coming back here."

He shakes his head. "I don't know, honestly. That's why I'm here, at this wedding. I need your advice. I came for Tom's funeral, but now . . . I'm not sure."

She tousles his hair. "Whatever it is, you seem more yourself. It doesn't take a rocket scientist—or a hotshot doctor—to figure out why. You're back where you belong, Sanjay. With MBH, the free clinic, Neil. With Emma. But you still have things to work out."

How does my big sister read me so well—and so quickly?

She puts her arm around him. "Just be careful, okay?"

Can she see the weight of Tom's death—and the car chase, the threats—on his face?

"Careful? What do I have to be—"

She slaps him on the wrist, her bangles stinging his skin. "Not you—her. Emma. The whole world doesn't revolve around you, you know?"

He raises an eyebrow. "Wait, it doesn't?"

They laugh.

"Neela, I need to ask you something. I—"

But before he can finish, the music starts. Mustached men in white uniforms appear out of nowhere, playing huge drums draped around their waists. As the trumpeters and horn players join in, Neela yells in his ear, "Don't overthink it. Head down, heart up, go, remember?"

Does she mean this wedding parade or everything else?

It's on. Soon their company of single adults merges with the main contingent—uncles and aunties, kids and grandparents; the groom standing in the back of an open red convertible—everyone dancing in the street and making their way to the wedding hall half a mile down. Back in the day, this was how the groom's family would go from his village to the bride's home, bringing the whole town along in celebration.

Sanjay feels out of place at first, the shift too fast from being in his own world to the one around him. But within minutes, he's throwing his hands toward the sky and dancing along with the crowd.

A wrinkled grandmother pulls him aside. She stands on the curb to match his height and wraps a pink cloth around his head, over and over. A minute later, his pagri is complete. He pulls out his iPhone and flips the camera. The turban looks surprisingly good on him.

He takes another swig of "pink lemonade." It's not tequila, but it doesn't matter. He belongs.

* * *

Twenty minutes later, the baraat reaches the wedding venue. Almost on cue, the men gather on one side, subdividing into the doctors and the nondoctors, while the women arrange themselves on the other.

Nonplussed by social convention, Sanjay's making a beeline for Neela when he hears, "Dr. Patel, over here!"

An Indian uncle, a cardiologist, is waving at him. He's standing with three other Indian men, whom Sanjay assumes are also doctors.

"Come, come, tell us, how's business?"

"Fine, Uncle," he replies, forcing a smile.

"Fine? My boy, you must be getting along better than that. Have you started using the new RPM billing codes?"

The others wobble their heads vigorously—the Indian head shake.

"My friend, Dr. Rupani—you know him?" one of the men says. "He cleared a hundred grand just from remote patient monitoring. It really adds up, yaar. In my clinic, those codes are the only thing keeping us afloat with all these Medicare cuts."

Sanjay's phone rings. *Thank goodness*, he thinks. The last thing he wants is another conversation about the cat-and-mouse game doctors are forced to play with insurance companies just to stay in practice.

"This is Dr. Sanjay," he says loudly, stepping away. He needs the men to know he isn't brushing them off; otherwise, it might reflect badly on his family.

"Dr. Sanjay, it's Harper Williams. You asked me to call when Mr. Vasquez was talking—the patient we extubated in the ICU earlier?"

Sanjay smiles, remembering how impressed he was with the ICU fellow. "Yes, of course. How's he doing?"

"Amazing. He's oxygenating well, and his pressure's holding up. We're hoping to transfer him back to the general medicine floor tomorrow. I just hope he doesn't bounce back."

"Why would he?"

"Oh, no reason. I'm just a black cloud."

Sanjay smiles at the doctor-speak. Despite their belief in science, residents and fellows can be surprisingly superstitious. Each year a handful get labeled "black clouds"—doctors who get more than their fair share of complicated patients.

"The past year I've had multiple patients get transferred back to the ICU for bleeding," she says.

"Bleeding?"

"Yeah. The worst part is, all of them were initially admitted for something unrelated." She clicks her tongue and sighs.

"Thanks for the update," Sanjay says. "Text me when he's on the floor so I can come see him."

He hangs up, an odd feeling nagging at him.

"Bleeding problem, is it?" Sanjay turns to find one of the Indian uncles standing surprisingly close. "I couldn't help overhearing," the man says. "I had a strange case of bleeding recently."

"Oh?" says another man in the group. "Do tell."

"Yes, a seventy-five-year-old man who kept having GI bleeding. We tried everything. Upper scope. Lower scope. Capsule study. It was a medical mystery! Finally, we asked him to bring all his medications to clinic. In his pillbox, he had two of the same blood thinner—Plavix the brand name and clopidogrel, the generic. All his bleeding was medication related."

The men laugh, but Sanjay isn't listening. As the man spoke, something about List C clicked in his mind.

"I have to go," he blurts, racing off to say goodbye to Neela before heading to Tom's office.

CHAPTER 25

THE NEXT DAY, Emma is back at Community Cares, heading up the stairs to her father's office. Sanjay texted overnight, told her to meet him here first thing in the morning.

The office door is ajar. Sanjay's reclining in her dad's chair, in bright red Indian clothes, his ear pressed to the phone. "No, you first. What are *you* wearing? . . . Oh, yeah? . . ." He laughs.

Emma feels her face flush.

"The Botox yacht patient? How much? . . . Nice . . . Don't transfer it to the 703 account, though, not yet. I need as much cash as I can get right now."

She knocks loudly, and he turns and waves, seemingly nonplussed that she may have overhead him.

"Cassie, Emma's here. I need to hop." Sanjay closes the call and smiles at her.

"What's with the Indian clothes?" she asks.

"Oh, it's a long story." He flaps his hand. "And I'm in a rush. I need to head down to clinic to see Carl Franks."

She raises an eyebrow.

"The patient whose home we visited? Who went into medical debt after his colonoscopy?"

Emma nods, remembering.

He pulls up a second chair and gestures for her to sit down. His face is serious now. Dark, even. "I need you to go to the blood lab. It's about List C."

* * *

Fifteen minutes later, Emma's descending into the depths of MBH. The only sound is the echo of her footsteps.

Janet Scully and Ecker's revelations about her dad are weighing on her. But after spending a day thumbing through old photographs of her parents and crying through two boxes of tissues, she's feeling lighter. Her dad's actions were deeply unethical, and she has questions, a lot of them—but they also tell her something profound.

Her father loved her. He loved her mom, too, and he was willing to sacrifice his career to save her.

Now memories of him replay differently. Her father wasn't always there when Mom needed him—not because he didn't care about her, but because it pained him to see her so sick. He didn't comfort Emma when Maria died not because he didn't want to, but because he himself was inconsolable. He threw himself into Community Cares not because he was obsessed with being a savior, but out of guilt for being a fraud.

Emma hasn't completely forgiven him. He should have been more vulnerable with her. He lost the wife he loved, yes, but she lost her mother.

But she's upset at herself, too—for not giving him more grace. For moving to Sweden when he needed her most. He wasn't perfect, sure, but he was her father.

He hadn't chosen between his work and his family. He chose both.

Maybe it's time for her to do the same.

Her mind turns to Sanjay. How he flew to Boston because her dad paged him; how he's making good on his promise to Carl Franks. How he looked at her in her apartment—all signs that, despite the life he's led since leaving MBH, he might be the same person she fell in love with years ago.

But some things continue to baffle and infuriate her. Like that call with his assistant. She could tell they were joking around, but still. And what about the money he mentioned, the 703 account? Was Ecker right to not trust him?

After multiple turns through the basement labyrinth, she reaches the hematology lab. Pushing open the reinforced steel door that warns "Hospital Employees Only," she steps inside and is immediately bathed in white light. After her eyes adjust, she observes the dozens of lab technicians scurrying about the 100x100-foot room. The lab is similar to hers in many respects, but it operates on a much grander scale—at any given time, it's processing thousands of blood samples from patients all over the hospital.

"Emma! What are you doing here?"

She turns to see Dr. Peggy Lin, the lab's director. Peggy wears a long lab coat over her thin frame, a pair of goggles resting on her head. Even under the harsh lightning, her skin looks perfect.

Peggy and Emma met a year ago at a major scientific conference. As the only two female scientists sent by MBH, they quickly bonded. At long last, Peggy had someone with whom she could share war stories of being the first and only woman in her department. Like the time she was pumping breast milk in her office and her chair barged in, asking, "What is that infernal noise?" Or the many, many times male scientists mansplained her PhD thesis to her.

Emma only wishes she'd replied to Peggy's frequent entreaties to hang out. They're cordial when they see each other in the hospital coffee shop or at interdepartmental meetings, promising to get drinks or dinner soon. But work always comes first.

More baggage from her dad she needs to throw out.

"I need your help," she says after she and Peggy catch up. "There's a patient on the floor that I suspect has a serious bleeding problem. I want to test him for a rare coagulation disorder."

Her friend looks puzzled. "We can't run tests down here without an order from the treating physician."

Emma knows what she's asking for is borderline unethical, but Sanjay was convincing. He has a hunch that one of the patients on List C has something wrong with his blood, something his doctors don't know about. Sanjay's many things, but he's rarely wrong about patients. Emma's planned for this question.

"I could, Peggy, but how is that going to go? I show up on rounds and say, 'Excuse me, Mr. Attending, I'm a basic scientist, not a doctor, and a woman, and I think you've missed a major bleeding disorder in one of your patients.'"

Peggy rubs her forehead, bites her lip. "Fine, I'm in," she says. "But to keep it from automatically showing up in the patient's chart and getting us into trouble, we're gonna do it the old-fashioned way—no computers."

Soon they're side by side, staring down a microscope. Peggy found a day-old sample of the List C patient's blood and spun it down to separate the blood cells from the plasma. Then she extracted the plasma into a second test tube and added calcium.

Under the light are a few milliliters of the solution. Carefully, using a long pipette, Peggy adds a drop of clotting factor to activate the blood clotting pathway and starts her timer.

Emma sees white bubbles form as the solutions mix. A minute later, Peggy looks up at her, her eyes wide.

"I've never seen numbers like this!" She whips off her rubber gloves and grabs her phone. "I'm calling up to the floor. This patient could bleed out at any moment!"

CHAPTER

26

SANJAY STEPS ANXIOUSLY into the lobby of Community Cares and looks up at the sign above the reception area: ABIERTA PARA TODO. Open for everyone. Years ago, as a medical student, seeing that sign would take all his worries away.

Not today.

After he sent Emma to the blood lab, Cassie called. A patient fired him. His first ever.

Sanjay offered to waive his retainer for two years, even promised to make the global lobbyist his first house call after Tom's memorial service.

The only concession? He'd stay if Sanjay left for London in an hour. For drinks. Not an exam. Not a medical crisis. Just drinks.

No chance. Someone tailed him last night. That means whatever Tom was investigating isn't over. Patients could be at risk.

On top of that, Mr. Franks is expecting him.

Is he being foolish? Probably. But with everything upside down, putting patients first is the only thing that makes any sense.

As Sanjay passes the front desk, a chorus of clinic staff greets him: "Buenos dias!" He salutes them wordlessly and heads to the back, where two physicians, a woman in dark jeans and a man with an orange beard and a flannel shirt, are hunched over an X-ray. They say hi, then Sanjay excuses himself and moves down the hallway to the nursing station.

"Dr. Sanjay!" In the corner of the crowded room is Nurse Kay. "I knew you couldn't stay away. A lot's changed, hey? We've got a big-time donor now. Anonymous, but they paid for actual chairs, exam tables, the works!"

Sanjay takes in the room around him and smiles weakly. The computers, the equipment, the staff . . . It feels like a real clinic now, not just a free one. A clinic patients deserved.

His eyes linger on the desks, then the chairs—just the ones he always dreamed of having here.

Nurse Kay claps, getting the attention of the medical assistants. "Folks, meet Dr. Sanjay, the best doctor this clinic has ever seen. After Dr. Carpenter, of course."

"Uh, hi everyone," Sanjay says, shifting his weight, almost apologetic. He feels like an intruder—and an impostor. "I'm just here to see one patient, then I'll be out of your hair."

Nurse Kay guffaws. "One patient? We've got a whole waiting room full."

He looks at the expectant faces of the nurses and medical assistants and shrugs.

"Fair enough, Nurse Kay," he says. "Where do you need me?"

"Aw, shucks. I thought you'd never ask."

* * *

The cases are amazing—urgent, messy—exactly what he's been missing. The first patient is a carpenter from El Salvador who hit himself with a hammer and is bleeding into his nailbed, causing severe throbbing pain. Using an eighteen-gauge needle, and with

Nurse Kay holding the man down, Sanjay manually drills into his nail until the blood spurts out. The second patient is an Amharic-speaking grandmother who fell and hit her head on the way to the bathroom. Sanjay checks her neurologic function, which is normal, reviews her medications to eliminate any that might cause dizziness, and counsels the family on fall-proofing their home with shower bars and nightlights.

Then there's a thirty-something Bangladeshi Uber driver who complains of constant exhaustion. As soon as Sanjay enters the exam room, he catches a whiff of nail polish remover and, on a hunch, checks the patient's blood sugar level—538 mg/dl, four times the upper limit of normal. He diagnoses type 2 diabetes and starts insulin.

Equally gratifying is how he's able to address the root cause of what's ailing his patients. Legal aid for the carpenter in case his boss demands he return to work too early. Social workers to set up home health services for the grandmother. An on-site pharmacy that dispenses insulin to the Uber driver for just ten dollars.

A reminder of what medicine practiced the right way can achieve.

"Healthcare that isn't out to get you? This I had to see with my own eyes!" Sanjay turns around to see Mr. Franks sitting in the hallway, getting his blood pressure measured.

Sanjay leads him to the exam room, and they both sit. "I know we're here to talk about your chest pains, Carl. But before we do, anything else you want to cover today? I want to chat about your preventive care, routine blood work, and vaccines, but we'll get to that."

Carl puffs out his cheeks. "Vaccines? Aren't they just for kids?"

Sanjay explains that adults need vaccines, too: tetanus booster every ten years, shingles vaccine after age fifty, pneumonia shot after sixty-five.

"Well, I'll be. I haven't gotten a vaccine in years, except for Covid—but I'll do whatever you say."

Sanjay nods. "Now tell me about your chest pains."

"Actually, they seem to have gone away."

"Oh?"

"The day after you left, I got an overnight letter in the mail. From the collections agency." Carl reaches into his jacket pocket and pulls out a neatly folded envelope. "Says all my medical debts from that colonoscopy have been paid. In full." He eyes Sanjay. "You wouldn't know anything about that, would ya, Doc?"

"Me?" Sanjay smiles and shakes his head. "I'm just glad your chest pains are better."

Nurse Kay pulls him aside after he finishes with Mr. Franks. "A patient just showed up in the waiting room," she says, her face worried. "She doesn't look good."

Despite being in her forties, the patient takes a full two minutes to walk the fifty feet from the waiting room to the back hallway, stopping halfway to catch her breath. When he finally gets her onto the exam table, Sanjay gently pulls her eyelids down and sees her mucosa is light pink, not red, a telltale sign of anemia.

At first, he suspects a gynecological problem, but she tells him her menses are regular and not particularly heavy. Then he asks about her stools, and she says they are tarry and dark. When he pushes on her belly, right below the sternum, she winces.

"I'm worried you have an ulcer," he tells her. "One that's actively bleeding. I'm normally a very conservative doctor, but you need to see a GI doctor and get scoped right away."

Before Sanjay can continue, she starts collecting her things to leave. "I'll be fine," she says, shaking her head.

When he presses her to stay, she tells him that she's a single mother to three young boys, with no money to pay for medical care and no time to find a specialist willing to give her a discount. Then she stands up, gets lightheaded, and nearly topples over. Sanjay has to steady her, help her back into her seat.

"Yes," he says. "You *will* be fine, but once you let me help you."

He asks Nurse Kay to monitor her, then calls Dr. Olopade, the GI doctor who used to work with Neil at MBH.

"Fuki, it's Sanjay."

"Dr. Sanjay, a pleasure. I was meaning to call you. That patient we discussed? She did indeed have mesenteric ischemia. We placed a stent, and she's already feeling better."

The follow-up makes Sanjay like Fuki even more. He's closing the loop, like Tom always did. "Glad to hear it. But listen, I need a favor. It's for a patient."

"I don't take care of any rich patients here. That's what MBH is for."

Sanjay laughs, then fills him in on the case.

"Sounds serious. Hand her the phone and switch to FaceTime."

A moment later, Fuki's speaking to the woman in perfect Spanish. She starts crying. Tears of relief. She hands the phone back to Sanjay.

"I got it from here. We're arranging for her to get two units of blood, then go directly to the procedure suite to find the source of the bleed," says Fuki.

Sanjay can't contain his surprise. Fuki's able to treat an uninsured patient, just like that?

As soon as they hang up, Sanjay's phone buzzes. A text. His first thought is Fuki. Has a senior administrator blocked the patient?

—ICU bed 12 successfully extubated x 30 hours. Transferring to gen med 5NW-14 later today. Telling bad jokes.

It's Dr. Harper Williams, updating him about Vasquez, the patient who's now off the ventilator. Sanjay grabs his coat, thanks the staff, and heads to MBH.

* * *

Forty minutes later, Sanjay is outside Vasquez's ICU room. Through the glass wall, he can see the patient laughing in bed. He's playing cards with his two daughters, their giggles filling the air, while his wife cheers them on.

Sanjay hesitates, not wanting to interrupt. But as he's about to leave, one of the nurses pops into the room and taps on the glass wall, drawing the family's attention his way.

"It's him!" the wife says.

The next thing he knows, Sanjay is being smothered in hugs and steered into a chair by the patient's bed. Hoarse-voiced, Mr. Vasquez says, "I hear I owe you my life. And let me tell you—it's the one I've been waiting my whole life to live."

Sanjay tilts his head. He's sat with countless patients in hospital rooms and ICUs, listening to their reflections in the face of death or serious illness, but he's never heard anyone speak about life quite like this. "How do you mean?" he asks.

"When I was younger," Mr. Vasquez says, "I kept trying to 'find myself.'" He makes air quotes around the words. "I traveled the world, changed jobs over and over. But the feeling you get when you're where you truly belong, doing what you're meant to do?" A slow smile spreads across his face. "There's nothing like it."

* * *

Twenty minutes later, Sanjay's in the elevator, heading down to the main lobby. For the first time in days, he feels optimistic. Maybe healthcare in America isn't all bad.

But all too soon, the feeling starts to fade. Emma's been feverishly texting him about an update on the patient whose blood she tested, and he's dreading whatever she's found.

He spots her in the coffee shop, on the phone, gesturing wildly.

"Let me know if he responds to the infusion," she's saying. "We gotta keep a close eye on it . . . great, great."

Sanjay's head is buzzing, but he gives her space to wrap up and heads to the coffee dispenser. Just as he's putting a lid on his cup, a slap on the back nearly has him spilling his coffee.

"Tell me how you knew!" says Emma as he whips around.

Breathlessly, she fills him in. The patient on List C's coagulation test was so high it was off the measurement scale. Even the simple act of brushing his teeth could have caused him to bleed uncontrollably. The treating team was skeptical at first, but when they repeated the test, they jumped into action.

"That was them on the phone. He just got transfused with plasma, and they're monitoring him closely in Neil's ICU." A big grin spreads across her face. "I have to say, it was pretty incredible. I helped a patient!"

Sanjay wants to celebrate with her, but he's filled with a sense of doom. Never in his career has he wished so hard to be wrong. "Did you bring the sample?"

"That was the hardest part." Emma takes a plastic specimen bag out of her purse and hands it over. "I owe Peggy big time."

Sanjay holds the bag to the light and eyes the purple-topped tube inside. His mind goes quiet.

Emma squeezes his arm and smiles. "You didn't answer my question. How did you know?"

"I didn't," he says under his breath. He isn't ready to reveal his diagnosis. Not yet.

"Does this have anything to do with the stolen absoluxir?" she asks.

Sanjay runs his fingers through his hair. His voice goes up in pitch. "I'm sorry, but I can't tell you right now. It's too crazy."

"Sanjay—"

Before he can stop himself, he grabs her shoulders, squeezing. "Emma, I need you to trust me! Can you do that? Can you trust me?"

He catches himself almost instantly, backs off, looks down at his hands. They're shaking.

When he looks up, Emma's face is frozen. It makes his stomach turn. He didn't mean to yell. He hasn't thought through the implications of what Emma's found out yet, but the bare facts have him scared. Worse, he doesn't know *why*.

He takes a deep breath. "I'm sorry, Emma . . ."

She rises on tiptoes to meet his gaze and looks into his eyes. "It's okay, Sanjay." She comes back down, and her voice evens. "You were right about the patient on List C, which means you're onto something important. What do you need me to do?"

"I need you to help me get into Ecker and DeSalvo's lab."

He expects her to push back. Instead, a crooked smile spreads across her face. "Then you're gonna need to trust me, too. Pick me up around six. We're going to our med school reunion after all."

CHAPTER 27

Emma stops outside Neil's office and takes a deep breath. She doesn't feel right going to the reunion with Sanjay, even as friends, without having this conversation. And between her lab, the absoluxir review, and her search for answers about her dad, she has no time to arrange a meeting elsewhere.

She knocks gently, and Neil looks up from his computer and grins. "Emma! This is a nice surprise."

"It's nice to see you too, Neil," she says as he envelops her in a hug. After a couple seconds, she pulls back, and he looks at her face, his smile fading.

"Is everything okay?"

His voice is full of concern. His eyes, too. A wave of sadness hits Emma. Neil's so sweet and kind, and he's always been there for her. He may not have Sanjay's spark, but he's consistent. And right now, she needs consistency—and friendship—more than ever.

She takes a seat in front of his desk. He seems confused, but follows suit, awkwardly settling back into his chair.

"Is this about Tom?" he asks.

"No, it's about us." Her voice comes out more matter-of-factly than she intends. "Neil, I value our friendship. You've always been there for me, in school, in Sweden. And especially after Mom died. Our two dates were wonderful, but it's not what I want right now. I'm sorry."

Neil swallows hard. "I understand, Emma. Is this temporary, or . . ."

"I don't know, Neil. I don't think so, but with everything going on right now, I don't trust my emotions."

"Then let's consider it temporary," he says, looking away from her. "We can revisit it in a few weeks."

She tries again. "Neil, what I'm trying to say is I'd like to be friends."

He slumps down in his chair. "Does this have anything to do with Sanjay being back?"

"It might."

"I knew it! Everyone's taking his side. Even the residents in my own ICU! They're all saying, 'Dr. Sanjay saved Mr. Vasquez's life.'" He throws his hands in the air. "There'd be no life to save if I hadn't built the ICU in the first place!"

Emma's breath quickens. "It isn't like that. Sanjay is just—"

"Just what?"

Neil's secretary sticks her head in. "Is everything all right, Dr. Desai?"

"Yes, I'm fine. Thank you." Neil smooths his suit jacket and squares a notepad on his desk. After his secretary leaves, he averts his gaze and says, "I'd like to be alone now, Emma."

The anger is gone. All Emma sees is hurt. She wishes she could reach over and give her friend a hug, but she's still shaken.

"Neil, come on. Three peas in a pod, right?"

He looks at her, his eyes red. "Please close the door on your way out."

CHAPTER 28

A N HOUR LATER, Sanjay wakes up in a dark, quiet room to the ringing of his phone.

"Good morning," he says to Cassie, his voice hoarse.

"Oh, were you sleeping? I love that manly voice you have when you're groggy."

"Well, if you'd just marry me already, you'd get to wake up to it every day."

They both laugh, then Sanjay flips on the light. He's in the resident call room, where he crashed for a nap. It's an old trick from internship. The call rooms are packed at night, but during the day, they're empty. The perfect place to recover from an all-nighter.

He sits up and stretches out his arms, then asks, "So, what's up?"

"I made some progress on Next Health. Six months ago, they announced a partnership with MBH. According to the financials from Barnett, around the same time, their numbers miraculously improved."

"That's also around when the ICU opened," says Sanjay.

"The article is vague about the actual purpose of the partnership. There hasn't been any more information since, at least not in the public domain."

He can hear the glee in Cassie's voice, and he laughs. "Why do I get the feeling you're about to tell me what's in the private domain?"

Her smile practically comes through the phone. "When I checked into MBH's finances and cross-referenced them against List B, I found out that MBH is overcharging the patients Next Health refers to them. To the tune of three *hundred* percent."

Sanjay whistles. Those costs would largely be borne by the patients' employers, but still, it's staggering.

"Which department within MBH is the biggest offender?" Sanjay asks. He hopes it isn't Neil's old department, GI.

"Can't answer that yet. I'm still cleaning the data files," Cassie says. "But I'd bet Next Health is getting kickbacks from MBH for those bogus referrals."

This could be the link Sanjay's been looking for. If the partnership with MBH is what's finally making Next Health profitable—and ready to go public—they'll do anything to keep that information from getting out. Including threaten Tom—or worse.

"I want to follow the money," Cassie's saying. "See what kind of arrangement Next Health has with MBH. There's just one problem. Next Health's head of security is ex-Mossad, so I can't hack their system from the outside."

Sanjay groans. "That's it, then? We're stuck?"

"The key phrase being 'from the outside.'"

Sanjay gulps. "You want me to break into their clinic?"

"Don't be silly, sweetheart. They'd eat you alive. I want you to get a checkup."

* * *

Cassie insists that Sanjay take the train. Whoever's tailing him might still be following the Range Rover.

While he stands on the platform, he tries to distract himself by checking his patients' labs on his phone. But it doesn't work. He finds himself repeatedly glancing over his shoulder, scanning the bustling crowd, trying to pick out potential tails. The threat Tom received suddenly feels more real—and more dangerous.

To make matters worse, he's headed to Next Health—straight into the lion's den.

But Next Health has dozens of clinics scattered around the country, three in Boston alone. He prays that a bit of luck, plus the false identity Cassie provided, will be enough to keep him safe.

An hour later, he arrives at one of Next Health's suburban clinics and tightens his blue ballcap, adjusts his sunglasses.

The lobby looks like a mix between an Apple Genius Bar and the sickbay on *Star Trek*. On the left, smart-looking staff with clear-rimmed glasses help patients check in on flat-screen computers. On the right, an array of gadgets allows patients to wirelessly check their vital signs and measure their body fat index.

No less impressive is that Sanjay was able to get the appointment in an hour, compared to typical wait times for a new primary care doctor of three to eight weeks.

But as Cassie explained, it comes at a cost. Unless your employer offers Next Health as a free perk, membership fees are $2,000 to sign up and $300 a month thereafter. And that's just for access to the facility. Visits to the doctor and medications are charged through insurance, and if Next Health isn't in-network or you don't have health coverage, those are extra. So much for their billboard slogan: "We're democratizing the future of medicine!"

A perky young woman in a bright red dress and matching lipstick approaches Sanjay, iPad in hand. "Are you here for an appointment?"

"Ah, yes I am. I'm Sam Gupta," says Sanjay. Cassie went with his 'pizza name,' the easy-to-pronounce nickname every immigrant kid has for takeout and coffee orders.

"Mr. Gupta, perfect. I have you right here." She smiles and flicks her bangs to the right. "Now, smile!" Before Sanjay can react, she lifts her iPad and snaps a photo. He grimaces, and she says, "Don't worry, it's just for your member profile."

"Member?"

"Oh, we don't use the term 'patient' here. That sounds so, you know, sick and everything."

"Ah, gotcha, we wouldn't want a clinic filled with sick people. Totally kills the vibe."

She brightens up. "Yes, exactly!"

"Thanks. Well, I'm here for a routine visit."

"Routine? We don't do 'routine' visits, either. Our visits are amazing! We have the best doctors. They're cute, too," she says with a wink. "You're so lucky that your work pays for this experience."

He frowns, confused. "As an employee, don't you have access to a membership?"

"No," she says with a sigh. Then she perks up again, as if remembering herself. "But they say maybe one day we will! Until then, I just stick to my juices."

Sanjay hopes her juicer also does Pap smears.

"Should I grab a seat in the waiting room?" he asks.

"Waiting room! Hello, 1990s." She laughs. "That's so outdated. It's what our founder says is wrong with medicine." She points at an oversized photo of their CEO on the wall. There's that smirk again. "We have a *lobby.* Here's the Wi-Fi code, and over there is our espresso bar."

"So you want me to wait in the lobby?"

She gives him a thumbs-up. It takes everything Sanjay has not to roll his eyes.

* * *

The exam room looks like a typical doctor's office—except for the large flat-panel screen embedded in the wall that reads, "Welcome, Mr. Gupta."

Before the doctor arrives, Sanjay quickly searches the room. There's no port to plug in the flash drive Cassie gave him. He tries to pull the screen forward, but it won't detach from the wall.

Damn it. His only hope is that this is one of those clinics where doctors go room to room, carrying their own laptops. If that's the case, how can he distract the doctor long enough to insert the flash drive?

But when Dr. Corbin, a polite, boyish, early thirty-something physician, arrives, Sanjay's hopes are dashed. The doctor only has an iPad. No USB port.

"So, what brings you to Next Health?" asks Corbin.

Sanjay sits forward, putting a hand on his chest. It's all part of the act. "My asthma's getting bad. Normally I get episodes like this once a month, but recently it's been every other day. At night, too."

"I see. That's concerning."

"Yeah, it all started when I lost my job—"

"Hmm, yeah, it's a tough economy out there. Do you have any allergies?"

"Allergies, no," says Sanjay, taken aback by Dr. Corbin's poor bedside manner. "I'm lucky my employer—well, former employer—is covering Next Health for another three months. But since I'm not getting paid, money is tight, and the inhaler I use is really expensive."

In spite of himself, he raises his eyebrows meaningfully. But Dr. Corbin doesn't get the hint. He's too busy staring down at his iPad.

"Here's what we're gonna do," he says, finally looking up. "We have this brand-new X-ray machine that can look into your lungs and see everything that's going on." He checks his iPad again. *Is he reading from a script?* "It even makes pictures in 3D, for an additional fee."

"I don't know. My medications are already so expensive—"

The doctor cuts him off. "Don't worry about that. Let's get this test done, and then we'll know what we're dealing with. Okay?"

"Okay . . ."

"After that we'll send you to a specialist. At MBH."

Sanjay knows he's supposed to act impressed, but he can't bring himself to do it. "A specialist? I just have asthma—it's pretty common. You're a doctor, right?"

"I *am* a doctor," Dr. Corbin says, looking toward the big screen. *Is someone watching them?* Sanjay pulls his cap down, just in case. "It's just . . . Don't you want an expert to see you?"

"I thought primary care doctors *were* experts in asthma."

"Well, we are. I am, actually. But Next Health—I mean, *we*—" His eyes dart back to the screen. "We prefer asthma be managed by pulmonologists. MBH is amazing. Besides, you have great insurance. It'll be free."

We're all paying for it, thinks Sanjay. *One way or another.*

"All right, I'm going to step out and get things set up. My assistant will pop in here to swipe your card and collect the fee for the 3D imaging."

"Okay, but before you go, I noticed you weren't taking any notes?"

Corbin smiles. "We have software that will take our conversation and automatically generate your clinic note. Pretty cool, right?"

"Yes, but does that mean our visits are being recorded?"

"Well . . . maybe. I'm not sure."

"Isn't that a HIPAA violation?" asks Sanjay, referring to the law that protects patient privacy and information.

Corbin's face reddens. "I suspect our terms of service agreement covers that, but I can turn off the auto-transcription if you like."

"Please do."

Corbin taps a small button on the far end of the room. A red light just below the screen turns off. "I'll be back," he says cheerfully.

He leaves, and Sanjay takes out his phone and calls Cassie. "There's something weird about this place."

"No surprise there. And?"

"And there's no computer in the exam room. Or on the doc."

She huffs. "I was worried about that." A pause, then, "Okay, time for Plan B."

* * *

Five minutes later, a black Mercedes S-Class jumps the curb in front of Next Health, nearly crashing into the front lobby. Out of the driver's side door and into the reception area stumbles a sixty-something woman, clutching her throat.

"I. Can't. Breathe," she chokes, falling to her knees.

"Oh my God!" someone shouts. "What do we do?"

The nearest receptionist walks up to her with an iPad. "Um, ma'am, can we help you? Do you have an appointment? Are you a member?"

The woman is rolling around on the floor, wheezing. No answer.

"I can't do this!" the receptionist screams.

"Call the doctor!" yells someone in the back.

Moments later, Dr. Corbin comes running in. He crouches down next to the writhing woman and checks her pulse. She's pointing frantically at her red wrist band. Bee allergy.

"Ma'am!" he yells. "Are you having an allergy attack?"

She nods her head.

"Okay, somebody call 911! And get the crash cart!"

"Crash cart! Crash cart!" The staff repeats. Then one of them asks, "What's a crash cart?" and more panic ensues.

A minute later, a gray crash cart rattles through the door, drawers clattering, supplies spilling.

"Where's the damn epi?" yells Corbin, flailing through the cooler of medications. While another team member continues the search, he turns to the EKG machine—but it won't turn on. The AED case is no better. A wire is missing.

And there's no EpiPen.

"This is a disaster," he mutters.

From his exam room, Sanjay hears the commotion, a mixture of shouting and crying. Through the doorway, he overhears one of the doctors say she isn't going out front. Her CPR certification expired, she hisses, and Next Health refuses to give her time off to renew it.

He waits two more minutes, then steps into the hallway.

Thumbing through the office blueprints Cassie sent to his iPhone, he finds his way to an unmarked door next to the janitorial closest and slips inside. The server room is quiet, except for the steady hum of cooling fans. Not wanting to attract attention, he feels his way through the dark to an open USB port and pushes the flash drive into the slot. He pushes it again, to make sure it's secure, then starts his count, as Cassie instructed. At thirty Mississippis, he pulls out the drive, slips it into his pocket, and feels his way back to the door.

"Hey, you!"

Sanjay is in the hallway now. He shuts the door behind him, then spins around to find his head level with someone's chest. Startled, he takes a half step back.

The man in front of him is at least six foot six, with slick black hair and dark, menacing eyes.

"What were you doing in there?" he demands.

"I'm trying to find the bathroom. With everything going on—" Sanjay gestures toward the chaos around him. "I got lost."

The guard eyes him suspiciously, then gestures at the sign for the men's room, mere feet away.

"Got it, thanks!" says Sanjay. He makes for the bathroom, but a massive arm shoots out, blocking his way, and he flinches. The guard doesn't seem like the usual clinic or hospital security type. More a professional killer.

"Listen, I have a bad case of prostatitis. My doctor is treating it, but for now when I need to go, I *need* to go." To add to the act, he starts hopping from foot to foot.

It doesn't work. Without another word, the man grabs his collar and pushes him toward the back of the clinic. Sanjay's heart is pounding. Mike's training includes martial arts, but an actual fight? He clenches his fists, a tidal wave of adrenaline rushing through him.

Just as he's being pushed through the emergency exit door, he hears a voice say, "Mr. Gupta?"

Sanjay's whipped around, and Dr. Corbin comes into view.

"Is everything okay?" Corbin asks, eyeing the guard suspiciously.

With a shove, the guard releases Sanjay, who turns his head to find the guard glaring at him. "I'm . . . fine," he says. "This man was . . . was helping me find my way. I'm ready for that X-ray scan, Dr. Corbin."

Corbin looks at him dubiously, then shrugs and says, "Er, well, follow me."

The doctor escorts him to the front of the clinic. Sanjay's mind is racing, replaying every step of the visit. Were there security cameras in the main hallway? Should he have wiped the door handle to the server room? He's way out of his league here, and he knows it.

The lobby is overrun with concerned members and staff. Sanjay's heart rate is still up, but he's relieved to be surrounded by people.

Corbin steps close to him, dropping his voice. "Listen. You don't need an X-ray. Or a referral to MBH, for that matter. You just need a cheaper inhaler and to actually use it every day." He takes a prescription pad out of his pocket and scribbles out a script for a generic.

"And Mr. Gupta?"

"Yeah?"

"I'm sorry you lost your job. At this rate, I may not be far behind you."

CHAPTER

29

Ten minutes later, Sanjay is hurtling down the highway in the black Mercedes sedan—the same one that nearly crashed into the clinic. He catches his breath, glad to be out of the clutches of Next Health and that guard, then inspects the older woman in the driver's seat.

He's asked a lot of Cassie this time.

A quick scan shows no sign of injury. She has on a fresh face of makeup and doesn't look a day older than when he met her six years ago. At the time, she was sixty-one and chief of staff to Alphonso Ballantino, an arms trafficker. She was also a former computer scientist and art lover turned Cold War operative. One of her many jobs for Ballantino was running security checks on anyone he did business with—including his private physician. When she screened Sanjay using a lie detector test, they instantly connected. They were both outsiders, pretending to be someone else: a doctor who was in it for the money; a computer whiz who didn't care whose side she was on.

A couple years later, when a rival killed Ballantino and Cassie was wounded in the raid, Sanjay was the first person she called.

After stabilizing her on his plane, he flew her to a hospital in Finland, where she underwent curative surgery on her spleen and left lung.

After the procedure, she insisted on recovering on his plane in case they were tailed. Though she must have been in pain, she lay on his bed, relaxed, smiling. Pointing at the bandages across her chest, she said, "Geez, Dr. Sanjay, is this your idea of making a woman feel special?"

Humor, Sanjay realized, was Cassie's coping mechanism. She'd lived for years as a spy, then worked as part of a criminal organization. Now she'd survived an attempt on her life. Laughter was what she needed to heal.

So he quipped back, "That's what every woman in my bed says."

"Ha! I mean, if anesthesia is what it takes to get them there, then we have to work on your game," she shot back.

Once she recovered, she happily accepted a job as his executive assistant. Ever since, their banter has been a staple of their relationship.

Now, confident that she isn't hurt, Sanjay says, "You outdid yourself in there."

She turns from the wheel and winks. "I always told you, I should have been an actress."

"You would have been breathtaking. Pun intended."

They both laugh. She changes lanes. "I'm glad they didn't have an EpiPen. Those things hurt. But good God, what kind of clinic doesn't stock one?"

"Don't get me started." Sanjay shakes his head. "Even the electronic health record was strange. I'm not sure, but I think it was literally scripting out everything the doctor said and did. Probably so Next Health can keep their doctors in line, make sure they're upcharging everywhere they can."

He tells her about his run-in with the guard.

"I think the entire visit was recorded, too."

"It was?" Her face tightens. Sanjay explains that he had the camera turned off before calling her, but she still looks worried.

"I'll go into their system and delete the recording," she says. "Can't risk them tracing the code we uploaded back to you."

He nods.

She pulls over on the highway and flips the hazard lights on, then pauses for a minute, eyeing her rearview mirror. Satisfied, she reaches into the back pocket of his seat and pulls out a laptop. Within seconds, the black screen fills with lines of code.

"We're in," she says. She gets to work, typing furiously. "And . . . visit deleted." She closes the laptop and exhales, visibly more relaxed. "There's still a chance they can ID you from the surveillance footage, but you did good, Sanjay."

That doesn't make him feel much better—but at least he's far away from that trained killer.

"Work with Paul Klein on this," he tells her. "He's at *The Globe*. We didn't talk long, but he seems smart. I'd bet he knows how to follow a money trail."

"Consider it done."

"Thanks. And thanks for taking care of the bills for that patient. In paying for his colonoscopy, you cured his chest pains."

Cassie smiles and says, "That's what the 703 account is all about." Then her face hardens. "Speaking of which—it's time to pay the piper."

She raises her eyebrows—like she's disciplining a child—and hands him a stack of papers.

"They all called the clinic line, same hour, with bogus symptoms that'd normally require an in-person evaluation. Clearly a coordinated attack."

The corners of his mouth turn down as he skims the top sheet: a letter signed by five patients—Kosaac, the syphilis guy, and four of his cronies. Citing delayed care from him and his NP, they're threatening breach of contract. They're demanding their full annual retainers back, with interest.

Over a million each.

Exactly what Barnett warned him about.

The legalese dredges up old memories: the email from MBH, the involuntary leave, the whispers behind his back, nurses looking away as he walked by.

He exhales slowly. Sure, he could return to Europe tonight—but what about the next time? If his mom gets sick? If Neela needs him? If he just wants a break?

He thought he'd set up the perfect practice. He was wrong. Again.

Beneath the letter is a hiring contract for a lawyer. It's solid—but could mean court.

Heat rushes up his neck, and a wave of nausea hits. He thrusts the papers back at Cassie, unsigned.

"No fighting," he says, voice shaking. "Just pay them."

"But Sanjay, if we cave, more patients may follow. We have some money stashed away, but not enough to—"

"I don't give a damn." It comes out louder than he intended. He braces for blowback.

Cassie just gives a clenched half smile and nods.

Which only makes him feel worse.

She turns off the hazard lights and merges back onto the highway. Her voice is lighter. "So, have you and Emma talked about the other night? At her apartment?"

"No, and I don't intend to. Everything's fine the way it is."

"Maybe this—" she slaps the stack of papers on her lap, "is a chance to start over. You don't need all the answers right now. Just start by telling her the truth about what happened after the anatomy test and why you weren't there for her."

"No. I already know what I need to do. Get everything back to the way it was. Before Tom died." He pauses, rubs his nose. "Besides, I don't really know how she feels about me."

Cassie pats him on the shoulder. "For a master diagnostician, you're terrible at reading women."

CHAPTER 30

SANJAY PULLS UP to Emma's apartment building dressed in a dark blue Brioni tuxedo and white shirt, no tie.

—*Here, take your time.* He texts.

—*Be down in 5.*

—*By 5, I mean 15.* She adds a wink emoji.

An hour earlier, she texted to let him know she'd had the talk with Neil. Sanjay wonders how his old friend took the news. He'll pull him aside at the reunion and check in on him.

For now, it's a moonless night and clouds are forming. He steps out of the car to stretch his legs, then turns to look at his ride. Cassie rented him another Range, but a different model and color to avoid possible tails.

Sanjay takes out the folded paper from his suit pocket and lays it on the hood of the car. With a few strokes of his pen, he updates his differential diagnosis to include his suspicions about Jim Hadley, Next Health's CFO.

There's more, but he isn't ready to put pen to paper. Not yet.

At the wedding, it dawned on him that many of the patients on List C went to the ICU for bleeding, which can be triggered by

	What?	Who?	Why?
List A	Unnecessary procedures	Neil	To be department chair
List B	Referrals from Next Health	Hadley	To pay back investors
List C	ICU transfers	?	?
Tom	Stroke; Murder?	?	?

medications. Given what he knew about absoluxir, he had to consider the possibility that the new drug was the cause.

But it was a long shot. Although absoluxir could theoretically cause bleeding, the clinical trial *proved* it didn't. Plus, the trial ended months ago. That's what made the blood test Emma ran on the one patient from List C who was still hospitalized at MBH so confusing—and scary.

The thought reminds him to call Feldman.

The senior pathologist picks up on the first ring. "Don't you have anything better to do than bother an old man on a Friday night?"

"Good to speak with you, too, Dr. Feldman." They both laugh. "Hey, have you run Tom's blood yet?"

"Sure did."

"And?

"Nada. Everything came back normal."

A wave of relief settles over Sanjay. While not every harmful medication Tom could have been given would show up in the blood, Feldman's results are consistent with a routine stroke. Maybe Tom died of natural causes after all.

Then a niggling thought hits him.

"Can you grab his coags for me? I want to make sure his blood wasn't thin."

"Thin? Heck, that's the opposite of a stroke. You darn internists . . ." Sanjay hears drawers opening and slamming shut. "Coags, coags . . . Okay, yes. Definitely not elevated. If anything, his blood was more clotty than usual, but that might be . . ." He clears his throat. "The manner in which the sample was procured."

The front door to the building opens, and Sanjay's jaw drops. It's Emma, wearing a dark green dress and clutching a black purse, her hair down.

"Hey, I gotta go—" he says.

"Wait, what do you want me to do with the rest of the sample?"

"I don't know. Ice it," he says, then hangs up.

When Emma reaches the car, he gets the door for her. "What, no driver?" she asks, ducking in with a smile.

"What can I say? I'm a man of the people." He smiles back and closes the door, then goes around to his side.

The rental is already smelling sweeter. When he turns the engine on, the radio's playing Marvin Gaye, "Sexual Healing."

"Trying to send me a subliminal message?" Emma asks.

"Is it working?"

They laugh.

* * *

While Sanjay drives, Emma explains her plan. Ecker Lab is strictly off-limits to visitors at night. But Matthew DeSalvo might be willing to get them in—if they give him a good enough reason.

"Okay, sure," Sanjay says with a frown. "But what?"

"At Bombo's, Matt suggested you use absoluxir in your practice. What if you tell him you want to learn more about the drug, see the lab where it was discovered?"

Sanjay frowns again. "What's in it for him?" Then Ana's words come back to him—her theory that Matt stands to make money from the drug—and he snaps his fingers. "He's very money minded. Maybe we can use that."

"Yes!" Emma's eyes are bright. "Think about what Ecker's secretary said. About how people are willing to pay to get absoluxir before it's FDA approved."

Sanjay stiffens. Is she suggesting he buy absoluxir from Matt? The thought had crossed his mind before—that Matt could be the one skimming the drug. He *had* insisted on there being no guards at night. But Sanjay wouldn't risk his patients or his practice by prescribing an unapproved medication.

"Tell him you might bring on a consultant," says Emma. "After the drug is approved, of course. I mean, wouldn't your patients pay top dollar to have *the* scientist who discovered the drug advise them on it?"

Sanjay strokes his chin. It's a brilliant ruse.

"You think Matt will go for it?" he asks.

"Maybe. Part of the reason I suggested the reunion is that it might help if you get him tipsy first."

Sanjay grits his teeth. He'll need all the drinks he can stomach to make it through that conversation.

* * *

The reunion is at the new MBMS medical education building, recently renamed the Stadler Center, after the investment banker-cum-philanthropist who donated $100 million to the hospital. Its centerpiece is a glass atrium where students can greet their classmates as they climb up and down an open staircase between lectures.

It's a classy event. Champagne at the entrance. String quartet playing Bach. Waiters in starched button-downs serving hors d'oeuvres. Mixed in are the classic props of a reunion: A photo booth with costumes. A map to pin where you live. Old-school R&B on the dance floor. And of course, pharmaceutical companies, with tables full of well-groomed reps handing out penlights and umbrellas emblazoned with the drugs they're peddling.

Sanjay and Emma arrive late. After awkwardly greeting a handful of classmates they barely recognize, they grab flutes of champagne and find respite in the gymnasium, empty now except for the DJ and ground crew getting set up.

An old Monica song starts playing: "Angel of Mine." A favorite of Sanjay and Emma's back in med school.

Sanjay pulls her close, and they start swaying to the beat. This isn't where he wanted the evening to go, not yet. Not until he's able to speak with her and truly clear the air.

"Emma."

"Hmm?" Her eyes are closed.

"I wanted to . . ."

Her eyes open. She's smiling at him. But that only makes him more nervous.

Just then, the music dies. The auditorium lights flicker on, and Sanjay lets out his breath. All around them classmates are filing in. It must be time for the main program.

Indeed, Neil bounds onto the stage and announces, "Welcome, everybody from the Class of 2014. The best med school class *ever*!" The crowd cheers uproariously. "I'm Dr. Neil Desai."

From the back of the room someone yells, "We love you, Neil!"

Neil smiles. "I'm a gastroenterologist and president of our dear hospital, MBH."

"We love you, MBH!"

"It's my honor to emcee one of the highlights of the reunion, a true MBH tradition, the class awards." More cheers. "The first is for 'best humanitarian.' And it goes to . . ." Neil opens a white envelope. "Dr. John Carnett, vice president of St. Alban's Pediatric Cancer Hospital. His heroic efforts have saved thousands of kids with cancer. Come up here, John!"

As John trots to the stage, Sanjay whispers to Emma, "Last year, they raised over two billion dollars in donations. But many of the families who travel there for treatment end up exhausting their personal savings. Meanwhile, their execs get paid millions."

"That's just wrong," Emma whispers back. She stops clapping.

As Neil doles out each award, Sanjay offers more dark commentary. The "best clinical teacher" hasn't seen a patient in ten years. "Best healthcare leader" is a management consultant who tripled a pharmaceutical company's sales of an addictive pain reliever. "Best patient advocate" is a health services researcher who publishes papers on how Black people have worse health outcomes than white people, but does not support local community groups trying to improve those outcomes.

Twenty minutes later, Neil's down to the last two awards, and Sanjay's never been more ready for a drink.

"And the award for 'best researcher' goes to . . . Dr. Matthew DeSalvo!"

The applause is noticeably light, and Sanjay wonders if Matt has already left. But he slinks on stage in a Ferragamo tuxedo and awkwardly accepts the plaque from Neil.

A nearby classmate whispers to Emma, "That award should have gone to you. Matt gives me the creeps."

"The last award of the evening is for 'best doctor.' Hmm. I wonder who that could be?" Neil opens the envelope and reads the card. "Woah, it says Neil Desai. I didn't know there was another Neil Desai in our class." He scratches his head dramatically. "Well, Dr. Desai, come on up!" The audience laughs, a warm sound that fills the room. "No? No Neil? Okay, well, I accept this award on his behalf, and on behalf of all the doctors, nurses, janitors—everyone who makes MBH the greatest hospital in the world. Thank you all, and have a great evening!"

The audience roars with applause.

Neil takes a few short bows. Just as he's putting the microphone down, he spots Emma and Sanjay, standing close together, their arms touching. Emma's leaned into Sanjay, and Sanjay sees the look of surprise—and jealousy—on Neil's face.

Frowning, Neil picks up the mic again. "Actually . . . one last thing. I dedicate this award to my dear friend, Dr. Sanjay Patel!" He points, and the crowd turns toward Sanjay and Emma. Sanjay hears people gasp.

"Yes, everybody," Neil says, lips twisting. "The Botox King is here, and the first round of drinks is on him!"

CHAPTER

31

EMMA IS ABOUT to join Sanjay and several of their former classmates at the bar when she hears her name being called. She turns to find Matt DeSalvo. His tuxedo is slightly askew, giving him an awkward charm.

"Hi, Matt," she says, bracing herself.

He looks at her, his expression sheepish, almost vulnerable. "Emma, I just realized I never offered my condolences. For Dr. Carpenter."

Her breath catches. "Oh. Well, thank you, Matt—"

He rubs his elbow, struggling to meet her eyes. "Listen. It's no secret that I was angry at Tom. What he did to Jaewon back in med school was wrong. Jaewon made an honest mistake. None of us are perfect. But I shouldn't have expected your dad to be, either. It's time I moved past it."

Emma struggles to hide her shock. *Matt's burying the hatchet?*

He leans forward. "Listen, I have some concerns about our lab. I wasn't sure about you joining us, but honestly, you're exactly who we need right now. A person of integrity."

"Er, thanks, Matt," she says, her mind whirling. *Does this have to do with the missing absoluxir? Or is it something deeper?*

"And if you ever need anything . . ." he adds, his gaze softening, "I'm here."

"Actually, Sanjay and I—"

"I hope I'm not interrupting," calls a voice from over her right shoulder.

It's Dr. Henry Ecker, in a perfectly fitted tuxedo, whiskey in hand.

"Dr. Ecker, so nice to see you," says Emma. He makes for a hug, but she opts for a handshake. She doesn't want to seem too friendly in public. Especially with her review of absoluxir ongoing.

Matt mumbles something about going to the bathroom and scurries away.

"I just secured a grant to study the effects of absoluxir on tumor growth," Ecker says. He gives Emma a knowing look. "The applications for oncology are exciting."

The FDA meeting is less than a week away, and Emma hasn't found any issues with the drug. On the contrary, the data is impressive. Almost too perfect. She sees the potential synergy of combining their labs, but given her role on the review team, now isn't the time to discuss it.

"Based on the data you've seen on absoluxir, what do you think of it?" he asks.

Does Ecker know she's advising the FDA? "I . . . um . . ."

"Surely you must have read some of my published papers?" he asks with a coy smile.

"Dr. Ecker, if you don't mind, we're at a reunion, and I'm in a dress, not a lab coat." She pastes on a smile to soften the words. "It's hardly the place or time for me to offer a scientific opinion on your work."

Ecker nods. "I'd be happy to set up a tour of my lab—"

"I appreciate the offer, but unfortunately, I'm tied up for the next several weeks." She turns to walk away, hoping he got the message. She's heard he can be aggressive in recruiting donors and scientists, but she's never witnessed it firsthand.

"Emma, one more thing," Ecker calls.

She sighs and turns.

"On the other subject we were discussing . . ." He pulls out his phone. "I hate to be the one to show you this."

He's on Instagram—which Emma can't quite believe. But then outrage sweeps away her confusion. Because the screen shows a selfie of Sanjay and the woman from the hospital coffee shop—Ana, was it?—somewhere dark, faces pressed together. Looking more closely, Emma sees he's wearing the same Indian outfit he had on when she found him at her dad's office this morning.

Heat rises from her core. Does this mean he slept with Ana last night—and is now acting like he and Emma are on a first date?

And why is Dr. Ecker following the social media of a young female employee of MBH?

He seems to read her mind. "Someone has been stealing absoluxir from our lab. Ms. Nunez was a research assistant on the absoluxir trial, so our partners have been tracking her and anyone else who might have had access to the drug."

Emma feels her eyes widen.

"I even heard about a patient on the wards who had an unexplained coagulation problem," he says, stirring his drink. "Do you know anything about that?"

Sanjay instructed her not to tell anyone what she and Peggy found, but she can't lie to Ecker. She opts for silence—hoping Ecker can't see through her—then feels a surge of relief when she spots Peggy out of the corner of her eye.

"I need to go, Dr. Ecker," she says, waving over his shoulder.

He stops her with a gentle touch and leans in. "I don't know who to trust, Emma. I even have my doubts about Matt." She looks up. Ecker has never looked so human. He lowers his voice, frowning. "That's part of why I want you in my lab. The stakes are too high."

C H A P T E R

32

A THICK HAND SLAPS Sanjay on the back. He looks up from his tequila to see Nikhil Bansari, the CMO of Next Health. He's the same big-chested, big-mouthed guy Sanjay remembers from medical school, only now with a shaven head and designer clothes. He greets Sanjay with a handshake-hug fit for a rap star.

Sanjay wants to ask about Next Health, but Nikhil gets the first word in. "Dude, you are living the life! You gotta tell us the story."

Two other male classmates gather round.

"How's the money?" demands the first.

"And the women!" adds the second.

"Hah. Come on, guys, all rumors," Sanjay says, putting his hands up.

Out of the corner of his eye, he sees Emma, perhaps a hundred yards out, walking toward them but away from the bar.

"Bullshit, Sanjay," says Nikhil. "So you didn't diagnose a rich guy on a beach with Marfan's?"

"Well . . ." says Sanjay, surprised the European tabloid story made its way across the Atlantic. More high fives.

"And you didn't sleep with supermodel Jennifer Peters?"

"Well . . ."

The three men smirk at each other.

Sanjay needs to shift the conversation. "What about you, Nikhil? I hear you're gonna crush this IPO with Next Health."

"Yes, Nikhil, tell us!" says another classmate.

"Ah, it's nothing, man," Nikhil says, grinning. "We got lucky."

"Bullshit. It's hard work. I walked by one of your clinics the other day," says Sanjay. "The one by the Alewife T stop. It looked amazing from the outside. It's like the future of medicine."

"Cool. I haven't been to that one yet."

"You haven't?" Sanjay was already unimpressed, but now he's shocked. Nikhil's the chief medical officer of Next Health, and he hasn't even stepped foot in his clinic in the city he lives in?

Nikhil just shrugs. "They have me mostly meeting the press, doing conferences and stuff. The clinics are more for the operational and business teams."

The healthcare industry in a nutshell, thinks Sanjay. *Leave the medicine to the businesspeople and the marketing to the doctors.*

It also means Barnett was right. Nikhil doesn't have a clue what's happening at Next Health. Talking to him is a dead end.

Sanjay looks for Emma, but she's gone. He spins on his bar stool and sees her striding toward the exit. *She's leaving? What about their plan to get into Ecker Lab?*

He gets up. "Sorry, guys, I'll be right back."

On the street, it's dark and raining. She's halfway down the steps of the building when he spots her. "Emma!" he yells as he runs to catch up. Reflexively, he holds his hand above his head before realizing it's futile. He's getting soaked. Nothing he can do about it.

She pauses to open her umbrella. It gives him time to catch up.

"What?" she yells. He can't tell if she's raising her voice to talk through the downpour or because she's mad at him.

Then she looks up from the stair below, and her eyes confirm his fears.

"Where are you going?" he asks.

"Home." Her voice is cold.

Sanjay steps down beside her and nearly loses his footing on the slick marble. "What happened?"

"I don't know, Sanjay. You tell me." Her eyes are piercing.

"Emma, I literally have no clue what you're talking about."

"The money, the women, the Botox? That's the real you, right?" She jabs a finger against his chest. "I thought you'd changed. That the rumors were wrong." For a passing moment she looks more hurt than angry.

He pulls his fingers through his hair, sending cold water down his neck. "I mean, yes, a lot of that is true, but that's not me. At least, not all of me. And not anymore."

"A few days with me, and you're a different person?" She has her hand on her hip. "Is that what you're saying?"

"No, of course not. It's more becoming the person I was before. The person I truly am."

She scoffs. "Cut the enlightened shit, Sanjay. Were you with Ana last night or not?"

His jaw drops. *Is that what this is about?*

"Yes, I met up with her. But not like that. It was about your—"

"I don't care, Sanjay. I'm done. With the men in my life, their careers always come first. Either it's some patient you're trying to fix or some test you failed. It's never about us. About me. About putting the people you claim to love first."

"It's not that simple, Emma." He tries to take her hand. She swats him away.

"I mean it. I'm done."

She turns and walks down the steps. He can hear it in her voice: He's lost his chance somehow.

"What about Matt?" he calls. *A Hail Mary.*

She doesn't look back. "What about him? If I want to go to his lab, I'll ask Ecker in the morning. I'm leaving now. Don't try and follow me."

"Fine." Sanjay hears his voice rising. "That's who *you* are."

"What did you say?" she hisses. She's at the bottom of the stairs, fading into the dark.

"Nothing," he mutters.

"No. Go ahead," she turns and steps closer, slowly. "Tell me your diagnosis, Doctor."

"You think you have to choose between having a career and having a life. Whenever someone lets you down and you find out they're not perfect, you choose your career. Fine, Emma, you're right. I'm not saving the world. But at least I didn't give up on everyone I cared about because my mother died."

His head snaps to the right. He reels back, his left cheek stinging. It takes him a moment to realize that she slapped him.

Before he can recover, she's back on the sidewalk, hailing a cab.

He storms inside. *What the hell just happened?* One minute they were slow dancing. The next, screaming at each other in the cold rain. He's helping people and getting to the bottom of what happened to her father; doesn't she see that? Why is there only one way with these Carpenters?

Ignoring his classmates, he heads straight to the bartender. "Clase Azul Reposado, neat." He pauses, then adds, "Make it a double."

The bartender pours him a glass. Sanjay tosses it back. So much for sipping tequila.

The alcohol goes straight to his chest, stoking the fire within. He was a goddamn fool to come back here. Tom Carpenter is dead. Nothing can change that. And whatever is going on between Next Health and MBH is just more money games, more padding the wallets of CEOs and investors. Not worth any more of his time.

"Another." He puts down a hundred-dollar bill.

The bartender nods and refills his glass.

A gentle tap on his shoulder.

"Guys, I'm not in the mood to tell stories," he says, turning around.

But it isn't Nikhil and the frat boys.

It's Matt DeSalvo.

"I don't know about any stories, SAN-jay. How about we just have a drink?"

* * *

"Shhhhh," says Sanjay as the two men walk through the hospital to Matt's lab.

"What? Why?" yells Matt.

Matt places his arm around Sanjay's shoulder and with it, half his weight. "There's nobody here, anyway," he says, slurring his s's.

They can't get there fast enough. Hospitals are never empty, even at 2 AM. Sanjay hurries Matt across the bridge to the research building. Matt clumsily swipes at the door with his keycard, and Sanjay breathes a sigh of relief.

"We're *here*!" Matt proclaims, his voice echoing through the empty lab.

Sanjay ushers him in and closes the door before anyone hears them.

It was easy to get Matt onboard. Sanjay slipped the bartender a thousand dollars to keep his glass full, then shared the scheme Emma suggested, mentioning the millions Matt could earn advising Sanjay's patients. By the time Sanjay was ready to ask if he could visit the lab, Matt suggested it himself.

But now, as he sits Matt down on a lab bench, Sanjay curses himself. He intended to get him tipsy, not drunk. He asks Matt where the coffee is and goes to fix him a cup.

Over drinks, he learned a great deal about Matt and Ecker's research. The discovery of absoluxir was the culmination of decades of research on blood clotting. Of course when someone gets a cut, clotting is what helps them heal. If even a single protein is missing in the blood clotting pathway, patients can bleed uncontrollably, as in hemophilia.

But there's a negative side to clotting, Sanjay knows. Heart attacks often begin with the rupture of a cholesterol plaque, but it's the *clotting* around the rupture that blocks the artery. It's why people take aspirin for heart attacks. It "thins" the blood.

But existing medicines are too crude: Aspirin lowers a patient's risk of heart attack by only 20 to 30 percent. It also reduces clotting everywhere in the body and thins the lining of the stomach, causing hundreds of thousands of cases of gastrointestinal bleeding in the U.S. each year.

But Ecker and DeSalvo discovered the specific blood clotting protein activated when cholesterol plaques rupture. From that breakthrough, it was a relatively small step to creating an antibody to block that protein. That's how they came up with the name absoluxir: It stopped bad clotting, *absolu*tely.

Aspirin was a bazooka. What they discovered was a smart weapon.

"Normally, a drug like this would take seven to ten years to develop," Matt explained. "But MBH helped us bypass the outdated steps in the process. Ecker was keen to get it to market before a competing researcher at Hopkins could claim the glory. The hospital saw absoluxir as the key to regaining its top ranking."

When Ecker got the call that the trial was being stopped early, Matt and everyone else in the lab assumed the worst. The study was double blind—no one knew who got the drug and who didn't—but they'd all heard anecdotes about patients in the trial getting admitted to the ICU for bleeding. They assumed it was because of absoluxir, but it turned out to be a coincidence. The results showed that patients on absoluxir had even lower rates of heart attack than anticipated, with no major side effects or increased risk of bleeding.

Sanjay returns to Matt, hands him a coffee, and encourages him to drink. After a few minutes, as he starts to sober up, Sanjay asks, "How do you know how much absoluxir patients have in their blood?"

"What do you mean?" asks Matt, putting the mug down on the lab bench.

"You said the effect of the drug depends on the dose. Is there something in the patient's blood you can measure to see how high their absoluxir level is?"

Matt nods slowly. He seems to be weighing whether or not to answer.

"If there is a test," Sanjay adds, "we could potentially sell it to concierge patients. They love tracking their health data—fitness trackers, at-home DNA kits . . . This could be another revenue stream."

Matt perks up, finally. "Yes, of course. And I should say, that assay was my baby."

With a jerk of his head, he wheels his chair around to the far side of the lab. Sanjay follows him to a tidy desk with a light microscope station and an Apple monitor.

"You can't measure absoluxir itself, but that doesn't matter. All that matters is the *activity* level of absoluxir. How much it binds with the protein it targets." Matt fires up the microscope and calibrates it effortlessly, like it's an extension of his hands. "During the trial, we'd test patients at day one, three, seven, twenty-one, and sixty. We ended up doing so many that I had to simplify the assay." He does a fake eyeroll. "You know? So the lab techs could do it without . . ."

"Without being a double doctor?" asks Sanjay, stoking Matt's ego.

Matt shoots him a crooked grin. "Exactly."

He opens a tray and pulls out a vial of red liquid. Sanjay suspects it's some type of synthetic blood. "You place the sample here, enough to cover the base of the plate." He pipettes a few drops onto a plastic tray. "Then you add the binding reagent."

Opening a blue tray, he pulls out a vial of clear liquid. "This part has to be exact, 0.25 ccs. And . . . I can see immediately that the sample has the drug—or more precisely, the effects of the drug." He peers into the microscope, adjusting the focus and light source. "I'd estimate . . ." He continues to tinker. "That the activity level is, oh, 0.35 to 0.40."

He steps back to let Sanjay have a look. All Sanjay can make out is a sea of red.

"To make it easier, I developed a colorimetric test and integrated it into the microscope. You just run this software program I developed—" Matt double-clicks an icon on his desktop. An application window opens, and a loading bar starts spinning. He turns back to Sanjay. "Normal people, you and me, the activity level should be less than 0.05. People on absoluxir, anywhere between 0.2 and 1.0, depending on the dose and timing of administration. Higher than 1.0, and theoretically there's a risk of bleeding."

"Got it."

"And . . . voilà!" On the application window the number 0.38 appears. Matt was spot-on.

* * *

"Hey, you remember the anatomy test? End of second year?" Matt asks casually.

They're on the wet bench side of Ecker's lab, where the experiments are run, sipping beers that Matt had stashed in the back of the lab fridge.

Sanjay's been trying to wear him out with small talk, but this is the last subject he wants to talk about.

Matt laughs. "It was brutal. Especially for me."

Sanjay says nothing, hoping he'll stop there.

"I came down with mono," Matt continues. "Had to take the test a week later, all by myself. By then the cadavers were decomposing. I could barely tell a lung from a liver." He chuckles. "Just glad I passed."

Heat rises up Sanjay's neck.

Matt seems to sense Sanjay's emotions. "But hey." His voice is gentler now. "I just remembered—you didn't do so well. F—. Sorry to bring it up."

Sanjay looks up at Matt, who looks remorseful. "It's fine," he manages.

"I feel bad for Michael Hobbins, too. Not that you need anatomy to be a psychiatrist."

"Michael?" Sanjay remembers him. Nervous guy—but caring, gentle.

"Yeah, he failed, too."

Matt's still speaking, but Sanjay isn't listening anymore. He's back outside that cadaver room, waiting for his turn. Next to him is Michael—fidgeting, dropping his flashcards. They'd been the last two students to take the exam. Sanjay remembers him saying, "We had the most time to study, but also the most time to live in dread."

Both of us failed? And we were the final ones in the cadaver room?

"Those tests back then," Matt is now saying, "don't mean anything. What I remember about you is how you went to the free clinic every week. I don't know how you made the time, but that's what being a real doctor is about. Not memorizing some obscure body parts."

Hot tears well in Sanjay's eyes. He still doesn't fully trust Matt—but right now he's grateful.

Sanjay glances at his watch. 4:15 AM. He's running out of time. He wipes his eyes and forces the memories back down.

"I'm grabbing another beer," he says, rising. "Want one?"

Matt lets out a big yawn. "I don't know if that's a good idea. I'm beat." He takes off his glasses and rubs his eyes.

"Come on," says Sanjay, already heading to the fridge. "Just one more."

* * *

When he returns, Matt's facedown on the lab bench, fast asleep. *Finally.*

He speedwalks back to the microscopy station, adjusts the table to his height, and takes a deep breath. He was never great at benchwork. Closing his eyes, he plays back the steps Matt showed him earlier.

Then he reaches into his pocket and pulls out a plastic specimen bag. The blood from the List C patient.

After Emma gave him the vial, he kept it in the cold storage compartment of his medical bag. Right before picking her up for the reunion, he put the bag into the trunk of his rental. Over drinks with Matt, he excused himself and slipped out to the parking lot to get it, knowing the contents would remain cold for at least a couple hours.

Now he pulls the blood into the glass pipette. His hands shaking, he holds the tip over the plastic tray and pushes down on the plunger.

Just as the sample begins to release, his hand jerks, nearly spilling the blood all over the microscope.

"Damn it!" He stands up straight and takes a deep breath. If only Emma were here. This would be so easy for her.

It takes several minutes, but he succeeds. The loading bar in the software application on Matt's computer whizzes to life. A moment later, a number appears on the screen: 2.24.

Sanjay lets out an audible gasp. Matt said anything above 1.0 posed a risk of bleeding. Not only did this patient receive absoluxir, he received a dangerously high dose.

Sanjay's mind starts racing, but he forces the thoughts down. He needs to leave the lab as fast as possible. It's nearly 5 AM. Soon the first wave of staff will arrive.

Matt's still sound asleep. He considers waking him but decides against it. All-nighters are common in the research world; if Matt sleeps here until morning, nobody will think anything of it.

Instead, he slips his hand into Matt's suit jacket and fishes out the keycard to the lab.

"Thanks, old friend," he whispers.

CHAPTER 33

SANJAY'S FOOTSTEPS ECHO through the hospital parking garage as he makes his way to his car. The weight of what he just learned pulls at his every step.

There's no doubt about it: The patient on List C was dosed with absoluxir. Knowing Tom, that means the rest of the patients on the list were, too—which means someone is treating patients with dangerously high doses of an unapproved drug. It's terrifying.

His car's up ahead, partially hidden behind a pickup truck. As he approaches, a cold shadow passes over him. He scans the dimly lit garage, trying to see into the shadowy corners. Despite the early morning hour, it's filled with cars. But no people.

Could the guys that were tailing his car have tracked him down here?

He waits, straining to hear any footsteps. Nothing. He pulls out his keys.

Then, without warning, two hulking figures emerge from the darkness. Sanjay barely has time to react before the first thug slams him against the door of a nearby car. Pain explodes throughout his body as the second thug's fist connects with his stomach. He doubles over, the wind knocked out of him.

Heavy blows drive him to his knees, each hit blurring the world around him.

Then, just as abruptly, it stops. He's panting, struggling to focus through the pain. His eyes trace up from the military-style boots and pants to the men's eyes, glowering at him out of black ski masks.

"That was a warning," one of them growls.

"Leave town and stay the fuck away from Next Health," the other hisses.

They vanish back into the darkness, melting away like they were never there. Sanjay collapses to the ground, gasping for breath. Is someone calling his name?

He tries to listen, but everything goes black.

CHAPTER 34

BEEP. BEEP. BEEP.

Sanjay's eyes flutter open to the familiar sound of the cardiac monitor. Except this time he's the one looking up from the hospital bed.

Cassie's face comes into view.

"What happened?" Sanjay whispers, clutching at the stabbing pain in his chest. His hand touches a compression bandage. Grimacing, he feels around. His entire torso is covered in bandages.

"You got busted up pretty badly yesterday, that's what," says Cassie, crossing her arms. Tears gleam in her eyes.

Fear grips Sanjay. "Wait, am I at MB—"

He starts to push off the bed, but Cassie gently guides him back down. "No. You're at Boston Medical Center. Dr. Olopade admitted you under his supervision. I made sure of that."

"How—"

"John found you. I told him to track down the car that was tailing you, the green Pontiac." Sanjay nods, though the movement hurts. "He didn't get a look at the guys. Whoever it was clearly did this to scare you off. They didn't touch your face. Or break any major bones. It might be MBH. You were just coming from that lab. Maybe someone thought *you* were stealing absoluxir—"

"It was Next Health—or someone affiliated with them."

"What!" Cassie steps back, her eyes widening. "How can you be sure?"

Sanjay fills her in on his two assailants and their message to him: *Leave town and stay the fuck away from Next Health.*

"Sanjay, shit. They must have seen you on the security footage! I knew I shouldn't have sent you to that clinic. I feel terrible, I—"

Another deep stab to his heart. Cassie reaches over to help him, but he waves her off. She looks at him with pity. And he catches something else in her eyes.

"Tell me," he says.

"Emma texted that she doesn't want to see you anymore." She hands him his phone. "John found it next to you."

"Is she safe?"

"She's in her apartment. I have someone watching her, just in case. But if this is Next Health, she'll be fine. She knows nothing about them."

Sanjay sighs and rubs his cheek where Emma slapped him. He's made a mess of everything.

He looks up at Cassie. Her face is still tense. "What else?"

"Three more patients canceled their contracts. A dozen more are on the verge." She sighs. "I'm going to have to put the jet up for sale."

He shakes his head in disbelief.

"What do you want to do?" Cassie asks.

His practice is crumbling. Emma wants nothing to do with him. If he stays, he risks getting hurt again—or worse, ending up like Tom.

It all makes his decision easy.

"Get me on the first flight out of Boston. We're done here."

She looks at him, incredulous. "You're not going anywhere, Sanjay. You have bruises all over your chest and back, a broken rib—"

"Jacqueline can take care of all of that. I can, too."

Cassie crosses her arms, her face still, her eyes cold. "The police want to talk to you. When they're done, I have to show you what Paul Klein and I found out about Next Health."

"Burn it, for all I care. The police, I'll deal with. After that, we're leaving."

"What about Emma? What about Neil? And Tom?"

"What about her?" Sanjay says, his voice rising. "She doesn't want anything to do with me, and she's safer if I'm gone, if we drop this whole business. Neil and I will find a way back from this. We always do. And Tom?" He scoffs derisively. "That's all ashes and dust now."

He tries to turn away, but a sharp pain shoots through his chest, doubling him over.

"Why are you pushing back?" he asks after he collects himself. "Weren't you the one telling me to leave?"

Cassie sighs. "That was before we found out there's something really wrong with this place, Sanjay. Patients are getting hurt! Doctors, too. We need—"

"This place has had something wrong with it for a long time. And I can't fix it."

She looks away. She's disappointed in him, but he doesn't care. He closes his eyes, a wave of exhaustion crashing over him.

* * *

The next day Sanjay hobbles out of the hospital, braced against Cassie for support. Each step sends a jolt of pain through his chest, triggering memories of the past few days—Emma's sharp slap; the brutal attack; the chilling realization that patients were treated with dangerous doses of absoluxir.

As John drives them to the airport, Sanjay stares blankly out the window. He needs to find a way to share what he knows about Next Health and absoluxir with the police. The two officers who debriefed him at the hospital seemed sincere, but they weren't trained in medicine. Piecing together the complex medical science won't be easy—but it's the best he can offer.

His thoughts drift to Emma. How in a way, he's ghosting her again.

"Stop the car," he says, more loudly than he intended.

Cassie pivots to look at him, surprise flashing across her face.

"I need to say goodbye to Emma," he explains.

Cassie nods, and he sees a hint of a smile tugging at her lips. "We'll be fine," she says. "As long as we keep the car running and make it quick."

* * *

A young couple in running gear and headphones come jogging out of Emma's building, where Sanjay is waiting. They pause to gawk at his injuries, then feeling sorry for him, hold the door for him to step inside.

At Emma's unit, he knocks. He hears shuffling behind the door, but it doesn't open. He knocks again. "Emma, it's Sanjay!"

"Leave me alone."

"Emma, look. I'm sorry about the other night, okay? I'm sorry—"

An elderly man in house slippers emerges from the next unit and gives him a scowl on his way to the trash chute. After the man goes back to his apartment, Sanjay tries again, more gently. "Can you just open the door?"

Silence.

"I'm leaving and I wanted to say goodbye. The right way this time."

Nothing. He turns to leave. That's when he hears the deadbolt.

The door opens, and Emma's face comes into view. His heart lurches; he desperately wants to take her into his arms.

"Look, you don't need to—" She looks up from the door handle and freezes, eyes widening.

Sanjay shifts under her gaze, suddenly aware of how stiffly he's standing, his arm unconsciously bracing his ribs.

Her jaw drops. "Sanjay! What happened?"

She ushers him into her living room and settles him on her sofa. From the kitchen, she fetches an ice pack. "Here," she says, placing it over his chest. "For the swelling."

A new ache pulls at his heart.

"I'm okay, Emma. Thanks. But I need to tell you something." He sets the ice pack aside and locks eyes with her.

There is so much he needs to share—about the three lists, the threat Tom received, Next Health and their thugs, absoluxir. But first, what he should have told her years ago.

Head down, heart up, go.

* * *

It was the end of second year, the week before Sanjay, Emma, and Neil would leave behind lectures, labs, and exams and finally begin caring for real patients.

But first, there was the comprehensive anatomy exam.

Anatomy was considered the hardest test at MBMS—the last in the gauntlet. Although failing was unheard of, each year bright-eyed med students broke down in tears during the exam, adding to its infamy.

Sanjay entered the cavernous anatomy lab alone. No classmates; no proctor. Just rows of open cadavers—men and women of different ages, some healthy, some ravaged by disease. Each body had dozens of numbered flags marking specific structures. The task: Identify as many as possible.

The hour passed in a blur.

The next day, Sanjay joined the crowd outside the lecture hall to check the posted scores.

For once, he let himself believe he might've done well—and scanned the rank-ordered list from the top.

His name wasn't there.

He moved lower.

And lower.

Until he reached the bottom.

He had failed.

The gossip began before he could even walk away.

"Did Sanjay get too cocky?"

"I warned him he was spending too much time at that free clinic."

"Guess that rules out matching at MBH for residency."

How could I have failed? Sanjay wandered the campus, racking his brain for answers.

Sure, he had the late nights at the free clinic, and was distracted by his new relationship with Emma—but he had felt okay before the test and had crammed for weeks.

Was it possible the flags had been moved just before his turn? It would mean his answers would be marked wrong, even if he'd done everything right.

But how?

It was too far-fetched.

Occam's Razor: The simplest explanation was usually the right one. He had failed, plain and simple.

He thought he could do it all—get top grades, win Tom's respect, be with Emma.

But he'd lost focus. Let himself get distracted from the patient in front of him—just like the doctor who misdiagnosed his mother.

That was the real failure, and he deserved to crash and burn for it.

That night, he waited until dark to return to his dorm and pack. He wanted to say good-bye—to Emma, to Neil—but the shame was too much.

He boarded the first bus home and put MBMS behind him.

* * *

Now Sanjay sighs and forces himself to meet Emma's eyes. "That's why I just left. It wasn't the bad grade. I felt like I didn't belong at MBH—or with you. That I wasn't good enough."

Emma nods, tears filling her eyes. He looks away, the weight of her gaze almost unbearable.

As he relives it now, he wonders if he hadn't missed something crucial. The student who took the test right after him failed, too.

Didn't that make sabotage more likely? If his test had been tampered with, anyone who followed him would be impacted as well.

Emma's voice cuts in. "Sanjay, why didn't you tell me sooner? I cared about you."

"I tried to later, even after you told me never to contact you again," he says. "But in the moment? I was in a dark place. I didn't know if I'd ever come back."

"I understand."

But she doesn't. A wave of nausea comes over him. "It's worse than that. I . . ."

She puts her hand on his.

"When I got home, I told my parents I was dropping out of med school. But that meant they'd have to pay back my scholarship. Two years' worth of tuition. That night, I overhead them talking. To make ends meet, they'd have to work longer hours, miss a long-overdue trip to India to see family, even cancel Neela's dream wedding. It made me sick to my stomach. I was supposed to be my family's ticket into the middle class, and here I was, hurtling them into poverty."

Emma looks at him, her lips trembling.

"In the medicine cabinet, I found the oxycodone my mom took when her rheumatoid arthritis got bad. I can't remember the rest, but the ER doctors said I took the full bottle."

"Oh, Sanjay, no," Emma whispers. "No, no, no."

"I knew exactly what I was doing. But Neela heard me collapse and called 911 in time."

He hangs his head. He's spent.

"Oh, Sanjay, I don't know what to say." He feels her arms over his shoulders, rubbing his back, as if trying to knead the darkness away. "I'm so sorry."

He stares at the floor. "I didn't see your missed calls and messages, not until weeks later. My parents took my phone away, rightfully. When I came back to school at the end of the summer, after your mom died, I tried to get in touch, but you were so angry—and I don't fault you for that. I was too ashamed to tell you what happened. I'm sorry, Emma."

Emma lays her head on his shoulder.

"I never left you," says Sanjay.

"I see that now."

"And I always kept my promise to put patients first."

She lifts her head and looks into his eyes. "I'm beginning to see that, too."

They both take a deep breath. It's time to move on.

"Sanjay," she says, her eyes locked on his. "Tell me everything that's happened."

* * *

Ten minutes later, they're both leaning over his differential diagnosis, the sheet spread out on her kitchen table. He's been careful to fold the section about her father underneath. He still suspects Next Health played a role in Tom's death, but without a theory to explain how, he doesn't want to alarm Emma.

	What?	Who?	Why?
List A	Unnecessary procedures	Neil	To be department chair
List B	Referrals from Next Health	Hadley	To pay back investors
List C	Absoluxir	?	?

"Let me make sure I have this right," says Emma, pointing to the top of the page. "List A is unnecessary GI procedures, likely pushed by Neil to become head of his department. But all that's over now."

Sanjay nods. He left out the part about doing rounds with Neil and the unnecessary heart biopsy. It's not his place to get between friends, and after he leaves, Emma will need Neil even more.

"List B," Emma continues, "is patients who got referred by Next Health to MBH, in some sort of kickback scheme. No patients are getting hurt; it's all about profit. But they threatened my father and sent those thugs after you. Presumably to save their IPO and pay back the shady investors Barnett told you about."

Again he nods.

"List C is the scary one." She shakes her head. "Patients who got transferred to the ICU for bleeding after they were injected with absoluxir at potentially deadly levels. Outside of a clinical trial."

"Yes."

She puts the paper down and shakes her head. "This is insane."

It's impossible to disagree. *But ultimately*, Sanjay thinks, folding the paper, *the root cause is a system that puts profits ahead of patients.*

It's time to go. He squeezes her shoulder, a sigh catching in his chest at what might have been. "It's scary but fortunately, all the bleeding cases in List C were months ago—"

"But—"

"And none of the patients died—at least not from the injection itself." He feels a wave of nausea even as he speaks. It's a sorry excuse for leaving, and he knows it.

Still, he forces himself to stand, a touch of lightheadedness unsteadying him. "I have to go, Emma. Those thugs from Next Health are probably watching me. The last thing I want to do is put you in harm's way."

He strides toward the door, hyperaware that Emma hasn't left her couch.

"Stay and fight," she calls out behind him.

He takes a step back, shaking his head. He can't. He's running. Back to his lucrative practice, his private plane, the bottom of a thousand-dollar bottle of tequila. The system is fucked—the world is fucked—and he wants nothing to do with MBH.

But somehow, for the first time in two days, the pain in his chest eases when he hears her words.

Emma stands and walks over to him. "Remember what my father used to say about good doctors and great doctors? 'A good doctor treats the patient. A great doctor fights for all patients.'"

The words stagger Sanjay. He remembers the saying, but it never made sense to him. He stumbles back into the living room, slumps on the couch.

Should he have fought for his mom when she was misdiagnosed? Should he have fought for his job after MBH put him on leave? Should he have fought for Emma after she left for Sweden to get her PhD?

All his life, Sanjay has avoided fights. He thought great doctors needed to focus on the patient in front of them. But if he'd made different decisions, maybe his mom wouldn't be living in pain. Maybe he'd still be at MBH, and he and Emma would be together. He steadies himself before he lets himself consider one last thought.

If he'd stayed and fought, maybe Tom Carpenter would still be alive.

Is this why Tom paged him? Not to save himself. Tom knew it was too late for that. Not to uncover the scandal at MBH. In his dying moments, Tom couldn't have known that Sanjay would piece it all together.

No. Maybe Tom paged Sanjay to bring him back to MBH—and the fight—and give him a second chance.

He looks down at his bandages, then over at Emma, and he feels his resolve growing.

It's time to make things right.

CHAPTER

35

SANJAY EASES HIMSELF up the stairway to his jet and slides into his usual seat. His chest still hurts, but he feels better than he has in days—months, even.

"Good to be back?" asks Cassie, looking up from her computer.

Sanjay eyes the narrow quarters, the empty walls, and shrugs. "The plane—not really. But the chance to take the fight to these bastards? Hell, yes."

According to the *Globe* reporter, Jim Hadley, Next Health's CFO, has been traveling the country, doing a "road show" for the upcoming IPO. His next stop is an invite-only healthcare event in the Hamptons, an hour's flight from Boston. That's where they're headed now.

As a precaution, Sanjay asked Emma to leave town for a while. She mentioned taking the opportunity to visit an old friend in New Haven.

"All set here?" the captain asks, standing in the doorway to the cockpit.

"Nope, not yet," says Cassie.

Sanjay's lips purse. "Who are we—"

On cue, the port side of the plane tilts down.

"What the—"

Two huge men enter the main cabin, keeping their heads bent to avoid catching the roof. Sanjay can't believe his eyes. These guys are almost as wide as they are tall.

"Petrov sent them," says Cassie, and Sanjay smiles in spite of himself; hard to believe the Viagra overdose was only a week ago. "I know you think Hadley won't try to hurt you in front of his investors, but we need backup, just in case."

Sanjay just shrugs, and Cassie smiles, taking the win. "By the way," she says, "Petrov's cardiac stress test came back. He's getting two stents put in."

Sanjay watches the two men squeeze into their seats, still in awe of their size.

"I haven't figured out a way into the event yet," he says to Cassie. "Klein told me it's restricted to big-time players, people with enough money to invest in the IPO."

Cassie turns her laptop around and points at the screen. She sounds implausibly relaxed. "You're due to call Ms. Sophie Jansen. We got the results of the biopsy you did on the yacht in Italy. Melanoma, as you suspected. But the pathologist said you got all of it out."

"That's great, Cassie, but right now—"

"According to the fitness tracker data she shares with us," says Cassie, tapping the map on the screen. "Ms. Jansen is currently at her summer house. In the Hamptons."

One step ahead, as always.

* * *

The Hamptons event is everything Sanjay despises about healthcare, all in one place.

Health insurance CEOs colluding on next year's premium hikes over Beluga caviar. Impassioned speeches on health equity by hospital executives whose boards are made up entirely of old white men. Private equity investors bemoaning unfair competition on the back nine with senior administrators from Medicare and the FDA.

"I should have dressed up more," says Sophie Jansen as she enters the hotel, Sanjay at her side. "I thought this was a . . . work conference."

"For these people," he says, and he can hear the derision in his voice, "this is work."

Around the room, dozens of healthcare executives, nearly all men in dark suits and ties, sample oysters and lobster rolls. Lots of gray hair and shiny, bald heads.

But no bodyguards. So far, Sanjay's instincts are right.

"Hello! I was fishing for a compliment." Sophie puckers her lips and strikes a pose.

Smiling, Sanjay turns toward her. "Oh, I'm sorry, Sophie. You look lovely."

She eyes him up and down. "'Lovely'? Am I a painting?"

She's doing him a favor, so Sanjay steps back to take a proper look. In her green and yellow flowered silk dress, Sophie exudes a sophisticated yet sexy vibe. Which would normally be a real turn-on for him. But today, she might as well be a storefront mannequin. His focus is locating Jim. That's supposed to be the easy part. Getting him alone? That's the challenge.

He loops his arm with Sophie's and guides her to the check-in desk. Barnett said there would be side meetings happening, that they'd be his best chance of cornering Jim.

The host is dressed like an auctioneer at Sotheby's and has the same pretentious demeanor. When Sophie gives her name, he whisks her away to a private luncheon. Sanjay tries to follow, but a hand bars his way and a low voice murmurs, "Sorry, high net-worth individuals only."

Sighing, he picks up the conference agenda, embossed on scented paper, and sees that Jim's keynote is in an hour.

* * *

It's a scene out of a TED talk. CFO Jim Hadley stands onstage in a darkened room, wearing a microphone headset and facing one of two large projection screens. He and the audience are engrossed in a patient video produced by Next Health.

"I had no idea that lurking in my ovaries was a cyst. The day I signed up for Next Health, I got my full body CT." Dramatic music. "When the surgeons at MBH opened me up, that cyst turned out to be cancerous. Now I'm cancer-free and appreciating the little things in life." Uplifting music. "Thank you, Next Health."

The video ends to resounding applause. When it quiets down, Jim's voice booms through the speakers. "Guys, I'm here to talk about the numbers, but I can't help but start with our mission. Why we do what we do." He bows his head and presses his palms together to form a namaste.

Sanjay rolls his eyes at the video—and the gesture. For every patient like the woman in the video, a thousand more would be exposed to unnecessary radiation, which *increases* their risk of cancer.

But when he looks around the room, he sees heads nodding. There's even a tear or two.

Cassie's plan is to wait for the Q&A, then have one of Petrov's guys pull the fire alarm while the other grabs Hadley in the chaos. Not the most original—or elegant—approach, but it would have to do.

As the lights come on at the end of the video, the audience sees Jim as an enviable sixty-something fellow executive who in a few short weeks will be worth billions.

Sanjay sees something very different—and with it, a better way to get Jim alone. He texts Cassie to stand down.

Following the Q&A, people rush the stage. Probably investors hoping to get in on the IPO or hospital executives wanting exclusive partnerships with Next Health. Sanjay bypasses the line and slips Jim a folded note with his name and number on the outside. On the inside is a message: "How long has your urine been dark?"

* * *

An hour later, Sanjay sits across from Jim Hadley in Hadley's hotel suite. He's recording the meeting and Cassie's listening in, with Petrov's men on standby.

Light pours through the huge bay windows, and Sanjay sees that Jim's in even worse shape than he thought. His skin and pupils are yellowed, his face hollow. There's even a slight bulge over the right side of his belly.

"How'd you know?" asks Jim. The TED talk voice is gone. What's left is thin and tremulous.

"Pretty simple, honestly. Onstage, even under the artificial lights, I could see your skin was jaundiced. Jaundice has many causes, but you aren't just thin. The muscles on your temples are wasting. You don't get that from not working out. It's most commonly cancer. Cancer plus jaundice in an otherwise healthy sixty-year-old? I didn't figure you for a smoker."

"Never touched the stuff."

Sanjay nods. "I played the odds and went with pancreatic cancer. When the tumor is big enough to cause jaundice, it affects the liver and causes the body's bilirubin levels to spike. Conjugated bilirubin can only be excreted in the urine, and when it does—"

"The urine gets dark. Impressive, Dr. Sanjay."

Sanjay signed his note "Dr. Patel." Apparently, Hadley's done his homework, too.

Jim seems to read his mind. "I had my staff look into you. You wouldn't believe the crazies that try to get to me. But you? Apparently, you're one of the best doctors in the country. I texted your client, Richard Beane. He told me you saved his life. Twice."

"I get lucky sometimes," Sanjay says mildly.

"So here we are. I just haven't figured out why."

Right to the point. Sanjay will return the favor. He steels his voice. "I'm here to tell you and your murderous thugs to back off."

A flicker of recognition crosses Hadley's face, but he masks it. "I'm calling security," he says, reaching for his phone.

"I'm not here to hurt you, Jim. The cancer is doing that all on its own. I just want to talk."

Jim hesitates, then nods. "Fine. You have two minutes."

Sanjay leans in. "I know about the illegal dealings with MBH, the kickbacks."

"Kickbacks? That's absurd! I've never—"

"Cut the bullshit, Jim! You gave me two minutes, and now you're wasting my time. Here." Sanjay tosses Jim his phone, the device clattering across the table, open to the documents Cassie uncovered.

Jim's fingers tremble as he thumbs through the documents. "I don't know how you found these, but they weren't obtained legally, which means—"

"That they're not admissible in court? Do I look like a fucking lawyer?" Sanjay snatches the phone back, swipes to another screen, and thrusts it back at Jim, whose eyes widen at the draft post displayed on the app.

@medhack4ever: #hackerfans, Next Health should be called Last Health, as in the last place you should go for healthcare. These files I "found" show they are getting kickbacks on the backs of our bodies.

"I don't know anything about social media," says Sanjay. "But my assistant, she's a whiz, and I have celebrity patients with millions of followers. If you don't call off your thugs, she'll post this. Once it's out, it won't matter what a court of law says. Your investors will panic, and your IPO will collapse."

The remaining color drains from Jim's face. "Don't do this. Please. I'll do whatever you want." Sweat beads on his brow. "My wife, my kids . . . I'm dead already from the cancer. But the investors . . ." He swallows hard. "They said if something happens to their money, to the IPO, they'll hurt my family."

"Slow down, Jim." Sanjay doesn't like making people sick. His calling is the opposite. "Tell me everything."

As Barnett surmised, in the last round of funding, Jim Hadley took money from bad actors. The Russian mafia, in fact. When his initial attempts to turn Next Health around didn't work, they demanded answers. MBH had already approached Jim to set up a system of legalized kickbacks disguised as "value-based care." He initially refused, but now he had no choice.

MBH effectively paid Next Health for each referral. Overnight, a primary care visit that would typically bring Next Health one or two hundred dollars in revenue began generating thousands. And MBH kept its hospital full.

"I still have no idea how Tom found out. A month ago, he called me. I begged him to drop his investigation, but he wouldn't listen. Instead, he started questioning our doctors—"

Sanjay slams his hand down on the table. "So you had him killed?"

"No. My PIs only threatened him! I told them they wouldn't get paid if they hurt him!"

"You think that justifies what you did?" Sanjay lunges across the room, grabbing Jim by the collar. "What about what they did to me?"

Jim's whole body is trembling, and gripping him this tightly, Sanjay can feel how frail he is. The cancer is almost palpable, ravaging the man's insides, draining his strength. Disgusted with himself, he lets go, and Jim sputters, gasping for air. For a moment, they just stare at each other.

Then Jim says, "You have my word: No one will harm you or anyone else you care about."

Sanjay scoffs in exasperation. "Why should I believe you?"

Hadley's phone is already in his hands. "I've texted my head of security to join us."

A sharp knock sounds at the door, which swings open to reveal a hulking man, his grizzled facial hair and dark eyes radiating menace. Sanjay sits back, a chill racing down his spine. Even without a mask, he knows. It's one of the men who jumped him.

"Did you attack this man?" asks Jim.

"I did," the head of security replies, unapologetic. "He was a problem for our investors. We needed him gone."

"I explicitly said no violence!" Jim snaps. "You let *me* worry about our investors. I know what those criminals want, and it's high time I gave it to them. You're fired. Leave your badge and my hotel room key."

The man strides past Sanjay, a looming shadow. His belongings land on the coffee table with a thud.

"And if you want to keep your shares in the company," Jim spits out, "you'll never bother this man again."

The door slams shut, allowing Sanjay to breathe again. He locks eyes with Jim, then loosens his jaw and stands to leave.

"I didn't mean to hurt anyone," Jim calls out from behind.

Sanjay stops at the door and turns, his face twisted with disgust. "No. That's the problem with you healthcare executives. You hide in spreadsheets, pretending to wipe your hands of your decisions. But you can't. They're covered with blood."

* * *

Back in the hotel lobby, Sanjay hugs Cassie, then fills her in on his run-in with Hadley and his head of security.

"You did good," she says, patting him on the back. "I'm proud of you for fighting."

Sanjay smiles. They've stopped the danger from Next Health, and Cassie's coming up with a plan to tell MBH's board about the three lists. Although the illegal absoluxir dosing has stopped, the board needs to get to the bottom of who did it and why.

With luck, they'll also be able to wind down MBH's relationship with Next Health, too. Sanjay's only hope is that they don't scapegoat Neil for List A; the pressures he faced to order unnecessary procedures are as much the board's fault as anyone else's.

His phone buzzes in his pocket, interrupting his train of thought. It's Harper Williams, the ICU fellow.

"Dr. Williams, to what do I own the pleasure—"

"It's Mr. Vasquez," she says, cutting him off. "He's . . ." A sharp breath fills the silence. "He's been transferred back to the ICU. For bleeding."

"No," Sanjay says. Then, more softly, "It can't be."

He lets the phone fall to his side. Fear paralyzes him.

"Dr. Sanjay?" he hears. "Hello?"

Snapping back to the moment, he puts the phone back against his ear. "Do everything you can to save him. I'm on my way."

CHAPTER

36

THERE'S A SLIGHT breeze when Emma steps onto Yale's campus. The quad is filled with students tossing Frisbees or lying on the grass, reading. She envies them. Her world feels so much heavier.

Ever since Ecker told her what Tom did to get her mom into the clinical trial, something has been nagging at her. She needs to know the full story behind what happened a decade ago. And with her dad gone, there's only one person who knows the truth.

Professor Abigail Steinmetz insisted they meet outside, away from her lab and students. Emma finds her on a bench in the quad, reading an issue of *Nature*. She wears a heavy brown coat, though the day isn't cold.

"Professor Steinmetz?"

The woman looks up. She has small, bright blue eyes, and looks like the pictures Emma saw online. "Please, call me Abby."

"Thank you for meeting me."

"Of course." Abby looks intently at Emma. "My goodness, your eyes . . . Looks like your mother's genes won out. I wish I could have done more for her." Her hands tighten on the magazine. "But we were too late getting our work out there."

Emma nods, trying not to cry. "Can you tell me what happened? From the beginning?"

She, Tom, and Henry Ecker were classmates at MBMS, Abby explains.

"Your father was the best of us. Henry the most ambitious." There were very few women in the class, and most faculty expected Abby to marry a doctor and stop working. "Not Tom. He pushed me to go into science. That was my true passion."

Tom had no interest in research. He had served in Vietnam and knew he wanted to take care of patients full-time. And back then, physician-scientist spots were rare. Henry and Abby were the two chosen from their class. But at graduation, she bested Ecker to win the award for the best graduate research. "Our relationship went downhill after that," she tells Emma.

Years later, Abby was on track to become chair of medicine at MBH. She had done groundbreaking research in oncology and developed a promising new drug. "The first clinical application I went for was breast cancer," she says. "Because it was a woman's health problem, it got less funding than other cancers. I was determined to give those women a fighting chance."

To her delight, her clinical trial was oversubscribed. "Women started referring other women," she says, her eyes shining at the memory. "It was almost like a movement."

Then Ecker came to her with a request: Tom was desperate to get Maria into the trial, and he'd asked Ecker to assist. "He said Tom would never ask me directly. That he'd only be agreeable if I broached the topic myself. I had no reason not to believe him. I considered it for several days and ultimately decided it was the right thing to do. There's such a thing as compassionate use, as you know. We didn't call it that back then, but the idea was the same. In some ways, we were ahead of our time."

She says this last part with a sad smile, referring to what the FDA now calls Expanded Access—a pathway that allows patients with no other options to receive investigational drugs outside of a clinical trial.

"I went to Tom and told him I'd found a way to get your mother in the trial. In retrospect, he seemed surprised, but I chalked that up to anxiety. He asked me in every way possible whether giving Maria the drug would deprive another candidate. I told him it wouldn't, which was true. We didn't have a shortage. The only limitation was the number of patients the IRB allowed us to enroll in the trial. My plan was to give your mom the drug, but not include her in the study, so the results wouldn't be biased. She wasn't taking anyone else's spot."

A wave of relief crashes over Emma. What Tom did was wrong, but it didn't come at the expense of another patient. She'd have to find the right time to tell Sanjay. It might help him make peace with his mentor's memory.

"The decision weighed on him for days. But then your dad had an encounter with you, and it made up his mind."

Emma's heart flutters. "With me?"

"Yes. I remember it quite clearly."

Maria had been hospitalized for pneumonia, a complication of her chemo, and Emma had come home from med school to help out. After staying in his wife's hospital room until she fell asleep, Tom came home.

"Apparently you were reading under the covers of your bed with a flashlight," Abby says.

Emma smiles. A habit from childhood, one she picked up again when her mom got sick.

"When he saw you, he said, 'Emma, what's wrong?' And you said, 'If Mom dies, I'll be alone.' It broke his heart. That night he called, woke me up, and said, 'I'm in.'"

Emma can't hold the tears back anymore. She starts sobbing, and Abby holds her tight until she recovers.

"You know what happened next. But what you may not know is that, six months later, Ecker came to my office to tell me he was reporting me to the IRB for unethical conduct. If it went through, my research career would be over. I'd be lucky to get a job teaching at a community college."

Abby's blue eyes seem grayer now.

"I realized this was his endgame. The current chair of medicine was about to retire, and I was favored over Ecker to replace him. Chairs at MBH hold their position for twenty, even thirty years. Ecker had one shot, and he took it."

Emma cannot hide her shock—and disgust. Backstabbing is common in the competitive world of academia, but never anything this blatant.

"He offered me door number two. Leave MBH, find a position somewhere else. If I did, he wouldn't tell a soul what I'd done. That's how I ended up here." Abby purses her lips like she's tasted something sour. "Before I agreed, I talked to a lawyer. He drew up an affidavit for Ecker to sign. It stated that he not only knew what happened with your mom, but that he was directly involved. It was my insurance policy."

She pulls a plastic folder out from under her jacket and hands it to Emma.

"That was the last I heard of this business until a month ago. The MBH board contacted me, told me Tom was being considered for physician-in-chief, but they'd received an anonymous tip about the trial." Abby's eyes spark with anger. "In that moment, I knew."

Emma's breath catches, and Abby puts her hands on hers. "Only three people knew what happened with your mom—Tom, Ecker, and me. I made sure of that."

Emma needs to hear her say it. "So that means . . . ?"

"The anonymous tip telling the board to investigate Tom? It was Ecker."

CHAPTER

37

SANJAY ARRIVES AT MBH and scrambles up the stairs. As he reaches the main walkway to the ICU, he hears a code called over the PA, "Dr. Cart, ICU bed 14. Dr. Cart, ICU bed 14."

Someone has gone into cardiac arrest.

"Please don't be Vasquez," he says under his breath, breaking into a full sprint.

Plowing through the ICU doors, he scans for bed 14. He sees a dozen people in white coats and pink scrubs standing outside a patient's room, their faces tense. That's the one.

Through the din, he hears Neil barking orders at the code team. Sanjay pushes his way past the crowd. It's Vasquez, all right, lying on the bed. Two doctors stand over him, doing chest compressions. They're in bright yellow gowns, covered in blood. At the head of the bed, the anesthesia team is attempting to intubate Vasquez; below, two surgeons are placing a central line through his groin.

Pools of blood cover the bed, the floors. Even the walls are smattered with red and violaceous mucous. Sanjay suspects hematemesis, projectile vomiting of blood.

He reaches the foot of the bed. "Step aside," he says, elbowing Neil away.

Neil turns and gives him a look of surprise. "Sanjay? This is my ICU—"

Sanjay grabs the defibrillator paddles from Neil's hands. "I'm not asking." He looks at the charge nurse and says, "I'm Dr. Cart now"—the doctor in charge of the code—"pager number 3629. And I want quiet!" he yells across the room. "No talking unless it's about the patient. And anyone who doesn't need to be here—leave. Now."

Within seconds, all that can be heard are the grunts of the two men pushing on Vasquez's chest.

"What's the rhythm?" Sanjay asks.

A voice from behind him says, "PEA, Dr. Sanjay."

It's Harper Williams. A small dose of relief comes over him.

But PEA's not a shockable rhythm, he thinks, cursing under his breath. He runs the differential diagnosis in his head—hypoxia, profound acidosis, tension pneumothorax, drug overdose, sepsis—though the cause is obvious. It's spattered all around the room.

Still, he can't afford to miss anything. "Give me the story," he says.

Harper says, "Forty-four-year-old man admitted for acute respiratory distress syndrome, recently extubated, stable on the floor until he started suddenly hemorrhaging. First rectal bleeding. Then hematemesis. Transferred to the ICU for endoscopy before he coded."

"Hemoglobin level?" asks Sanjay.

"Six point one," says Harper.

"Two units packed red cells," Sanjay commands. "And type and cross two more."

"Already given," says the charge nurse.

"Well, give two more!" he snaps, and the code team jumps into action. "When was his last dose of epi?"

"Three minutes ago," the pharmacist replies. "Still have two minutes left."

"Do it. Now!"

She looks at Neil, but he says nothing.

After five more minutes of CPR, Neil turns to Sanjay. "Dr. Sanjay, there's nothing more we can do—"

Sanjay thinks of Vasquez's daughters. He can't give up now.

"Your compressions aren't deep enough!" he barks at the residents.

He stands with crossed arms for ten seconds, then takes matters into his own hands, pushing aside one of the residents. Blood spatters over his clothes and face. He pushes harder.

"Dr. Sanjay," calls out Neil.

He ignores him.

"Dr. Sanjay! Sanj!"

Sanjay looks up.

"It's time to call it," says Neil, his eyes soft. "I know you care about this patient, but this isn't the way." He sighs. "We've been at it for fifteen minutes. He's been in PEA the whole time. There's just too much blood."

Sanjay looks around the room. Everyone seems to be nodding in agreement. Through the glass wall, he sees Vasquez's wife, a look of horror on her face. He looks back down at Vasquez. His face is waxy and blue. *I'm just mutilating her dead husband's body now*, he thinks.

He feels himself pull away.

"Time of death—" says Neil.

"7:27 PM," says Sanjay, looking up at the clock.

He looks at Vasquez's face one last time, then steps away. He quietly thanks the staff, exits the room, and turns to Vasquez's wife, who stands motionless. Probably in shock. She's alone because of him—a feeling that will never go away.

"I'm so sorry," he manages to say, putting a trembling hand on her shoulder.

Then he stumbles out of the ICU and collapses on the ground, blood from his gown smearing the tiled wall and floor.

How many more times will he miss the diagnosis? How many more patients will get hurt before he finally figures out what's going on?

Vasquez was dosed with absoluxir. He's certain of that. But who would do such a thing?

The ICU door hisses open. It's Neil.

"Sanjay—"

Sanjay leaps to his feet and grabs Neil by the collar. "Did you have something to do with this?"

Neil's face twists in shock. "What? Why would you—"

He yanks Neil closer. "Did. You. Do. This?"

"I'm not even sure what you mean," Neil stammers, confusion etched across his features.

"You didn't inject him with absoluxir?"

Neil's pupils dilate, a flicker of fear flashing through his eyes. "What? No!"

Sanjay releases him. "If you did, and I find out—which I will—you're dead to me."

The ICU door hisses open to reveal Vasquez's wife, and Sanjay instinctively steps back from Neil, lowering his gaze out of respect.

"Thank you, Dr. Desai and Dr. Sanjay, for everything you did for Eddie," she says, her voice trembling but composed. "You both are incredible doctors, and I'm so grateful to you."

On the final words, her facade cracks, and she breaks down, sobbing. Sanjay wraps his arms around her and holds her tight. "I'm going to make this right, Mrs. Vasquez," he whispers.

She pulls away and looks up at him, eyes red. "How can you? My husband is—"

"I promise you, I will," he says, and takes his leave.

CHAPTER 38

"I CAN'T BELIEVE IT," says Emma.

They're back in her apartment, standing over the kitchen counter. Shortly after leaving the Hamptons, Sanjay texted her that it was safe to return to Boston. He's just shared the devastating news about Vasquez. Together with List C, Vasquez's death points to a disturbing pattern of patients being illicitly injected with absoluxir—one that's far from over.

"Why would anyone treat a patient with an unproven medication?" Emma's face contorts. "Who would do such a thing?"

Despite his confrontation with Neil, Sanjay refuses to believe it's him. "What if someone was testing the drug on those patients?" he says slowly.

"Testing it?" Emma sounds horrified. "Is that what you think this is about? Secret experiments on patients?"

Sanjay nods gravely. "When I looked at List C again, I noticed that nearly every patient had a bleeding complication. That suggests they received higher doses of absoluxir than the ones given in the clinical trial."

Emma's jaw drops. "But there are over two dozen patients on that list!"

"Twenty-six, to be exact," he says. His face darkens. "Plus Vasquez."

She collapses onto a counter stool, the blood draining from her cheeks. "This is a disaster, Sanjay. It violates every ethical principle in human subjects research. This single action could set us back fifty years or more!"

"What do you mean?" he asks.

"Think of the Nazi medical experiments. Physicians conducted awful tests on thousands of concentration camp prisoners without their permission." Her voice rises. "Or Tuskegee! The U.S. Public Health Service enrolled hundreds of Black Americans in a longitudinal study of syphilis. But they never told the men they had syphilis, even after penicillin was discovered and they could have been cured."

Sanjay recalls the lectures from med school. The photographs of men with tertiary complications of syphilis—brain damage, skin changes, and blindness—still haunt him.

"Even now communities of color mistrust doctors and science because of it—and rightly so," Emma continues. She starts pacing the room. "What I can't figure out is why someone would risk giving patients absoluxir in the first place."

It's the right question. From everything Sanjay's heard, absoluxir is a game changer. For Ecker and DeSalvo, it'd guarantee their place in the annals of medicine. For MBH, it could mean reclaiming their number one ranking. Why risk that? If word got out about the unauthorized experiments, Ecker Lab would lose its funding, and the institution could face severe penalties—even criminal charges.

It's too much to lose for everyone involved.

Then Sanjay recalls something Tom taught him: When you can't solve a case, go back to the data and question each piece. What if the sodium wasn't low? What if the blood culture wasn't positive?

It's a habit from before medicine became digitized, when lab results were sometimes entered incorrectly or filed on the wrong patient.

"What if Ecker and DeSalvo *aren't* on the verge of a major breakthrough?" he says slowly.

Emma frowns, furrowing her brow. "What do you mean?"

"This whole time, we've been assuming absoluxir worked. What if it didn't?"

"The clinical trial showed it was effective. You're saying someone manipulated the data?" She puts her hands on her hips, thinking.

He nods. "Then started secretly testing it at higher doses, before anyone found out."

Emma shakes her head. "But who? Only Ecker and DeSalvo are senior enough to have that kind of access. Clinical trial data is highly guarded."

Sanjay bites his lip. "I know how you feel about Matt, Emma, but after spending a whole evening with him, I don't think he could have done it."

Emma falls back against the kitchen counter, her body trembling. "Yeah, Matt approached me at the reunion to talk about my father. I don't think it's him, either. Ecker . . ."

Her voice trails off. Sanjay senses she has more to say, but she's hesitating. Impulsively, he draws her in for a hug, and she buries her face in his chest.

Then she pulls away and tells him what she learned from Abby Steinmetz. That Ecker backstabbed Tom Carpenter and lied about it to their faces.

Sanjay's shocked and disgusted. It takes him a minute to collect himself. "But why did Ecker report Tom to the board?" he asks, frowning. "So he could become physician-in-chief instead?"

"That's what I thought at first, but it doesn't make sense. That job is prestigious, but it'd come with heavy administrative responsibilities that would take Ecker away from his research—right when he's on the verge of a major breakthrough."

Sanjay takes a minute to think. "What if it's all related? What if Ecker found out that your dad knew about his illicit experiments, and he tried to get him fired before he told the board?"

"My God," Emma whispers. She turns to her window and gazes out. He gives her space to think. At length, she turns and says, "I need to tell the FDA about this."

"The FDA? Approval for absoluxir could be years away. We have plenty of time to—"

"Actually, more like three days."

Sanjay stumbles back. "Three *days*?"

"This is strictly confidential, Sanjay, but given the circumstances, I need to tell you. The FDA is meeting to review absoluxir next week. I know because I'm going."

"Wow," is all Sanjay can manage.

"I'm not reviewing the trial data, but if it looks as good as the preclinical data, it'll get approved. Once that happens, it could take months, if not years, to pull it off the market. Best case scenario: Absoluxir isn't ineffective, and no harm is done. Worst case? It causes serious bleeding and tens of thousands of patients—or more—are harmed."

Images of ERs and ICUs around the world filling up with patients like Vasquez flood Sanjay's mind—a nightmare scenario.

"What won't Ecker do to make this drug a success?" he wonders aloud.

Emma isn't listening. He can almost see her mind working as she plans her next move.

"There's something I need to do," she says, and his stomach twists in knots. "I believe your findings, Sanjay, as a colleague and a friend. But the FDA will only listen to hard proof. The results you got in Ecker's lab need to be validated."

"But Emma—"

"I'm going to my lab." She's already at the door, grabbing her car keys. "I'll create my own assay to test the blood from the patient on List C, the same patient you tested in Ecker's lab, and, if I can find them, samples from Vasquez, too."

"Do you even have enough time?"

"Not sure. I'll get Janelle to help, but if we can get Matt on board, it'll go a lot faster." She locks eyes with Sanjay. "If you get proof he isn't involved, text me."

CHAPTER

39

When Sanjay arrives at the nondescript Starbucks across from MBH, Ana Nunez gives him a big smile. "What, no Indian outfit this time?"

One look at her and Sanjay regrets not making his intentions clear. Although they texted just a half hour earlier, her hair is blown out, and she's put on makeup.

He takes a seat across from her and leans forward to hear her over the coffee grinder. She seems to take it as a cue and reaches her hands out across the table. He leans back.

"Ana, I'm so sorry, but I'm not here socially. I need to ask you about MBH."

"What?" She sits back, tilting her head to the side. "What do you mean?"

"It's important, Ana." He lowers his voice to emphasize the point. "When was the last time you gave a patient absoluxir?"

The smile is gone. "We're really doing this?"

He waits. It's unlikely Ecker would risk dosing patients himself. Ana's the natural choice. She assisted with the clinical trial and knows how to administer the drug. Ecker might have convinced—or duped, or bullied—her into helping him.

"The last patient was in February, eight months ago." Ana's voice is icy.

"You sure?" Sanjay quickly calculates: February was before the trial ended.

"Yes, I'm sure. That month, my abuela, she had another heart attack. I went home to Mexico City to see her. When I got back . . . I started working with Dr. Desai again."

Her story seems plausible. "What about giving the drug to patients outside of the trial?"

"What? No." But her pupils dilate. His words have triggered her sympathetic nervous system—her "fight or flight" response. He's onto something, but he can't afford to scare her off.

He'll appeal to her clinical side.

"Listen, Ana, someone's been stealing absoluxir and giving it to patients. Without their consent. I think either Ecker or DeSalvo is behind it."

Ana's face is white, her lips pressed together. "It couldn't be Matt," she says, forcing the words out. "He doesn't even know where the absoluxir is kept."

Sanjay sits up in his chair. "What . . . what do you mean?"

Tears form in Ana's eyes, and her body starts trembling as she holds them back. Sanjay instantly recognizes her reaction. It's not fear. It's shame.

"That second heart attack? My abuela almost died. And here I was in America, thanks to the sacrifices she made, giving patients a miracle drug that prevented heart attacks. So I . . . I took a vial of absoluxir. Just one."

Sanjay tries to hide his shock.

"Ecker caught me on video, a security camera. He said if I didn't help him, he'd make sure I couldn't get a PA position anywhere in the country. My family . . . It would crush them." She starts sobbing. He takes her hand, trying to comfort her.

"After that, Ecker moved the absoluxir somewhere safe. Outside the lab. He didn't allow me to administer the shots anymore, but I was the only one he trusted to retrieve the vials. Only the two of us and a handful of security people at MBH know the location."

"But surely, Matt, as co-head of the lab, knows?" Sanjay asks.

She shakes her head. "No. Once during the clinical trial, my car broke down. I was waiting for a tow truck, but a patient in the study was due for her injection. Ecker was out of town. DeSalvo called and demanded I tell him where the vials were, but I refused. I was too scared of what Ecker might do to me."

She puffs out her cheeks, as if the memory is too much. "Bottom line: If someone stole absoluxir, it could only be me or Ecker. And it wasn't me."

He takes out his phone and texts Emma: "Definitely not DeSalvo."

When he looks up, Ana looks like she has more to say.

"Listen. Ecker?" Her voice is low. "He's a creep. Remember that doctor who died, the one all the patients loved, Dr. Carpenter?"

Sanjay's heart skips, his pulse quickening. "What about him?"

Ana's expression darkens. "Last week, Ecker called me. Told me to go into Dr. Carpenter's chart and remove any details about his condition."

Sanjay feels a rush of blood to his head. He grips the table. "Do you remember any mention of blue toes?"

Ana looks surprised. "Yes. That's not something you see every day." She takes a tissue out of her purse and wipes her nose. "I knew it was wrong, but I need this job. Dr. Carpenter was dead, right? And Ecker's a powerful man."

"Did he ask you to do anything else?" Sanjay asks.

"He told me to call the path lab and tell them not to do an autopsy. And if they asked, which they didn't, to say the order came from Dr. Desai." She starts sobbing again.

Sanjay shakes his head, fear and disbelief washing over him.

"You know the worst part?" Ana's face is wrecked. "I didn't even give my abuela the absoluxir. I got too scared. I know it's silly; the trial didn't show any major side effects, but so many of the patients in the study ended up in the ICU. I just . . ."

"That's not silly, Ana. To me, that shows you'll be an excellent doctor one day."

She smiles weakly at him through her tears.

"My advice?" he says. "Get away from this damn place. As fast as you can."

CHAPTER

40

Emma can barely keep her gray Audi sedan on the road. She's a mess, oscillating between fits of anger and tears. Fortunately, it's still early for rush hour and traffic through the city is light.

The thought of Henry Ecker, a man she trusted and admired, injecting patients with a potentially deadly drug makes her sick. And angry.

Ecker betrayed her dad. He betrayed Abby Steinmetz. And he betrayed the trust held in him as a doctor and a scientist.

On one level, what he did goes against everything Emma knows about him—that he's an impeccable scientist and widely respected physician leader—but on another level, it all fits. The way Ecker seems to know everyone's business at MBH. The way he's tried to curry her favor, bring her lab under his control. Her dad's distrust of him.

An underlying current of unbridled ambition has long defined Dr. Henry Ecker. She just chose to look past it.

Not anymore.

Over text, Sanjay made her promise to go straight to her lab. She feels guilty for telling him a half truth. She *is* headed there, but she's making another stop first.

She wants to test the List C patient's blood to prove he received absoluxir. But she also wants to prove Ecker was behind it. If he was, he should go to jail for what he did to Vasquez, to all those patients. She won't be able to do either in time without Matt's help.

At the next stoplight, she calls him.

* * *

"I need to sit down." Matt DeSalvo slumps over, his face pale. He looks like he's about to vomit.

They're in Emma's office. She's just finished telling Matt what she and Sanjay have uncovered about absoluxir. Now she goes to the sink to get him a glass of water.

"Matt, it's going to be okay. Drink this."

He takes a sip, then says, "I wanted to keep testing absoluxir before we went to trial. I was worried that some patients would metabolize the drug more slowly, which might mean an increased risk of bleeding even at normal doses. It's also possible that some people have rare genetic mutations that completely alter the effects of the drug. But Ecker insisted I was being overly cautious."

Emma nods. Matt needs time to process everything she's told him, but time is something they don't have much of. The clock is ticking on the FDA review committee—and for anyone Ecker dares to experiment on next.

Matt stands and paces the room. "There was this brilliant postdoc in our lab, a woman from Mexico . . . She suspected Ecker of tampering with the results of an experiment. Nothing was ever proven, and a couple months later, MBH dropped her work visa. But when I heard the rumors, I knew they were true. I was just too wrapped up in our success to say anything."

He turns to Emma, his eyes reddened.

Emma knows the pressures of science. Only one in ten grant proposals get funded—the very dollars that pay her salary. If her experiments don't work, the chances of getting funded again drop dramatically. Enough failures, and she'll end up teaching biology to high schoolers. It's an infuriating system that keeps scientists from taking the big risks that often lead to breakthroughs. It can also incentivize scientists to overstate or outright fabricate results.

"When we found out vials of absoluxir were missing, I freaked out," Matt says. "But Ecker didn't. His only concern was making sure word didn't get out. Maybe this is why." Matt slumps down in his chair, shakes his head. "But experimenting on patients without their consent? I never thought he was capable of that."

"I have a plan, Matt. We can fix this." Emma puts her arm around his shoulders. "Where is he right now?"

"Ecker? New York. He's giving grand rounds at Columbia-Presbyterian tomorrow."

A breath of relief. She's caught a break—but there's still the security guard to contend with. "Great. I need your help."

* * *

Five minutes later, Matt is rushing up to the security guard in front of his lab.

"Hey!" he shouts. "I just saw someone without a hospital ID badge hanging around the absoluxir storage unit!"

The guard whips out his phone.

"There's no time! Get over there, now! I'll make sure the lab's data is secure."

The guard takes off. A second later, Emma peeks around the hallway corner and gives Matt a thumbs-up. "Nice work."

"Thanks," he says, catching his breath. "I don't know exactly where the absoluxir is kept or how long it'll take him to get there and back, so we need to be quick."

Within a few minutes, he's given Emma a crash course on the drug and how to re-create his assay. All around his desk are spec sheets and notebooks he's spiraled open. He's also given her three test samples to calibrate her results with.

Emma is starting to believe she might actually have a shot at validating Sanjay's theory in time. She just needs one last piece of evidence: Ecker's logbooks.

"He keeps them in his personal office," Matt says, his face tight with tension. "Let's hurry."

They find dozens of black binders in a heavy metal cabinet. Most are chronologically arranged, the year and month written on the spines. But a few are loosely scattered to the side. They start with those.

"That's weird," says Matt, thumbing through the pages. "This one seems to be about patients. But the dates are recent—"

"After the clinical trial ended?"

They look at each other—and nod. Without another word, they start putting the cabinet back in order. When they're satisfied that it looks unchanged, Emma slips the logbook into her tote, and they swiftly make for the exit.

Neither of them notices the tiny red light coming from a security camera hidden above the cabinets.

CHAPTER 41

As he speeds to Tom's office, Sanjay reruns his differential diagnosis.

Tom used to say the best doctors don't just diagnose. They uncover root causes. Otherwise, their patients risk suffering from the same illness again.

Sanjay believes Ana. He believes Ecker ordered her to remove details from Tom's ER record and cancel his autopsy. But *why*?

The anonymous tip to the board at least made sense. Ecker wanted to get Tom fired and keep anyone from finding out about his illicit experiments. But why would he care what was written in Tom's chart, or whether an autopsy was performed?

At the back entrance of Community Cares, Sanjay puts the question aside and turns to something that's been nagging him from the moment Emma left her apartment. He told her that "nearly" every patient on List C had a bleeding complication.

Did he mean that?

At Tom's desk, he takes out his handwritten notes. Sure enough, for two of the twenty-six patients, there's no mention of bleeding.

Tom didn't make mistakes. Not with patients. If those names are on List C, they're there for a reason. He logs into Tom's computer and goes through the records of the twenty-four patients with bleeding complications. They all follow a similar pattern: Hospitalized for something else—pneumonia, heart failure, post-surgical infection—just as they were starting to recover, they wound up in intensive care.

As Sanjay rereads their records, he notices that all of them were transferred to the new ICU, the one Neil runs.

For most of the patients, the doctors suspected bleeding from the moment their condition deteriorated. But for some, the cause initially went undetected. In one case, the patient had an acute drop in her blood pressure. They thought she had sepsis, but by the next day, it became clear it was anemia.

Now he turns to the two patients without bleeding complications. One was admitted for pneumonia, the other for gallstone infection. On the surface, they look no different from the other patients—no bleeding when admitted to the hospital; improvement within days; then, suddenly, the ICU.

The only difference? No mention of bleeding.

But minor bleeds can easily go undetected. To make sure the ICU doctors didn't miss anything, Sanjay pores through the records with a fine-toothed comb. He opens every blood test result and every diagnostic report. Nothing.

Desperate, he summarizes the cases aloud, speaking slowly, hoping to trigger a new thought.

"One patient was transferred to the ICU for a heart attack—a blockage in his left anterior descending artery. The other developed a blockage in the major artery of the leg. When surgeons went in, she was found to have an unusual number of smaller clots, too." His voice softens to a whisper. "Instead of bleeding, the patients had the opposite problem."

So all the patients in List C had a blood clotting problem. Most had too little. Two had too much. What's the common diagnosis?

Usually when he's stumped on a case, Sanjay turns to old case reports for answers. But this time, he decides to phone a friend, a brilliant scientist and professor with a PhD in biology from one of the top universities in the world.

Besides, he misses her and wants to know if she's okay.

Emma picks up on the third ring. "I'm in the middle of something; what's up?"

She sounds different. Not thrilled to hear from him, but not mad, either. *Maybe this is Professor Carpenter in work mode?*

"I have a clinical question, or more of a science one. Most of the patients who got absoluxir had bleeding, but two had clotting. I'm not sure what to make of it."

An audible sigh. "Don't you remember anything from first-year basic science?" she asks, a hint of teasing in her voice. "Two percent of Caucasians have a natural mutation in the Factor II protein. It's usually not a problem; in fact, it probably conferred a survival benefit at some point in our evolution. But some people experience increased clotting as a result."

Sanjay is still confused. "So . . . ?"

"The same could be true for the protein that absoluxir targets. A point mutation at its binding site might mean Ecker's antibody can't bind there. It could even cause absoluxir to *activate* the protein, increasing clotting."

Sanjay is speechless. It's a brilliant explanation.

"Look, Sanjay." Emma's voice switches back to nonscientist mode. "I know we have stuff to talk about. But I'm running out of time, and I need to finish this assay ASAP. I'm putting my phone on silent. I'll call you when I'm done."

They hang up, and Sanjay stares out the window of Tom's office. He can just make out the ICU tower in the distance. A dark cloud looms over it.

If Emma is right, the possibilities are deeply disturbing. Patients with this genetic mutation who are dosed with absoluxir could clot anywhere. In the brain, leading to a stroke, or in the tiny vessels of the feet, leading to . . . blue toes.

A new diagnosis dawns on Sanjay.

CHAPTER 42

Sanjay leaves Tom's office at 3:10 am. Ecker and DeSalvo's lab should have emptied out long ago. But to be certain, he has the hospital operator transfer him to the main lab line. It rings five times before he hangs up. A good sign.

First, though, he heads to pathology. Feldman has cleared out for the night, but the instructions he gave Sanjay over the phone were simple enough. He pushes through the double doors and turns on the lights. The autopsy room is empty, but the smell of formaldehyde remains.

The cryofridge is in the far back. Sanjay dons a pair of gloves and grabs the door handle. It takes a surprising amount of force to pull it open. When he does, a fog of cold air envelops him. Then it clears, and he makes his way through the fridge, sorting past specimen containers and vials of blood. He finds a metal tray labeled "Dr. Feedback" and smiles sadly.

It's Tom's blood. He grabs it.

* * *

There's no security guard outside Ecker and Matt's lab. Sanjay scans the hallway to make sure the coast is clear, then opens the door using the keycard he took from Matt. The main lights are on, which isn't unusual for hospitals, but to be safe, he pauses to listen for any sounds. Nothing.

Quickly, he moves to Matt's station and sets up the assay. Reaching into his jacket, he pulls out the plastic specimen bag and says a small prayer. *Please work.*

He preps the sample. This time, everything goes smoothly. He turns on Matt's computer and opens the software program.

Just when he thinks the loading bar is frozen, the result appears: 3.14. Well above the therapeutic range of 0.1–1.0.

Sanjay takes a deep breath and tries to push the implications out of his mind. He needs to run it again.

When he tries to remove the sample tray from the microscope, his right hand is shaking so hard he has to steady it with his left. He closes the software program, counts ten Mississippis, then reopens it. With both hands, he places the tray under the microscope.

He holds his breath and stares at the loading bar, willing a different result.

3.15.

His worst fears are confirmed. Tom was killed with absoluxir.

* * *

"Damn it! Pick up!"

Sanjay races out of the hospital, his heart pounding. He's phoned Emma five times already—and sent multiple frantic texts—but his calls keep going to voicemail.

He's already checked her lab. When he arrived, it was a mess, beakers and Erlenmeyer flasks in every direction. Dozing in the corner was Janelle White, whom he startled awake. In her sleep-deprived state, she explained that she and Emma had just finished replicating Matt's assay and were about to start testing samples. She didn't know where Emma was, but guessed she'd gone home or snuck off to a call room to nap.

The cold night air hits him as soon as he steps outside the hospital. Other than an empty bus squeaking to a stop nearby, the city is quiet. But inside Sanjay's mind, all he can hear is muffled roaring.

Should he call the police? Go to Emma's apartment? Confront Ecker?

He can no longer convince himself that Tom died of natural causes, that the anomalies around his death were any sort of coincidence. The elevated absoluxir level, the revelation that Ecker was behind the skipped autopsy, and the editing of Tom's medical records all scream one truth: Ecker murdered Tom.

But can he prove it?

Sanjay replays the case in his mind, working backward through the facts he's uncovered. On Ecker's instruction, Ana had wiped Tom's chart. Tom died of a stroke. Tom received absoluxir. Tom figured out Ecker was running experiments illegally. Tom did a diagnostic work-up on MBH. Tom was asked to be physician-in-chief. Ecker fudged the results of his clinical trial. Ecker and DeSalvo discovered absoluxir.

But how did *Tom* get injected with the drug? Like nearly all antibody treatments, absoluxir has to be given intravenously or intramuscularly, like a vaccine.

Which might explain why Ecker only tested the drug on patients in the hospital. Nearly every hospitalized patient has an IV, and each day dozens of people go in and out of patient rooms. It'd be easy for someone to walk in and inject absoluxir into an IV line without anyone getting suspicious—especially if the culprit was a doctor.

But how did an injectable drug get into Tom? What is Sanjay missing?

Back at the free clinic, he logs into Tom's record. There: The morning Tom died, he had an appointment at MBH's primary care clinic. A nurse-only visit. For the flu shot.

The clinic note is brief. Tom's height, weight, heart rate, and blood pressure readings were all normal. At the end is a prefilled template: "Patient counseled. Allergies reviewed. Influenza vaccine administered in the right arm," followed by the vaccine's lot number and expiration date.

Nothing seems out of the ordinary.

Then he sees it. Next to the phrase "Vaccine administered by," no name is entered. It's blank.

* * *

"Tell me again what happened," says Sanjay. "Every detail."

"I'm so sorry, Doctor," the nurse says, dabbing her eyes. "I didn't mean to cause any trouble."

She starts crying again. Sanjay hands her a tissue box, giving her a moment to recover.

It's 7 AM, and he's in an exam room at the MBH primary care clinic. It's not yet open, and the only staff in attendance are nurses and medical assistants, readying the rooms for the morning rush. Across from him, awkwardly sitting on the exam table, is Samantha, the nurse who signed Tom's note for his flu shot appointment.

Sanjay observes her carefully. She's in clean scrubs, wearing a simple gold locket and minimal makeup, her hair up in a ponytail. She reminds him of so many nurses he's worked with. No-nonsense but kind. Vulnerable yet strong.

He wants to be mad at her, but it's impossible. Nurses are almost universally deferential to doctors, to a fault. Given her older age, this is truer for Samantha. She comes from a generation of nurses that did what they were told, even when they disagreed, unless it put a patient in immediate danger—in which case, all bets were off.

She begins her story again: "I got to clinic early because I'd noticed Dr. Carpenter on the schedule. His appointment was our first slot of the day, eight AM, but I knew he'd come earlier so he could be out on time and get to his patients."

Sanjay nods, encouraging her to continue.

"I'm in room eight when I hear them. Out in the hallway, two men, arguing in whispers. They get closer, and I can tell one is Dr. Carpenter. The other guy keeps saying, 'Tom, I need to talk to you. I can explain.' And Tom, I mean, Dr. Carpenter, keeps saying, 'There's nothing to talk about. I have patients.'"

Despite everything, this makes Sanjay smile. Tom was himself to the very end.

"I didn't want to interrupt them, but I had a job to do. So I opened the door, and there they were. It was Dr. Carpenter, like I thought. The other guy, I recognized his face, but I couldn't remember his name at first." She balls up the tissue in her fist, rubs it against her nose. "Dr. Carpenter sees me and says, 'Nurse Samantha, how are you? How's your mom?' He was always like that.

"The other guy was just glaring at me. Before I could answer, Dr. Carpenter says, 'Could I trouble you for my shot? I'm due back at Community Cares.' I say, 'Of course, Dr. Carpenter. Someone must have known you were coming, because they got your shot ready, with your name on it and everything.' The nurses all loved Dr. Carpenter and were always doing special things for him, so neither of us thought anything of it."

She looks up at Sanjay, her brow furrowed, as though waiting for reassurance. He nods, and she continues. "He starts to head into the exam room, and the other guy says, 'Tom, you really need to hear my side.' Dr. Carpenter says, 'I'm busy, unless you want to come in here and give me my shot.' I think he was being sarcastic, but the other guy says, 'Sure, why not?'"

She starts crying again. "What was I supposed to do, Dr. Sanjay? He grabbed the tray, and I saw his ID badge. That's when it hit me. I recognized his face from the monthly newsletter. *The President's Corner*. Dr. Neil Desai."

The knot in Sanjay's stomach tightens.

"And Dr. Carpenter?" he asks. "He didn't look sick after he got the shot?"

"Honestly, I didn't see much, but he definitely walked himself out. Only later, I wasn't sure how to fill out the note. I wasn't going to lie, but I didn't want to call out Dr. Desai and risk my job. So I left it blank."

"Okay. I want to go over the part about the syringe being ready."

"Sure, I—"

His phone rings. He yanks it out, hoping it's Emma.

It's Cassie. "I have something for you," she says.

Sanjay looks at Samantha and recognizes a shift in her posture. Clinic is about to open, and she's not ready for her patients yet. But she's hesitant to tell him that she needs to go.

"Hang on." He puts the phone on his chest and looks squarely at her. "Nurse Samantha, you did nothing wrong. I know you have patients. If you think of any more details, call me."

"Thank you, Dr. Sanjay." Samantha hops off the exam table and hurries out. Sanjay follows.

"Okay, I'm listening," he says, putting the phone to his ear.

"I just finished my analysis of MBH's financials," says Cassie. "Guess whose department got the most revenue from Next Health?"

"Neil's."

"Damn it! How'd you know?"

His head spins: *List A, Next Health, Vasquez and now Tom*. An image of his final differential diagnosis flashes in his mind.

	What?	Who?	Why?
List A	Unnecessary procedures	Neil	To be department chair
List B	Referrals from Next Health	Neil	To increase revenues
List C	Absoluxir	Neil	To fill ICU
Tom	Murder	Neil	To silence him

"Because we've been wrong all along. Tom's diagnostic work-up wasn't of MBH. It was of Neil."

CHAPTER

43

EMMA'S BACK IN her lab, fuming. And exhausted.

She's been awake for almost twenty-four hours. It took longer than expected to replicate Matt's assay. The reagent was finicky. But after three tries, they got their measurements within 0.01 of the controls Matt gave her. More precise than she needed, perhaps, but it reaffirms her belief in doing science the right way—a certainty she needs now more than ever.

And at last, she's done. Their experiments have proved, in a way the FDA can validate, that the List C patient illicitly received absoluxir. Emma tested the sample three times: 2.23, 2.23, 2.24. When she was done, she ran back to the blood pathology department and convinced Peggy to give her two samples of Vasquez's blood. The results were confirmatory.

With a sense of grim satisfaction, she sends Janelle home. Once she's alone, she picks up Ecker's logbook. Only she has touched it. During periods of downtime, when her instruments were calibrating or Janelle was setting up the next experiment, she pored through his notes, page by page.

The first half, his reflections on the clinical trial, confirms her suspicion that the trial was manipulated. Patients in the absoluxir arm had a lower rate of heart attacks, but they also had a high rate of major bleeding complications. Ecker's theories about why are insightful. Brilliant, even. No matter how much she despises him now, Emma can't help but be impressed by his scientific mind. His conclusions suggest that some patients naturally have higher activity levels of absoluxir and point toward the development of a diagnostic test that would allow doctors to tailor an individual's dosage in advance. His hypothesis is sound, and Emma suspects that he is on to something important.

The second half of the logbook takes a disturbing turn.

It follows the hospital course of more than twenty patients admitted to MBH after the clinical trial ended. None of the entries mention absoluxir or any drug—Ecker's too smart to leave a paper trail—but each one contains a suspicious timeline. The early days of hospitalization are labeled "5 days before event." "3 days before event," and so on. Then comes a tick mark labeled "day 0," followed by sequential entries—"day 1," "day 2," etc.—many of which document a bleeding event.

The data presents a compelling case that Ecker was secretly experimenting on patients—possibly to test his new hypothesis. Emma can't be sure. But what is certain is that his ambition knows no bounds. He will do whatever it takes to have a blockbuster drug to his name and claim his place in medical history.

If he intentionally harmed patients, what else is he capable of?

Her mind jumps to Sanjay, and a chill passes through her. Where has he been all day? Why hasn't he called?

Then she remembers: Her phone is on silent. She fumbles through her pockets before realizing it's in her purse.

She turns to grab it and freezes.

Ecker is standing six feet away.

* * *

"Emma! I'm so sorry. I didn't mean to startle you." He steps toward her, a big smile contorting his features.

Wasn't he supposed to be in New York? Did someone tell him what I've been up to?

The thought sparks a flame inside her. Ecker experimented on people without their consent. He hurt them. Images of patients and families in the ICU—suffering as the direct result of his actions—fuel her anger, and she takes a step forward, snaps, "I know what you did. The unauthorized experiments. And I have proof."

Ecker furrows his brow, then smiles again.

She spews out everything she's learned. The lists of patients on Tom's computer. The List C patient's coagulation test. Vasquez's horrific death. Ecker's logbook.

"Ah. I was wondering where that one went," he says.

Why isn't he more worried? Or angry?

He takes a stool and sits down. "That's quite a story, my dear. With everything going on, how are you holding up?"

He's giving her a look of genuine concern. For a moment, with him in his white coat and her in an over-exhausted state, it seems like Ecker's her doctor, consoling her.

"I wasn't close with my father when he died," Ecker continues. "But when my mother passed, I was lost. Angry at the world. She had cancer like Maria, and we had so few good treatments back then."

Emma's head is spinning. Did she run her experiments correctly? Did she jump to conclusions too soon?

"I haven't told many people this," he continues. "But that first week after she died, I had some dark thoughts. Not suicidal ideation, mind you, but thoughts of hurting the doctors and nurses I faulted for not saving her. It took me a while to realize it was an atypical grief reaction."

Emma shakes her head. "But the tests . . . I saw patients in your logbook—"

"Did the logbook mention that I gave the patients absoluxir?"

"No, but—"

"Did it mention absoluxir at all?"

"No. But that patient in the hospital tested positive for it! So did Vasquez."

"Did they?" Ecker stands up and walks toward her. "Did they test positive for the drug itself? Or for a clotting disorder—one that could be caused by absoluxir, but could also be from a genetic defect of some sort?"

"Sanjay said there were dozens of patients with major bleeding. They couldn't all have had a defect. And Sanjay—"

Ecker is now a foot away from Emma. Even if it's foolish or dangerous, she can't back down. This man needs to be stopped.

"Sanjay," he says, stepping closer, placing his hand on her shoulder. "I know you have feelings for that boy, but he's a disgraced physician. You and I, we're scientists. Look at the data. First, Sanjay was basically *fired* for failing to admit a patient that might have had a stroke. True or false?"

"True."

"Second, he flies around the world rendering his services to billionaires and doing heaven knows what with supermodels."

Tears fill her eyes as she looks up at him. "That's all true, but—"

"Third, Sanjay is not a good doctor."

Emma snaps back, "False." She pushes Ecker's hand away. "Sanjay may be many things, but he's a great doctor."

"So, you and Sanjay believe I experiment on patients and you intend to tell the world? Fools."

He pulls a loaded syringe from his lab coat. The sweet doctor is gone. All that's left is a man—aggressive, cold, and clinical.

Before she can scream, he grabs her.

CHAPTER

44

Dr. Neil Desai is at MBH, desperately looking for Emma.

An hour ago, he got an urgent page from Joanna Collins, the head nurse of the primary care clinic. She had disturbing news. Sanjay was in the primary care clinic, asking questions. One of her nurses had told him Neil and Dr. Carpenter had argued the day before Carpenter died. Afterward, Sanjay raced out of the clinic on his phone.

Was he calling Emma? Did he know what they were arguing about?

Emma needs to hear Neil's side of the story.

Just like her dad did.

Neil knew Tom Carpenter was next in line to be physician-in-chief. He was excited to partner with him; he had big plans for what they'd accomplish together. But then he learned about Tom's diagnostic work-up of MBH.

Worried, he had the chief technology officer log him into Tom's account. It confirmed his worst fears. Carpenter was tracking a list of patients that had received absoluxir. Somehow, he'd pieced together that Neil was aggressively filling up the new ICU and cutting a few temporary corners along the way.

For a full week, Neil tried to meet with Tom, but Tom's assistant claimed he was unavailable. As president, Neil had full access to the outpatient and operating room schedules. When he saw Tom had an appointment for a flu shot, he cornered him in the clinic. It was risky, but it was early morning, and he hoped no one would overhear them.

Stupid, he thinks. *Another stupid choice.*

Neil crossed a line; he knows that. But he was careful. During the absoluxir trial, he saw that the old ICU was fuller. Then the trial ended early, and the numbers plummeted. It could have been a coincidence, but he had his suspicions.

Convincing the hospital's head of security to reveal the location of the absoluxir was easy. The hard part was the first few injections. With each patient, he gradually increased the dose until he found the right one—high enough to cause bleeding that warranted a transfer to the ICU, but not so high that it caused permanent harm or death. With each ICU patient who fully recovered, it got easier and easier.

He shudders at the memory. But it's all behind him now. Thanks to his attempts to court local clinics like Next Health, the ICU is in the black.

This is the burden of leadership. What's demanded of the best. His parents sacrificed everything for him. Now it's his turn to sacrifice for the greater good.

And his ICU *is* the greater good—it's saved lives that would have otherwise been lost. And this is just the beginning. Now that he's hospital president, he plans to fix so much of what's wrong with MBH: the surprise bills, the cap on Medicaid patients, all of it.

The ends sometimes justify the means. He doesn't care what people think.

But he does care about Emma.

A month ago, when he mustered up the courage to ask her out and she said yes, he felt redeemed. He knows they can be the ultimate power couple: him, CEO of MBH; her, the dean of MBMS. And as soon as he finds her, he'll remind her of that possibility. He'll figure out a way to win her back.

As he scours the hallways of MBH on the way to her lab, his mind turns to the last time he desperately searched for Emma. It was the end of their second year of medical school. He'd just gotten a call from Bethesda, saying he'd won a Royston, a two-year research fellowship at the National Institutes of Health, awarded to only four medical students in the country each year. If he accepted, he'd be packing to go after the last exam of the year, anatomy.

But when he put the phone down, he experienced a profound moment of clarity.

He didn't want it.

Getting the Royston had been his parents' dream. Research was the fast track to success, and many Royston winners ended up as department chairs, vice deans, even hospital presidents. But if it meant two years apart from Emma, Neil wanted nothing to do with it. All that was left was to tell her how he felt.

Emma had mentioned studying at Sanjay's after class. The door was ajar, so he let himself in. That's when he saw them. On the sofa, facing the TV on the far wall—the same spot where the three of them used to binge watch their favorite shows—kissing.

Neil managed to slip out without being seen. He took the Royston fellowship. And he swore to himself: He would never be second again.

* * *

The entrance to Emma's lab is up ahead. He quickens his pace, swings the door open—and falls back in shock.

Henry Ecker is holding Emma from behind, pulling an empty syringe from her neck. When he sees Neil, he lets go, and her body slumps to the floor.

"Emma!" Neil shouts.

His reflexes kick in. He runs to her, slides to his knees, and puts his ear to her chest, his finger on her carotid artery. No air, no breathing, no pulse. He scrambles up, places his hands over her breastbone, and starts compressions.

When he gets into a rhythm, he stares up at Ecker, who is watching him impassively. "What have you done?" he shouts.

CHAPTER

45

SANJAY HURTLES THROUGH the stairwell doors into the main hallway of the executive offices.

That Neil is behind Lists A and B, he can understand. But deliberately hurting patients?

The new ICU meant intense pressure. Neil's job was at stake. And bleeding events in hospitalized patients almost always require intensive care. Inject enough patients, and overnight his new ICU would be full.

The logic's there, but Sanjay still can't picture Neil tiptoeing into a patient's room and injecting high doses of an unproven drug into the IV line, then standing by as the patient starts bleeding. Doing it to another patient the next day. And again, and again.

Patients like Mr. Vasquez. Chills rack Sanjay's body.

But nothing can compare to the discovery that Neil killed Tom. There's no explanation or justification for that. It's murder, plain and simple.

He bursts into the executive offices and flies past Neil's assistant, who yells, "Wait! You can't go in there!" He ignores her and pushes the door open, his eyes darting across Neil's desk and working space. Empty. He feels his heart rate rise. His sixth sense is telling him something is wrong. Very wrong.

Think. Neil could be in the ICU. He could be in the boardroom. He could be injecting another patient.

Damn it. There are too many options. And he's running out of time.

In the distance, he hears an overhead page from the main hospital. That's it. He whips out his phone and calls Cassie.

"I need to find Neil. He always has his pager. Can you locate him?"

He hears furious tapping on the other end of the line. "I should be able to triangulate his position. I still have backdoor access to their IT system—"

"Do it!"

More tapping. "I'm in. I just need to . . ."

Standing there, holding his phone, feeling helpless, Sanjay is flooded with images of Emma. The day they met. Their first date. Dinner at Il Paloma.

He has to find her, too.

"I got it! He's on campus. In the main research building. Room 608."

Sanjay's heart sinks to his stomach. "That's Emma's lab! Call the police! I'm heading over."

He runs, fearing the worst.

CHAPTER 46

"NEIL, THIS IS our way out. After this business—" Ecker gestures toward Emma's limp body. "We can go back to the way things were."

Neil is on his second cycle of CPR. Emma still has no pulse. While he pumps her chest and counts compressions under his breath, he keeps his eyes on Ecker.

"I know you've been injecting patients with my drug," says Ecker.

Neil's whole body tenses, and his arms freeze mid-compression.

"Of course I know, boy. Do you think I'm stupid?" Ecker snaps, then sighs loudly. "When one of my guards spotted you coming out of the absoluxir storage unit, I was dumbfounded—and furious. Then I realized your scheme. Transfer patients to the ICU, get heads in beds. Nobody gets hurt, not really, and MBH is back in the black. You must have gotten the idea from the trial."

It never made sense, he thinks. *The drug was proven to not cause bleeding.*

Ecker seems to sense his confusion. "Absoluxir worked. Heart attacks dropped by more than eighty percent. Just imagine how many lives we could save! But there was one little setback. Five percent of the patients had increased bleeding, too. I needed time to figure it out, so I switched a few labels."

Neil reaches his thirty count. He puts his ear to Emma's mouth and places his finger over her carotid artery. Still no breath. No pulse. He tilts her chin back and continues.

"Your . . . experiments gave me additional data points. Thanks to them, I'm developing a new blood test that will help doctors choose the right dose of absoluxir. This is how science makes progress: in fits and starts. Maybe you and I can publish our findings together."

"I'm not doing anything with you!" Neil spits out.

"Of course you are. Otherwise, I'll tell everyone you killed Tom. After all, you're the one who gave him absoluxir. But this time by switching out his flu shot."

Neil's whole body goes cold. In spite of himself, he stops the compressions, just for a moment. "That can't be. He had a stroke."

"Yes, another failed experiment. I had no idea Tom had a genetic mutation in his blood clotting proteins." Ecker pauses and stares down at the ground, shaking his head.

Tom was murdered? Now Ecker's framing me? Neil pictures himself in the exam room, giving Tom what he thought was a routine flu shot. He'd been able to access Tom's medical record to know he had an appointment that day. Which meant Ecker could as well.

A wave of nausea overwhelms him. Tom was always good to him; he offered to mentor him when he became president.

Now Emma has no father, and MBH has lost its statesman.

"He didn't deserve to die," he grits out.

"No, he didn't, the damn fool. I just thought he'd have a small bleed and be out of commission for a few days, long enough for me to cover your tracks." Ecker swipes at his eyes and looks away. "If only he'd *listened*. He took your data to our general counsel. And because of attorney-client privilege, the lawyer's hands were tied—he couldn't tell anyone, not unless there was an imminent threat.

But Tom wouldn't let it go; we found out he was going to the press." He exhales hard. "I tried to get him to back down, be reasonable. MBH's reputation is everything. It's why we get the chance to save lives!"

"So you killed him?"

"I loaded the gun. You're the one who shot him." Ecker's face has gone cold. "But think of the alternative. No more grants, no more research. Patients would leave. Your precious ICU would be empty!" His voice rises to a yell, his composure shattering. "I've spent my career making Man's Best Hospital what it is. And it would have been ruined in a minute!"

He takes a deep breath. "We have to be smart now, Neil. Put it behind us."

"You have no proof I killed Tom. I'll fight you."

Ecker shrugs. "You can try. But what about Vasquez?"

Neil stops mid-compression, whispers Vasquez's name under his breath. "That was you?"

Ecker just folds his arms. "They were getting too close. Emma wouldn't admit it to me, but she'd figured out someone was giving patients absoluxir. I had no choice but to place the blame on you." He looks off onto the distance, his voice softer. "The dose? A terrible mistake."

Neil remembers the look on Vasquez's wife's face, the blood on the ICU room walls, and feels a wave of nausea overcome him.

Ecker's right, he thinks. This all started with Tom's diagnostic. But Tom is gone. Neil is president, and he has the ear of the board. He'd be in the clear if it wasn't for Emma and . . .

"Sanjay," he whispers.

"What about him?" scoffs Ecker. "He's a disgrace to the profession. If we need to, we can just OD him in his hotel. He's probably on drugs anyway."

Neil shakes his head in disbelief. He and Sanjay might have their differences, but Sanjay believed in him when his own parents didn't.

It's time for another breath. He tilts Emma's chin back. Then he pauses to look at her. Even now, her soul radiates goodness. There's time to save her, too.

He looks up at Ecker, his eyes burning. "I'm getting the crash cart."

Ecker pulls a small gun from his lab coat. "I'm sorry, Neil. But you'll do no such thing."

CHAPTER 47

SANJAY BURSTS INTO Emma's lab.

The first thing he sees is Ecker, pointing a gun at Neil.

Then, on the ground: Emma, lifeless.

He runs toward her, inspecting her from head to toe. No breathing. No obvious trauma. No blood. Pale. Has she been drugged?

Out of the corner of his eye, he sees Ecker turn toward him. A banging sound, and Sanjay hits the ground with a thump. Has he been shot? No; he feels no pain, no wetness. His body instinctively threw itself to the ground. But where did the bullet go?

He turns to his left, gasps out a loud choking sound. A body is splayed across the floor.

Neil. He must have jumped between Sanjay and the bullet.

Standing on the other side of Neil is Ecker. The muzzle of his gun is tipped toward the ground, a look of shock frozen on his face.

Sanjay propels his body forward, toward Ecker, every muscle—well practiced from years of blocking drills with his trainer—pulling in the same direction.

Ecker sees him too late. Before he can re-aim his Beretta, Sanjay tackles him head on, and Ecker falls back against the lab bench. Hard. The force causes the wooden shelves that rise up from the granite countertop to teeter, knocking loose a compound light microscope from its perch eighteen feet above.

Sanjay watches it wobble, then fall. Ecker traces Sanjay's gaze, but before he can react, the microscope crashes down onto his forehead, right above the supraorbital ridge. Ecker crumples to the ground, out cold.

Without wasting another second, Sanjay turns to Emma. Neil's already kneeling beside her, hands on her chest in the CPR position. The bullet must have only grazed him.

"What did he give her?" Sanjay asks, nodding toward the empty syringe on the ground.

"I don't know," Neil says, resuming compressions. "Couldn't have been absoluxir. It wouldn't have caused this."

Sanjay eyes the needle, a list of common cardiotoxic drugs running through his mind. *Potassium chloride?* He can't be sure. "I'm going for the crash cart."

A minute later, he returns. "Let me jump in at the next cycle."

Neil nods. He starts counting his compressions out loud. "Fifteen-and-sixteen-and-seventeen-and-eighteen . . ."

At thirty, they wordlessly exchange positions.

"How long has she been down?"

Neil grabs the paddles out of the crash cart. "Three . . . maybe four minutes."

They exchange a knowing look. The chances of a full neurologic recovery decrease with every minute the brain goes without oxygen. Sanjay pumps harder.

"Hold!" calls Neil once he sets up the defibrillator. They stare at the screen, willing it to hurry up. A moment later, a flat line appears, inching across the screen.

Asystole. A shockable rhythm.

Sanjay is back on the chest compressions while Neil charges the device.

"Two hundred—clear!"

Sanjay jerks his arms and legs back. Neil pushes the paddles against Emma's chest, shocking her with two hundred joules of electricity.

Immediately, Sanjay jumps back on compressions while Neil gets in position behind her head to feel for her carotids. "I have a pulse!"

"You get an IV. I got the 12-lead."

Within a minute, Neil has a 16-gauge in Emma's left arm. Sanjay hooks her up to the EKG machine, keeping hold of her wrist. Her pulse is thready, but it's there.

"One milligram of epi?" asks Neil.

"Let's do it," says Sanjay.

Neil reaches into the crash cart for the epinephrine. He pushes it, then signals Sanjay, who flips on the EKG machine. A second later, QRS waves bounce across the screen. Where there should be short and narrow waves, they see tall and wide ones.

"Peaked T waves!" they shout in unison.

"KCl," says Sanjay, and Neil nods in agreement. That bastard Ecker gave her potassium chloride, the drug of choice in state executions. Heart muscles rely on a potassium gradient. Too much potassium, and they don't contract. Emma needs something to counteract the potassium—and fast.

"Calcium gluconate!" Sanjay yells. "Ten milliliters."

Neil grabs the drug from the crash cart and loads the syringe. This time he hands it to Sanjay.

Calcium gluconate is a slow push, given over two to three minutes. To keep his fingers on the pulse and steadily inject the medication, Sanjay wraps his right arm around Emma's left.

Within a minute, her skin feels warmer, and her color starts to return. He gazes at her, feeling his heart swell, then averts his eyes. *Not now*, he tells himself.

But even as he thinks it, the door bursts open, shattering the quiet. The code team and police dispatch have arrived at the same time, arguing loudly.

"This is our damn hospital and our damn doctors," says the woman in charge, giving a nod to Sanjay. He's relieved to see it's Dr. Ciroli, the chief resident from the ER. She pushes past the last policeman, snapping, "It's not like any of them are running away."

Within a minute, Emma is up on a gurney. She's breathing on her own and doesn't need to be intubated. Her BP is 80/40, not great, but good enough for now. The code team unlocks the stretcher and starts pushing her toward the hallway.

That's when Dr. Ciroli's pager goes off. She looks down at it, then back at Sanjay, wide-eyed. "Shit, another code."

"Isn't there a second code team?" he asks.

"No, cost-cutting measures," Ciroli looks like she's about to say more, but her eyes move to Neil, and she stops herself.

"You take the other code," says Neil. "We got this."

The code team hesitates. Ciroli eyes Neil's clothing, and Sanjay follows her gaze, sees a splotch of blood.

"I owe you one, remember?" says Sanjay, taking his position on the other side of Emma's gurney.

Ciroli nods. Before she can say anything, her male colleague shouts, "Come on. Let's go!" and she runs out the doorway behind him.

Neil and Sanjay move quickly down the corridor. The gurney is more cumbersome than Sanjay expected, but they manage. Their reward is the steady beat of the heart monitor, letting them know Emma's okay.

They take a breather in the elevator, heading down to the first floor. Smiling sadly, Neil says, "We're three peas in a pod again."

Sanjay observes him closely. Blood is soaking into his shirt and left pant leg, and beads of cold sweat are forming on his forehead. "You're bleeding out."

"I'm fine," says Neil. "I'm fine." But his voice is weakening.

"You're not." As the gurney clears the elevator, Sanjay sits Neil down on the ground. With all the new construction at MBH, the ER is still five minutes away—time Neil doesn't have.

Sanjay peels open Neil's shirt, looking for a place to apply pressure. The bullet entered the tenth intercostal space along the axillary line, hitting Neil's spleen, maybe even the left lower lobe of his lung.

"You made it worse by doing chest compressions," he breathes. "By wheeling her to the ER."

"I made it worse a long time ago." Neil winces. His breathing is labored. "I made mistakes, Sanjay. Too many. I didn't kill Tom. Or Vasquez." He grabs at Sanjay's arm, pulling him close. "I'd never kill a patient. I was being careful. But the pressure—"

"I know. I know," Sanjay says softly. He wraps Neil's shirt around the wound as tightly as he can. He tugs it once more to assuage the pain. The motion brings up the memory of their first trip to the free clinic, Neil wrapping the stethoscope around his neck. Then of late-night tutoring sessions over cold pizza and the encouraging text messages that got him through residency.

Neil's always looked out for him. Now it's Sanjay's turn.

Neil's hand clamps onto Sanjay's arm—his grip surprisingly strong.

"Sanjay," he whispers. "I'm the one who messed up your anatomy test."

Sanjay sits back, shocked into stillness.

"I saw on the exam schedule that there was a break right before your turn. I moved a few flags. You were top of the class, a few points ahead of me. I thought you'd just get a lower score—not fail." Neil seems to sense Sanjay's ambivalence. "You're a great doctor and a good friend. You always were."

He sputters. His body is going into shock. There's not much more Sanjay can do.

"You and Emma were the only people in my life to love me for who I am. When I saw you two together . . . The only thing that mattered after that was being first. I'm sorry, Sanjay. So sorry."

A dark cloud Sanjay didn't realize was hanging over him all these years lifts. What's left is love for his friend—and Emma. "It doesn't matter now, Neil. None of it matters."

Neil's body is shivering. Sanjay pulls his head into his lap.

"Emma—she loves you, Sanjay. I know it. Tell her I loved her, too, and that I'm glad for it. Take care of each other."

Sanjay holds his friend to his chest while Neil lets out his last breath. Then Sanjay just sits in silence, listening to his own breath.

CHAPTER

48

TWO DAYS LATER, Sanjay takes a last look out the window at the dozens of bouquets and cards on the front lawn—left there after yesterday evening's candlelight vigil for Emma. Then he closes the blinds on the hospital window to reduce the glare from the setting sun and jumps on his Zoom call.

Emma regained consciousness early this morning. She quickly fell back asleep, but not before the doctors—and Sanjay—had a chance to do an exam. Miraculously, she showed no sign of neurologic deficits and could be discharged as soon as tomorrow.

Even so, Sanjay hates diverting his attention from her—almost as much as he hates once again having to play Dr. Sanjay, private doctor to the uber-rich.

"Dr. Patel, thank you for attending. We would have preferred this meeting be in person. We know you're busy."

The MBH board members are arrayed around a semicircular conference table. Through the laptop screen, it's hard to make out who everyone is. That everyone is old and white doesn't help. Sanjay can't help but think of the firing squad he'd have faced had he not resigned from MBH all those years ago.

The man at the center of the table goes first. "Before we begin, we must kindly ask that this meeting not be recorded. Do you have any recording devices with you now?"

He must be the general counsel, Sanjay figures, the one Tom met with before he died.

Sanjay just stares in reply. "Give them nothing," was Barnett's advice when Sanjay called him for a quick lesson on board meetings and negotiations. "Not a damn thing."

The lawyer looks at the colleague to his left, a woman—perhaps Janet Scully?—and shrugs. "All right, then, let's get started."

The board was "surprised" by the revelations about Ecker, the woman says. The loss of Tom Carpenter is "unfortunate." Sanjay can see the hospital's lawyer mouthing along as she speaks. A ventriloquy act gone bad.

"As you may know, Dr. Thomas Carpenter was meant to be our next physician-in-chief. It has come to our attention that you were his protégé. Your record of service as an attending at MBH was exemplary until . . ." She falters. "Until the alleged incidents surrounding your departure."

Alleged?

"Pursuant to the board's charter, we have unanimously voted to install you as MBH's next physician-in-chief. Congratulations."

As if on cue, all the board members look into the camera and smile.

Barnett anticipated they'd try to buy his silence. But nothing could have prepared him for this.

"Of course," the lawyer states, "you'd be doing so with certain preconditions."

Here it comes.

"You'd forfeit your right to disclose the . . . events of the past week, your right to sue the hospital, your right to pursue criminal charges—"

The lawyer drones on. Sanjay looks over at Emma, craning his neck to check her vital signs on the monitor.

"But in return, all your privileges as an attending physician at Mount Beacon Hospital would be restored and—"

"I have a proposal of my own."

The lawyer keeps talking. The board member beside him reaches over and shushes him.

"I said, I have a proposal of my own," Sanjay repeats. "I'm not coming back to MBH. But I will agree to your preconditions—if you meet two of mine."

The lawyer crosses his arms. "And those are?"

"First, you make Dr. Fuki Olopade the next physician-in-chief of MBH, not me. He's an exemplary doctor and will do more to fulfill Tom Carpenter's legacy than I ever could."

The room erupts, the board members talking over each other and yelling questions into the camera.

"Decorum!" yells the lawyer.

"Second, you unaffiliate Community Cares from MBH. Make it its own 501(c)(3) nonprofit, with an independent board of directors, half clinicians and half members of the community."

The discord resumes, this time less dramatically. Sanjay speaks over them.

"I have a patient to see. Discuss my terms and get back to me with a decision by end of business today. After that, any offer is off the table."

Just as one of the board members starts to ask him a question, Sanjay pushes the laptop screen down. He takes a deep breath and walks back to Emma. She looks comfortable. He takes a seat on the edge of her bed and puts his hand on hers.

"Hey," he whispers. "I think I just did the right thing. You wouldn't totally hate it."

* * *

An hour later, he hears a soft knock. He squeezes Emma's hand and opens the door. It's Cassie.

"Sanjay, look outside!" she whispers excitedly, moving past him to the window.

"I saw. The flowers from the vigil are beautiful. I'm sure Emma will appreciate—"

"No, not that. Look."

Cassie opens the curtains and lets the light in. It takes a moment for his eyes to adjust.

"Paul Klein's article in *The Boston Globe* just dropped. He linked Ecker and Neil's actions to wider systemic issues at MBH." Cassie raises an eyebrow. "Apparently it hit a nerve."

On the front lawn, hundreds of people in white coats and stethoscopes are walking up the road to the entrance of MBH. In their hands are signs: "Patients, not profits." "No caring, no care." "Understaffed, Overworked, Undervalued." Following close behind are nurses in blue scrubs and medical students in white coats over jeans.

"They're out in droves," marvels Cassie.

It's not just the residents and junior attendings. Sanjay sees the chair of cardiology and MBH's top neurosurgeon. And everywhere are iPhones, no doubt being used to post images and messages on social media for the world to see.

Tears form in his eyes. Dr. Tom Carpenter's final lesson echoes in his ears: "A good doctor treats the patient. A great doctor fights for all patients."

"Rapport not damaged." She [illegible] moving past him to the window.

"There. The flowers from the vine are beautiful," [illegible] will [illegible] here."

[illegible]

Sam opens the curtain and lets the light in. [illegible]

"That's [illegible] in 24." [illegible] just dropped. He [illegible] and [illegible] a month [illegible] syndrome [illegible]. Apparently [illegible].

On the [illegible] lawn, hundreds of people in white coats and [illegible] gathered [illegible] in the [illegible] of [illegible]. [illegible] following [illegible] doctors and nurses in their scrubs and medical students in white [illegible].

[illegible]

[illegible] the residents and junior [illegible]. Sam sees the [illegible] of cardiology and ABP's [illegible]. And [illegible] where [illegible].

[illegible] a good doctor treats the patient [illegible].

EPILOGUE

THE MEMORIAL SERVICE at Community Cares is the service Dr. Tom Carpenter would have wanted. As soon as they finish with the last patient of the morning, the clinic staff goes to work. They clear out the plastic chairs in the waiting room and lay out food—homemade pupusas, pork al pastor, rice and beans—on folding tables in the back. The interim executive director and Nurse Kay welcome everyone, then invite Tom's patients to speak.

The highlight is a sixty-eight-year-old grandmother who shares a story about the first time Tom gave her a gynecologic exam—he hit his head on the examination lamp, nearly knocking himself into her private parts. A few days later, instead of calling with the results, he showed up at her house to tell her she had cervical cancer and promised he'd be with her every step of the way. By the time she finishes, everyone in the room is half laughing, half crying.

Professor Emma Carpenter-Flores is the last to speak. For those who knew Tom and Maria, she's a perfect melding of her parents, both outside and in.

And then it's over. Someone turns on light Latin music, and everyone grabs a plate and talks among themselves about their beloved doctor and friend. The few MBH execs who came leave as soon as they can.

Sanjay and Emma sit in a corner together. At last, they're alone, and Sanjay's able to fill her in on everything that's happened.

With Matt's help, the police found a thick binder of notes in Ecker's office: the files Tom mentioned to Emma. After Tom died, Ecker apparently broke into his office and stole them. They outline everything Tom had discovered about MBH. Ecker, the police reasoned, must have kept them as insurance, as most of the evidence pointed toward Neil.

Other than a concussion, Ecker is fine—clinically speaking. He's being held without bail, thanks to Paul Klein's article in *The Globe*. More is expected to come out as reporters and investigators dig into the absoluxir story. Paul's theory is that MBH pushed Ecker to cut corners and accelerate development of the drug to regain the hospital's top ranking, and he suspects the scandal goes as high as the board.

So far, Matt DeSalvo has been proven innocent. Sanjay hopes it remains that way.

The truth has come out about Neil, too. But to Sanjay and Emma's pleasant surprise, he's received more sympathy than Ecker, as doctors across the country have confessed on social media to feeling the same pressures that led to his horrific actions. The hashtag #IAmDrNeilDesai is trending, a call out to the effects of moral injury on doctors and nurses everywhere.

The FDA rejected absoluxir's new drug application. After Emma's injury, Janelle White sent the data they'd collected to the committee. They were so impressed with Janelle's work they offered her a role in the FDA's Office of Minority Health and Health Equity. Though Emma will miss her, she knows no one is better suited to champion the inclusion of minority and rural communities in biomedical research.

Mrs. Vasquez's wife insisted on attending the FDA review to tell her husband's story, an unusual occurrence for a formal scientific meeting. Zooming in from his wake, she gave a human face to the dangers of absoluxir and of rushing medical science.

William Barnett sent Cassie's analysis of Next Health's finances to the SEC. When their investigation was announced, the IPO was postponed indefinitely, and thousands of patients canceled their memberships.

Jim Hadley? He died alone in a freak explosion on his yacht, days after taking out a $125 million life insurance policy. Sanjay suspects this was Hadley's plan for repaying his investors and protecting his family. According to his obituary, he will be remembered as a "tireless advocate for value-based care."

Sanjay's practice is in good hands. Barnett surprised Sanjay by offering to backstop every one of his patients, covering the past twelve months of his retainer plus interest, provided they sign an airtight, five-year contract. Then Sanjay surprised Barnett by asking Harper Williams, the ICU fellow, to take over the practice full-time, making him a silent partner. Vasquez's death made Williams realize that ICU medicine isn't for her; she prefers keeping patients healthy in the first place. Besides, she's always wanted to travel the world and has a thing for designer purses. Barnett had his reservations, but after two hours of intense questioning, he gave his seal of approval—which was enough to get the rest of Sanjay's patients on board.

Community Cares is well on its way to becoming a truly free clinic. Initially, there were concerns that it wouldn't survive financially. But then it emerged that over the past five years, it hasn't relied on MBH for any of its funding, which was all coming from an anonymous donor.

Dr. Fuki Olopade accepted the physician-in-chief position at MBH. Although he won't officially start for three weeks, he's already making the rounds, working to understand what the administration can do to make physicians' jobs easier.

Perhaps the most stunning development is The Mount Beacon Declaration. After the walkout by hundreds of MBH physicians, pharmacists, nurses, and medical students, a group of clinicians calling themselves The Mount Beacons began circulating a Google Doc of demands. They were angry about what administrators had done to their patients and their beloved hospital and were determined to make sure it never happened again. Sanjay and Olopade made the final edits, and just this morning, they submitted a formal petition to the hospital board.

Sanjay hands Emma his phone so she can read it.

The Mount Beacon Declaration

I. Don't sue patients. Hospitals should never subject patients to debt collection, lawsuits, and garnishment of wages.

II. Insurance equals access. No more VIPs, no cap on Medicaid patients, no surprise bills.

III. Charity care does not equal indebted care. Uninsured patients should have a clear and transparent process to apply for free or subsidized care. No bills after the fact.

IV. Represent the community. More than half the hospital board should be made up of patients who reflect the diversity of its patient population.

V. Pay for value, not volume. Hospitals should be paid for what they do for a patient, not to a patient. Eliminate fee for service.

VI. Equal pay for equal training. RVUs and physician productivity measures incentivize more care and less caring. Doctors in the same specialty should earn similar amounts and be paid a fixed salary.

VII. Practice makes perfect. Every level of hospital leadership up to and including the board should include doctors and nurses who still see patients. Having an MD or RN degree is not enough.

VIII. If conflict, no interest. Researchers should not be allowed to earn money from drugs they discover, technology they invent, or research they conduct.

IX. Right to unions. Doctors, nurses, and trainees should be allowed to self-organize.

X. Patients are the mission. The tripartite mission of academic medical centers is broken. Put patients first. Teaching and research are secondary.

Emma reads the declaration twice. "I love it, Sanjay. This is exactly what Dad believed."

"Dad?" asks Sanjay. "What happened to 'my father'?"

"Time to move on, I guess," she says wistfully. Then she scrolls to the end of the page and says, "Wow! There are hundreds of comments already."

"I'm getting emails, too. Doctors all over the country are being pressured to choose profit over patients—they're desperate for guidance."

"Will you help them?"

Sanjay pauses. He hasn't asked himself that question yet, but he knows the answer. "Yes. I will teach them how to fight."

"Ahem," comes a voice from above them.

Emma looks up, sees an older woman with tortoiseshell glasses.

"Hey, you," says Sanjay. "I was wondering where you were."

"Funerals and memorials get me all sappy." The woman straightens her suit jacket. "I just needed a minute."

"Wait, were you crying?" Sanjay teases. "I didn't think you had lacrimal ducts."

"I'm thinking about getting them surgically removed. Do you know a good doctor?"

They laugh loudly, and Emma looks at Sanjay curiously.

"Oh, don't bother with him. He's hopeless." The woman reaches out her hand. "I'm Cassie, Dr. Sanjay's executive assistant. I'm sorry for your loss."

Emma can't hide her surprise.

"Not who you expected?" Cassie says with a laugh.

"No, it's just . . ." Emma feels herself blushing. "I overhead you two talking once."

Cassie laughs harder. "Oh, you mean, about what I'm wearing? It's usually plaid PJs and knitted sweaters. It's a bad inside joke between me and Sanjay."

Emma unsuccessfully tries to stifle her own laughter. Sanjay excuses himself to grab a plate, and she and Cassie talk about her plans in the coming days. Emma needs to get back to her lab, but her near death experience and insights about her father have her questioning her life choices—including the decision to not take care of patients.

"He loves you, you know," Cassie says.

"Who? What? No," says Emma, feeling her face redden again.

"He does. I don't think he ever stopped. He's just too proud or too stupid to tell you. I can't tell which."

The two women share a smile.

"Tell you what?" Sanjay says, returning with a heaping plate of pupusas.

"Oh," says Cassie, giving Emma a wink. "That we got another cash transfer." She stands up and grabs Sanjay's arm. "Be right back with him, I promise," she says to Emma.

The clinic is about to reopen for the afternoon. As Cassie and Sanjay step off to the side, the music stops, and Cassie's voice carries a bit too loudly. "Should I send it to the 703?" she asks, pronouncing the number "seven-zero-three."

A young Black man with headphones around his neck turns to Emma and says, "'Seven zero three.' That's funny." In his hands is a waiting room form.

Emma cocks her head to the side.

"You must not be from around here. Here we call it the 'seven-oh-three.'"

Emma's confused. "Call what the 'seven-oh-three'?"

"The clinic?" He gestures around the room. "Where we are, right now?" He looks at her like she's crazy and slides over a seat. "You know, 703 River Road."

The answer was in front of her the whole time. Emma can't help but laugh at herself.

Sanjay returns, beaming. Something is clearly on his mind. "I have an idea," he says. "They're short a doctor for the afternoon."

Emma feels herself brighten. She stands up and takes his hand. "Let's go see some patients."

THE END

The chance is about to expire for the chairman. [illegible] Carter and [illegible] step out to the side, the most urgent and [illegible] [illegible] brightly. "Should I send up to the [illegible]?" she asks, pronouncing the number "seven-zero-three."

A young Black man with headphones around his neck turns to Emma and says, "Seven-zero-three. [illegible] [illegible] it is [illegible] four."

Emma cocks her head to the side.

"You must not be from around here. Here we call it the [illegible]."

Emma [illegible] the seven-oh-three?"

"The number," he [illegible] we are [illegible] He looks at [illegible] over a [illegible]

He [illegible] in front of [illegible] the whole [illegible] Emma can [illegible]

[illegible] on his [illegible] "There is [illegible]"

[illegible] stands up and takes his hand, [illegible]

THE END

SUGGESTED READING AND RESOURCES

In Life of Pi, Yann Martel wrote: *"That's what fiction is about, isn't it, the selective transforming of reality? The twisting of it to bring out its essence?"* So too it is with this book.

For those interested in exploring the real-world issues behind the story—corporatization of American healthcare, moral injury, and the harm it's causing—these works offer insight, evidence, and hope for change:

- *An American Sickness: How Healthcare Became Big Business and How You Can Take It Back*, by Elisabeth Rosenthal
- *Code Blue: Inside America's Medical Industrial Complex*, by Mike Magee
- *If I Betray These Words: Moral Injury in Medicine and Why It's So Hard for Clinicians to Put Patients First*, by Wendy Dean
- *Never Pay the First Bill: And Other Ways to Fight the Health Care System and Win*, by Marshall Allen
- *The Price We Pay: What Broke American Health Care - and How to Fix It*, by Marty Makary

Free clinics are real, vital places—and a lifeline for many. To find a clinic near you and support their work:

- The National Association of Free & Charitable Clinics: https://nafcclinics.org/find-clinic/
- Society of Student-Run Free Clinics: https://www.studentrunfreeclinics.org/
- State-level resources (for example, the Virginia Association of Free and Charitable Clinics https://www.vafreeclinics.org/)

ACKNOWLEDGMENTS

I BELIEVE BOOKS CAN change the world. I wrote this one hoping to change medicine.

To my fellow doctors and healthcare workers: as a kid, I dreamt of taking care of patients. What I never imagined was the kinship and inspiration I'd find among my fellow healers-in-arms. This novel is, in many ways, your story—our story. It's about what's happening to our noble profession and the patients we've been entrusted to serve.

To my patients: thank you for trusting me with your lives and your stories. You've given me more meaning than I ever dreamed possible. The hugs, the handshakes, the bins of cookies, the holiday cards—they stay with me.

To my early readers—you know who you are, even if I can't name you here—thank you for encouraging me when this story was just a shaky idea and for helping it become something more. Your belief in it meant everything. A special thanks as well to Dr. Rahul Banerjee and Dr. Reza Manesh for fact-checking the medicine and science. Any errors, of course, are entirely my own.

To the writers and editors who helped along the way: Jess Taylor, Genevieve Gagne-Hawes, Rosemary Ahern, Caroline Leavitt, John Paine: thank you for your talent, your generosity, and your conviction that I could write fiction, even though I hadn't written a word of it since high school. You didn't just make this book better—you made me a writer (albeit a novice one).

To my entire publishing and distribution team: my agent Susan Golomb and the team at Writer's House including Sasha Landauer and Tom Ishizuka; my editor Sara J. Henry and the team at Crooked Lane; at Macro, which optioned the TV/film rights—Jamila Hunter, Jordana Guarino, Reena Singh; at BookSparks, my publicists Crystal Patriarche, Grace Fell, Leilani Fitzpatrick: thank you for saying yes to this story not despite its mission, but because of it.

To the writers I've met on this journey—retired professionals, dreamers, storytellers—I can't wait for the world to hear your voices.

To my family: the original spark for this novel began on a walk with my mom during a vacation in Florida. A lifelong Bollywood fan, she immediately wanted to know more about this South Asian doctor—part Sherlock Holmes, part James Bond. My dad read every draft, offered edits, and even penned a few sample chapters of his own. My sister approached it as she does all of my endeavors, with concern for the time it would take away from my family, and then wholehearted support once she saw why it mattered so much. To my daughters, who peppered me with questions as I narrated plot twists during school drop-offs—you helped me find the story. And to my wife, who humored this wild creative detour and picked up the slack at home while I rewrote, revised, and rewrote again—I owe you everything.

And finally, to you, the reader: medicine is built on trust, the kind that comes from you. So speak up for yourself, your loved ones, and the healers who care for you. My sincerest wish is that your world, too, is better off for it.

—Shantanu Rai